TOO
LATE
TO SAY
GOODBYE

MARK ATLEY

TOO LATE
TO SAY
GOODBYE

TULSA UNDERWORLD BOOK 1

4 Horsemen
Publications, Inc.

Too Late to Say Goodbye
Tulsa Underworld Book 1
Copyright © 2022 Mark Atley. All rights reserved.

4 Horsemen
Publications, Inc.

4 Horsemen Publications, Inc.
1497 Main St. Suite 169
Dunedin, FL 34698
4horsemenpublications.com
info@4horsemenpublications.com

Cover by 4HP
Typesetting by Michelle Cline
Editor Laura Mita

Library of Congress Control Number: 2021951207

Print ISBN: 978-1-64450-461-1
Audio ISBN: 978-1-64450-459-8
E-Book ISBN: 978-1-64450-460-4

DEDICATION:

T HIS BOOK IS DEDICATED TO MY WIFE AND family and to the real Gene Orr, who is nothing like my character, but whose death inspired this book. I will forever remember my evening on watch. I'm glad you were my friend.

ACKNOWLEDGMENT:

WANT TO THANK THE FOLKS (GIRLS) AT 4 Horsemen for taking a chance on me, and I hope to make it very worth their while. I want to thank those of you who follow me on Twitter and offer encouragement, including Martine, Craig, Gareth, J. Todd Scott, J.B., Stephen, Eric (Beetner—Long live Writer Types), Max, Neil, Alec, and many more who I've interacted with over the years. To my coworkers and family who have put up with me during many story breakdown sessions. A very special thanks to my wife—for putting up with me.

And always, thank you to each and every one who reads this novel. Without you, this would not be possible.

TABLE OF CONTENTS

CHAPTER ONE:

TONY MORA

DEA AGENT ANTONIO "TONY" MORA crouches through the open door into the backseat of a tan 2004 Buick Regal belonging to a guy known as Stevie Gragg to complete a drug deal. It is two o'clock in the afternoon and twenty degrees outside.

The sedan is in a McDonald's parking lot in a suburb north of Tulsa, backed into the parking space, running with the heat on full blast. The McDonald's is quiet. The lunch rush has come and gone; they are far removed from the hectic morning breakfast crowd. Through the windows, a mom and a child walk back toward the restrooms, a couple of people stand at the counter ordering, and an employee mops the floor; otherwise, the place is like most McDonald's off a highway in the mid-afternoon in winter, a sparse parking lot with some light traffic in the drive thru.

The two men in the vehicle have been waiting for Tony, so neither of them pays much attention to him as he slips into the car. The guy in the passenger seat tells the driver

1

who's smoking a cigarillo, about his shoes. He lifts his foot and rests it on the dashboard to display the sneakers. "They're genuine Air Jordan's, never worn, my size, white like a polar bear's ass—" Tony slams the car door shut, and both men check him out; the passenger glances at Tony, mid-sentence, "a sweet find."

The passenger is Franklin Hayes, a black man, bald, fit, with no distinguishing features except for a wicked scar running across the left side of his face, horizontal from his lips to his ear. Franklin wears a cheap gray suit with a crisp white collar and apparently genuine Air Jordan's. Tony knows from surveillance Franklin bought them from a pawnshop that specializes in knock-off footwear. Franklin's a salesman.

Stevie, the driver, scans Tony from the rearview mirror. He's a white man, large—some would say fat—with a full beard. Stevie wears a tan work jacket, a Carhartt, and a stocking cap. He says, "I always liked LeBron better," in response to Franklin's comment about the shoes.

Franklin, Tony knows a lot about, but Stevie, Tony knows very little, other than the guy buys Black & Milds by the boatload and his brother's a killer who goes by the name Leon.

Stevie ashes out the cracked driver's side window, which lets cool air into the cabin, and after a moment blows smoke through the crack as Tony settles into the backseat. He's eyeing the old man inside the McDonald's who is reading a newspaper, flipping pages slowly as he reads, drinking coffee. Tony puts his hands up to his face, blows warm air into his gloveless hands, and studies his surroundings. This spot works, but it could be better. His partner, Clyde, is parked a couple of spaces down, nose in a parking spot with Clyde low in the driver's seat so that he's harder to see. Not that Tony can see him. Just they've done this a hundred times, and that's how they operate. Clyde's his partner, so Clyde's the closest guy. He's the oh-shit guy. His closest support if things take a turn for the worse.

Besides Clyde, there are others. Across the street, there's a car with two agents. Lawrence Johnson and Nader Kahn, both fuckups, but enjoyable to work with. They're watching the Regal through binoculars. Then, there's another vehicle two businesses down. Eliza Cortez, competent, tough, and very pregnant. And one street over, the arrest team's set up and ready to go should things go sideways, which consists of Tony and Clyde's boss Marque Boykin and five others. Today, Boykin plays host to Assistant United States District Attorney Eli Buchanan, who's pretending to be junior field man, so he has a better understanding of how things are done.

This morning, at the mission briefing, Eli Buchanan, Bucky to most, bull-nosed his way into Clyde's briefing and explained how knowing how they worked will help him explain things better in the courtroom. On the way over to the meet, Clyde told Tony that's bullshit. Bucky just wants a story to brag about so he can get laid.

All of them are waiting for Tony's signal.

Or lack of signal.

Because today's deal is supposed to go forward with no problems. Tony is just supposed to set the deal and confirm the drugs, nothing else. No hang-ups. Flash the cash so to speak, except he doesn't have the cash. Bucky wouldn't let them withdraw what they needed, partly because Franklin kept changing the meeting location, three times with no explanation, which is what Clyde calls "doper-time," and partly because Bucky didn't want to release the money until they saw the product. When Tony protested showing up to a drug-deal without the funds to purchase the drugs, Bucky told him to be creative. He didn't trust the deal, or rather, didn't trust Franklin. So Tony's supposed to record the interaction and set another meeting for another day.

Today, Tony wears black over black, black leather jacket older than him over black jeans, with an off-white t-shirt underneath because he's still the good guy, wearing what Eliza calls his millennial greaser look. He chose black on black for working with criminals. Easy to clean and easy to blend in. Doesn't stand out too much, goes with his dark hair and olive skin, hints of his Cuban heritage, and doesn't distract from his average height, average build, and green eyes. Tony can be nobody and anybody. He's an ethnic jack-of-all-trades.

Franklin slips his foot from the dashboard and rotates, placing his hand on Stevie's seat to turn his body, to get a look at Tony. "You paying attention?" Franklin looks back at Tony, but Tony's not paying attention; he's watching the old man inside, letting Franklin's voice wash over him.

Tony drops his hands from his mouth. "It's cold outside," he says and transfers his attention from the old man with the paper to Franklin, dropping his eyes, but doing it slowly to show he's not going to be pushed around.

Franklin asks again, "I said, did you bring the money?"

Tony repeats, "It's cold outside." Then adds, "I've not been in the car two seconds, and you're already coming at me like this. Let me warm up a bit before we get down to it."

Franklin throws his hands up. "Hey what can I say, it's two o'clock in the afternoon," he taps the gold watch on his wrist with his index finger, "and I got better things to be doing than sitting here jibber-jawing with the likes of you. You think I try this shit with my woman, go in cold, and try to get her jump-started without any of the sweet stuff? Only when I don't want to wait for a good time— and well, buddy, I don't want to wait for any time with you any longer."

"Jibber-jawing?" Tony says. "Who talks like that? Look, this was supposed to happen at the Home Depot at ten. That's ten this morning." Tony taps Franklin's watch with his forefinger to make his point. "If anyone should be upset about things, it should be me, not you."

"You want to do this or not?" Franklin asks, sliding his wrist away from Tony. "Because like I said, I've got other shit to do."

"Well yeah," Tony says, "of course, but like, what's so important that you got to blow me off for a couple of hours and then give me a hard time like I'm the one that's late to the party? I got things to do today too, man." Tony crosses his arms. "So, what's got you in such a hurry now?"

The cloying, sweet smell of geranium, lavender, and something reminiscent of peppers fills the cabin with an arrogant, self-assured swagger. It must come from Franklin, who absently runs a finger over his forehead, stroking the prominent ridge above his left eye. "We wanted to see how flexible you would be," he says. "And by we, I mean my boss, because Stevie and I couldn't give two fucks if you're flexible or not. But I'm tired of wasting your time and mine, and the boss is the boss, you know? So, we do what he wants up until a point. Consider that fucking point reached. And just so you're aware, we got Thunder tickets for tonight's game. Stevie here says he's not been to one. I'm going to change that. Say it's a thank you for a job well done. I closed a major deal the other day. Stevie brought them to the table. So, we want to get this taken care of so we can get to the city before too long. I want to get to the city before it gets too late because I want to have dinner at this place down in Bricktown."

From the driver's seat, Stevie says, "What's the point of going? They're no good this year."

Franklin turns to him. "The point is when you're a fan and your home team's playing at home, you go. Doesn't matter if they're good or not. You go. You support them."

Tony asks, "What you got, like season tickets?"

Franklin shakes his head. "No, but I've not been to a game since Durant took off."

Stevie says, "See, that's what I'm saying. Without him and without what's his face, the short one that wore the glasses and dressed like a clown trying to sell used cars— you know who I'm talking about?"

But Franklin doesn't know who Stevie's talking about because his face twists into a strange look trying to determine if his partner's serious or not. "No, I don't know. Who the fuck are you talking about?"

"The short guy."

"What short guy?"

"The guy that just left."

"Who the fuck just left?"

"Not Durant, he made everyone mad leaving, you remember how they treated him?" Stevie says. "He goes on to make more money, try to get a championship ring and all that. And everyone's pissed off at him for having an opinion on his own career. I mean the other guy, the one that stayed behind. Everyone loves him."

"Westbrook?" Tony provides from the back seat.

Franklin glances at Tony and then back at Stevie. He asks, "Do you mean Westbrook?"

Stevie just shrugs, his large shoulders banging up and then slouching in a fall, with one hand still on the steering wheel.

Tony adds, "Russell Westbrook; he left a couple of years ago."

"If you mean Westbrook," Franklin says, "fucking say you mean Westbrook. Do you mean Westbrook? He's not short."

Stevie puffs on the cigarillo, blows smoke out the window, and says, "He's shorter than Durant."

"It's the NBA," Tony comments. "No one's short in the NBA."

Stevie says, "What about that guy with the Golden State or whatever? The one who's got the curly hair, and everyone loves him, he's not tall."

Tony tells Franklin, "He's got a point."

"What the fuck's wrong with you two?" Franklin says, twisting in the seat. He pounds the dashboard. "You two doing a stand-up bit? Is that it? You two doing some comedic bullshit, who's-on-first-type-fuckery, where the new guy in the back knows what the fuck you mean, but with me, I've got to play fucking charades with you, twenty-fucking-questions?"

Stevie says, "No, I'm just saying, they're nothing without the guy with the colorful outfits."

"Outfits?" Franklin says, "Who the fuck wears outfits? What the fuck is an outfit?" Franklin reverses in the seat, asks Tony, "You wear an outfit?"

Tony shakes his head.

Franklin goes on, "What are we just like fucking toddlers, is that it? You're like a fucking first-grader, your mother dressing you. Dressing you in outfits? You want to wear a sailor's outfit, with the little white cap and all that bullshit? Look like Donald Duck?"

Stevie shakes his head.

"That's what I thought," Franklin says. "Now, if you don't mind," he hangs his hand out toward Stevie, "I'd like to get on with business with the gentleman in the back seat unless you have something more you would like to add?"

Stevie doesn't move and doesn't say anything either. He just wraps his lips around the cigarillo and takes in some of the smoke, which adds to the noxious mixture of Franklin's cologne and makes the car smell like gummy bears, and he stares intently at Franklin.

"We done?" Franklin asks, clarifying, "Or you got some other bullshit you want to get off your chest, anything more you want to spout? How about you do this—you drive. Stick to driving. Let me do the talking. Now, where were we?" He turns back to Tony. "Oh that's right, do you have the motherfucking money or not?"

"I've got the money," Tony says and puts his hands up. "But it's not on me."

Stevie's eyes flash up toward the rearview mirror.

Franklin says, "What'd you mean you don't have the money on you?"

Tony shrugs. "What'd you mean what I mean? I don't got it on me."

"Why not?" Franklin demands, jutting his hand out as if he's expecting a tip before closing his hand into a fist, squeezing tight until his skin turns white at the edges, and he presses his fist against the seat, speaking in a slow

controlled manner before his words out-race his indigna-
tion. "Why come to a deal without the money? Do you
go to dinner without your wallet? Tell the hooker, sorry
babe, put it on my tab? Buy the lemonade from the kid, tell
him you'll get him next week? Because if you did, then I'd
get to thinking you like fucking people over. You trying to
fuck me over? Is that it? Is that what you're trying to do?
Man, I do so much business I don't have time for these
bullshit little kid games. Either you buy the product or
not, but don't sit here, in Stevie's fucking car, and tell me
you didn't bring the money. That's disrespectful. Hey, what
you smiling at?"

Tony doesn't tell him. In his head, he hears Clyde's
voice, telling him to breathe. Stay calm. The voice telling
him don't let Franklin get to you. No reason to get upset.
He's just blowing steam. It's the stress. It's nerves.

Tony shrugs. "I left it with my partner."

Franklin repeats, "You left it with your partner," testing
the words out as if he doesn't understand them, as if they
taste bad, turning them over with his tongue. "What
the fuck?"

Tony places his palm on the seat next to him. "You got
the drugs?"

Franklin leans back, puts his hand on the driver's seat,
fingers covered in gold rings, and smiles. "We left it with
our partner."

Tony brings his hands together. "See we're all even then."

Franklin kicks his foot out, striking the underside of
the dash. "What do you mean we're all even? Of course,
I've got the fucking drugs. They're in the duffle bag next
to you. Who comes to a deal without their end of the

9

bargain? What sort of fucked up bullshit is this? Who do you think I am?"

"I've got the money," Tony says. "I just don't *got* the money."

"What good does that do me?" Franklin asks him, rocking in the seat. "Call me a selfish man, but I wouldn't be who I am today if I understood whatever the fuck that means. What's that do for me? What good is that for me? These are the questions I ask, but here and now the most important one is, where's my motherfucking money?"

"Easy," Tony says, hands up again, fanning the air. "I've got it. It's just not on me."

Stevie sways in the seat, pulling the zipper of his jacket down and pulling the folds open at the neck. "Maybe he's got a reason."

Franklin pauses while his attention shifts to Stevie without looking away from Tony. "Maybe he's got a reason?" he says. "What sort of fucking reason could this guy have for not having the money?"

With the cigarillo stuck to the corner of his mouth, Stevie shrugs again while shouldering his way out of his jacket but due to his size he can't get his arms out without lurching back and forth, which serves to agitate Franklin more. The cigarillo bounces in the corner of Stevie's mouth as he explains. "Just saying, you've not really asked. Maybe you ask. Maybe he tells you. I don't know. We did fuck him around for a few hours. Maybe he got spooked or something."

Franklin's eyes snap toward him. "You being a fucking racist asshole again? Spooked. Who the fuck got spooked, white bread? What the hell does that mean?"

Tony holds up a finger. "I think he means scared like as in a ghost—boo."

Franklin slaps at his finger. "What the fuck's wrong with you? Now you come into my friend and I's conversation?"

"We're not friends," Stevie interjects, freeing one arm from the jacket.

Franklin jams his hand on the driver's seat thrusting his body back until his elbow locks and he's against the window, eyeing Stevie. "We're not friends?" Franklin is offended and exerts pressure against the seat and window. "What the fuck are we?" he asks, shaking the car in a fit.

Using his free arm to hold the sleeve of the trapped arm, Stevie says, "More like work associates."

Franklin starts to say something but then stops and sits forward in the seat, crossing his arms, calm. "I'll do this slow so your thick head can understand what's happening right now because obviously, you don't see what's going on—"

"—I'm just saying, we're more like work associates," Stevie says as he puts the burnt-out cigarillo in the ashtray and retrieves another from above the visor, placing it in his mouth as he tries to retract a lighter from his pants pocket, leaning his large body to the side to where Tony can see the gun in the seat next to the center console. Stevie succeeds in dragging the lighter out of his pocket and holds the lighter to the cigarillo in his mouth. Stevie's thumb flicks the lighter to life as he says, "I mean we don't go and hang out or anything. You're only taking me to the basketball game because your date cancelled on you. And don't you try to pretend otherwise."

"Fine," Franklin says. "I didn't want to invite you, but out of the kindness of my damn heart, I said to myself, 'Self, why don't we bring Stevie along? Maybe educate the man on what it means to have a passion?' Say, 'Stevie, let's have a closer relationship, be friends, have a beer, hell, I'm buying tonight, budgeted a couple hundred dollars.' Tell you job well done and all that bullshit."

Cigarillo in hand, waving around like a conductor, Stevie stabs out toward Franklin, stopping him. "And don't pretend you're not just bringing me along so someone can drive your ass to the city."

"Fine," Franklin throws up his arms, "I need you to drive because I don't have a car right now because that bitch took it, okay? Is that what you want to hear? I broke up with her. We're supposed to go to the game tonight, but this morning, she's bitching and complaining about me staying out late with your ass, and I'm not dependable, reliable, and a bunch of other able-shit, meaning I'm not the right guy to be around her and her shit-spawned kid? Is that what you want to hear? Hear about how she fucking took off in my Cadillac, and I've not tracked her down yet to put her in her place, slap a bitch, tell her what's what because we've been fucking with this asshole all day and we're going to the game tonight? Is that what you want to hear?"

"I mean it'd make a difference." Stevie restores the cigarillo to the corner of his mouth. "Hearing something like that."

"Do I need to come back?" Tony asks, laying his hand on the duffle bag, palm sweaty, making like he's going to leave.

Franklin flips around in the seat. "No, you don't fucking need to come back. Don't leave either. Get your hand off the merchandise. You've not paid for it. It's not yours."

Tony lifts his hand from the bag with his fingers splayed out wide. Stevie blows smoke through the crack in the window.

To Stevie, Franklin says, "Now before you rudely fucking interrupted me, I was going to ask you if you know what's going on here." But Stevie just looks at him. So Franklin goes on. "I'll take your dumb face as meaning you don't know what's happening right now. How you don't know that our illustrious friend in the back here's not who he says he is?"

Tony false grins through tight teeth. "What are you talking about?"

Franklin ignores him as he explains it to Stevie. "See, the way things are, I've been in this business a long time, gives me certain skills like smelling when something's about to get rotten," he says. "You know like how you know the milk's turned in the fridge before you pour it into your bowl of Fruit Loops or whatever the fuck it is you white people eat. Doing this for as long as I've been doing this, I know what sort of people don't bring the money to the deal."

Franklin opens the glove box and pulls out a 1911 handgun and puts it up to his face next to his cheek. "The type of people that don't bring shit to the meet are either people getting ready to fuck you over, rob you, or cops. Either way, someone's getting fucked. So, which one are you?" He drops the muzzle of the 1911 on Tony, pointing it right at him. "Are you a cop or you just getting ready to rob me? It doesn't fucking matter what you say because nothing you say's going to make me feel any better about you or think you're not fucking me over."

But Tony, who's been in this situation before and knows exactly what to do, plays it cool, letting everything happen the way it should, doesn't break character. He asks for the benefit of the wire he's wearing, "You ever watch *Psych*?"

"What the fuck?"

"*Psych,* the show about the psychic detective. I love it—you see it?" Tony pauses to assess the hesitation creeping across Franklin's face, the same hesitation saying he's willing to entertain the tangent because after all, he's a businessman, not a killer, but it better be worth his time. "Did you know every episode has at least one *pineapple* and a fist bump in it?"

Franklin laughs out loud. "Pineapple? Fist bump, that's what you're going to say with a gun pointed right at you—talk about fucking pineapples? Talk about some fucking show? What sort of last words are those?"

Tony shuts his eyes and braces himself for impact, thinking Franklin should really see the show. It's about partners, about friends. Pineapple equals help and cue the oh-shit guy—Clyde.

And it's at this point, Stevie sees what's coming, with his eyes locked on Franklin's window, so much so the cigarillo tumbles out of his mouth as his left hand immediately juts to the ceiling, bracing himself as his other hand grabs the center console, his brain processing what's happening faster than his mouth can communicate. The cigarillo bounces down Stevie's large body, rolls over the center console, and flips end over end into Franklin's lap. Franklin jumps in the seat, removing the gun from Tony, as he brushes his hand down once, the back of his hand batting the cigarillo away, sending a flash of embers while saying, "What the fuck?"

Then, the taillights of Clyde's Chevy Impala glare red, the high-single-gear whir rising in sudden intensity heralding his arrival, as the vehicle rams, full speed, into the passenger side of Stevie's Regal, crushing plastic and breaking glass. The impact throws Franklin into Stevie's lap as Stevie's head bounces off the driver's side window, and Tony's left side slams against the door. Glass flies everywhere. Tires screech in protest after the crunch of plastic as the Impala pushes the Regal over half a parking space before Clyde lets off the gas. Then, Clyde's up and out of the driver's seat of the Impala, door open next to him, and withdraws his sidearm from under his black sports coat. He aims as Franklin recovers some and reflexively picks up his hand with the 1911, and Franklin manages to squeeze off three rounds toward the sky. Clyde shoots back, once, twice, three times, and his bullets impact the passenger door, and one flies through the windshield, which catches Stevie in the stomach, who lets out a groan as if someone's punched the air out of his lungs. Franklin brings the gun around for another shot, but Tony grabs for Franklin's gun hand, as Stevie's right-hand goes to his stomach to inspect the wound and comes away with blood.

Franklin twists his body away from Tony, so he has leverage, yanking to free his hand and the gun, and slithering farther, his head and body, across Stevie, who leans to the side now against Tony's arm, pinning Tony's arm against the seat. Stevie frantically gropes for his gun from between the seat and the center console, but the gun has fallen some because of the impact and is just out of his reach. Franklin spins his head out of Stevie's lap and away from the blood, like an upside-down turtle, head near the glove box, feet in the air, kicking out toward Tony to knock him loose, like a fighter fending off an on-coming assailant in the ring.

Clyde fires again through the windshield, and this time he hits the big man on purpose, putting two in Stevie's chest in successive bursts, pow-pow. As the bullets strike him, Stevie's hand latches around the handle of his gun, jerking it up from between the seat and center console, and he lets off two rounds into the sedan's radio near Franklin's head, who is working his sneakers between his body and Tony's, and Franklin kicks out violently to knock Tony back with his size fourteen Air Jordan's. Franklin's kick whacks Tony's hand off the gun and flattens Tony's back against the back seat, who then, deciding to get off this ride, reaches for the door beside him, works the handle, popping it open, and swings the door open. Tony bails out of the car, flopping to the pavement and rolling clear of the Regal as Lawrence and Nader arrive on the scene, ramming their car into the driver's side of the Regal just as Clyde did, rocking the entire vehicle and moving the cars a few inches, jarring Franklin, trapping him inside, and pinning the Regal in place.

Clyde steps forward, nearing the impact site of his vehicle, and tries to get a better angle on Franklin but Franklin's at an awkward angle: the right one for Franklin; the wrong one for Clyde. Franklin fires twice more, the bullets punching Clyde in the chest. He drops to the pavement.

Tony scrambles away from the cars. Lawrence and Nader exit their vehicle, with their guns drawn, before their car has stopped rocking. Tony rolls to his side, protecting his head with his arms and bringing his feet to his stomach. He claps his hands over his ears as Lawrence and Nader unload their firearms into the Regal, shooting with precision and a cadence. Their searing-hot shells clatter beside Tony, bouncing with golden metallic clinks. Then, both men run dry, first Lawrence and then Nader. At the same time, they drop their magazines in one smooth motion, slamming home new magazines, and unload that one into the vehicle as well. Now, Tony scrambles out from under the rain of shells and around the back of the Regal, his body scratching and crawling across the pavement and broken glass.

The shooting stops. Lawrence and Nader reload the third magazine and approach the Regal slowly, clearing it like they were trained, working as a team, taking their time.

But now that the shooting's over, Tony's up and jumping over the back end of Clyde's Impala, landing next to Clyde. He's down, on the asphalt, sitting, pulling Clyde into his lap. Clyde's bleeding, two holes, both above the vest, one of them just under Clyde's throat. Tony places the palm of his hand on the throat wound and presses down on Clyde's body to apply pressure. Clyde's hand brushes against Tony's chin, his fingers gripping the side of Tony's neck. His blue eyes stare up at Tony as his warm blood pumps out of his body and between Tony's fingers.

CHAPTER TWO:

ELIZA CORTEZ

T HE CALL GOES OUT OVER THE RADIO and
Eliza Cortez's heart drops; Tony's in trouble, he said
the word: *Pineapple*. Then, through her open window, as
she's slipping her white Ford Taurus into gear, she hears
a crash, the telltale crunch of plastic on plastic, gunshots,
and another crash. Then, more gunshots, dozens coming
in a staccato. Finally, Tony's voice on the radio, screaming,
"Clyde's shot. He's bleeding out; we need a car now! We
need to get him to the hospital."

Seconds later, Eliza pulls onto the scene, crossing
traffic, and her eyes quickly scan the area, taking it all in:
faces in the McDonald's windows watching the mayhem
outside, the parking lot empty except for Larry and Nader,
who've pinned the suspect vehicle in the parking space
with their car, dozens of bullet holes peppering the driver
side of the suspect vehicle, with at least one suspect dead in
the driver's seat. Jerking the wheel, Eliza brakes hard, tires
screeching as she comes to a stop, and the smell of warm

ceramic lingers in the air, drifting in through her window. Larry and Nader load both Clyde and Tony into her back seat without saying a word, Tony holding Clyde's head. They slam the door, and she peels out of the McDonald's parking lot, making for the closest hospital. She's in and out of the parking lot in less than thirty seconds.

A block away from the McDonald's, two marked patrol units join her and clear the way, lights and sirens blaring the whole way. The entire time she's driving, Eliza isn't sure Clyde's alive or not because no one said anything, and in the car, Tony's not talking. But he doesn't have to talk because there is always a plan for things like this, where her role in the plan is she's the hospital car in case something bad happens, which was the only job Marque would allow her to do today, blaming her pregnancy, saying she was too far along, too pregnant, and shouldn't even be on the op, but Marque needed her because she's one of the best watchers they have. Eliza disagrees with the negative reasons. She's not too far along; she still has two more weeks until she goes on maternity leave, which means she's only at the seven-month mark. Though, the baby is a problem in and of itself, one to be worked out later. Today, she needs to be here because of everything going on in her life, the stress of her marriage, the issues between her and Tony, and the looming delivery of the truth—work, this work, her work, is the only thing keeping her going, the only thing keeping her sane—and she's glad she's here today because something bad did happen, something to Tony—to Clyde.

She can't help peek in the rearview mirror at the scene unfolding in the back seat; Tony in the seat repeating over and over, "Stay with me, stay with me, stay with me," with Clyde cradled in his lap. Tears stream down Tony's face as he cries and pleads for his partner to stay alive. When Tony finally looks up at the mirror, his eyes are cloudy, sobbing, pleading. And Eliza is alarmingly aware of how silent Clyde is.

At the hospital, the medical staff's already standing outside, waiting, and as soon as the vehicle stops, they yank Clyde out of the back of her car, nearly ripping him from Tony's hands. Tony follows Clyde's body out of the backseat, climbing out of the car with his hand still pressed against the wound. Bright red blood seeps between his fingers.

Then, half a dozen people crowd around the car and block Eliza's view of Clyde. She gets out of the car to watch the scene unfold as one of the nurses, a female shaped like a pear with purple hair, physically stops Tony, slapping her hands on his chest, pushing him back, once, twice, palms on his shoulders, telling him to stay. "*Stay here.* We've got him," she says. "Stay here."

Two nurses yell something about Clyde being alive as they transfer him from the car to a gurney. Then, they yell about a pulse. It's weak. The chaos rolls from just outside the car through the front doors of the hospital where a doctor meets them at the doors. He checks Clyde's vitals with a stethoscope while running alongside the gurney, yelling commands.

They disappear from view, which leaves Eliza alone with Tony outside. He stands dumbfounded next to the car holding his shoulder, face in pain, a vacant stare, skin white, in shock.

Rushing around her vehicle toward him, Eliza examines the vehicle and Tony. Both are soiled in blood. The side of the Ford is covered in blood, all of it Clyde's. The backseat's a mess and smells of freshly tilled soil and iron. And Tony, his white shirt, under the unbuttoned jacket, is reddish-pink, and the jacket is a haggard representation of Tony's outward expression. His right hand clutches his left shoulder. Eliza asks, "Are you hurt?"

Tony shakes his head as if part of him has returned to the present and mutters something about it being dislocated—an old soccer injury.

In this moment, Eliza's glad she's here, glad she was part of the operation, glad that Marque's a weak supervisor and let her bulldog her way on today, but most importantly, she's glad she's here for Tony. Part of her wants to comfort Tony while the other part wants to know what happened—how did things go so wrong? But she knows better than to ask. Explanations can come later.

Tony steps toward the hospital as Eliza rounds the backend of her Ford and cuts him off from the hospital doors, forcing her body against his in a violent embrace. Tony ventures a half-step to go around her, but Eliza collides against him, stopping him, and attempts to draw him in deeper into a warm caress, a hug, but her stomach separates them and is a reminder of their weaknesses. They spin in place, Eliza spinning with him, seizing him, delaying him from going forward. "Let them handle Clyde," she pleads. "Give them space. It's okay."

But it's not okay, and she sees that in Tony's eyes, which stare at her with detached coolness, as if Tony has left and someone else has taken hold of his senses, occupying his body, all of which is delivered in his haunted vacant look as his eyes traverse her, the hospital, and the car without seeing or conceiving any of it.

"It's my fault," he croaks as he breaks her grasp, freeing his hand, rejecting her affection, and sidestepping her a second time. He staggers his way into the hospital, still holding his shoulder.

Eliza stumbles behind him and urges him to stop. "Tony, come on. We need you to get checked out, get that shoulder looked at."

But Tony shakes his head and continues, barreling toward the ER suite, careening off the white walls with a light olive-green stripe in the middle and pastel color accents. Staggering drunkenly forward, skimming stationed equipment that loiters outside of rooms, he even brushes a tray of food to the ground. Eliza trails in his wake, righting equipment, picking up what she can, and watching as his hip sideswipes the nurses' desk, which turns him and nearly jostles him to the ground. When Tony reaches the ER suite, he freezes at the door, which gives Eliza time to catch up with him. She stops at his side, where she feels she belongs.

Tony stares at the scene unfolding in front of him, at what's happening with Clyde, who's on the bed in the room as the staff yanks the mattress out from underneath him. The room's not large enough for all the people and the equipment, and they bounce and skip off the walls as the doctors and medical staff work frantically to save his life. Someone yells about the bleeding. "Give me something to control the bleeding." They cut Clyde's shirt away as someone says they're monitoring his breathing and heart rate, but then, the shout goes out that his breathing has stopped, causing the gears to change, going from seemingly just under control and methodical to something frantic and hectic. And then Eliza watches with bitter disgust as

Clyde's intubated, the nurse slipping the silver curved tool down Clyde's throat, opening his airways—the tool looks like a large guitar clamp—followed by some tubing. Then, they hook a large plastic bulb to the top of the tubing. A nurse scales the side of the bed, climbing up to sit on top of Clyde, straddling his midsection, back straight and upright, hands pressed high on Clyde's chest pushing against his sternum while another nurse pulses the plastic bulb in her hand rhythmically to control his breathing as the others work around her to try to stop the bleeding, and Clyde's body is eclipsed by the whirl of motion and bodies.

All Eliza can see is the small stream of blood, dripping to the floor, trickling down Clyde's side and off the side of the bed—drip, drip, drip. A passing nurse throws a gown on the forming puddle. The blood drips mutedly onto the gown as a large swath of it turns from white to a brownish red.

Eliza reaches out for Tony, finds his hand, and squeezes it...

———

THE TIME OF DEATH IS ANNOUNCED at 15:30 hours after which Tony refuses an ER room no matter how hard the redheaded nursing supervisor tries to herd him. He doesn't want to move from his spot, from Clyde. He sits on the floor outside the ER suite, back against the nurses' desk, eyes forward, watching them clean the blood from the floor and unhook the equipment, Clyde's body still on the table. After the death's declared, the conglomeration of heightened emotions and the blur of activity transforms into an antiseptic, sterile environment as nurses return to stations, doctors evaporate into the hospital, and emotions decrease into unhindered professionalism. Others begin to arrive, some of the arrest team, importing a variety of badges, stenciled jackets, and an assortment of bodies, clamoring radios, and grumbling prattle.

The nursing supervisor hands Eliza some ice and a sling and threatens to kick Tony out of the hospital if he doesn't take it. Eliza assures her she'll handle it, although she doubts the woman would carry out her threat, and explains, "It's a cop thing—nobody's left alone," to the nursing supervisor who doesn't argue. "He's just lost a friend." After the nursing supervisor waddles away, Eliza squats awkwardly at Tony's side, to the best of her pregnant ability, and forces him to accept the ice by slapping it against his hurt shoulder and wresting his hand, which rests limply in his lap, to his shoulder to hold the ice in place.

As Eliza slips a sling around his arm, working the strap over his shoulder and down his neck, Tony looks up at her, knees pulled to his chest, and says, "Someone needs to go talk to Iris." His tone suggests he wants to be the one that goes and talks to Clyde's wife as his vision tracks back to the room and Clyde. Except he can't be the one to go talk to her. He's a wreck, and it breaks Eliza's heart to see him this way, in pain, this pain.

A nurse scoots a stool over for Eliza. She settles on the stool, hands in her lap, frustrated that if she sat on the floor next to Tony like she feels she needs to, she's not sure she'd be able to get up without help. Perched on the stool, she runs a finger along her forehead, whisking a strand of dark hair out of her face and tucking it behind her ear, and says, "You're not doing that."

Tony turns and gives her a look almost as if he's challenging her to stop him, but Eliza refuses to back down. She looks right back at him and knows she'll win this staring contest, and he should know it too, but still, he points the ice pack at the room. "I was his partner."

"Which means you need to be here."

"But she needs to be here. She should be here. That's her husband in there."

"Yes, she should be, but she's not. You are. And yes, that's her husband in there, I agree, but you're in no shape to do anything but sit here and be with me."

Tony whips his head away from her, trying to conceal his tears, but Eliza grabs his chin with her hand, her nails digging into his cheek, and she pulls his face back toward her.

"Look at me." Tony jerks his head out of her hand, bottling his emotions, and turns away again. "*Antonio*, look at me."

Reluctantly, he relents and turns back to her with tears streaming down his cheeks. He drops his head toward the white tiled floor, dipping his chin to his chest as the rigidity of pain flees his body, crumbling under her gaze, his shoulders drooping as he kicks out his legs in front of him.

"He's gone," Eliza says with a soft voice. "Worry about yourself. This is the point where you need to stop and look around, assess the situation, figure out what happens next."

"Assess the situation?" Tony lifts his head as anger rises in his voice. "The situation is my partner was just killed."

"And the man that killed him is on his way here," she says. "Iris can wait. She doesn't need to be here for that. She doesn't need to see any of this. But you, I'm worried about you, and I'm talking about you. You and I both know this is not the time for you to leave or do anything. Tony, I'm here with you." Eliza pauses. "Besides you know a whole helluva lot of things have to happen now. Let someone else worry about his wife."

His voice softer now, barely above a whisper, "She still deserves to know."

"And she will know," Eliza assures him. "But you're not going over to his house looking like this. She can wait. You can wait. Someone else will go. Marque can handle it."

"I don't trust Marque to handle it," he says. "It has to be me. It can't be anyone else."

"Tony—look at you," she says, pained that she has to expose the reality of the situation. "You're covered in Clyde's blood."

Tony inspects himself, studying his hands, his wrists, his fingers. He touches his neck. His fingers come away with tacky blood; his white shirt and jeans are red with it, saturated in it.

And attuned to Tony in ways only Clyde would understand, Eliza differentiates the acceptance from the anguish in his face, and it breaks her heart to see him this way. "You know I'm right. You need to listen to me."

His eyes flick to the ER suite and then back to her, compartmentalizing, working through his continuum of emotions. His eyes gaze at her—bold, blazed, watery, and sad. "It has to be me," he utters again, but he doesn't sound sure of himself.

Eliza sighs, summoning internal strength born from the looming inevitability of motherhood and the intimacy between them. "I'll do it. I'll have to change first, but I'll go."

Tony starts to protest again.

"You have to stay here. Marque and Bucky are going to want a full report. I'm sure someone will come to ask you questions. I just drove, so there's no reason for me to stick around. I'll go."

Tony accepts Eliza's proposal and nods in consent.

———

CHAPTER THREE:

IRIS KING

IRIS KING ROLLS OVER AND CRAWLS OUT OF bed, nude, leaving Renaldo asleep under the covers with his back to her, sculpted and tanned. The covers are pulled down just enough to show the disappearing V-shape of his lower back muscles with cute dimples on both sides of the bottom tip of the V. Iris reaches for her blush pink silk robe with black fizzy furry lining draped across the nightstand as the knock that woke her from her afternoon nap comes again, a little harsher this time.

Extending her lithe, delicate leg to the floor, Iris pauses to study Renaldo sleeping to see if the noise woke him; it didn't. She delights in the shape of his body; she has dimples like his. As she departs the confines of the bed, it occurs to her that it was warmer under the covers with him, warmer when her body was pressed against his back, and it was hot earlier, so much so that when finished, they were both enveloped in a sheen of sweat. But now, outside the covers, as she throws the robe over one arm and loops the other behind her back to find the sleeve, she's cold; the room's cold. The winter afternoon seeps in through the large bay windows on the far wall, drapes askew and tossed to the side to allow the last hints of the evening to contrast against the warm glow of the bedroom's lighting.

Iris checks the alarm clock on the nightstand for the time. The red numbers on the display tell her it's sometime after 5 p.m. The sun will be gone soon, and she'll have to wake Renaldo. He has to leave before Clyde gets home. Their marital agreement is one of ignorance, and ignorance only goes so far. Sight unseen. Like a child. This is his way.

Iris adjusts the robe, pulling it together over her body, glad she met Renaldo and thankful for how young he makes her feel. She's fifteen years younger than her husband, in her mid-thirties, but she's older than Renaldo, yet she feels that doesn't matter. He loves her. She sees it in the way he looks at her, lingers just a beat too long, or smiles when he doesn't think she's looking. He may say he doesn't. Renaldo likes to brag that he isn't attached to anything, and there are times he pretends to be emotionless, but her relationship with him isn't a normal flirtation or a common extramarital dalliance. For him, it is something more, but for Iris, it is a power move—calculated and beneficial to her. To believe otherwise would be what's expected, and Iris doesn't do what's expected. She likens herself to Lana Del Rey's musical persona, which is appropriate because she's playing on the stereo on the dresser opposite the bed: jazzy, smoky, seductive, glamorous, romantic, a little bit of a bad girl, a lot of naughty, threatening to some, and alluring to many others. No, Iris doesn't do normal; she does everything but, and she relishes this about herself, and so too does Renaldo.

The knock comes again, downstairs, from the front door, abrasive and gruff. Iris wraps the folds of the robe around her thin frame, pulls the flaps across her body until they nearly come together at her back, and ties the sash in a loose knot in the front over her left hip. She trots over to the stereo and stops the soft music, filled with cinematic wistfulness, thinking it's a good thing she doesn't wear any make-up. She doesn't need it. She wouldn't want to answer the front door looking like she'd just had a heavy make-out session, even though she did. Iris touches her cheeks, warm, still flushed from her time with Renaldo, and a glance into the mirror confirms her suspicions. Her hair is a mess and probably says exactly what she's been doing. She tosses it, pulls at the sun-kissed brunette loose curls highlighted with hints of gingerbread and cinnamon, puckers her alarmingly bright red lips, puffy and full from the kissing, and wipes the flakey drool from the blissfully induced siesta from the corners of her mouth.

The knock again, but this time followed with the push of her doorbell: impatient, chafing, abrupt. The ding-dong of the tone resonates throughout the house, and Renaldo stirs in the bed, groaning some. She says go back to sleep as she surveys the results of her quick fretful touch-up in the bedroom door's mirror, figures it will have to be good enough, and then licks her lips, detecting hints of Renaldo, which causes her lips to curl into a wicked smile.

"I'll be right back," she tells his dozing form.

The doorbell sounds again; it hurries her along. She doesn't like the doorbell, the ding-dong tones, and she doesn't like how they play throughout the entire house. If it were up to her, she'd rip the damn thing out of the wall, but Clyde likes it. He lobbied for it, explaining to her he spends too much time in his workshop out in the garage, and she won't answer the door, obligingly adding because no one tells her what to do, which is correct. No one tells Iris how to act or be. But in the garage, he won't hear when packages are delivered, so he needed some sort of solution. Iris came up with a compromise, and her compromise with Clyde was the purchase of an exquisite front door, one they barely could afford without a bit of creative bookkeeping, her specialty, because if she has to have something as rude and abrasive as a ding-a-ling bellowing at all hours, casting forth anxiety and stress, then she needs something pretty to go with it.

At the top of the stairs, the doorbell ding-dongs again, chiming obtrusively, and she curses under her breath and hurries. Her nails are cold against her bare legs, which are thin and toned with hints of muscle, developed from her time at home trying to look like the perfect housewife. Of course, Clyde does all the cooking and the cleaning when the cleaning woman's not over, and he hasn't complained about her body or her creative inputs to their budget. She doesn't hide anything. Clyde knows everything about her and loves her for who she is.

"I'm coming," she yells, treading one step at a time, passing the peach-colored walls devoid of accouterments like photographs and other such knick-knacks and paraphernalia. But when another knock booms, her eyes fixate on the front door, narrowing her features and furrowing her brow. It sounds like Clyde when he's locked himself out of the house, and if he has, then she's going to express her displeasure loudly and for many minutes until she chases him into the garage. For a brief moment, her heart skips in panic as she half-turns to look back up the stairs, to the bedroom, knowing Renaldo is still there in their bed. As she nears the door, she makes out two hazy figures in the frosted glass, obviously not Clyde, and from here she can tell the two forms are a woman and a man, one standing still while the other, the man, sways nervously from side to side. Both cast shimmering shadows in the dying winter light across the foyer's floor; a golden chandelier dangles above, painting crystal refracted rainbows on the marble tile.

Clearing the last step, Iris drums her toes against the cold floor, double-checks her robe, and reaches for the handle as the woman figure, the smaller and more shapely silhouette of the two, knocks and jabs the doorbell in quick succession, several times as if she's annoyed.

Iris rips the door open and lodges herself in the doorway. "Yes, what is it?"

The woman steps back as if pushed by a wave, surprised by the sudden burst of Iris's appearance and anger, or maybe, it is just Iris's appearance, the robe, the thin, almost see-thru material showing a lot of skin. The woman is the opposite of Iris, short but not tiny, petite maybe, dark-haired with dirty blonde highlights, Mexican or something, very tan or dark skinned, and very pregnant. Despite this affliction, she looks good; her skin glows, probably from the pregnancy.

The man is the woman's opposite, haggard, older, taller, balding, with a hint of a ring of hair on top, and he seems surprised by Iris's appearance and is instantly uncomfortable. He has thick sideburns and a drooping mustache, which are similar to Clyde's—but where Clyde's is all dark, brown, and healthy-looking, this man's mustache is tinged with gray. The man is slim, with hints of the musculature that used to be, but he has the belly of a man who drinks too much. His complexion behind the hair says the same: thin lips, a red nose, the type of man to worry and unwind at the same time, usually to the benefit of whiskey or a welcoming watering hole.

Both wear jackets; the woman's light gray with a hot pink blouse, and the man's dark gray with a white shirt. No tie. Blue jeans and battered cowboy boots. They look like a couple of Jehovah's Witnesses.

Neither of them speaks, they just stand there gaping at her like a couple of bunnies that lived in her front bushes unsure when they see her if they should run or continue eating.

"What is it you want?" Iris says. Both figures blink once, twice. She says, "Well, say something. Don't just stand there looking like that—makes me think something bad has happened. What is it?"

That's when the woman's face twists to something sour, a grimace as if this is going to be just as painful for her as it will be for Iris, which reminds Iris of when her father tried to discipline her when she was a kid. The woman shifts on her feet, sweeping the folds of her jacket to the side to show her the badge. "Ma'am, I'm—"

Iris pushes the door closed, but the man jams his foot in the way.

"Mrs. King..." the man starts to say.

Iris backs away from the door, repeating, "No. No. No," not knowing why they are here, but knowing why they are here.

"May we come inside?" the woman asks.

She might as well let them in. They won't go away and whatever they have to say won't be any easier with time.

With a flip of the robe and walking ahead of them, Iris shows them into the living room, stepping down from the foyer's marble tile to the white carpet of the living room, walls of gold. The furniture's white and the TV's black, which works as an accent because it was something Clyde wanted—so she went for the biggest best thing she could find and afford, not that money's an issue, 72-inches, a whole wall, just for football and baseball—the black of the TV, being so large, breaks up the intrusive white and gold. Furniture in the living room is scant because Iris likes sparse and clean. And like Iris, this room's beautiful to look at, warm on the first impression, but cold and hard—or so Clyde complained to her.

Once everyone's seated, the two across from her with her gold coffee table with glass panels between them—not that she's ever served coffee on it—Iris takes a deep breath and says, "He's dead, isn't he? That's why you're here?"

The two look at each other and nod.

Iris says, "This was always a possibility, but that doesn't mean this is any easier to hear. So, I wish you would get on with it and say what it is you have to say."

The woman, who introduces herself as Eliza Cortez, says she worked closely with her husband and follows it with, "Clyde is dead," delivering the line without an ounce of emotion.

The news hits Iris hard, harder than she thought it would or should. Stuns her really. She blinks a few times, unsure of herself. She knew, but now she knows. "Dead?"

The woman repeats, "Clyde's dead" as if the second time will make hearing it any easier.

Iris isn't used to this, being the one playing catch up, because usually she's the one in control. That's how she wins. She controls her emotions. Her face. Her actions. Everything calculated and played to effect. She doesn't let the cards excite her just as she tries to not let life excite her. She barely feels emotion except the thrill of winning.

The man, Marque Boykin—Iris remembered who he was when she saw the badge: Clyde's immediate boss—displays a look of empathetic shock to the Cortez lady's matter-of-fact-manner. "That's to say," Marque says as he leans over and pulls on his belt, trying to work it over his gut, "he was killed."

The Cortez woman's face flushes annoyance as she bites her lips to keep silent, but her eyes tell Iris everything she wanted to say without words, like that's what she said when she said Iris's husband was dead.

Then, it is as if Iris is watching the scene from outside her body. This happens when she needs to think. She sees herself seated on the white loveseat, smoking a cigarette from a long black holder that her mother said reminded her of something Cruella de Vil would use, and she sees herself sitting with her legs crossed, robe loose, and the cigarette perched between two fingers, hanging at the edge of her mouth, listening to them talk as they try to explain why they're here, but nothing they say makes any sense nor is it going to make it all right.

The two keep stepping over themselves, trying to explain what happened, how this could happen. Iris shuts her eyes and focuses on the invisible hand gripped around her heart, squeezing her from the inside and pulling her heart up through her throat, but it seems like they just want her to cry. And she should cry, but Iris won't cry, not in front of them and certainly not for Clyde. But crying would be a normal response.

It is similar to something the man says. "I understand if the news comes as a shock. It's very upsetting news."

Opening her eyes, Iris locks on to him. "It seems like you want me to cry," she says, tilting her head to the side, going on the offensive, and getting to the point. "That's what it seems like you're trying to do right now." She addresses the man but guards herself against the woman. "Make me cry. Draw this out. I know what you're here to say, and I understand it's difficult news to deliver. But I'm not going to give you the pleasure of breaking me. No one does that to me."

The woman says, "No one wants to make you cry."

Iris suppresses a smile by wrapping her lips around the tip of the holder, drawing in smoke, narrowing her eyes. She pushes the smoke out through her nose. "Well, it seems that way. You were rude, inviting yourselves in like that."

"I didn't want to do this at the front door," the Cortez woman says. Her eyes rove around the room. "It didn't seem you wanted—"

"—Clyde and I have only been married for five years," Iris says, cutting her off. "So when I saw you at the door—when I saw the badge—I knew why you were here. Two badges don't just show up at your door to deliver good news. Clyde had told..." but she can't continue. She has to pause to swallow hard and think about how to play the situation best. She was going to say they've talked about it, that he always said it could happen, telling her what would happen when it did. "He said it would be something like this. Told me to let you in and act right. But I never thought it would be anything like this. I never thought I'd feel this way."

The Cortez woman leans forward, trying to reach for Iris to provide comfort, but there's too much of a gap over the table; the table acts as a barrier between them, and that's on purpose. Iris likes barriers. It's one thing that helped in her marriage.

The Cortez woman asks, "Is there anything we can do for you?"

"That's a stupid question," Iris says, aware her lover's upstairs, asleep in her bed. She glances over her shoulder, checks the top of the stairs, willing him to stay upstairs. How would it look if he came downstairs now? Then, she's aware of how naked she is under the robe, of how short the robe feels now—tugging at the edges with one hand—of how she must look in it, of how she's not a good wife, covered in Renaldo's sweat and other ... *substances* with her sex-hair, and Iris knows she's not a good person. Neither is Renaldo. Or Clyde... they've been...

Iris recovers some. "But that's what people say in a situation like this, isn't it?"

The two women lock eyes. The Cortez woman seems to be trying to put forth some sort of sympathetic comfort, but Iris's whole demeanor is defeating her efforts. The woman can't empathize with Iris because it's becoming clear to the Cortez woman Iris and Clyde weren't close. That's how Iris is reading the woman's face because, at first, she looked on with care, but then her expression turned into barely hidden disgust.

Clyde's boss is in her peripheral vision, nodding his head like a bobble-head, missing this revelation completely, but such are men—silly and uninformed. Marque says, "We can call someone for you if you wish."

"No, that's alright," Iris says, patting her thigh, smoothing the robe. "I don't know who I would call. I'm not religious. We don't have many close friends." She doesn't say she spends her time at the casino, which is where she met Renaldo, and Clyde spends all his time in that damn woodshop in the garage or here watching this fucking TV. She takes another drag of the cigarette, leaning back against the loveseat.

Marque starts to say something, but the Cortez woman cuts him off. "Clyde's at the hospital right now. He'll go to the Medical Examiner after. They'll do an exam, and then he'll be released to a funeral home."

But with the words *funeral home*, the cogs in her mind turn things over. Everything she's going to have to do over the next few days. Funeral. Expenses. The house. Taxes. His body. Who to invite, how to let them know, all the phone calls she'll have to make. She doesn't even know where to begin. Does she know anyone willing to help her? Who would help?

This certainly wasn't part of the plan. Clyde wasn't supposed to get hurt.

And then the last thought strikes her: these two are watching all of this happen across her face.

"Did Clyde have a will?" the Cortez woman asks. "Did he have any wishes in the case of death? Maybe a funeral home or something?"

"Yes, he did," Iris says. "I should've asked about him, I suppose. Ask what happened. What happened?"

"There was a shooting," the Cortez woman says, answering her before Marque can say anything.

Marque, dejected, looks like he doesn't know why he's here; he's uncomfortable, and it shows. He pulls at the collar of his shirt. "A routine drug deal gone bad."

"That doesn't tell me what happened."

"I know," the woman says.

"So, what happened?"

Marque leans in, trying to smooth over the Cortez woman's abrasiveness. "We can't get into the specifics at this time."

But it doesn't matter. Iris is playing a role now, the grieving wife, playing it something like Keira Knightley in *London Boulevard*, which is one of her favorites because of Colin Farrell and, honestly, one of his better performances, a sort-of remake of *Sunset Boulevard*. Her mind brings her to that movie because it's fitting; Knightley and she resemble each other, tall, slim, graceful, no curves, but that's okay—money changes everything. Clyde compared her to Blake Lively, but he sure wasn't Ryan Reynolds, and Iris is not as hippy as she is and doesn't have the boobs she has, nor is she as young. So, Iris plays it like Knightley and exudes depressed indifference, but playing Knightley comes with a downside of giving off hints of sensuality, which has plagued her for her entire life. Iris smokes her cigarette and keeps her eyes locked on the two in front of her. Something in the woman's face tells Iris that she doesn't buy her act; perhaps it's the sensual nature she's developed over years of using her femininity to her advantage. She casually crosses her legs, making sure to point her knees away from Marque, who does try to steal a glance anyway.

All of them are playing different roles than what the scene calls for, which to Iris is ... interesting.

"Tony's with him right now," the woman says.

Iris likes Tony. He reminds her so much of Renaldo. Maybe Reni's just a stand-in for Tony, who's always stealing glances at her when he's over here. Usually sitting right here, right next to where she is sitting now. Looking at the spot now, she almost perceives the specter of his form on the loveseat with her, dressed nicely, looking good, smelling better than Marque. Completely devoted to Clyde, he sees... no, not sees... saw Clyde as a mentor and friend. But that's not his real name; not what Clyde called him. What was it... Antonio? That was his full name. His real name. And what Clyde called him, which is something Clyde took pride in, knowing someone's real name, because Clyde liked to name drop who he knew. That was annoying and a liability at times. Clyde was never very good at hiding his emotions or thoughts. Like when Clyde brought Tony to the house, he was ecstatic to introduce Tony to his wife. Clyde introduced him as Antonio, going on about how great he is, and she'd heard a lot about him. But then that was her husband; she always knew where he stood on things he liked. He wouldn't shut up about his partner; in bed, before going to sleep, Clyde would be talking about his day, Antonio this and Antonio that; at the breakfast table more Antonio; on Sunday afternoons, Clyde on the phone with Antonio—and when she met him, Tony corrected Clyde, "No, just Tony." So humble. Embarrassed even. Cute.

Sadness, she should be sad right now, and in a way, she is. She didn't hate her husband, doesn't hate him, but she didn't love him, not in the traditional sense, and that was okay with them both. Clyde knew where he stood. He was a solution to a problem: security and comfort. Just as Renaldo is and just as maybe Tony can be. Overall, he was useful.

Rocking slowly in her seat, reminding herself of what she is supposed to be feeling, Iris says, "That's good. He's a good man. I'm glad. Was… was anyone with him when it happened?"

The woman swivels to Marque, attitude saying he's the one that should be talking since he's the supervisor, but the man sits mute and just seems uncomfortable with Iris's questions. His eyes are on the door as if he's ready to leave. But not the woman—she's taking in the entire living room, looking past Marque now, past everything, looking around, perhaps looking too close. Then, Iris sees it as Eliza sees it. Renaldo's brown leather bomber jacket, fur collar, draped over the back of the recliner.

The woman, back to her, says, "Tony was with him." But her voice really asks *is someone else here?* "I drove him to the hospital where he was pronounced."

"But rest assured, we will conduct a full investigation and prosecute those involved," Marque says.

"You didn't catch the guy?" Iris says. "He wasn't there? Weren't you all there?"

"I was around the corner," Marque says and then adds, "with the arrest team."

"I wasn't close either," the woman says, "but Tony was with him the entire way. Your husband saved his life. You should be very proud of him."

Iris nods a few times, processing the revelations. "That's good. Clyde adored Tony. I'm glad Clyde saved him. He always cared deeply for Tony. Clyde would like to have gone out that way, saving a friend. Is Tony okay?"

The woman dismisses her, waving her hand in front of her body. "He's fine." She pauses. To Iris, it sounds possessive. The Cortez woman adds, "Couple of bumps and bruises, nothing serious."

Marque, perched on the loveseat, shifts back and forth between the door and the two women, and misses all of this. He's a man. Sometimes such subtle things go unnoticed. It always did with Clyde. Marque says, "We do need to get back. There is an investigation. If there's not anything else?"

"—what happened to the man that shot him? Where is he?"

"The hospital," the Cortez woman says. "For now, but he'll be arrested for the murder of your husband."

"That's good." Iris takes the cigarette holder from her mouth and drops her hands to her lap. She plucks the cigarette out of the holder and uses the remains to light another cigarette, softly blowing on the embers, coaxing the end to glow orange. She jams it into the holder and puts the tip between her lips, asking, "So what happens now?"

Silence.

Neither of her husband's coworkers know what to say. The silence ushers a brittle tension into the room; it lingers over them and highlights the friction between the two women. From upstairs, she hears a turn of a faucet and the flow of water; it's slight, but she hears it, and so too does the Cortez woman.

Then, Marque stands and straightens his jacket, and now everyone's standing, which is good because Iris is starting to sweat. She checks the folds of her robe, pulling at them again, cinching the robe tighter against her body, wicking away the sweat beading on her spine. She starts to show them out. Marque turns to say something and catches her fixing the robe. He thinks better of his comment and shuts his mouth.

At the door, with refracted rainbows landing on her large midsection, the Cortez woman tries to peer around Iris, to look up the stairs. "We'll do our investigation, but right now, I suggest you contact someone to comfort you in your time of need."

Iris bites her tongue, annoyed at the insinuation, embarrassed, feeling some guilt about it but not enough to not go crawl into the shower with Renaldo. As they step out of the door, she slams the door behind them.

CHAPTER FOUR:

GENE ORR

G ENE LEARNS ABOUT CLYDE KING'S death while playing cards at one of Renaldo's minor poker games; that's an important distinction, minor over major. It's like music notes—some are bigger than others, and Gene knows his place and where to be because when Kevin explained how this had to happen, he said it had to be a minor game. He said it had to make Renaldo look like he doesn't have control anymore. Kevin added, "And of course he doesn't. I'm pulling his fucking little strings. He just doesn't know it yet."

Gene knows it just as he knows the minor games used to belong to that girl, the King woman, but she's a girl to Gene. Somewhere along the way, like all good things, Renaldo showed up and started running her games and backing her bank, which effectively pushed her out of her own poker game. It's not something Gene would be pleased with, but the woman's sleeping with Renaldo, so she must have been okay with the arrangement, according to Kevin, which just plays into Kevin's master plan. Then, she started playing at Renaldo's minor games as a side attraction for the players, which was the end of a good thing and the start of something else. Renaldo didn't seem to mind her staying around. Why would he when he's fucking her? Usually, when the family moved in on something, whoever had it before either disappeared or was cut out, but Renaldo let the girl stay behind. And this is why it had to be a minor one because Kevin said the girl's important.

Right now, Gene sits his happy fat blond ass in this dark little makeshift room stuffed in the back of a sporting goods store, which is sandwiched somewhere between the managers offices and hidden amongst the warehouse shelves with boxes of Nike and Adidas shoes decorating the walls around him so much so that he's not sure if there are walls or shelves. A couple of floor lamps encircle the table like Tiki torches as if they're on one of those game shows where people try to survive, but everything's pre-fabricated bullshit, i.e., Reality TV, which is basically what this looks like: a set for a poker game.

Gene's one of four at a little felt-topped table, plus Jaramillo the dealer, and they're playing Texas Hold'em.

In the corner, just outside the light, a big guy in a dark suit, little jacket, goes by Mastodon because of his size— Renaldo's trusted enforcer, who isn't specifically tied to the Siriano family—sits hunched over on a stool. His dark eyes watch everything and everybody from the shadows with perpetually furrowed brows, and his dark hair is slicked back, which almost makes it shimmer in the refracted light. A computer with two flash sticks and an external hard drive sits in the corner with him on a small table. It's Mastodon's gateway to the outside world, specifically banking accounts that need to be accessed, which is really to say Renaldo's "book" and Gene's mission. Well, part of it.

Gene stares at the computer as the news of the DEA agent's death comes over the airwaves pumped into the small space through the little TV perched on the TV stand, the type of TV stand Gene's used for a dining-room table his whole poor life. The TV is in the corner somehow plugged into the wall with an extension cord. The cord runs off between the shoeboxes disappearing into the ether of the back of the store, so Gene's not sure if it's plugged in or not. It could be magic; he doesn't know. But the TV's on, and he doesn't have to get rained on to know if he needs an umbrella when the street's wet.

On the TV, the Six O'clock Evening News breaks the story first, a talking head, male, all distinguished gray hair, saying a DEA agent was shot dead today. Then, the screen flashes to a reporter standing outside a Ronny Mac's, who breaks down the story. But it's the headline that gets Gene's attention first, *DEA Agent dead,* as the first of his two cards lands in front of him, sliding to a stop next to his fat fingers. His eyes shift to the table with the words echoing in his head. *DEA Agent dead* and he knows what he's done and what he's about to do, and how it is all for a friend, an ex-boyfriend.

Normally, Gene stays away from Renaldo's poker games because Renaldo's into some heavy shit connected to the Siriano family, and Gene knows better than to get involved with Renaldo because that means getting involved with Siriano beyond his wonderful business relationship, but selling guns isn't gambling. Gene's one weakness, well one of few, is gambling, and every now and then Gene will play one of the girl's games. She is nice and always caters good food. But since Renaldo's taken over, he's not wanted to chance owing Renaldo, and the family, any money. That's what he told Kevin a month ago when he said, "He's not someone you want to owe a lot of money to," meaning Renaldo, which meant Siriano. "He's connected to some major players."

Renaldo's the bagman for Siriano, which isn't just *somebody;* he is *The Guy*, meaning Renaldo's the second-in-command of the number-one guy. He's got some pull. But Kevin, who's a lower rung guy in Siriano's organization, told him that's not going to be a problem any longer. He said that's what he's been working on, separating Renaldo from Siriano, saying, "We're going to get him ousted."

It's all part of Kevin's grand-master-fucking-plan of climbing the ladder in the Siriano organization because, to quote Kevin: "I'm sick of taking orders from a spic upstart. He's not even Italian."

This conversation happened in Kevin's bullshit club that he uses to rob people blind, with Kevin sitting at a high-top table drinking a mixed drink, sucking it down through the little stir stick straw, wearing a baggie hoodie, dressed like a Fred Durst stunt double, complete with a flat bill hat.

And at the table, all Gene said was, "How the fuck are *we* going to do that? And why is it *we* all of a sudden? I don't work with Siriano. That's *you*."

But what he really wanted to tell Kevin was that he's not supposed to suck through those straws. Don't you watch movies? Ryan Gosling told everyone exactly what that looks like, but then again, it just reminds Gene of their past.

Kevin told him, "This is what you're going to do—"

"—no, answer me first, when did it become *we*... you and I... we're friends. Yeah, okay. I get it—we shouldn't be friends any longer but no hard feelings. I still like you. We work together. It's a good relationship. I fence your shit, but look, why is this connected to me? Yeah, I move your guns, that's the other part of what I do, low-level bullshit crime, low-level the keyword here, and yeah, we work together from time to time—"

"—this is what you're going to do." Kevin talks like Gene didn't say nothing. "You're going to make the call to that Cuban-fucker, the one the ATF agent in my pocket told me was DEA. He's been after Siriano for years. Guy said the Cuban is trying to work his way into the Siriano organization by using your gun deal as a cred builder."

Gene threw up a hand. "Hang on, hold up. ATF agent? What ATF agent?"

"DEA doesn't deal with guns, so don't worry. Besides, you're a *low-level* bullshit crime guy. What's it matter to you?"

"The ATF deals with guns. That matters to me."

"The ATF won't touch you," Kevin said. Gene asked how he knew that. "What's it matter? You're already fucked—hence why I said we." Then, he said, "Do you want to hear my plan or not?"

"And then what are *we* going to do?" Gene asked, playing like he wanted to hear the plan but knowing this could only spell trouble and playing along was the only way for Gene to clear his name. But more importantly, what he really wanted to know was why his guy didn't let Kevin in on the fact that the feds were involved with Gene's business in the first place. His business has been paying people at the manufacturer and end-seller to do some creative paperwork having to do with gun returns and destructions that don't really happen. Those same guns find their ways into Gene's hands, then through guys like Casper, he offloads them to the street sellers. Or into Kevin's hands. Gene asked, "Why didn't you let me know about the feds?"

But at the table all Kevin did was smile and say, "We'll get a friend of mine to do the deal. He's independent, so when the indictments come down, we'll get him kicked off the warrants. My guy won't argue with me about it—we're keeping it business and he loves business."

"ATF agent going to help *us* with that part?" Gene asked. "Or you want me to see if the Cuban-fucker's going to get on board, or a raft, with us and give us a reach around after we fucked him in the ass?"

"That's not how a reach around works."

"What about Renaldo? Isn't he going to have a say in it?"

"Are you listening to me?"

"No, because this will go bad, and I'm going to be the one left holding the bag."

"How could this go wrong?" Kevin asked, sitting back on the stool pleased with himself for working this out in his head. "Here's what we do... we put the DEA on to Siriano and blame Renaldo. If there's something I know about Siriano is he doesn't like rats. Even perceived ones. And Renaldo's an uppity fucker who needs to be knocked down a few pegs. What could go wrong?"

"Everything," Gene said. But what's he going to do? Kevin just informed him, this guy who he's still in love with even if he's not in love with him, that he has his ass tight in a vise. "So where do you want *me* to come in?"

Kevin told him and then told him how he'll set this all up. "What we have to do is find someone that we can pin everything on when this all comes downhill,"

Gene asked, "Got anyone you want to suggest since we're playing Machiavellian schemes now?"

"Don't be like that."

"Like what? The fact that you're punching above your weight doesn't concern you? It concerns me. This is going to go bad, and you still haven't told me what you want me to do because it sounds like you want me to do something other than being the cred builder for the DEA-fucker."

Kevin told him, "We're going to blow the wheels off the wagon."

"What the fuck does that mean?" Gene asked, and then after Kevin told him what he wanted Gene to do, Gene told him this plan was shit, but fine, he'd play along.

"Get Casper to help you," Kevin said. Casper is the kid Gene rescued off the streets and now Casper's involved because Kevin, probably out of misplaced jealousy, said, "We'll fuck Casper. His time's come anyways."

So now, Gene's at Renaldo's minor game, getting ready to rob the man, and by extension the Neanderthal, Mastodon, repeating the mantra minor over major, trying not to think about the fact the girl should be here and is not here, and that's what's important for this to work. Kevin told him to come here for the girl. Said she's something to look at. Said she's the key.

A dead DEA agent.

And here he got to thinking today was a good day.

Gene asks the table, "Where's the girl?"

The old burglar, Bronson, who sits across from him with his dark weathered skin, cracked and dry like riverbeds, deep, the color of red clay, like leather, with wisps of white hair scattered across his body like scrub brush in the desert, says, "She's not here tonight."

"I know that," Gene says, checking his cards, bending them just so he can see them without showing anyone else. Ace/king, not bad, but then he knows the cards can always turn. "What I'm asking is, where is she? She take a day off? I like her."

Which gets a laugh from the table.

Tania, young—younger than Gene—dark hair, oriental, says she's Chinese, but not mainland Chinese and Gene doesn't know what that means, asks him, "Does it matter?"

"I guess not," Gene says, but it does.

Shrugging, Bronson sets his cards flat on the table and says, "Sometimes she's here. Sometimes she's not."

Tania says, "It must matter."

"What do you mean?" Gene asks.

She glances at her cards. "I mean, for you to ask, it must matter to you."

"I wondered the same thing too," Wilson Notaro says. "I think she's pretty."

Kevin said Wilson's a minor player in the Siriano organization. He is Italian and handsome. No other way to describe him. Imagine Rob Lowe, and that's pretty much Wilson. Rumors, for those that believe in such shit, say he's Siriano's illegitimate son. Some say he's a spitting image of the big man himself. He comes around to the small games because he likes to socialize. He's dashing and handsome and likes Renaldo, so he's not going to rat him out to the old man. He never wins, but he doesn't always lose either. Wilson says, "But be careful what you say—that's Renaldo's girl."

The dealer, Jaramillo says, "She called in. Family emergency," while adjusting the stack of cards on the table.

The group at the table gives the dealer their attention.

Then, Wilson folds, telling Gene, "There you go. That's your answer," and tosses his cards toward Jaramillo.

The cards slide across the table as Gene's phone rings, vibrating on the table, which wakes up the big man in the corner.

Mastodon straightens his body. "Don't you know the rules? No phones."

Gene picks the phone off the table. "Look, I still got business to conduct." He holds the phone in one hand, pointing it at Mastodon. "Unlike the girl, apparently, I don't take days off. I don't know what a day off is. What I know are opportunities and pitfalls. Losing some money can be a pitfall, but that doesn't mean I stop trying to make money. You want to take this call? You want to do my business while I sit here and play a fucking game? How's that going to look to the guys underneath me? Them seeing me blowing off work just so that I can sit here and jack off with you."

"No phone calls," Mastodon says again, with more force in his voice. "Those are the rules. Do I need to get up and show you what I mean when I say no phones?"

Gene mocks him, extending his arms out in upside-down arches, a monkey act. "No phone calls. You know what, you mind if I fold and take the call outside? Will that work for you, you big lumbering fuck?"

Tania stifles a laugh. Bronson closes his eyes and sighs. Wilson just looks at him and shakes his head. The dealer deals.

Mastodon grumbles unhappily. "Fine, step outside."

Gene stands from his chair and says into the phone, "Hold on a second." He bows toward Mastodon like he's exiting the mat of a dojo, feigning respect, and steps out from behind the shelves, briskly walking toward the door. Outside, Gene puts the phone to his ear, "What do you want?"

It's Kevin, at his club... his alibi. He asks, "Things still on track?"

"What do you mean on track?"

"I mean are you in position?"

"Yeah, I'm outside right fucking now, but listen, did you see the news—"

"—Casper know what he's supposed to do?"

"—the girl's not here—"

"—you explained to him no one gets hurt, right?" Kevin asks and then says, "What do you mean the girl's not there?"

"Did you see the news?"

"No, why would I need to see the news?"

"Oh, I don't know. It might have something to do with the dead DEA agent."

Silence comes through the phone. Gene can hear a band warming up in the background, and then Kevin says, "That might not be related."

"What do you mean, not related? How many DEA agents are in town doing deals? How many named King? And how many are married to the girl that could be involved in such deals?"

"Could be several."

Gene sighs. "It's related."

"Still we don't have time to call this off. This will work in our favor."

"How's this going to work in our favor?"

"We'll have to get the girl later," Kevin says. "Do everything else we planned. I need the drives. Do you understand?"

"I'm not fucking stupid. I get it. I still don't see why you couldn't just break in and steal them."

"Because I'm good at that which would bring suspicion on me, but if we force Renaldo to look in one place—specifically at Casper—he won't know what the hell happened. In fact, now that I'm thinking about it, the DEA agent dying's just going to sweeten the pot. Sucks for Frankie but helps us. Might push things a little faster than I planned though, but I'll adjust."

"You'll adjust?" Gene asks. "What happened to *we*? Now it's *I* again?"

"Get rid of this phone when we're done."

"You didn't answer me—how's this going to work in our favor? And I think I'm starting to see a pattern in how you treat your friends."

But Kevin ends the phone call, so Gene stares at the phone for a moment longer and then slips it into his pocket. Get rid of the phone—why would he get rid of something he can still use?

It's his prevailing business philosophy. Don't trash perfectly good items. It's how he got involved with the gun business. That and hustle.

Casper comes around the corner, gun in hand, mask on face, and ready to go. His shitty white jeep with the black ragtop idles beyond the back of the building, keys dangling from the ignition.

"You're just going to leave the keys in the car?" Gene points to the car behind him. "What if it gets stolen?"

"What?" Casper asks. "You think I should have them on me? I was thinking if I had to get out of here fast, it'd be better to have it ready to go, you know?"

If Gene wasn't about to fuck Casper over, he might take the young man, who when Gene met him was a woman, to the side, arm over his nineteen-year-old-shoulder and explain to him how the world works, not that he hasn't already done that. He would also explain how people like Gene don't want people like Casper to think things over, or how Casper, no matter how hard he tries, will find the world a little bit hostile to him, just like with Gene.

Gene says, "You know what, never mind."

Casper nods and hands Gene a matching ski mask and jumpsuit. "You ready?"

Gene says he's not, but then he says go ahead, closing his eyes, clenching his fist while grabbing the lip of his pockets, bracing for the impact. Casper smacks Gene hard on the forehead with the butt of his pistol. Shattering shards of bright lights fill his vision, and Gene loses his balance and staggers, amazed at how quickly the headache comes like a surge of rushing water through a garden hose. Small at first, the pain waits at the edges like horses on the ridge, but then it's hard and fast like Huns down a mountainside, full-on master blaster.

He inspects his head with his fingers. The blow didn't cut him open. That's fine. He wants the goose egg. More visually appealing. He slips the mask on and steps into the jumpsuit—now he matches Casper. He says to the kid, "When we run out this door, I'm going to shed this shit and you take it with you. Okay? I'll stagger back inside and tell them you left as you're leaving. Slow them down. Got it?"

Casper says sure he's got it.

But Gene's not sure. "I'm not fucking around. You going to be able to remember that or not?" Casper nods. Gene says, "And just the money."

Casper pauses as his strawberry blonde curly hair stabs through the mask's eyeholes. "No girl?"

"No girl," Gene says. "I'll get the computer."

"Should we call this off?"

"No," Gene says, although he thinks they should. "We go forward. Do what we came to do."

"You ready?"

Again, he's not, but Gene says, "Yes."

CHAPTER FIVE:

RENALDO LUNA

RENALDO OPENS THE DOOR to his third-story empty apartment and steps inside, rolling his shoulders under the heavy leather jacket with the fur collar, and checks the sleeves of his grey button-up shirt, which poke out of the arms of the jacket.

His hand reaches for the switch on the wall and flicks the lights on before throwing the deadbolt on the door. He turns toward the living area, and the first thing he notices is the balcony door open, which is surprising, considering he didn't leave it open or unlocked. Then, he spots Kevin Alexander, a white male—although grey would be a more appropriate description—a doper and an eager underling, an errand boy with ambition, sitting in a chair shielding his eyes as they adjust to the light. It is not surprising.

Yeah, sure, okay, maybe it's surprising, but Renaldo plays like it isn't. The old man has begun to rely on Kevin more than Renaldo would like. If Renaldo had to guess, he'd say it was because Kevin is Irish-Italian, not some

Mexican who looks more Italian than half the men in the organization, and despite the inroads Renaldo's built while working for Siriano, who traditionally hasn't cared about lineage, the rest of the families have been leery of Renaldo and his *pedigree*, as one particular man from Kansas City said.

Kevin sits at Renaldo's card table, which is near a small TV. The table has four folding chairs and is a utilitarian solution for Renaldo's preferred living arrangements. The rest of the apartment is empty. Renaldo's bedroom is not much different, mattress on the ground, a couple of blankets, a pillow or two. The kitchen is standard with all the furnishings and appliances one comes to expect in a kitchen: a couple of plates, a fork, and a mug next to the sink. The only luxury items in the apartment are Renaldo's clothes filling his closet, expensive pieces, colorful, all bought with his earnings, one of his few indulgences—beyond Iris that is—and the liquor and food in the fridge.

Although slightly startled, Renaldo plays it off, pushing the flutter in his chest down, shrugging his shoulders, and strolling from the door to the kitchen while shedding the leather jacket and tossing it on the kitchen counter. In the kitchen, Renaldo withdraws a glass from a cabinet and fills it with tap water from the sink. "I could've shot you," he says with the glass up to his lips as his other hand reaches behind his back and removes his gun from the waistband holster. He drops the gun on the countertop next to his jacket.

Kevin uncrosses his legs. "Welcome home," he says and then takes an exaggerated look around the apartment. "You should really invest in some furniture."

Renaldo drinks the remaining water from the glass and refills it. He asks, "Do you want something?"

"Thirsty, are we?" Kevin says, ignoring the question. Renaldo reads the man's face, the smug expression, the self-assuredness, the hollowed look of someone who isn't in control of his impulses, and sees Kevin wants something. "Where were you?"

"That's not any of your concern," Renaldo says.

He was with Iris, although he wouldn't say he was really with her, not at the end, because she wasn't with him; her mind was someplace else. Unlike Kevin, she's hard to read; he likes that about her, but whatever it was that was bothering her, she wasn't letting on, not until he was walking out the door, and she was checking down the street, looking for something or someone it seemed, half-expecting to see it. That's when she told him her husband had been killed. Of course, she was dressed then, not in the robe she came back into the bathroom wearing, where he was taking a shower, shedding the robe, and climbing inside with him for another session, not uttering a single word. He knew something was wrong, where he could have sworn she was crying during all of it, but it could have been the water. When he was leaving, after she told him what was wrong, he asked her if she wanted him to stay. She crossed her arms and told him no and that he should go.

Renaldo knows Kevin will keep prying until he gets some sort of usable answer—the man likes to sniff through other people's secrets—so Renaldo says, "With a girl."

Kevin wags a finger. "Be careful: girls can kill you. It's why I stay away from them."

Renaldo doubts that is the reason.

Then Kevin asks, "Who is she?"

Renaldo finishes the water. "That's my business," he answers. He steps away from the counter, still playing unconcerned about Kevin's unwelcome and unexpected presence. "Can I get you something to drink?"

"I'll take some of the vodka you have in the freezer," Kevin says, hinting he's had a look around and he's been through the apartment, but then again, that's Kevin's specialty. He's a burglar whose specialty is coming and going without leaving a trace.

"Didn't you use to joke about shitting on people's rugs?" Renaldo says. "That's something I've never understood, going through the trouble of breaking in, moving around, and being in someone's place without disturbing the place, only to fucking shit on the carpet."

"It's so they know—makes them feel violated," Kevin says, grinning before he metaphorically shits on Renaldo's rug and shows he knows about the vodka by adding, "you know the stuff you have in the back of the freezer under the waffles—I'll take that."

Renaldo nods. "That's my hold out for bad days."

Kevin smiles wider. "And you have the really good stuff in the cabinets above the fridge. I'm a bourbon man myself, but if all you want to offer me is vodka, I'd say I want the waffle vodka."

Kevin doesn't faze Renaldo any. He's careful and doesn't keep anything compromising at his apartment. Doing what he does for who he does it, he's learned it's better to be a ghost among the living. There's nothing that gives any indication about the man who resides here, except for the closet, and that's an acceptable risk because if Renaldo's learned anything in his life, or from his mentors, is people do *judge books by their covers*, and he'd rather start on strong footing than play catch up.

And Kevin is Renaldo's opposite; he doesn't dress well: baggy hooded sweatshirt, gray, blue jeans, distressed and acid-washed with pre-made rips and well-worn holes, Birkenstock sandals, bare toes. A black flat bill ball cap sits on the card table next to three phones, the shiny sticker still on the brim.

"What are you doing here?" Renaldo asks as he retrieves the Grey Goose vodka from the freezer. He's not a barbarian. Money buys luxury; he just applies the luxury to what he considers internal extravagance, food, drink, and clothes—not toys. That's how the taxman takes notice and, by extension, the law, which is a lesson anyone who's idolized Al Capone or Mickey Cohen has learned.

"Don't skimp on it, will ya?" Kevin says. "Plenty to go around." Kevin points his thumb toward Renaldo's bedroom. "You'd think for all the clothes you got packed in there, you wouldn't wear something like that." Kevin flicks the lapels of a make-believe jacket. "Think maybe this guy's got some jewelry or watches or something—but nada. I might have hit the bottle earlier, but I've been waiting a while, and I got to do this first before I can do anything else, express, chop-chop, and all that."

"Why are you here?"

Kevin picks up one of the phones and offers it, getting to it. "He wants to talk to you?"

Renaldo retrieves two shot glasses from the cabinet and uncorks the vodka. "Who?" he asks, knowing who. He turns to the counter, laying everything out, filling each of the glasses, letting the clear liquid pour into the two stubby glasses.

"Who could it be?"

"The boss?" Renaldo says. "Yours or mine? Because if I remember correctly, you're looking at yours. So, you must mean mine, and mine doesn't talk to me like this, not directly that is."

Kevin raises an eyebrow. "You're going to do that right now?" he says. "Look, I'm not happy about being here. Just so you know—getting in here was nothing. That door was unlocked," he points at the open balcony door, which is allowing a breeze to blow in, adding a chill to the room, "just sloppy, considering who you are, but I've been here," he checks his watch, "a couple of hours. Got hot. Opened the door again. Where the hell were you? You know what, never mind, that's not my business. My business was to contact you. So here, just take the damn phone—this is a special request."

"What's so special about it?"

"I'm not saying it out loud here," Kevin says, eyes slanting from side to side, body saying you never know who's listening as he taps his ear with his index finger. "But let's just say it's special. Something that needs your *personal* attention."

"Yeah, sure, okay," Renaldo says. "Everything these days seems to require my special attention. Why didn't he call me? Why send you?"

"As I said, special request," Kevin says. "This is a one-time phone call on something considered to be clean. He went through the trouble to make this happen. Let's just say it's an inconvenience for me. I had a job planned for tonight," he glances out the windows and pauses, "but I had to put that off to be here. There's a lot of effort and planning that goes into setting up some shitty-ass half-baked band at my place just so I can lift some poor fuck's wallet and keys, get to their place, steal their shit, and get back before the sets end." He acts out the next part, playing the two roles, saying, "Standing behind the bar, like I'm running the lost and found. Dumb fuck coming up to me, 'oh sorry sir, but I've seemed to misplaced my wallet and keys. Anyone happen to turn them in?'" He does the dumb fuck's voice in a British accent for some reason. "'Why no. I've not seen anything. Let me check with the other bartender...' Wait for a beat... 'Hey yeah, seems someone did,' act like I'm reading his license, 'This you? A Mister Dumb Fuck?'"

Listening to him, Renaldo sips the vodka, savoring it, rolling it over his tongue. He swallows and says, "That doesn't sound like something he usually does. I should know."

"Yeah, well, this requires your attention and this ain't something normal," Kevin says. "So, take the damn phone."

Renaldo steps around the counter, sipping his vodka, and hands Kevin his glass but neglects the phone. "You telling me what to do?"

Kevin accepts the vodka and then puts the phone down. "No, just, I'm hoping to get back, maybe get lucky, get in someplace, not lose out tonight, you know?"

No, Renaldo doesn't know. "Don't ever tell me what to do."

"Wouldn't dream of it," Kevin says.

"Good, that's better," Renaldo says. He sips his glass.

Then, Kevin says, "But just so you know, you're to consider the pushiness as coming directly from the big man." Kevin's lips twist into a grin. "So, you know, take the damn phone and call him—sir—so I can leave."

"Yeah, sure, okay," Renaldo says, finishing the vodka, setting the glass on the table, switching glass for phone, swiping the phone from the table, a flip phone, old-school, easy to dispose of. "How's he want to do it?"

Kevin leans his whole body back, tilts his head back, glass to his lips, eyes on Renaldo, and slings the drink back. He slams the glass on the table. "I'll make a call, then we wait—this is where someone on the other end's relaying I called." Kevin points at the phone in Renaldo's hand. "Then, he'll call that phone."

"Yeah, sure, okay. Make the call."

Kevin retrieves the other flip phone from the table, hits one button—speed dial—and holds it up to his ear. A short moment later, he's saying, "Yeah, it's me." Silence. "Yeah, he's ready—yeah, I know it's been a couple of hours. I didn't know where the fuck he was, but I was doing my part—you know what? Just do your prison shit and send the message. We're waiting." Silence. "Yes, I know he's waiting too. You know what? Just do your thing. I'll do my thing, knowing I'm fucking glad to be getting to do it on the outside, you stupid fuck."

Kevin flips the phone closed and slips it into the hoodie's pocket. Renaldo's eyes stay on the man while holding the phone down at his side.

Jittery and enjoying himself, Kevin says, "Now we wait."

"Yeah, sure, okay," Renaldo says. "You going to leave or just stand there looking—"

"—I got to take the phone with me. Get rid of it," Kevin says, "when we're done."

The phone in Renaldo's hand buzzes. He flips it open and holds it to his ear. The voice on the other end doesn't wait for him to say anything.

"I'll take it you still don't know how to fucking answer a phone," Siriano says.

"Yeah—"

"—sure, okay, you ever say anything fucking different than that?"

"Yes," Renaldo says. Short answers are best with Siriano.

"You know what? It doesn't matter," Siriano says. "Look, sorry to send that fuck-tard around to you, but this is a special request—we've experienced some problems that need to be dealt with quickly. Where were you? I was expecting to make this call sooner... my shows are on right now." Primetime entertainment is something Siriano takes very seriously. Currently, it's all the Chicago melodramas. He goes on. "I need you to take care of a couple of things."

Silence.

"You there?"

"I'm here," Renaldo says.

"Well, you have to fucking talk, or this is a weird fucking conversation."

"Yeah, sure, okay."

"Don't do that, 'okay.' Really. I can't fucking stand it when you do that."

"What do you need done?"

"Good," Siriano says. "That's better. I like that about you, straight to the point. We've got some problems that need to be handled. You hear about the fuck up?"

Renaldo shakes his head. "No."

"Seems some of our boys sold to the wrong customers— the motherfucking government."

"Who?"

"Frankie Hayes and Stevie Gragg," Siriano says. "Things went bad. A cop got shot. DEA I hear. Stevie's dead."

"They're independents," Renaldo says. "Not directly involved in our chain."

"Yeah, well, talk to Kevin about that. He was in charge of their distribution."

Interesting... Renaldo didn't know that and that's not happened before. Sure, Siriano used Kevin as a messenger but never as a facilitator, not anything like that without running the idea through Renaldo.

Renaldo's eyes are on Kevin. "Consider it done."

"I'm not done yet," Siriano says. "It doesn't seem like you're writing anything down. You might need to write this down because there's a couple of things to do."

"I don't write anything down," Renaldo says. "I'll remember it. Amateurs write things down. That's how they end up..." but he doesn't finish the sentence because he was about to say prison.

"Still, you should write something down," Siriano says. "Doesn't matter. Frankie's alive. Cop dead, I hear. So, he'll need to be taken care of, you get it? Make it look like someone else."

"Yeah, sure, okay."

"Look I don't care what order of things you take care of first, but Frankie was put on to those guys by that little shit-stain Casper, so you're going to have to find out if he knew if he was working for them, and then take care of it— don't care if we get answers or not if you get what I mean."

Renaldo does. He nods and stays silent.

Siriano says, "Casper's the kid who works for Gene Orr. He's the one that buys and sells stolen guns to and from people like Kevin there and works his magic on them, getting them into the hands of people that need them. Gene's a regular Eddie Coyle, but then again, last time I went down, I read that book and what happened to the title character. Guess that's what's going to have to happen to Casper. Gene'll understand."

Renaldo doesn't say anything.

"Again with the silence," Siriano exclaims. "Your mother never teach you how to take a phone call? You know what? Don't worry about it. I'll knock some sense into you as we go forward. I'm getting out of here soon—lawyer says technicality—I say bribery, but we'll see. So you get that, talk to Casper, then take care of Frankie. I hear Frankie's in the hospital."

"Got it."

"I don't believe Frankie put them on to us," Siriano says. "Wouldn't be beneficial to business, and we know how seriously he takes his business. If there's no money in it, then there's no Frankie in it. But look, Stevie didn't do it either. I don't need his brother Leon getting involved in things. Personal feelings need to be left out of this, so you might put Frankie at the top of the to-do list because if Leon gets to him—doing what he does, probably going through whoever's on Frankie—then that's a whole other level of shit we don't want to deal with. Leon needs to understand we had nothing to do with the government getting involved... meaning his brother's death."

"Yeah, sure, okay," Renaldo says.

"We haven't used Leon in a while, so I don't know where he stands, but last I heard he was working..."

"I understand. Make sure Leon knows we didn't get his brother killed."

"Last thing—we have a leak," Siriano says, "and that's the last thing we need right now. I hear rumors of indictments, but with this blowing up in the news, the DEA wouldn't dare try to come after me on this, lay this at my feet, that'd be fucking stupid. So I don't care how you figure it out, but if it's not Casper, then we need to know how they got on to my business arrangement. I compartmentalize for a reason, and still, they're there. I don't like it."

"Yeah—"

"—sure, okay. I'll take that to mean you've got it handled."

"I have it handled."

"Hand the phone back to Mr. Alexander there and get to work," Siriano says. "Have any questions?"

"Just one," Renaldo says. "Who was the cop that got killed?"

"Some fucking dick engorging agent named Clyde King."

Iris's husband.

And then Siriano adds, "Oh and final thing, forgot to mention it... when you find out Casper's the one that set us up, take care of his handler for me, and then the dead cop's partner—send a message—he was in the car. Keep it clean. Again, make it look like someone else. Maybe we'll get lucky, and they'll be the same. Two birds and all that shit. I can't stand people not being loyal or even appearing as if there's any infidelity. I pay good money for loyalty. If they don't need my money, then they don't need air either—free ain't free."

Renaldo hangs up the phone, flipping it closed, and hands it to Kevin, who slips the phone into his pocket and points at the table, at the other phone. "That one's for you when you do whatever it is you're supposed to do. The number's already programmed in it. Get rid of it when you're done."

CHAPTER SIX:

GENE ORR

GENE UNLOCKS THE FRONT GLASS DOOR of his pawn shop, struts inside, only to find someone sitting behind the glass counter in his chair, which makes Gene nearly jump out of his shoes and grab at his heart, dropping the morning paper. On second thought, the guy looks like he's nearly asleep, so Gene takes a moment to get control and quiet the storm raging in his chest cavity. Gene says, "Jesus, you scared me." Tony stirs awake now as Gene fights to bring the adrenaline coursing through his system down. "God, I can't breathe right now. My heart's beating like a goddamn drum." Gene retrieves the paper from the floor. "You freaking scared me. What's the hell wrong with you doing that to a guy?"

Tony's feet are up on the counter and through heavy-lidded eyes, with stubble stippling his chin giving his whole expression a dark haze, he says nothing, looking like he hasn't slept all night as he stares at Gene entering the place.

"You been crying?" Gene asks, straightening, the paper pressed against his hip. "Your face is all red, and there's something dark on your shirt. Is that blood? Why're you covered in blood? And why is your arm in a sling?"

All Tony says is, "We need to talk."

Gene locks the door behind him, flips the switch for half the fluorescent lights, which blink and buzz to life, and glances out the windows, making sure no one can see Tony inside. *Oregon Pawn and Gold* is located in a small strip center off the main drive in a small East Tulsa suburb. Like Gene, the place has enough legitimacy decorating the walls and plastered to the exterior to pass as a real business, but in reality, it's as crooked as they come, and it's where Gene runs his little half-assed empire of dopers, burglars, and thieves, which really are all the same type of criminal— fuckups and rejects. The showroom's nothing more than four white walls, a couple of shoulder-high shelves with scattered random items, and a nearly empty glass L-shaped showcase and counter running along two walls. Gene runs the legitimate gun store next door, too. A door in the back connects both businesses.

Wheeling back around from the front door, Gene asks, "What do you mean we need to talk? What are you doing here?"

Tony says again, "We need to talk."

Gene toddles across the open space and halts in front of the counter, standing in front of and peering down at Tony in Gene's chair seated at Gene's makeshift desk with Gene's desktop computer screen next to Tony's elbow. With his hands on his hips, paper flaring at the side like tail feathers, Gene asks, "What do we need to talk about?"

"What happened to your face? You look like you have a black eye."

"That's because I do, but don't ask me to explain how it happened because I don't want to get into it. And I do know why you might be here—maybe, just maybe it might have something to do with the dead DEA agent, but pretend that I don't know that so you can tell me and I can be surprised, but if it were because of a dead guy you know, then I'd say that's a big fucking problem."

"We're going to play this game?" Tony drops his feet off the counter to the floor with a clomp. The chair squeaks as he shifts his weight. He rests his hands on the counter glass. "Now of all days, the day after you fucked me in the ass, you're going to pretend you don't know what happened? The day after my friend was killed, you're going to play stupid?"

Gene holds up a hand. "Hey, don't talk to me like that. I get it. Your friend's dead. He died. But you need to understand a couple of things. I said pretend that I don't know what it is you want to talk to me about because I don't. How could I? I'm not you. I can't read your freaking mind. You want to sit here in the dark and nearly give me a heart attack, fine, but don't sit there, in the dark, and say mean things. I didn't do anything to you or your friend, and I ain't stupid. So, either talk to me like I am a person, you know mean something to you, or get the hell out."

"My friend's dead," Tony says, his voice dropping out for a moment as sadness creeps across his face and features but then recedes. "And you're the person responsible for that, so forgive me if I forgo the humanity of the situation and cut straight to the point of asking how the fuck did Frankie know I was a cop?"

"And I'm sorry about that," Gene says, not responding to anything Tony just said, "but I don't have nothing to do with that."

"You set it up."

"No, Casper set it up, and I don't control him," Gene says. "He's not a fucking dog. He's a person, which is something you need to remember. You work with people. We're not all fuckups. Alright? You got that? I don't appreciate you treating me like I don't matter. I matter. Casper matters. But I'm not a dog. He's not a dog. Do I look like I own dogs? Own him? Is Casper on a leash? Like one of those baby strap tether things. Am I holding on to his tether, walking him through the park or zoo or wherever fuck you see people walking their children instead of being parents? Harness like little sports bras across the kid's front? Come to think of it, maybe that's what's wrong with society. Too many people treat their pets like kids and kids like pets. Oh, sorry, I can't put a leash on my fucking dog because he don't like it, goes *cowf cowf* every time I put it on him, coughing his little head off making like the leash is choking him, but I sure as hell won't let my kid have any ounce of responsibility. No, my kid can't wander off. No, my kid can't be paid attention to like a parent should. No wonder kids are fucked up these days."

"Casper's not my informant," Tony says. "You are. You're responsible."

"Yeah, I am, but that's because you got me by the balls," Gene says. "What do you think happened here? You been to bed yet? No, don't answer that question. I can tell by the way you look and are looking at me, you came here after doing whatever the fuck you've been doing. So what do you think I'm going to do? Try to set up a deal and get you whacked, is that what you were thinking's going to happen? Although it did cross my mind, I dismissed that very course of action because how do I know killing you's going to stop them from investigating me? Just means someone else comes along and rips them free from me, my balls I mean."

Tony says he didn't think he was going to have him whacked. "You're not that smart," he expresses. "But Casper works for you—"

"—like I said, how was I supposed to know that something like that was going to happen," Gene explains again, getting more comfortable now, the redness fades from his cheeks and he can breathe better. "But just so we are clear because I can't read your mind. What happened?"

"Frankie pulled a gun on me," Tony exclaims. "Said he knew I was a cop."

"That's you. No fluff. Just the facts. My boy Friday," Gene says. "I don't know where he would get such an idea—maybe he's got some information I don't have. You know I'm not part of the Siriano organization. In fact, I avoid them at all costs. But you come to me, hat in hand, and ask me to set up this deal as a cred builder, and I did."

Tony leans forward in the chair, making Gene suddenly feel very uncomfortable. "You know how this works, right?"

As if quoting from the legal document, Gene utters, "Yeah, I know how this works. I have to fully cooperate in every manner, yadda yadda yadda," he rolls his hand over and over, "... leads to Siriano's conviction, blah blah blah, bullshit." He says it like people say *bah bah black sheep*. "That's what I got to do, and that's what I'm doing. Again, you've got my balls in a vise. I don't like it. You're over there fondling them like they're some Chinese medicine balls, but I'm not stupid. I know what I need to do. Wear wires, record phone calls, take pictures, and introduce—"

"—undercover officers if necessary," Tony finishes.

"And I get how this drug shit works with you all. You explained it to me." He uses air quotes as he talks. "The *federal government* looks at the drug system as a whole. So, using easy math, if someone moves twenty pounds of coke and if the street seller offloads an ounce, but that coke can be traced through the entire criminal tree, everyone goes down for the same damn twenty pounds. So yeah, I get how this works. I'm sorry that someone bought some guns from me with a half-pound of meth. I don't like drugs, but I'm not going to pass up an opportunity, something I can sell, which is how you and I have formed this wonderful friendship."

"I'm just making sure."

Gene stares at Tony for a moment, and Tony relaxes, dropping back into the chair. His arm in the sling rests limply against his chest. His face is still a mess. Tony's not changed his clothes since whatever happened, happened, so Gene adds, "And I don't know how Frankie would know if you were a cop or not."

"He knew."

"Maybe he didn't?" Gene suggests. "Maybe it was a test. You know, say 'hey motherfucker I think you're a cop,' and see what you do."

Tony makes a noise as he mulls over Gene's suggestion. "Maybe."

"A test you failed by the way."

"You think so?"

Gene raises his hands in mock surrender while maintaining eye contact. "Hey, don't get shitty with me," he says. "I did my part. I got you in with Casper, who got you in with Kevin and Frankie. You want Siriano. I did my part."

"Where's Casper?"

"I don't know."

"What do you mean you don't know?"

Gene tugs on his ear. "I mean I haven't seen him. Remember, he's not my dog," he says. "I don't have him on a leash. Better, he's not GPS tagged. You know, I don't have his belly tattooed saying Property of Eugene Oregon," he gives his full name, "but considering that shit was blasted across the news last night, Casper's probably dust now. In the wind. Made for greener pastures or sleeping with the fishes. Take your pick of clichés because it all just means you're not going to fucking find him asking me."

"Siriano will want him dead." Tony stands and stretches some, wincing as if his shoulder's tender. He walks with a slight limp, no major damage in the walk, just slow to get going. "I wanted to let you know that there could be some blowback."

Now, Gene's putting on the sarcasm. "Thanks, I didn't figure that out yet."

Tony moves around the counter's edge to stand in front of Gene. He mashes a finger against Gene's chest. "I've still got your balls in a vise. Don't forget that."

"How comforting it is to know that they're in a safe place with you."

"I thought you might want to play it safe for a while since there could be some significant blowback coming your way."

"I'll be fine."

"Casper needs to stay gone or turn himself in."

"You looking for him?"

Tony says, "Unofficially, I'll take him, but officially... well... I figure everything's off now. Meaning you start over in six months, or the AUSA decides fuck this shit, we got one guy for the murder of a federal agent and another on some federal gun violations."

"I don't want nothing to do with a courtroom," Gene says.

"I know that."

"I've done my work; I've been a good boy."

He hasn't but what else is he going to say: *yeah, I been moving guns and conducting business as if everything's happy-go-lucky-sunny-day-normal?*

"I don't want to end up in prison. I don't want to lose my gun license. So let me ask you something."

"Isn't that what you been doing?"

Gene ignores that jab. "What's going to happen now? What are you saying? Are you saying they're going to come after me?"

"I'm saying you need to be careful," Tony says. "I thought I'd give you the courtesy of telling you to your face."

"What about Casper?"

Tony shrugs. "If you see him, either tell him to disappear or have him find his way to me, and I'll figure something out."

Gene softens some. "When's the funeral?"

"Couple days," Tony says. "Some things have to happen first. I'm sure you understand. There's a process."

"Tony, I'm sorry about your friend," Gene says.

Tony tells him he appreciates it and starts to move to the front door to leave.

"Tony?"

Tony rotates just enough to look at Gene over his hurt shoulder. "Yeah?"

"Use the back door."

———

LATER THAT DAY, Gene gets another visitor: Renaldo and his man Mastodon. Renaldo's wearing a navy-blue button-up with the gray cuffs rolled-up and pressed tan denim jeans. Mastodon is in a black suit with a white shirt; his face is all bandaged up. That's Gene's work. He thought it would be funny to give the big man a similar blow to his— that way when he was playing like he had been jumped outside, he could say he had the same injury. Basically suggesting, *see it wasn't me.*

Mastodon enters and locks the door behind him. *So that's how they're going to play it? Does he know Kevin's my friend?* No, Kevin didn't want Renaldo knowing anything about Gene. But Gene's not stupid. He knows who Renaldo is and what he's capable of, but he'll play stupid. So, Gene tells his girl Ashley to go to the back and shut the door. She does as she's told, leaving Gene in the empty showroom with the two men.

After she's gone, Gene says, "Can I help you?"

"Yeah, sure, okay," Renaldo says, dismissively, eyes flickering across the showroom. He smiles like a shark, with his shiny white teeth, probably veneers. They go with the rest of his expensive look-at-me-outfit. "I was hoping you could help me find something."

Groaning some and with protesting joints, Gene wriggles to his feet from and leans over the counter, placing his hands on the glass, gripping the edge, all done to keep his knees from quaking. He has to play this cool.

Gene says, "Certainly, what are you looking for? How can I help?"

And then with lurching strength and abrupt fury, Renaldo strikes, lashes out, and grabs Gene's collar before Gene even feels the hands at his throat. With brutal efficiency, wrenching with his entire body, Renaldo yanks Gene forward, snatching Gene off his feet, over the counter, and dragging him over the glass, hauling Gene over the edge of the counter, and then lets momentum and gravity do the rest, dumping Gene onto the floor. Gene rolls over to his back, heaving, and spots for a split-second Renaldo's fist blotting out the fluorescent lights overhead as Renaldo punches him once in the face. The blow lands across Gene's lips. Then, with the second, everything below his nose goes numb, somehow making the showroom smaller and darker.

Gene's eyes flutter wildly as he tries to work his tongue over his teeth to make sure everything's in place, nothing's missing. There is blood. Gene manages to mutter, "What's going on?"

Mastodon joins Renaldo.

Renaldo's leg lashes out, kicking Gene in the side. Gene drops an elbow to protect the spot from a second kick. "Don't talk unless spoken to. We have business with you. Two topics. Neither good for you. Which one do you want to discuss first?"

Still blinking rapidly, Gene holds up his index finger but doesn't say anything, and then, he thinks better of it. "Why come in here like that? You coming on too hard, kicking and beating people like that. Does that work for you?"

Squatting at Gene's side, Renaldo's hand latches onto the finger, and he bends it backward. Needles of pain radiate through his wrist, up to his forearm, and into his brain. Renaldo doesn't break the finger, bending it that way, but gets it right to the edge. "Where's Casper?"

Fear slithers through Gene's body. *Does he know? No, no way he could know.* Things didn't go like they should have, but considering what they were doing, not failing was better than failing, and Gene didn't fail. Improvised sure. He did that. He had to.

So Gene lies. "I don't know where he is."

Renaldo kicks him again, the tip of Renaldo's hard leather shoe catching the crest of Gene's elbow.

Gene groans. "I told you. I don't know where he is."

"I find that hard to believe," Renaldo says. "He works here. You raised him. Her. Whatever. Where do we find him?"

Gene delays by taking his time to prop himself up on his elbow, the good one, not the one with the bruise forming. "What do you need with him?"

"That's not your concern."

Gene motions a hand to Renaldo. "Really might be, considering you're here kicking me," he says. Renaldo goes to kick him again, but Gene blocks the foot with his forearm, deflecting Renaldo's shin. It hurts like a bitch but has the desired effect of stopping the kick. Renaldo drops his foot to the floor, more tenderly than before. Gene points out the door. "I don't know. Try his apartment."

Renaldo stares down at him thinking it over and then snaps his finger. "Help him up," he orders Mastodon while taking a step back from Gene's prostrate form, tenderly, trying not to show the pain from the block. He rubs the back of his head as Mastodon picks Gene off the floor and stands him up.

On his feet now, although held at the armpits, Gene asks, "Now, I'll ask again," he brushes himself down, "what do you need with Casper?"

"I need to find him," Renaldo says, face to face. "Beyond that, it isn't any of your concern."

Gene doesn't press his luck, sure he wants to, but he replies, "Yeah, it's my concern. He's my guy. You came in here and beat me up over it thinking I own him like a fucking little doggie." Gene whistles. "Here boy, here boy. Nope nothing. I've not seen him."

Renaldo frowns. "Well that's a problem," he says and takes a step back. He jumps to sit on the counter and crosses his legs at the ankles.

Mastodon releases Gene.

Putting space between the big man and himself, Gene rubs his armpits, working on the constricted skin, and then sniffs his hands, discerning the smell of sweat, his sweat, and fear.

Renaldo insists, "I need to talk to Casper for my own reasons, but then, I hear from Mattie this morning, who is convinced he knows who robbed my game last night, isn't that right?"

Mastodon nods. "Don't know who the other guy was. But I think it was Casper."

Renaldo says, "He said it was something about the voice."

Mastodon adds, "And hair."

"And the hair," Renaldo repeats.

Gene scratches his head. "So, is that why you're here? The poker game?"

"Yes and no," Renaldo continues. "Mattie, explain to Mister Orr, or is it Oregon, which is it?"

"Oregon, but I go by Orr."

Renaldo, tilting his head, glances at Mastodon and then back at Gene. "Why?"

Gene crosses his arms. "You grow up a warden of the state, named after the town you were found in, and then you come back to tell me how you feel about your given name," he explains. "People have been making decisions for me my whole life, telling me it's in my best interest. Making assumptions about me. Telling me what to do. Where to sleep. How to eat. But most importantly, telling me I was nothing, unwanted, not fit to have a family. So forgive me if I want to control something like my name."

Renaldo smiles. Both hands grip the edges of the counter. "You want to have some control, huh? Well, I can understand that. I don't know if you know this, but I came from nothing."

"I didn't," Gene says, straightening his back, but that's a lie because Kevin's bitched about Renaldo so much that he knows the guy's whole life story.

"Mattie, explain to Mister Orr how I feel about my game getting robbed."

Mastodon punches Gene in the stomach, which doubles him over.

Renaldo says, "That's for letting them in the back door. Now, what did you see?"

"Nothing," Gene moans. Again a lie. He saw everything. "They came out of nowhere. Arrived in a Jeep, must have had another driver or something." Gene holds up his fingers as if he's counting. "That'd make three right?" He throws more doubt and deception into the story. "Two go in, one in the jeep, don't know why that one drove away, you know? You'd think you'd hang around when someone is inside waving a gun around."

Except that's not what happened.

What happened was the very thing Gene told Casper he was worried about, leaving the keys in the jeep. While Casper was inside, someone jumped in the Jeep and drove off. That was a fucking problem. Outside the door, Gene stripped off the gear; Casper hit him again, this time breaking the skin. Fresh blood. Gene threw him his keys, saying, "Take the damn Sebring."

"Three huh?" Renaldo says.

Gene counts on his fingers again, playacting. "Yeah, but two gunmen, wearing jumpsuits, masks, carrying pistols."

"That's how you got the shiner?"

"Yeah, see that fuck next to you," he says it while staring at Mastodon, daring him to hit him again, "wouldn't let me answer my phone at the table."

Renaldo says, "House rules."

"Right, so I folded my really *good* hand," Gene continues, stressing the inconvenience of taking the fake phone call outside, "and stepped outside. Talked on the phone, lit a cigarette, and then POW! Hit me right here. I fucking saw stars. Laid me out. Next thing I know, the door's swinging open and those two fucks are running out, jumping in my fucking car. Must have taken my keys when I was out."

Renaldo searches Gene's face, staring at him for a moment, trying to see if Gene is telling the truth or not, but Kevin and Gene spent hours coming up with the script for this little play and then rehearsing it. "Yeah, sure, okay."

Mastodon tells Gene, "They took something valuable, shoved it in a backpack."

"Like money?" Gene asks, playing dumb.

Renaldo says, "Something like that. So we circle back to what I want to know, need to know. Where's Casper?"

"I told you... I don't know," Gene says. "I don't own the kid."

"Who called you?"

"When?"

"At the game, who called? When you stepped out to take the phone call, who called?"

Shit. Kevin didn't talk about this. What's he tell him?

"Casper," Gene says, feeling shitty about throwing the kid down. Gene's looked out for him for years. Kevin knew Mastodon was going to recognize him. That was the whole point. But Gene still doesn't feel any better about it. Growing up in the system, it was killed or be killed, and Gene doesn't want to be killed.

"What did he want?"

"I don't know," Gene says, "something about a gun purchase or something. That's when the guys showed up, smacked me in the head, and stole my car. I don't remember. The blow to the head might be why."

"And robbed my game," Renaldo adds. "So it seems Casper robbed my game. So where is he now?"

"Man, I've told you. I don't know." Except Gene does know, sort of. He told Casper to get lost and told him where he could go.

Renaldo slides off the counter and taps Mastodon on the arm. They start to leave Gene's shop, but at the door, Renaldo, over his shoulder, says, "When you see him, you call me. Got that?"

Gene nods enthusiastically while fighting back the overcoming sickness and the urge to throw up.

CHAPTER SEVEN:

FRANKLIN HAYES

FRANKLIN JERKS AWAKE IN THE HOSPITAL, body shaking in the bed. He opens his eyes and for a moment doesn't know where he is, but he pulls his right arm away from his side and is suddenly constricted—handcuffs—then his mind goes over the last two days and fills in his memory like water rushing into the bottom of a hole.

He's alive.

Shot.

But alive.

Shot something like five times—that's what the nurse told him the first time he woke—but he was on some heavy shit. Good shit. But heavy.

Arrested, hence the handcuffs.

He blinks a few times, licks his lips, lifts his head, and sees the cop, a Fed—DEA—sitting across the room. Some Pakistani-looking fucker. The guy's in a recliner near the window, wearing a dark suit, looks wrinkled, been here a while, magazine, *Sports Illustrated*, laying upside down in his lap like he's five fucking years old.

Who is this guy?

Franklin orders his thoughts.

Is there a way out of this?

Not right now.

How's he get out of this? No idea.

He's thirsty though. His lips are cracked and mouth is dry—tastes worse than it does the day after a severe hangover, like a motherfucking desert. It almost makes him wonder when he ate sand—he didn't but that's what it feels like and he wonders when's the last time he's had anything to drink.

He doesn't know.

Franklin spots the water cup. It's on the table to the side of the bed, on his right. Without thinking about it, he reaches for it with his right hand, but the clink of the metal cuffs and sudden pressure on his wrist remind him those fucks did that on purpose.

He lets the arm drop back in the bed. Then, he yanks against the cuffs a couple of times in frustration, scraping the cuffs against the bed's metal rails.

Next, he tries to reach for the table with his left hand, rolling over on his right side, arm outstretched, fingers scraping against the edge of the table, but it's too far.

Of course, it is.

They did that on purpose.

Because he's a cop killer.

That's what this is all about. He broke the code. Killed one of theirs. Something his granddaddy told him never to do. His granddaddy told him, "You ever kill a cop, just go kill yourself. Save you and them the trouble because they're nasty fucks when you whip them into a frenzy."

He killed a cop, but he didn't really mean to. He was just trying to protect himself. The guy never identified himself as a cop. He just rammed Stevie's car and started shooting.

How was Franklin supposed to know he was a cop?

Besides, the shit with the gun, waving it in that guy's face, that was all just for show. See how he handled himself. Nearly made him lose it talking about that damn show—he found it humorous. The guy handled himself all right though, well, until the car backed into them and the shooting and shit.

He killed a cop.

Damn. He's fucked.

They probably got the product. That's a problem. But he's alive, so he can figure out how to work it to where it's not a problem. Franklin needs to see the upside. Something else his granddaddy taught him. "See the good in all opportunities and you will never run out of opportunities," like a fucking Zen master.

Still, he's thirsty, and the cup's right there, out of reach.

Stupid fucks.

A nurse enters the room, well-built, with what he'd consider a well-shaped booty, meaning big white ass, little waist, dark hair, nearly midnight black, good looking enough, if the lights were off. Pussy's pussy after all.

When she enters, the Pakistani-looking fucker jolts awake, grabbing at the magazine.

The nurse, seeing Franklin looking her over, studying her features, says, "You're awake—good," as she steps to the right side of his bed, moving the table even farther away from him, pushing the water farther out of reach.

Good? What's good about it, he thinks. *Why does she care?*

The whole way in and even now with her nearing him, he eyes her, watching her as she leans over him, her tits, heavy and full, something he likes, hang right over his chin with her sports bra showing, black and purple.

He might as well go play the lotto. She's prime nursing material, not the fat old hags he's seen puttering around every ER he's ever visited. But some days, some days, you get just lucky enough to get a young good-looking thing. And today's his day.

With the tits obscuring her face, she says, "We nearly lost you there." Her accent shows she's from up north, Minnesota, or something. "Nothing life-threatening— slight infection." She checks his forehead with the back of her hand; it's warm against his skin. "Good, feels like the fever's down." She reaches forward, pulls a digital thermometer off the wall where it's tethered, and runs the little rubber piece across his forehead. "You thirsty?"

He nods and tries to talk, but he finds resistance. Wanting to say something, he realizes his voice's not coming to him. Mouth open. No sound. The lack of internal humidity's stolen his voice. After a considerable effort, more than should be normal, he's able to croak out an affirmative answer.

She nods; she gets it.

The nurse replaces the thermometer in its cradle and turns around, picking up his cup. She starts to hand it to him, with his right hand up, handcuffs limiting his reach, ready to receive it, but then she pulls the cup away from him at the last moment and reaches into her pocket. She brings out a plastic purple bendy straw. She takes the straw out of the wrapper, loops one end into a circle, and sticks the other end into the plastic cup. He reaches for it again, but she shakes her head, foot hitting the pedal to raise the bed. Holding the cup down near his chest, where he can barely reach it, the straw just at his lips, she says, "Bullet wounds aren't like what you see in the movies. They can cause very little physical damage in the grand scheme of things, but they bring all sorts of nasty bits into your body. Clothing, bacteria, whatever. Can make you sick. Like it did in your case."

Franklin's finally able to work his lips around the straw to suck in the water, which raises through the straw, does a circle in the purple loop, and into his dry mouth, but it's like throwing a cup of water on a fire. The nurse, amused, smiling softly, showing off one cute dimple, not two, slowly pulls the cup away, more drifting out of reach as she's talking, saying, "Not too much. Don't want to make you too sick. But you've had the best medical care in the state—you'll live."

She sets the cup on the table and steps away from the bed. It's farther away than it was before.

The Pakistani-looking Fed asks, "You going to be in here a little bit?"

She nods as she pulls the computer pedestal from the wall.

"I have to hit the head. You alright with him for a few?"

She nods a second time as her fingers click-clack on the computer.

The Fed drops the magazine in his seat and exits the room.

After he's gone, the nurse asks Franklin, "How are you doing?"

Still struggling to speak, mouth dry, he manages to say, "I'm tired," while keeping his eyes on the plastic cup on the table, mentally trying to will the table to move his way. They can do that in the comic books, right? Move shit with their mind?

He used to read X-Men comics. He liked how they made him feel ... not so persecuted; being black, like there was a whole world out there beyond Wellston, Oklahoma that understood. Though, he's not read them for some time, not since his granddaddy found out he was reading after curfew in his bed under the covers with a flashlight. His granddaddy came into the room because he must have seen the light, yelled at Franklin about how he needed to be sleeping or working, "There's nothing else in this world," and ripped the comic from his hands. Then, his granddaddy collected the rest of the comics out of his backpack on the floor, taking them, and Franklin by the arm, out to the 55-gallon metal drum in the backyard, and he threw all the comics into the drum to light it all on fire. He squeezed the white bottle of lighter fluid starting low, raising as the long stream, shooting out until the pressure in his hand released. Then, he handed the bottle to little Franklin, said, "Now you." Little Franklin tried to protest, but his granddaddy wouldn't hear of it. Franklin squeezed the bottle until it was empty. Then, his granddaddy took the bottle of lighter fluid out of his hand and handed him a box of matches, telling kid-Franklin to, "do it." And Franklin did it. Only after it was done and the fire going, did Franklin tell his granddaddy that the comics came from the local library. All his granddaddy said was, "Well if you had been working or sleeping, nothing would've happened to them."

Now, Franklin licks his lips and asks the woman, "What's your name?" From over the top of the computer, her eyes peruse him as she says, "Vera," and she stands, pushing the wall-mounted pedestal back toward the wall, and strolls over to the side of the bed. First, she hands him the pitcher of water, putting the straw in the pitcher, and lets him finish all the water in the pitcher. Then, she leans over, pulling the nametag clipped to the V-neck of her scrubs, pulling the scrubs down with the nametag, showing him her name, and giving him a show to what's under the scrubs. The tag says her last name's Rose.

Vera Rose, a delicate flower, ripe, and he does mean ripe, for the plucking. "*Vera*," he repeats the name, working it out in his mind, saying it out loud for her, putting some sweetness, honey, in his voice, "I like Vera. Don't know too many Veras. Sounds like you were named after someone— who you named after?"

Vera cackles loudly and blushes while moving closer. "What do you mean? How do you know I'm named after someone?" Her breath is hot and wet against his cheek, and it feels good to be this close to a woman, feeling the heat of her body coming from those big full breasts.

Cute smile. Smells good too. Like flowers. Roses. Fitting.

She takes the empty pitcher away and sets it on the table.

"Vera's not a common name," Franklin says. "I mean, it's an older name—not calling you older, just saying it's not common nowadays. Sounds like something someone from my granddaddy's generation would be named, yeah?"

Vera nods and takes a step back, cocks her hip to the side, and plops her large thigh on the edge of the bed, down by his feet, where the rail ends. "My grandmother," she says, "if you must know."

He can feel her body heat through the covers down by his feet. Franklin smiles. "She as good looking as you?"

Vera slaps his leg. "I'm not good looking." She smiles, trying not to laugh while her hand stays on his leg.

"You been my nurse the whole time?" he asks as his mind's working her over, figuring out the best way to play her because Vera's easy to read, and he needs to find a solution to his immediate problems.

Siriano has a reputation. Franklin wants to tell him and his people that he won't talk. He'll do his time if it gets that far, but he's no snitch. Tell his people to leave him be. But most importantly, he'll tell them he wants to stay alive. If five bullets couldn't do it, then he doesn't want some prison shank correcting the problem.

"Just during the night," she says, nodding, "but I've been working since you came in." She pauses to glance over her shoulder at the door to see if the Pakistani-fucker's come back. He hasn't. In a quiet voice, she adds, "Did you *really* do all those things they say you did? Did you kill that man?"

Franklin thinks about the question for a moment before answering because with women like Vera, there're only a few ways to play it and each one has its pitfalls. Sure, he could deny it, but then she's going to know he's full of shit, and he'll lose that spark that's happening right now. But on the flip side of that coin, he could say yeah, he did it, play like he's proud of it even though he's not—see where that takes them—but then with some mousey ladies, that's a bigger turn off than him lying to her.

And he doesn't want to lose this spark, because her hand's still on his leg, palm spreading warmth through the sheet and all over his leg. "Vera," he uses his cuffed hand to talk, pointing at her with his index finger and then back at himself with his thumb, "you and I, we got something. I don't know what it is, but there's something here. I feel it. I see it in your face. A spark—*say*...," he plays like he's surprised now at his own words, "... a spark—that's what we'll call it."

"Oh, we will?" she asks, playing along with him.

That's a good sign.

"Oh, we will," he repeats. "I'm saying it's a spark. You know there's something here. Some little of something. Something so delicate and special, I don't want to ruin it by lying to you. See I could do this a couple of different ways. I could sit here and deny the whole thing, but let's be real—"

"—Let's—"

"—that'd be a whole helping of bullshit because I wouldn't be here with that fucker over there if there weren't some truth to what they're saying, and being that I've been out of it the last few days—with the fever and such—I don't know what they been saying, but let's just assume I think I know what you're talking about and so no, I'm not going to deny it because like I said, there's some truth to the matter."

She cuts in. "They're saying you killed that cop."

Franklin, playing it well now, stays quiet, nodding along with her, licking his lips, eyes cast down on that hand on his leg, inching its way up, aware of how his body's responding because after all, he's on the downslope of the infection hill. He's a healthy youngish man in the presence of a woman who's obviously digging him.

Now, ever so slowly, bringing his eyes up, flaring his nostrils a few times, getting the tears started, not over-doing it, but doing it just enough to make it look like he does after a good sneeze or before a good sneeze, all watery, red, and welling.

"Vera, I'm not going to lie to you," Franklin says. "I won't say I did, but I'll say I didn't necessarily either, you get what I'm trying to say? I don't know if there's any sort of cameras or something, some recording devices about."

"There's not," she says, fingers crawling his way, her body leaned into him. "Hospital wouldn't allow it. I care about my patients. I don't care what you might've done. If you're my patient, I see to your every need." Her hand squeezes his thigh now, once, twice. "I try to keep an open mind about the people that lay here. See not everyone's guilty of what they say someone is, you know? Like those boys up in New York, the five something or other that just got out of jail, that all them people been hooting and hol-lering about on Netflix. They didn't do that murder they were accused of doing, but everyone saw some poor black boys and judged them guilty even though they weren't."

This will be easier than he thought.

"See, then you get what I'm saying," Franklin says, rocking his head back and forth. He places his left hand over Vera's on his leg. His fingers strike her hand and wrist as he talks, working the lines down between her fingers, over the back of her hand, to the veins in her wrist. He says, "See, so I won't tell you I didn't do it because, you know, there's some truth to the things they're saying. But they don't tell you my side of things. I could, if we want to pretend I'm being hypothetical," he pauses for a second to make sure she understands, even winking some; she winks back, "I could say, yeah, I shot that guy, but that's not my side of things. That's not the whole story. How was I supposed to know he was a cop? He didn't say, 'hey shit-bird I'm a cop.' If he had, I would have said, I'm giving up." He holds his hands up, both of them together, cuffs clanking on the right. "Be a good little boy and give up all righteous and shit. Let's be real here—a drug charge for me ain't nothing. I'm not the driver. My hand ain't on the shit. They don't got nothing on me. Gun in the glove box, again, I'm not the driver. Possession being nine-tenths of fuck all—that's an easy rap to beat. All I got to say is I'm the passenger, not my shit, prove me otherwise. Do you know what would happen? Nothing."

"They wouldn't arrest you," she says, showing she's bought in now because her voice drops low and seductive.

She likes her bad boys.

Smiling as wide as he can, he says, "Oh no, they'd have arrested me. I'd be in jail for some time, but I'm looking at it in its totality. That's what you have to do. That's what cops do. Look at everything up against everything else, you dig?"

She nods.

He says, "Yeah, sure, I might go to sit in some six-by-six fucking box for a month or two, or less—if you get what I'm saying because money talks baby and I've got it—but I'll get a good attorney. Like I said, you know what would happen. Nothing, because in this great country—just like I am today, outside of this hypothetical we got going—I'm innocent until proven guilty. Remember that when you strut your fabulous booty out that door here in a few, I'll be watching, trust me, that I'm innocent until proven guilty. So consider this little question of yours, like Mr. Scrotum's cat—you won't know what I am until you know what I am—and at the end of the day, I'll be me and you'll be you. And I hope we'll be passing some of the time getting to know each other."

"Schrödinger," she says.

"What's that?" he asks.

"Schrödinger," Vera says again. "That's the guy's name. The one with the cat in the box. Schrödinger."

"What'd I say?"

"Scrotum," she says, giggling.

"Oh well, baby, that's funny," Franklin says, smiling. "Cuz, I was just wondering what my boys would feel like in your touch."

Now, she's bright red, slapping his leg, landing just above the crease in his thigh to hip, telling him to stop it. He feels himself jump in response, hand right there, just a fabric fold away. He can feel the warmth just rolling off the tips of her fingers, almost touching him.

"Oh yeah, that's what you were wondering?" Vera waits for his answer, but she doesn't get one. "What makes you believe I'm that type of girl?"

"Because you like the way I say your name, Vera," he says, adding it at the end, putting some emphasis on it. "*Vera*," he says it slowly, "you like how I say it, but what'd I like to know is how you're going to say mine." He drops the line and lets it sit.

Because this is the moment.

What's she going to do?

But then the Pakistani fucker steps back into the room and breaks the moment, destroying all his hard work, saying something about how all that blood, his blood, ruined Franklin's knockoff shoes.

Vera jumps as the Fed enters the room, jerking her hand away from him, trying her best to not appear flustered. She smooths her scrubs and says something medical about checking his blood pressure and leans over him to check something on the left side of the bed.

"Do me a favor, baby," Franklin whispers, not asking, telling her to do him a favor. Her large doe eyes smile back at him and that's all the confirmation he needs. "When he leaves to piss again, let me use your phone to call my granddaddy, let him know I'm alive."

As she turns to step away from him, she mouths: *Okay.*

Franklin throws his head back against the pillow. Ripe for the plucking, a delicate Vera Rose, an angel from his medical induced dreams, happy and good, and seeing an opportunity in all things. For her, helping him mend, maybe something more, but for him, there's always an angle.

CHAPTER EIGHT:

RENALDO LUNA

ALEJANDRO GREETS RENALDO AT THE doors, turning the open sign from closed to open, jerking the dead bolt to the side, unlocking the door, opening it, and letting Renaldo inside.

Renaldo pushes the rest of his way in and parks himself on a stool at the counter. He asks his old mentor and friend, "Is your nephew Filiberto still working at the hospital?"

After letting the door swing closed, Alejandro holds up a finger, which is his signal for Renaldo to wait.

Alejandro's *Morning Joe Café* is a small place, situated in a small corner of a squatty office building in East Tulsa. Barely deep enough to have inside seating, it has a counter and a scattering of tables. Everything's white and chrome with red chairs to refresh the palate.

The café's little owner trails behind Renaldo silently, shuffling awkwardly, wearing thicker glasses than Renaldo remembers, and slips behind the counter where he picks up his stained white apron, large brown stain, probably coffee or grease, just above the front pocket. He flips it once, holding it out wide in front of him, and then ties the apron around his body, looping it under his gut, and tying it high on his waist, just above the belt of his blue jeans.

Alejandro withdraws a pen from his light blue button-up work shirt and writes "coffee" on the ticket. He tears the ticket out of the book and places the ticket on the counter in front of Renaldo. Then, he runs his hands across the remnants of hair, just two white tufts above his ears, and reaches under the counter, withdrawing an old cabbie-type hat, grey, and fixes it on his head.

Renaldo gets comfortable in the seat as Alejandro washes his hands, telling him the kitchen will get going as soon as Flavia and Omar get in, a married couple, make good eggs. Renaldo says that's fine, but he's not here for the food. He just wants to talk, and he thought he'd visit because it's been a while.

Turning, fixing his thick black glasses on his nose, Alejandro nods and disappears into the kitchen. Renaldo watches him work, moving back and forth in the kitchen, through the kitchen window, turning on the ovens and griddles, hearing the clicks of the dials. Alejandro gets everything warmed up for the morning, leaving Renaldo sitting on the stool and remembering when he used to sit at this counter morning and night, doing his homework because Alejandro wanted him to finish school, his books spread out before him. Sitting here now, he can almost see his smaller self with the pencil in hand, writing on the paper. He'd be a couple of seats down from where he's sitting now, on the other side of the pie display, which still sits in the same place, smashed against the wall with no elbow room.

But that was a long time ago. A different time.

A time when his mother worked in the office building, a cleaning lady. Nothing for East Tulsa. Nothing in the eyes of the people she worked for. Nothing for the people whose office she cleaned. Nothing. But Alejandro Danois never saw her or Renaldo as nothing.

They were alike. His people.

And Alejandro was his protector. Mentor. Confidant. Friend.

But Renaldo's come a long way from that little kid.

Exiting the kitchen after completing his morning duties, Alejandro finally answers him. "Grandnephew, maybe great-nephew, I can never remember which." He waves his hand in front of his face as if he's swatting the memory in place. Then, he turns away from the counter, biting his lip, tongue sticking out at the corner, selects a mug from the four-story rack of eggshell-colored mugs, and carries it over to the coffee pot. He sits the mug down next to the coffee pot and wraps his hand around the black handle of the industrial filter tray, withdraws the filter tray, and sets it next to the mug on the counter.

"Right, but does he still work at the hospital?"

"At night, yes," Alejandro says. "He still does."

"I need his help."

Alejandro laughs. "You need his help? What about your friends? They're not available for helping you? Here, you come visit me—say when was the last time you came and visited me? Sometimes, I look down at the wall," he points where Renaldo used to sit, "and I feel like if I squint some, I'd see you sitting there. Not you as you are now, but you as you were. I liked you then. I don't know you now."

Then, Alejandro waves his arm in the air, dismissing the question and the memory.

Renaldo mumbles, "It's been a while."

"Far too long," Alejandro says, putting a filter and coffee in the filter tray. "We are family, Renaldo. You and me, blood, if that matters to you anymore. There was a time that mattered a great deal."

"We are family," Renaldo says. "It still matters."

"Family comes and visits each other." Alejandro presses the button for the coffee machine, starting the brewing process. "You should come and visit me more often. I need to see your face. It's been too long. Neighborhood changes. I change. Faces change. You change. Tell me about yourself? Do you have a woman?"

"There is a woman."

Renaldo's mind flips to Iris. He's avoided her, and she hasn't called—probably because she has bigger things going on, but still. It hurts a little more than he thought it would. She said it was nothing, a fling, something to do when no one was around, but now no one's going to be coming around, and he's not sure she's going to keep up the intimate side of the relationship.

"She good looking?" Alejandro leans against the counter. He folds his hands together. "Perhaps too good looking for you, no?

"She's good looking," Renaldo says. "White girl but good looking."

Alejandro scrunches his nose in disgust and pushes himself back from the counter. "But here you are visiting me; you must be here because you need something, no?" He touches his temple with one finger. "That's why you are asking about Filiberto. When's the last time you visited your mother?"

"It's been a while."

"Too long I would guess. And it's morning. You're dressed too nicely for a place like this. This is how I know you need something." He sticks his hands out, palms up. "You don't come to my greasy spoon—that's what you called it—you don't come anymore because you thought you'd enjoy the finer things in life. Said something about leaving home. Said there were better opportunities. I suspect you've treated your mother much like you've treated me. I haven't seen much of you, so I don't think she has, and I don't know what sort of opportunities you've enjoyed, but reading your face—now there's something worth seeing—says to me, your face, says things maybe aren't so nice, right now, no?"

"Yeah, sure, okay, I do enjoy the finer things. That's true, but—"

"I'm not done," Alejandro snaps. "You tell me, you say, 'Al, I can't come around no more because I have a nice job working for some heavy hitters'—white men, if I remember correctly. I said don't work for no white man; they don't see you as the same. Never will. No matter how hard you try. No matter how silly you dress. You can look like them, but you won't ever be them. I warned you. Said your mother should have taught you as much. Seeing what they did to her. You say, 'they're going to take care of me.' Grabbing at your collar, popping the lapels, in a shirt very much like the one you're wearing now, and telling me you've moved up in the world. You told me they let you be the top dog. Added, 'on the outside'—I remember that—you adding 'on the outside,' like that should mean something to me."

Renaldo knows what's happening right now: The old man's chastising him, and he's the only one left in this world that probably can chastise him. If he's going to ask Alejandro for his help, then he's going to have to sit here and take the verbal lashing, but it's not easy listening to the man dress him down. There was a time he greatly respected Alejandro and what Alejandro said. Just as Alejandro could snap his fingers and things would happen in the neighborhood, Alejandro was the embodiment of power in Renaldo's mind.

Renaldo says, "I am the number one guy on the outside."

"Which implies there's a number one guy on the inside, no?" Alejandro switches to Spanish. "Meaning you're the number two guy overall. You might as well be nothing. I taught you better than that."

"You taught me to see opportunity and take it."

"You could have had all this."

"What, washing dishes for you?"

Alejandro folds his arms over his chest, hands holding elbows, and gives Renaldo a look, eyebrows dropping with the corners of his mouth. He returns to what he was saying before, in English. "So, you tell me—you don't want to come around here no more. You don't want to be seen at this greasy spoon. 'Caught dead,' I believe. Smug-like when you said it. Cocky when you said it, yes?"

"Yeah, sure, okay," Renaldo concedes. "I said those—"

Alejandro lifts his hand off the elbow, holds it up. "Oh, I'm not asking for an apology; I forgave you the moment you said those words." He does the sign of the cross. "Your mother, she comes around still, can you believe she's in charge of maintenance in this building? It's her life. She stayed with me. I treated her right. I made that happen. She's very good at what she does. Come a long way from the quiet cleaning lady who vacuumed at night and stuck me with her child." He laughs. "So did the white man in prison do something to make you believe you might need to return home?"

Renaldo stays quiet for a moment, giving the coffee machine time to do its thing, watching the dark liquid drip into the coffee pot, then a steady stream, and then sputter. It clicks. Alejandro turns away from him, picking up the mug and the coffee pot. He pours coffee into the mug as Renaldo says, "There was a time that you were the example of power."

"What changed?" Alejandro puts the coffee pot down, turns, and places the mug on the counter.

"I changed," Renaldo says. "The world changed. Things changed. Priorities. Opportunities."

"How did you get hooked up with those white boys I wonder? Oh, I remember, it was because of me. You should be grateful." He points at him. "You should have visited more. You should have shown gratitude and respect."

"I should have," Renaldo agrees.

Alejandro's right. Renaldo, in all his ambition, left this neighborhood, went out into the world, did his thing, and now has come running back to this neighborhood because he doesn't trust the foundation of the relationships he's built.

With eyes on the coffee mug and in a small voice, he tells the old man, "And that was my failing. I should have come here. I should have seen you, talked to you, but I didn't. I wanted to be my own man. I wanted my own thing. It's been good."

"But you fear," he says, "it will no longer."

Renaldo nods.

He can't help himself. Thinking about what's going on the last few days, his mind's been turning over the fact that Siriano went to Kevin, working it like a Rubik's cube, trying to put what's right in its place, but all his mind's wanting to do is match the colors, and he's coming out with the same solution that shows him he ain't the right color. And it doesn't matter how he works it. He doesn't miss the one undeniable truth: Kevin's the same color as Siriano. No matter how hard he tries, no matter how much he wants it to be different, the white man in Siriano has finally come out and shown himself.

Alejandro pours a mug of coffee for himself. He takes a sip and places the mug next to Renaldo. Half-turning his body, he faces the windows and stares out at what's beyond his café. A parking lot, a street, a scattering of trees. Then, after a time, he turns from the window, picks up the mug, takes a sip of coffee, placing the mug back down, and says, "Why are you here, Reni?"

And there it is, forgiveness personified.

"I need your help."

"Tell me what's going on."

So, Renaldo tells him because he feels like he can. The weight of whatever tension he and Alejandro had is gone. It doesn't matter that he hasn't come around in the last few years. Alejandro said it himself: he forgave him the moment of the transgression.

Renaldo tells him everything, starting with the woman. "The girl I've been seeing, her name's Iris," he says. And then he tells him who her husband was: "Clyde, the cop who just died. The one in the paper." He continues, "He's why I started seeing her, sort of. I found out her husband was a DEA agent." And then, "Siriano owns a casino of sorts; I run operations, my side business, my thing. I built it. It's separate from the drug stuff. But I give Siriano the credit. That's how I met her."

"I thought he was white," Alejandro says. "I don't know any white man that owns a casino around here. The other red meat has those." He spits on the floor.

"Not a legit place," Renaldo says. "Siriano set up this place, an underground place in an old warehouse. We run some good poker games. Iris plays poker. That's how we met. She had some underground games. Good money."

Something in Alejandro blooms when Renaldo says this, but Renaldo ignores it.

"I saw them come in one time and then saw him, Clyde, in court, testifying about a friend of mine. He didn't recognize me. I barely recognized him. When I saw him, he had this big beard. In court, just this dinky mustache." Renaldo runs his finger over his lip to demonstrate. Alejandro smiles. Renaldo goes on, "Iris plays poker really well. Almost too well sometimes. But sometimes not too well also. I have to stake her money. She owes me some, a lot, but not enough I don't think she won't be able to pay it back. Plus, she plays so that means others play. They like looking at her, and she likes the attention. It's beneficial to everyone."

Alejandro takes another drink of the coffee and tells him to go on.

"Sort of like *Molly's Game*—you see the movie?" Renaldo asks. Alejandro shakes his head. "Well, it was the story of this female skier who opens her own underground poker game. Siriano's organization's like the criminal one from the movie, and Iris started like Jessica Chastain's character in the movie. Building her little poker palace here in Tulsa. She brought in some big names. She used to live in L.A., which where she learned all this, but she moved here after some heavies started leaning on her just like the movie, but instead of New York, she came here. That's where the parallels end. Although Iris's got a body like the Chastain lady.

"The difference between her and that movie was Iris likes to play, but she can't play at her own games no more. I took her games. So she comes and plays at mine, which is where I saw Clyde. Once you know where to look, you see what you want to find. Iris and I got to talking, and it seemed beneficial to both parties if we combined resources and started holding games together. Higher stakes. I backed her bank. So now, some games, she doesn't play. Some she does."

"What's this have to do with her husband?" Alejandro asks.

"After seeing him in court and knowing what his wife does, I got this idea. I wanted to get close to Clyde to work it, the idea, it being so I could be close to the DEA, work the man as leverage, maybe turn him, start getting information. It would be pretty advantageous to me in my position to know what the DEA knows about Siriano's organization, knows about me, but I've not gotten that far."

"How far did you get?"

Renaldo smiles. "Far enough to tell you I think Iris might be a redhead, but no one else knows if you get what I'm saying."

Alejandro does. He sips his coffee and says nothing.

Renaldo says, "I wanted to get close to Iris, so close that if anyone were to look at it, at Clyde, at the surface of things, that when anyone looked at it, they'd only see dirt—whether it was true or not—because he'd be so interconnected with me, he'd have nowhere to go. Like you told me once. Perception is reality."

Renaldo takes a drink of his coffee that's gone cold as he talked, and he studies the old man's face with something like pride displayed across his features.

Alejandro nods. "What's gone wrong?"

"This wouldn't be a problem if he didn't work around me," Renaldo explains. "Siriano, if he hadn't worked around me, this wouldn't be a big deal, but Clyde went and got himself killed. Now, I have to do clean up."

Alejandro nods, understanding Renaldo's predicament even if Renaldo hasn't come right out and said it. "You didn't tell Siriano about your plan. The girl. Her husband. And he doesn't know how close to the DEA you are."

"No, I did not," Renaldo says.

"And now, Siriano wants to know how the cops found out about the deal." Alejandro guessing at the matter, looking at it. That's what made him a great mentor—he knew how to look at things. "And he's going to see your connection, sooner or later, and get the idea that you were the leak."

Renaldo chaffs at the insinuation, but then again, this is his fear. "I wasn't the leak."

"It won't matter. When he sees it, he'll think it."

"Because perception is reality."

Alejandro hums as he thinks it over. "What do you need?"

"People," Renaldo says. "Not associated with me so that I can handle what I need to handle to keep that perception from getting out there. Siriano wants me to handle a couple of things but—"

"—I'll send someone to you. What else?"

"Guns," Renaldo says. "I have to do this completely separate from Siriano's organization. He can't find out about it. I figured I do this; it takes care of several problems and crosses some of those things off Siriano's list. I'll just pretend it's serendipity."

Alejandro nods. "What else?"

"A truck, a big one."

Alejandro lifts a bushy eyebrow. "That's a big ask."

"What I have to do isn't going to be easy," Renaldo says. "Which is why I need the people, guns, and the truck."

Alejandro is silent.

"And why I need to know if Filiberto's still working at the hospital."

CHAPTER NINE:

GENE ORR

"I HATE MYSELF RIGHT NOW," Gene says, standing with Casper in the men's section of Target. "I just can't do this to you. I thought I could fuck you over, but I cannot. I'm sorry."

They're meeting in the men's section of a Target Supercenter because the meeting had to be clandestine. Gene didn't want Kevin, Tony, or Renaldo knowing he was meeting with Casper because the kid's supposed to be in the wind, but Gene's known where he was the entire time.

After throwing the car keys to the kid, Gene told Casper to go lay low at one of his stash houses, one he uses for storage when he's selling something of a particular value, usually substantial. A house no one in Gene's world knows about and no one, means no one, which makes it the perfect place to stash Casper while Gene tries to figure a way out of this mess, but it's only a matter of time before someone figures out what he's done, or where Casper is, then it'll be Gene holding the bag and that can't happen.

Sure, Gene still loves Kevin, and he thought he could do this, but no matter how he looks at it, he's fucked, and he can't do this to the kid. He didn't intend for the kid to be an unwitting sacrifice. It just happened too quickly.

And as Gene slipped the stocking mask over his face before the robbery, the words about the dead DEA agent kept eating at him, and then when things went sideways and not the way they should have, meaning Casper got his freaking car stolen, Gene called an audible, threw the kid his keys and told him where he could hang out, telling the kid "Don't you fucking call anyone or go anywhere." Saying it to him like that was always part of the plan. Gene forced some concern into his voice so that the kid would believe it. Not that the kid wouldn't do what Gene says... well in some ways.

Gene is the kid's savior, raising him since he was fifteen. He was a girl then, but things change. Gene's tried to teach the kid some sense, and as the kid's gone from a kid to a dumb young adult, Gene realizes he can't keep Casper safe either, but maybe that's how parents feel about their kids. He wouldn't know. That's what he told Kevin just last week, saying, "I never had parents—I don't know what the fuck I'm doing." And Kevin only told him it wasn't going to be a problem any longer. Kevin made it sound like he was doing Gene a favor. Besides, the kid wasn't actually Gene's kid.

But he is, and Gene can't do this to the kid; he wants to save his own ass, but he can't, especially looking into his dumb doe eyes and seeing all the experiences and things they've shared and done together over the last couple of years. Casper's a dumb shit, likes to get high, went through an identity crisis—Gene remembering when it dawned on him as a kid he was different—but he's Gene's dumb shit, and Casper doesn't deserve this. So, Gene has to make it right; he has to figure out the right play here—see all the angles because this is one of those only one-shot type situations.

Now, walking behind the kid as they try to look like your everyday shoppers, moving around the section at a slow meandering pace, careful to put some distance between them and anyone else, Gene says quietly, "Look the reason why I hate myself right now is for having a change of heart. I thought I could do this to you, kid, fuck you over, but I'm not that guy. Yeah, I thought I could. Thought it would be easy, but looking in your big blue eyes right now, I'm telling you, I can't do it."

"Can't do what?" Casper asks.

He's wearing dark blue glasses even though he's inside, a ball cap, and flat bill pulled around backward, and he looks like he robbed a fraternity of their clothes, wearing a checkered white shirt, pink shorts—excuse him, salmon-colored shorts—with leather sandals, no socks. Actually, the whole get-up, matched with his wispy strawberry blonde hair, kind of works for the kid. It gives Gene some hope for him.

Casper pretends to look through the racks of clothes, thumbing over the different hangers and pulling on sleeves to check the color. "What are you talking about?"

Gene confesses. "I just thought I had it in me. I thought, you know, Gene, there's this kid that owes you a shit ton of money... that you've done a lot for... that you've tried to get clean, tried to keep clean, tried to look out for, and here I'm telling myself, this kid needs to be taught a life lesson if he's serious about living in this world. So, then this thing came along—understand, kid, I'm in a bind here. I'm getting fucked two ways and I don't like it; I want it to stop—I see this opportunity to handle you, teach you the lessons you need taught, while at the same time handling both of the guys that are fucking me. But it's like the nuns always told me, you know, after having sex, the parts about how you feel guilty. That's what I'm feeling right now: guilty. I thought doing what I had to do, I'd feel better, but I don't. I just can't do this."

"Do what?"

Gene sighs. "Fuck you over," he says. "I'm over here confessing to you in a fucking Target of all places, and you're not following me on what I'm trying to tell you. You need to follow me. It's all-important, and you need to know that. You got to understand where I'm at on this."

"What?" Casper pretends to pick up a shirt and look at it. "What are you talking about?"

"I thought," he starts to say but lets the words die on his lips.

What did he think? Did he think he doesn't have a conscience? Because he has one.

He's not like Kevin.

Maybe that's why he's never gotten into the burglary game. He just couldn't take people's stuff. Sure, he'll sell it. Heck, he'll hide it, but when it comes to stealing people's shit, that's not him. In his mind, when he gets the products, it's not whoever's it was before he got it. It belongs to the guys that brought it to him, guys like Casper or Kevin.

"I just want out of this," Gene says. "That's what I want. It's what I've always wanted. I just want to be my own man. Is that too much to ask for?"

"What are you talking about?"

"What I'm saying is I just want to be left alone, do my own thing, and make some money," Gene says, but the kid's face tells him he doesn't understand. "I work for myself. Always have. I hustle. It's how I survived in the homes and how I've made it on the streets."

Casper closes his eyes and shakes his head as he thinks over Gene's words. Then he says, "Wait, you were going to fuck me over? Fuck me over with who? How? The robbery?"

Gene waves his hand as if he's swiping away the concern. "Doesn't matter. Don't worry about it 'cause what's done is done. We can't change that. What we have to do is focus on what happens next."

Casper stomps his foot and pushes a shirt into Gene's chest, like he's seeing how the shirt would look. "Well, excuse me if I'm going to worry about it."

Then, Gene realizes the kid's actually shopping right now. "Look, what I'm saying is, there's nothing we can do to change what's happened."

"What happened?" Casper asks. "Other than robbing the game." He puts the shirt back on the rack.

"Speaking of, where're the drives?"

"They're safe."

"That doesn't tell me where they are," Gene says, fighting to keep the annoyance from building inside his skull, which is pounding. "They at the stash house? They someplace else? Where? I need them back. They're still part of this plan—"

"—the one where you fuck me over?"

"No, yes... they're a part of that, but what I'm trying to tell you is we need them to get you out of what I've done. I'm going to need them back."

"No, it doesn't tell you where they are and no, they're not there," the kid says. Gene starts to ask what he means, but the kid holds up a hand, stopping him. "But that's all you're going to get until you tell me what the fuck you are talking about. You don't make any sense." Then, he asks again with a little more force. "What do you mean you were going to fuck me over? You haven't explained that part. I think that's important."

Gene ignores all that and stays focused on the drives. He'll need them. He needs them. Kevin's already breathing down his neck asking for them, texting, calling, sending fucking smoke signals.

"Safe like how?"

"I'm not telling you," Casper says.

"I need you to tell me where they're at. I need them back. I got to get you out of this. You don't understand what's going on."

Casper glares at him, his eyes saying he doesn't like being told what he understands or thinks. "Look, I'm not the smartest, but I've figured some things out. Society doesn't accept you and it doesn't accept me, but I know when something's valuable. Fuck the money we got. Yeah, it's nice, but it's not worth the risk of messing around with someone like Renaldo—yeah, I know whose game we robbed. I didn't know it at the time, but then I saw the big guy, the one you cracked over the face, and I knew."

"They're looking for you." Gene says like it's a threat. "If they find you..." He lets his voice trail off as if they both know whatever terrible outcome will happen if Renaldo and company catch up to Casper.

"*You think?*" Casper says, sarcastically. "But what I'm saying is, I know I got a piece of something. Something to negotiate with."

"What do you mean negotiate?" Gene says. "No, no one's negotiating. Just give me the drives like we would normally do on a job like we agreed... Hell, keep the money ... and be done with it. Be mad at me, but get out of town, and give me the drives." Gene rubs the back of his neck. "See this is what I get for having a change of heart, which means, right now, I'm hating myself for it. You go thinking you can do something. You can't do nothing. You're a kid. Just a kid. You can't. You can't do nothing. This is and has always been bigger than you. You don't know or see what's happening right now."

Casper rolls his eyes and blows air over his lips. "Whatever."

"Don't whatever me." God, he sounds like a parent talking to a teenager because that's how he feels. That's what they are. That's how he sees his relationship with the kid. Gene says, "You're like a dumb kid. I'm over here, telling you we got to save your ass—"

"—and why is that?" Venom touches each word. Casper rolls his eyes again. "Because of you? Because you're trying to fuck me over? Or is it because of the robbery? Or, as you say, I don't know what's happening, it could be for something else."

The kid's got a point.

"'Cause...'" Gene starts but then pauses to think about how to phrase things without actually revealing his hand. Playing it like a poker hand. "I told you. I'm getting fucked over every which way but Sunday."

"Oh, so because you're getting ass raped you thought, what? That you'd just throw me in as a side piece?"

"I'm trying to help you."

"You're trying to help yourself," Casper says.

It is true, so Gene half-shrugs. "Yeah, I guess I am, but now I got to help you."

"Because you fucked me over, and now you're having second thoughts about it?"

"Well, yeah," Gene says. "That's the whole point of putting you up some place safe and talking to you now. I'm trying to tell you that I'm sorry and get us on the same page so that we can figure a way out of this mess because we're in a fucking mess... You might not see it, but I do."

The kid slams a shirt back on the rack with a metallic screech and walks away. "No, I don't see it."

"I need the drives."

Talking without turning, still walking away with Gene following, Casper says, "You're not getting them."

Gene, behind the kid, utters, "Don't act like that."

The kid wheels around. "Act like what?"

Gene talks with his hands. "Don't act like the stupid teenager you were when I met you. Act like we've been through something. Act like you understand what I'm trying to do here. I'm trying to make it right. Renaldo's a scary fuck, and he'll kill you."

"I know that." Casper points at him. "Why do you think I've not gone anywhere or why I'm wearing this stupid shit? I know how serious he is. After you cracked his guy over the head with your gun, I realized who we robbed, and I know I'm fucked if he figures it out."

Gene finds the familiarity in the situation. "You're like me. I see it in you. I came from nothing, and I made something. Sure, I had to do some stupid shit to get to that point, but you're a lot like me. Maybe that's why I took you in? I don't know, but like me you got no family to speak of. You hustle. You work hard when you want to, but you're like every other two-bit criminal, you've got the brains to turn a battery, paperclip, and a light socket into a lighter. But you can't keep a job for more than three days or see when things are outside of your control. Don't have blind ambition. That's a lesson you need to learn. I'm asking you to trust me, so trust me."

"I'm not like you at all," Casper says. "And you're not my parent. That's not what this is."

"No, I'm something more and something less."

Casper looks him over, real good, considering what he's told him.

"Don't be stupid," Gene says, concern in his voice, genuine concern. "You're not stupid. I know that; I'm just hoping you can see it too," he pleads softly. "You're not stupid. You got to see what's going on. You can see angles just as well as I can. You got to see how this is going to end with someone like Renaldo being involved."

Casper shrugs, shoulders sinking in defeat. "I don't want to be fucked," he says. "I mean... I do... but not like the way you're talking about... I don't want to die, and I don't want Renaldo finding me. What do I need to do?"

Gene nods. "Our options are limited, but I think I know a way out of this... maybe, we'll see... but if I do this right, I won't be getting fucked over anymore. And we can get you some place safe, but you have to trust me and do what I say."

Casper bobs his head a few times. "Alright, but you have to tell me what's going on... all of it."

CHAPTER TEN:

TONY MORA

Tony takes the overnight shift watching over Clyde's body at the funeral home with his arm still in the sling—the 8 p.m. to 8 a.m. shift—wearing jeans and a t-shirt with a light jacket. He stands over the casket in the backroom of the home and sips coffee from a gas station cup with a lid. He surveys his fallen brother, his friend, his dead partner. Clyde is in the casket, lying on his back, hands together in front of him, face slack, dressed in a grey suit—he always looked good in grey—which goes with the skin under the makeup.

Laying there, Clyde looks like a cheap version of Bobby De Niro from *Heat*, if the character had been allowed to age a few years and not get popped in the last five minutes of the movie, but the figure isn't Clyde. That's not his friend. Sure, the body has his friend's face, but like every dead person Tony's ever encountered, the essence of the person—some call it the soul; others call it the spirit—isn't present. His friend's gone.

What's left is this—nothing but meat and bone. A body but not his friend, a husk.

The room's rectangular in shape, almost claustrophobic, white and red walls with white trim. It is dark outside just as it is dark in here, except soft lighting, multi-setting orange glowing stand-lamps in the corners of the room. The setting turned to low and soft. On one side of the room, there is nothing, empty space, but along the wall, there are a couple of chairs, and on Tony's side of the room is the body in a grand-looking polished brown casket, with two flags, the nation's and the state's standing guard over Clyde, adjacent to each end of the casket.

That's good. Clyde believed in his country. He was a Marine.

It's past midnight, and Tony's already been in the room for a few hours. Even though he brought a digital e-reader, his gaze has been absorbed with the walls, engrossed with thoughts about Clyde. Him in the casket. Him as he was. What he wanted in life. What he's missing out on now. Tony processing what happened in the McDonald's parking lot, the blood in the backseat, the gunshots, going over the events of that day, and deliberating what comes next: what he's going to do, how does he want to live his life, and most importantly, what's going to happen to Franklin Hayes or to the Siriano investigation?

Neither Franklin nor Siriano should get away with this.

And they won't, which is the resolution Tony's mind confirms in this rectangular, claustrophobic room.

Two hours ago, the night staff left, but before leaving, they offered the entire facility for whatever Tony might need, and for some reason, he and they whispered when they spoke—perhaps it was for the dead contained within the walls.

With them gone, Tony stands over his friend for some time, auditing all the little details the mortician imparted to Clyde with care and precision, to make the body more Clyde and less death, but Clyde's not here. Looking down at his friend, Tony says to the empty room, "Whoever did your make-up sure got the mustache right."

Silence—

—greets him.

But what'd he expect? Did he expect his friend to get up and talk back to him? No.

And if he did, what would Clyde say? He might ask Tony why he let this happen? Not the dying part, but the being here in the casket. Tell Tony, *"Antonio, you know that's not what I wanted."*

And it wasn't what Clyde wanted, but that doesn't matter. Others more important than Tony made those decisions. Iris made those decisions. And when a compatriot dies in the line of duty, they aren't left alone. Someone stays with the body from the moment of death until the body's put in the ground. Just as Tony wouldn't leave the hospital until Larry promised to stay at Clyde's side. Larry spent the first night in the Medical Examiner's building and came out the next morning bitching about the smell.

Someone has been with Clyde ever since, and now, it's Tony's turn. This process, this ritual, is beautiful, simple. People don't see the grief law enforcement officers feel, but this time alone, with the dead, allows them time to grieve the fallen, absent from gathering eyes and attention.

When the funeral does happen, everyone will put forth a stoic front, stone-faced, and wear their dress blues or whatever the official uniform for that agency is, and with Clyde being a Fed, it means others will be coming from all over the country. But Clyde said he didn't want full honors. Clyde said, "*If I'm dead, it's my right as the dead guy. Don't do all that pomp. Just cremate me, spread my ashes,*"

Bucky wanted it, and after all, Clyde died on Bucky's little field trip, and so Tony guesses Iris went along with it.

But Clyde had his wishes though: "*Antonio, I don't want people in uniform, twenty-gun salute, a flag to the widow, and all that bullshit, because it makes me feel like I was nothing more than a jackbooted thug.*"

Clyde hated authoritarianism; he didn't want to be remembered as a jackbooted thug. He said he was a living, breathing, human being, who possessed a heart, and although his brothers and sisters behind the badge would remember his heart, all the people, the others as he put it, the civilians, "*will only see the shadows of authority in every respect.*"

———

AT A STAKE-OUT, Clyde had told Tony what he wanted to do when he retired; the two of them sat in an old Pontiac Grand-Am, sipping coffee, doing what partners do—talking and waiting. Clyde in the driver seat, turned, put his coffee in the cup holder—he liked to talk with his hands—and said, "You're a young guy, right? What you want to do when you retire?"

Tony, taking a sip of his coffee, staring out the window, watching the business front, and waiting for the guy to come by and make the delivery, answered, "I don't know. Haven't thought about it."

"I've thought about it." Clyde waited for a beat to see if Tony would say anything. Ask him about his plans. He didn't. So, Clyde told him anyways: "I want to make health shakes."

"Health shakes," Tony said. "What the fuck's that?"

"You know like protein and vitamins and shit."

"Why do you want to do that?"

"Something Iris's got me on," he said. "I've been drinking them."

"You drink health shakes?" Tony leaned in the seat to get a look at him. "I saw you eating a fucking cheeseburger yesterday."

"I didn't say I'm great about it," Clyde said. "But yeah, in the mornings I've taken to having one." Clyde stopped, took a sip from the coffee, put it back in the cup holder, and continued, "You know, I've got the woodworking thing, yeah, but let's be real, details aren't my thing—you seen my dining room table—I made that. Got the measurements wrong. So, I had to take off a couple of inches on the legs; it's lower than it should be. Nothing terribly wrong with it, not what a layperson would notice, but no one would buy that shit. So yeah, when I retire, I got a hobby I enjoy, but I don't have the touch for it, you know? No talent. That won't make me health insurance money. But I do have a talent—I can talk to people, and well, we got this idea for when I retire… you know it's not too far off." He waves his hand in front of him as if he could see it just over the horizon. "Open a health shake shack or store… still not out on the brick and mortar aspect of it, but I'm telling you, a shack—well not a shack—a food truck."

"—but without food?"

"No one likes a smart ass, Antonio," Clyde replied. "But yeah, a food truck, except it's health shakes, get hooked up with some company, like Herbalife—although I think they're all a pyramid scheme—have bananas and shit, fruit, granola, tea, and a couple of blenders. Buy those machines that put those fancy little seals on the top of the plastic cup. Invest in some bio-degradable straws—for the environment. Get a food truck, maybe an old one, get like an old ambulance or something, cut a hole in the side, park the truck outside a busy office building or something, a city park, get an awning. I can see it now. Maybe go to Sedona. Do it there. I like it out there. I can breathe. You can't breathe here."

Tony said, "I can breathe."

"I can't," Clyde said. "Allergies. I go out of town; I can breathe. I come back to Oklahoma; I can't breathe. Happens within hours. Too many allergies. Snot wall right here." He points to his nose. "I like it out there; in Arizona, I can breathe there. Desert air and all that. Clean air, big skies, blue, I like it. You been to the Grand Canyon?"

Tony shook his head. "It's just a hole in the ground."

"It's more than that—you got to go," Clyde said. "Before you die, you got to go. There's nothing quite like it. Nothing I've seen, media that is—TV, photos, and such—capture what it actually looks like. It's... *majestic*... There's nothing like it... nothing I've seen—although, I will say Thomas Moran's painting's the closest thing I've seen."

Tony knows Moran's popular with the Gilcrease Museum in town—Clyde's favorite place to visit on his day off and favorite painter to see when he's there.

Clyde said, "Really there's nothing like it. You got to go. Antonio, promise me you're going to go."

Clyde just stared at him.

Tony turned away from his eyes. "Yeah, alright, I'll go."

"Promise."

"I promise."

Clyde touched Tony's shoulder. "No, not your shitty I'm-pretending-to-say-something-just-so-this-guy-goes-along-with-it-leaves-me-alone promises. I want a real promise."

"You want me to stick my pinky out?"

"Will that get me a real promise?"

"Just hook yours around it. We'll say 'I pinky promise.' Is that what you want?"

"I ask again, will that get me a real promise?"

"Get outta here with that shit." Tony play-punched Clyde's shoulder.

"How about this?" Clyde said. "Make me another promise."

"What's with all the promises? The shit about going to Grand Canyon's done?"

Clyde smiled. "No, well yes, but no. I'll really ensure you get your ass out there sometime."

"Oh yeah, how are you going to do that?"

"No one likes to talk about death—"

"—then why are you bringing it up?"

"You know, Antonio, no one likes a smart ass either. You do that too well, and you're going to find yourself in trouble sometime and be at a loss for words, you fuck," Clyde said. "But what I was saying is no one likes to talk about death, but you know, we all die. You'll die. I'll die. Iris will die, probably fucking because she can't get enough—she's wearing me out, Antonio—she's going to be the death of me. My heart will go." He grabbed his chest, fingers bunching his shirt, and pretended to have a heart attack while humping the air in his seat. "Get my blood pressure up. Too much, then pop! There goes the old ticker. That's what I get for marrying a younger woman."

"Now, I have to scrub the image from my mind. Thanks."

Clyde slapped Tony's chest, the back of his hand landing softly against Tony's shirt. "No, listen, we all die. It's just a matter of time and numbers. You never know when your number's going to be up. So, with what you and I do, we're not exactly what you'd classify low-risk, doing undercover shit. We could kick the bucket at any point." He waves his hand over the dashboard as he did before like it's just on the horizon again. "One day we're here, fucking or whatever—in your case being a smart ass—and then the next, nothing. Gone. It could happen."

"Yeah, well I don't want to think about it," Tony said. "But with you, I know I don't have a choice, do I? We're going to talk about it all night long, aren't we?"

"You know me too well," Clyde said. He paused and took a drink. "Listen, if I should die in the line of duty—"

"—no, we're not doing this right now," Tony declared. "I got it. You don't want the shit that comes with a death while working. No flags. No guns firing. No nothing. I got it."

Clyde smiled. "That's not what I was going to say, but you have that right. All that's bullshit. I'm nothing. I'm not a hero. I'm a dope cop. Maybe on a bigger scale, working for the Big Man, but I'm still just a simple dope cop. I'm nothing. Nothing. So, you're right. Don't do the full honors. I've still got enough of my hippie parents in me to not like the fact that all anyone's ever going to see is a jackbooted thug getting put in the ground. You know I'm not that, and I couldn't stand people seeing that and that being their final impression of me. I'm not The Man, you know? I just happen to work for him."

"That's why you grew the mustache, isn't it? So that you could be a cop without looking like a cop."

"You watch TV, growing up?" Clyde asked. "I did—*Miami Vice*, saw it while in college. You ever see or read or whatever the fuck it is kids do now, something, and know that something's what you want to do with the rest of your life. That's what it was like for me. I wanted to be that cop. You know this was the eighties, and it was rip-roaring fun, you know?"

"No, I don't know," Tony said. Clyde's reached his *you know* quota for the night.

"Look, I like being a dope cop, but that's only going to last so long. I'm surprised it's lasted this long. So, here's what I want to happen. If I should ever die in the line of duty, you're going to take my ashes to the Grand Canyon and spread them out there. I already got it all written down. That way you get to see the Grand Canyon, and I'm not just some jackbooted thug. You get it?"

Tony nodded. "I get it."

"Promise me, Tony," Clyde demanded.

———

NOW, STANDING OVER CLYDE, Tony knows what he has to do. Clyde had his wishes. It's time to carry them out.

Tony reaches in his jacket pocket and pulls out the postcard he bought yesterday. He unfolds the postcard and carefully removes the pushpin from his pocket. He slips his arm out of the sling and throws the sling in the casket. Then, using both arms, he pins the postcard to the bottom side of the open casket, pushing the pin through the hardwood surface, just above Clyde's face, to give him something to look at in his afterlife.

Thomas Moran's Grand Canyon.

CHAPTER ELEVEN:

IRIS KING

RIS APPROACHES THE BACK DOOR, long before they open, when almost no one's around except whatever cop's taking the night shift of the *watch* over her husband, so she can have a moment with her late husband without anyone getting on to her about what's she going to do or how's she going about doing it. She figures she'll tell the cop, who's standing guard over Clyde, to get out of here for a few, go get a drink or something down the road. Say she'll take the watch.

But the *watch* seems kind of silly to her, watching over a dead body because whoever it was isn't anymore. They're gone. Gone on to the great beyond or something like that. Iris doesn't believe in an afterlife, not that she believes in much other than herself. She sure as hell doesn't believe in trusting others because she's always been on her own and thinks this while closing the doors and walking down the hall.

That, and this wasn't what Clyde wanted: a burial.

He made her promise not to do this to him, years ago, when they first met, but she told him, "What do you care what the living people do when you're gone? You're gone. Isn't the funeral a celebration for you so that people left behind can process their grief? Who're you to tell people how to grieve? You're dead."

Clyde never saw it her way. He said, "We'll agree to disagree."

And disagree they did, pretty much on everything, which at times had her wondering what she saw in him, but then she'd get to thinking about how they met. It'd make her smile, remembering how smooth he was and how polite, how caring. Remembering a time they did like each other—couldn't get enough of each other—but times change.

Looks and personality wise, Clyde always reminded her of Paul Newman, specifically Newman in *The Color of Money*, which was one of the first movies Clyde made her watch because he was a Scorsese fan, but not just a Scorsese fan, a movie fan. He said it was Scorsese's most commercial movie and even came in under time and budget. He asked what artist doesn't want to bloat their egos and budgets? When he made her watch it, they had a marathon. They watched all of Scorsese's movies over a week. In the movie, Newman's a lady's man, older, weathered, good-looking, and dashing—Clyde was the embodiment of Fast Eddie Felson, with the same damn mustache too. And funnily, she's like Tom Cruise: younger, a flake, but incredibly good at what she does, playing a game—in her case poker. It's how they met and the only time Clyde's ever played her. But their story didn't end on a freeze-frame.

Though, what was wrong with their marriage had nothing to do with them not liking each other; it had everything to do with her. So, being the reasonable rational person she is, she proposed a solution—an *open marriage*. That's the phrase she introduced him to. She explained that there's a whole lifestyle built around it, being this is the modern age. Clyde told her being his age there was another way to put it—*cuckold*: an old word but appropriate to the situation. He yelled at her *his situation*. He said that's what she's doing to him. She contended that, no, what she's done is fuck him whenever he wants, not like he hasn't enjoyed that bit about her being younger, and it's not her fault that he only wants it every other week or so. She said that she's there on his arm anytime he wants and argued that what she does with the rest of her time should be up to her. He said he never wanted to feel that way, *cuckold*, and never wanted to see evidence of it either.

So, agree to disagree—the motto of their union.

His body is in the room just beyond where she's standing now. The ADA convinced her to go against Clyde's wishes. Clyde never wanted the burial with honors. Eli did and does. It's why he had her come to his office the other day, so they could discuss it. He explained that Clyde had put Eli in charge of his will. He was an attorney and friend. Explaining to her, he said the estate would be left to her; there were some limitations and issues, but as far as the burial went, he felt it was good for morale, a show of force is how he put it, to do the honorable thing and go against Clyde's wishes. It was okay after all; he was dead. Eli said it was up to her; she could make the decision, but he'd support her in whatever decision she made.

Iris decided to follow his advice. She hasn't done this before, bury someone, although not only did it feel like Eli was getting his way about Clyde's funeral, but it also felt like Eli had her come to his office for something different.

Iris steps into the back room, lights on low, and finds Tony—Antonio—standing on the opposite side of the room looking down at Clyde with his back to her, wearing a jacket, sipping on some coffee. No sling this time. The last time she saw him, in passing, at Eli's office, Tony was wearing the sling.

Iris checks her outfit and runs a hand down her body, making sure her black blouse is down and tucked right into the waistband of her black slacks, slim fit, no belt, doesn't need it with her frame and black shoes, flats because the heels come later.

Iris clears her throat so not to startle him. "The house is so quiet with him gone. I never thought I'd miss the noise. He could be quite loud when he wanted to be. Talked loud. Played that music loud—Led Zeppelin—yelling at me from his shop about how it's the blues but not the blues. I never really knew what that meant. Do you know what that means? Know what I mean?"

Not surprised to find her, Tony turns. "He did like to talk loud," he says, acknowledging her. "Couldn't whisper very well either. One time, we were in a bad situation, and he tried to tell me something, but the guy across the room heard him."

Tony glances over his shoulder, which acts as an invitation, and she forgets her plan of telling the cop on the watch to go get something to eat. She wants him to stay. She steps forward. "What'd he try to tell you?"

She crosses the room, stopping next to Clyde's casket, next to Tony, and her eyes notice the postcard pinned to the lid.

"He was trying to tell me the recording device strapped to his body was malfunctioning," Tony says. "Because of a budget crisis, we pulled this old-school thing out of the back closet. Neither of us knew when the last time anyone used it was. He was trying to tell me it was shocking him—electrocuting him."

Iris snorts, laughing loudly. She fills the entire room with genuine laughter and realizes it's the first time she's laughed since the Cortez lady came to the house.

Tony says, "So this guy, who was about to sell us a couple of pounds, turns around and asks us, 'What was that?' Reaching his hand in his waist band. And Clyde's dancing a jig, right there in his living room, grabbing at the device at the small of his back, hands trying to get at it, but he couldn't reach it."

"What happened after that?" Iris asks.

But Tony doesn't say and collapses into silence. He turns his attention back to Clyde. "What are you doing here so late?"

Iris strokes the hair out of her eyes. "I couldn't sleep. I was thinking about him. Thinking about what's going to happen in the morning. I never thought—"

"He'd die like this—me either."

"He told me he wanted to retire soon. Told me the whole world was losing their minds when it came to drugs. He said he didn't know what he was fighting for anymore. Things seemed topsy turvy. We liked to watch *Fargo* on TV; you know it? Well, in the third season, there was a line where this guy comes home after everything very Fargo-ish happened, and he tells his wife he doesn't recognize the world anymore like it's not his world or something like that, and Clyde turned to me on the couch and said, 'I feel just like that, especially here in Oklahoma, passing laws where basically everything's a slap on the wrist and always going to be a slap on the wrist.' He said, the Feds aren't like that, yet, but he was sure by the time his ticket came up for mandatory retirement, he'd be without a job, saying, 'What's the Drug Enforcement Agency going to do when there's no drugs to go about enforcing?'"

Tony listens to her. "He told me he wanted to go to Arizona for retirement." Then says, "I was just thinking about him telling me that—said he wanted to do health shakes?"

"Oh yeah, the health shakes," Iris says embarrassed now, admitting it was her idea. "A dumb one, but not as dumb as Clyde's other ideas like the one where he wanted to go out to Florida, of all places. That's as cliché as it comes: an old cop retiring to the sun to get salt-pickled by the ocean. He wanted to go out there and open snow cone shacks because apparently, he had a buddy who worked in some sales field, who had a mid-life crisis, and quit his life here to go out there and do that. Buddy told Clyde there was an open market out there; snow cones weren't a thing. How's that not a thing? It's just shaved ice with sugar water."

"Colored sugar water," Tony adds.

She smiles. "Clyde said his buddy wanted him to come out and help, but I think the guy just wanted some other sucker to come out there and pour his retirement down the drain working for somebody else, him."

Tony sips his coffee. "That's worse than Clyde's wanting to open a movie theater idea. Used to bitch up a storm that all the dollar movie places were closed. Said he loved them. Grew up going to the theaters, basically was his afterschool specials—the dollar theater being special." Tony shrugs. "His joke. Not a good one. Though, the theaters were probably cheaper back then for him. I'd ask him how he thought he'd turn a profit if he's only charging a dollar, and he said he'd figure it out."

"I don't think he ever did because that idea came and went," Iris says. "You know what was better than that one was when he thought about opening a breakfast bar at that old oil-lube place. You remember that one? The half-circle joint with the garage doors, used to be called the G-spot? Which by the way, is interesting in its own right, calling itself that and being a lube place."

"Very Freudian."

"Shouldn't that be a name for a strip club or something? The G-Spot. I feel like that would work."

"Or a porno," Tony says. "Although I don't think the city would take too kindly to a strip place being right off Main Street of a sleepy suburb calling itself the G-Spot."

"But a lube place calling itself that was okay," Iris says, giggling. "Anyways, he'd tell me he wanted to serve breakfast in the morning, and then after say, eight in the evening, open it up as a bar. Have a full bar. Said he'd even serve it in the morning."

"I liked that idea though," Tony says. "It made more sense to me than say the health shake one. You know alcoholics need a place to go when the sun comes up. Like cockroaches, it drives them indoors. What better place than somewhere where there's food and booze?"

"I'll get to the health shake one," she says. "But he was always looking for something to turn a quick buck in retirement. You'd think, working for the government, especially the Feds, he'd want to relax or something—not work again. But not him."

"He detested not working. Always complained that's the one difference between his parents and him."

"There were a lot of differences between his parents and him."

"You know he never smoked grass," Tony says. "You'd think being in the DEA he'd at least know something about drugs, maybe tried it out. I've smoked grass. Did it in high school, not heavily, but enough to get an idea for it. Never anything else though, at least not off the clock," he winks at her, "but he never abused drugs or drank to get drunk. Kind of amazing when you think about it."

Iris says, "He said with his parents walking around naked at the commune drinking and smoking sort of took the appeal out of it for him. He said people would just start fucking right there."

"That was a different time."

"More like a different place," Iris says. "I still wonder— and have since I met him—why he decided to work for the federal government, especially the DEA. You would think with parents like that he'd be a little more against working for *The Man*, as he put it."

"That's easy: the retirement."

"But he never wanted to actually retire from working."

"No, everything transferred over from his military time," Tony says. "He used to complain about being a marine, sitting in the desert doing nothing."

"Probably bragged he could breathe better there."

"No kidding. That's why he said he wanted to go out to Arizona," Tony says. "Said the desert air helped him breathe better. I don't know about that. He said Arizona because of the Grand Canyon."

Iris's eyes flick to the postcard. "I've not slept well since they gave me the notification." Tony shifts his weight, and Iris catches the shift and wants to ask about the notification, why he wasn't there, but continues, "So I've been thinking a lot about what he wanted and wanted to do. Dying, death, I guess it makes you think about things like that. Think about life."

Almost as if he read her thoughts, Tony says, "About the notification."

"Don't worry about it," Iris says.

"No, it should have been me. I wanted it to be me. I wanted to come to you."

Iris processes what Tony's telling her. He's right it should have been him. Clyde would have expected it to be him. It would have been easier had it been him and not that bitch. But maybe it wouldn't have been. Just because someone she's attracted to comes to break the bad news doesn't make the news not bad news. And he was where he needed to be, here beside her husband, so she says, "You were with Clyde."

Tony relaxes.

Iris looks down at her husband for the first time. "Is that your sling?"

"I didn't need it any longer, figured he could use it. Being he's dead weight and all. I guess that's dark humor. Goes with the job."

"Not appropriate, but Clyde could be that way too," Iris says. "I think the real reason he wanted to go to Arizona was—I think he wanted to get back to his roots. To live out where there's some kooky people, living way out there like his parents did, because you know, he's getting older, wanted to remember his parents. He left home at seventeen, went to sign up for the military, lied about his age, got turned away, worked for a year, living on the streets, and flipping burgers, went back to the recruiting office, and shipped out a week later. He said anything was better than living on the commune."

"Not everything," Tony says. "He always said tanning was better. Even. No lines."

Iris chuckles. She slicks her tongue over her bottom lip. "Well, you don't have to live in a commune to walk around naked."

Tony gives her a look, almost a double take. And then there's Clyde looking back at her, all that life and the Newman-ness gone from his face.

"He wanted to be cremated."

"Spread out over the Grand Canyon," Tony says, waving his hand forward like he's staring out at the horizon.

"He told you?"

Tony nods. "I'm not really surprised to find him laying here after dying on the job. Kind of comes with everything. The bagpipes, drums, guns, and salutes."

"Think they're going to do the flag draped over his coffin or is that just in the movies?" Iris asks. "Who do you think will give me the flag?"

"You were in his office yesterday, and he's probably the reason Clyde's right here." And with that, Tony excuses himself, telling Iris he needs to go to the restroom and asks if she needs coffee or anything from down the way. He's going to get out of there for a few, clear his head. "I'll let you be alone with your husband."

CHAPTER TWELVE:

ELIZA CORTEZ

ELIZA FINDS TONY AT A SPORTS BAR around the corner from the funeral home, sitting at the bar, alone, sipping a beer, staring down at the bar top, his fingers digging a quarter into the coaster, a stack of split coasters discarded to the side.

From the doorway, letting in the fresh light into the already well-lit place, Eliza prepares herself, takes a breath, and marches inside. Inside, everything's golf-themed, clean, and gleaming. The bar is freshly polished, and several TVs line the walls showing SportsCenter. A couple of patrons are scattered throughout, and a couple of waiters are talking in the back. They glance at her, but she points to Tony at the bar. She walks over to the bar and passes a molded golf putter striking an overly large ball on the wall, and from the kitchen, the smell of hamburger meat on the grill drifts her way. The bartender fills a sink with water, preparing to wash glasses. Tony, sensing her presence, pauses what he's doing to glance her way and then goes back to digging the quarter into the coaster. The bartender opens his mouth to offer her a drink but scans her body and stays silent. Still, he does smile at Eliza as she takes a seat next to Tony, straddling the stool, which is more difficult than it looks with her belly getting in the way, hopping up and throwing her upper body on the bar top to pull herself up. It's uncomfortable and takes considerable effort. She says, "What are you doing here?"

Tony shrugs and returns his focus to the edge of the quarter indenting the coaster, nearly through to the bar. "Didn't know where else to go."

The bartender, a dark-headed male wearing tight jeans, comes over and drops a napkin on the bar top in front of her. Eliza tells the bartender that she'll take a tea. Pointing to Tony, she asks, "How long has he been here?"

The bartender, who calls himself Wesley, says, "I showed up at seven to do inventory, and he was sitting against the doors out there." He points to the glass doors of the outside seating. Eliza spots the knocked-over table and the toppled chairs. "Had a coffee cup with beer cans beside him, knocked over, and he was crying. I asked what's up. He told me about his friend. I figured what the hell, I couldn't turn him away. So, I let him inside, told him he could sit there while I did my thing. I told him just don't take nothing."

Defensively, Tony spouts, "I didn't take nothing."

The bartender nods. "But he did ask for a drink. I said no, but then he showed me his badge. And I figured why not. Cops got weird hours too. Been here ever since." Bartender adds, "I lost my best friend a couple of months ago—overdose. So I get it, losing a friend. Is there anything you want other than the tea?"

Eliza nods along to his story and shakes her head. "No, Wesley, I'm good." Then to Tony, "Why here?"

"Only place open," Tony says, checks his watch, "Officially open at ten-thirty. Figured I might as well get a beer."

"Yeah, but why?" Eliza asks. "And he just said you've been here for a couple of hours, being a sad sack, moping about."

Wesley laughs. "All right, I'll leave you be to get your tea."

Eliza thanks him, and he disappears.

With the bartender gone, Tony says, "She hit on me," sinking deeper into himself, elbows out sprawling across the bar top.

"Who hit on you?" Eliza asks.

"Did it over the body of her dead husband too," Tony comments. "Sounds like a bad joke. Woman flirting with a man over the body of her dead husband—like I'll do it over his dead body..." His voice is animated for the effect, but then it falls flat and fizzles out. He repeats the first line but never gets to the punch line. "I'll do it over his dead body."

"Sounds pretty disgusting if you ask me. Not that you are."

"I'm not."

"Don't be like that," she says, which causes Tony to stop what he's doing and turn to listen to her. "Don't be rude. I've been worried about you. I haven't heard from you. No one has. We didn't know where you were. Iris said you left this morning around four, and she never saw you again. Then, Larry got there, talked with Iris, called me, told me he showed up for his shift, and said you weren't around. He waited a bit and then called me again, asking if I could come look for you. He figured you were probably somewhere close. He didn't think you got too far."

Tony listens but then goes back to pressing the quarter into the coaster as he explains what happened. "I couldn't stand being in the room with her doing that cutesy shit."

Eliza says, "And not a bad-looking woman, you know? She likes to use it on men." Testing him to see if he reacts, dropping her line like bait in the water, hoping to hear a specific answer, to see if Tony gobbles up the worm.

But then Eliza's transported back to the notification, replaying her memories of that moment, about how she was ninety percent sure someone was upstairs, and being that it was evening time and Iris was naked under that robe, again, who does that? Eliza's pretty sure Iris was cheating on Clyde and just had sex when they came to tell her about his death. Hair is always a dead giveaway.

So, to Eliza, it's no surprise Iris hit on Tony. Five minutes with the woman, and Eliza had her pegged for just the type of woman, the one that would do something like that, judged her for what she is.

Tony says, "You know what the worst part about it all is?"

Eliza does, but she supplies the answer anyways. "You liked it, and you're not upset with her as much as you are upset with yourself."

Tony's head swivels her way, eyes wide. "How'd you—you know what, never mind." He nods and swats the idea away, eyes back on the coaster, sinking even more on the stool. "Yeah, okay, I enjoyed it. That's what disgusts me the most. I enjoyed her flirting with me. All of it happening before I knew what was happening. There I am, my friend the dead guy looking up at me, and I'm flirting back with her, his wife, cracking jokes. So yeah, I'm not disgusted with her for flirting with me in front of her husband's body—"

"I am. That's disgusting."

"—I'm disgusted with myself for flirting back." Tony sips the beer and shrugs.

Tony's disgusted with himself for biting the wrong bait because that worm must feel funny twisting in his throat like that.

Then, Tony comments, "It's what it is. I suppose. Some people grieve differently."

"You're not going to give me that bullshit about the *Five Love Languages*, are you?"

Tony's voice runs high as he says no, but that just means yes. It's the same spiel he gave her for justification for what they did. The problem was he wasn't too far off the mark, but she's too stubborn to admit he was right.

Tony shuffles in the seat some, bringing his body up in the stool. "Some people need to find comfort in others. Why does she have to be any different? Look, Clyde told me all about what sort of shenanigans they got up to, how they met, how they lived their lives. It's not like it's a surprise to me."

"It is to me," Eliza says. "But I don't know anything about that. I don't want to. Clyde was his own man. He did his own things."

"He was pretty sure she was sleeping around."

Eliza raises an eyebrow. "Really?" She debates with herself about telling him about the notification, about the nice expensive jacket over the loveseat, the sex hair, and the shower starting when they were about to leave.

"They discussed having an open marriage. I asked him if that meant he's going to be out there hound dogging other women. You know what he told me?"

"He told you he'd be out there doing just that."

"No," Tony says. "He said, his parents had that at the commune." Adding, "Oh yeah, Clyde grew up on a commune, by the way. Not sure that's ever come up before."

"You're shitting me," Eliza says, everything about Clyde making a lot more sense. "You're not shitting me. That's true?"

Tony splits the coaster with the quarter. He brushes the two sides away and picks another coaster from the stack. "He didn't want anyone to know, but he told me. He tells me a lot... told me... anyways, he told me she's the only woman for him. He can't see himself with another woman. 'A one-woman man' is what he said. But he did think she was sleeping around. I mean, I guess she told him she was. He just never told me who. He thought it—"

"How about you don't tell me anything more about their marriage, alright?"

"Yeah, whatever."

"So, you're disgusted with yourself because you're attracted to her?"

Tony nods. "I mean I guess so. Who wouldn't be?"

"Me," Eliza says.

"That's not what I mean."

"Well, I can tell you, for sure, Eli's not turned off by her. Did you see that shit yesterday, him meeting with her in his makeshift office in our conference room? He's only there because Clyde's dead and they're doing damage control, trying to decide what to do. And he brings her in, goes to the room, shuts the door, and through the windows, before dropping the blinds, looks like a kid at Christmas."

"I saw," Tony says. "He's a snake."

"Speaking of yesterday, what's going on, Tony?" she asks. "You left without telling me bye. Now, today, you're here doing this. What's going on with you? This isn't you."

He doesn't answer. He finishes his beer and sinks farther into the stool, body hunched over the bar. "Does it matter?"

"You're not doing this to me today," Eliza says. "I came here to get answers from you. Not the other way around. Today's already hard enough, burying Clyde." Eliza stands her ground and adds, "So yes, to me it does."

Tony searches her face as she reaches out and takes his hand; she squeezes. Tony squeezes back. "I had to leave. Marque told me to go home."

That doesn't answer her question, but he's going to keep whatever's going on to himself.

"Marque says there's too much exposure. Siriano would be there in the future. Try again. You know the drill."

"So we're done?" Tony asks. "What else did he say?"

"He didn't say much else," Eliza responds. "But Eli came to the briefing, said they're going to lay off Siriano. Said things went bad, saying two people dead, one a DEA Agent, one of our own, dead, which is unacceptable. Like we had any control over it. He said with the other in critical condition, it means there's too much exposure to really go after anyone. He wants to close the investigation for now. Clean up what we have and try again later."

Tony absorbs what she's saying. Then, with anger in his voice. "So, you're saying they're saying Clyde's death will be for nothing." He puts it out there because that's what they're both thinking. Then, he changes the subject. "Did you call Eduardo?"

Her voice is cold. "When?"

Pain and shame swell under Tony's tone. "At the hospital, after everything that happened, after Clyde, did you bother to call him that evening or did you wait until later, after you talked with Iris, or did you just pretend nothing happened?"

That's cruel. Tony shouldn't bring her husband up like that, asking the question the way he is. Yes, Tony's hurting, his friend is dead, and she delivered bad news, but he shouldn't lash out at her, of all people. And although she may understand and recognize what he's doing, it doesn't make it any easier for her. She doesn't like it. It's not fair.

"Yes, I called my husband," Eliza says, but that's a lie. She didn't call him until after it was on the news and after he'd sent a text message, which was just a question mark with a link to the story on social media. "What type of woman do you think I am?"

But Tony knows what type of woman she is, and Eliza knows what type of woman she is. He doesn't have to say anything, and maybe that's why Iris disgusts her so much. Infidelity damaged her marriage to the point that she's not sure the pieces can be put back together, although she's trying. And Iris is out there rubbing it in everyone's face, not caring, even flirting with Tony over her husband's dead body. It isn't what Eliza did—her marriage is essentially dead, just neither party wants to admit it.

Eliza drops her hand to her stomach and changes the subject back to Clyde. "I don't want to look at it like this is all for nothing. We will get him eventually. Siriano will know what's happened."

"But that's what they're saying. He died for nothing."

"That's what Marque's saying. Eli's saying the same. Said Siriano is a smart man, smarter than most. He'll put two and two together. Closeout business wherever Franklin touched it. We have Franklin. He's ours. Under arrest. We'll have to let the other stuff go for now."

"So, what's that do to my source?" Tony asks. "He's in danger. He trusted us... me... Siriano will want to know how we got on to him. He'll figure it out."

"Have you talked to him? What's your source saying, anything?" It's what she wanted to talk to him about yesterday, but he wasn't around.

"I haven't reached out to him yet," Tony says. "He's already in danger. I didn't want to make it worse. He may be dead already."

Tony's source is a dead man. They both know it, and she can tell he's lying. If she knows him as well as she knows she does, Tony's already reached out.

"Well, you might try," Eliza says. "Tell him we're done for a while. Keep his head down. Whatever we might have gotten is what we've gotten. Tell him I think we're done."

"I'm not done." Confidence lifts Tony's body, adds some strength in his voice, and even makes him sit straighter, shoulders high.

No, he probably isn't. That's probably what he's been doing while sitting here wallowing in his own version of self-loathing, deciding what he's going to do now and how he's going to get his revenge for Clyde. Eliza knows Tony too well, knows him enough to know this is personal for him. But knowing is half the battle. She wants him to tell her what's going on in his head, tell her what he thinks he's going to do about it.

"What are you saying?"

Tony is silent.

"Tony, we're done. Siriano will chop off whatever's been infected like a limb gone bad, you know that. If you go after him, he'll go after you. So that's it for us, for now. That's what they're saying. Marque and Eli. I know it sucks, but that's what it is."

"That all he's saying?"

"Marque or Eli?" she asks.

Tony says either but means Eli.

"They're saying you need to take a few days off, for the grief and stuff, heal up," Eliza says, "and come back to work on your other cases. After the meeting, I asked them where you went, and they said they weren't comfortable with you in the office yesterday. Said you just stared at your computer. So, Marque said he sent you home to rest. Still, you should have told me goodbye."

"If you knew, then why did you bring it up? So, he just gets away with it?"

"Who? Franklin? He's going to be prosecuted for it. Siriano? We'll get to him. It's never the end."

"That's not right. He's not going to get away with it."

"No, listen to me Tony, the Siriano investigation is dead," Eliza says. "Marque said we'd get something on him. Those guys can't help but fuck up, but right now, there's nothing we can do. Franklin will go down for Clyde and that's that. You will heal. We," her voice grows softer, "will bury our friend, and we will work on starting a new case on him. But right now, we need to heal and figure out what comes next."

"So, I'm supposed to just be happy with pulling out?" Tony asks, except his tone isn't pleasant and the insinuation chaffs her. "Clyde and I worked hard on getting this far on Siriano."

"Of course, you should be," Eliza remarks, anger getting the best of her causing her blood pressure to rise and with it a dull headache. "But if you knew how to do that, pull out of anything, I wouldn't be in the situation I'm in— or rather, we're in." Something that's taken her months to work up the courage to say. "It's only going to cause more problems."

Tony presses down hard on the quarter, and it squirts out from under his thumb, bounces away. He doesn't say a word. He watches the coin jump once on the floor, flashing silver on the second strike and disappearing out of sight under one of the stainless-steel sinks.

Finally, he asks, "How's Ed handling it?"

"Eduardo's handling it the best he can."

What else is she supposed to say? She's pregnant with Tony's baby.

"I suppose the best anyone can. He's excited for the baby."

"So you haven't told him?" Tony asks. He picks up the tone in her voice, the apprehension of talking about her husband and the baby in the same sentence and knows what that means.

"Tell him what exactly? Tell him that you and I fucked a couple of months back at a conference, both of us hammered and going at it like a couple of dogs in heat? How he and I were separated... how you and I..." But she can't even finish what she's saying because she's just as disgusted with herself as he is with Iris hitting on Tony over the body of her dead husband.

Disgusted would be an understatement. It is more like self-loathing. Hatred.

"Why'd you tell me?"

It's a legitimate question, and one Eliza can't answer. She doesn't know why she told him. Weakness? Hope? Shame? Absolution? She could have kept it to herself.

"You could have kept it a secret," Tony says. "Kept it to yourself. I mean, I enjoyed what we did, really enjoyed it. But you and I, it wouldn't have changed anything. We could have still been us. It was the first time. You could have pretended it's Ed's, and we would have been us," he motions to himself and her, "and nothing would have been different. Why'd you tell me?"

Eliza refuses to answer because she's asking herself that same question. Why did she tell him? What did she think was going to happen? Did she think that she'd just turn those sultry pregnancy eyes toward him, let the fabled pregnancy glow work him over, as she says, *it's yours, I'm sure*? And he'd, what, beg to be with her? Her life's a shit-show. Why would he want any part of that?

And if she didn't tell him, he's smart enough. He would have figured it out. Then, would he have let things go back to the way they were? Because everything changed the moment he came inside her, which was something that hadn't happened before, him going without a condom. They were drunk. She was hurting, angry. He was available. Who was she to think anything different would happen? Her Catholic upbringing's taught her better than that. It taught her that what she was doing was a sin, a mortal sin, a go-to-hell-don't-pass-go type of sin. But what'd she do after finding out her husband was in love with someone else but didn't have the balls to end it with her? Go fuck Tony.

166

What was she thinking?

She wasn't thinking, and she's sure about the father; the baby is his.

And now she's thinking: where the hell is Wesley with her tea?

"Ed's been throwing blanks for two years," Eliza says. "Why do you think we were separated? Yes, he cheated on me; he did it for years. Said he was in love, but really, the no-baby thing had stressed our relationship out so badly that we weren't happy. Never talked about it. Kind of figured that's how we got to that point, so far apart. Not talking. But I forgave him—put him through hell for it—but I forgave him because what was I supposed to do. What was I supposed to say to him, 'Hey honey, sorry for busting your balls about cheating on me; I'm pregnant with a coworker's baby?'"

"I thought we would be more than that at this point." Tony's unfulfilled hope shadows his face. "Friends at least. Maybe more."

What does he want from her? For her to leave her husband, so she can be with him? That's silly.

"I'm married, Tony," she says, letting the annoyance creep into her voice. "What do you want me to say? I can't be dealing with your shit all the time when I can barely deal with my own."

Tony shrugs, and his hand disappears into his pocket, which comes back with a thick black wallet. He fishes out a coin from the folds, quiet the whole time. Now, with a new quarter between his fingers. "Do you know if it's a boy or a girl?"

Eliza crosses her arms. "I'll tell you when I tell you."

"Meaning I find out when I find out." Tony accepts his place at her side. "How's this going to work?"

"I don't know. I'll have to tell Ed at some point, but the longer I wait, the harder it gets."

"Kind of like saying goodbye to Clyde."

"No, it's nothing like that."

CHAPTER THIRTEEN:
FRANKLIN HAYES

FRANKLIN SAYS, "Hey Larry," and almost on cue the DEA agent—this one called Lawrence, with a bit of a southern twang in the way he says his name, accentuating the *law* part of it—decides he's done and stands to exit the room. He withdraws his phone from his pocket, disgusted with all the times Franklin, laying in the bed, yells out, "Hey Larry."

Franklin would say, "Hey Larry, can you get the nurse?"

Lawrence would just stare at him from behind his magazine, the Pakistani fucker's *Sports Illustrated*, and would say, "There's a button."

Then, Franklin would say something like, "Hey Larry, can you get me some water?"

And Lawrence would say something like, "Why don't you get it yourself?"

"Hey Larry, ain't that why I have you?" Franklin would say. Doing it just to mess with the guy. "Hey Larry, can you get this?" Or "Hey Larry can you get that?"

"Hey Larry..."

Every time the room grows quiet, the bustle of the hospital falling into a lull.

"Hey Larry..."

Franklin expects nothing, but it doesn't stop him from asking or messing with the guy. It's easy to get under his skin. That and Franklin's pretty sure that Larry's one part of the goon squad, him and the Pakistani guy, the same two that rolled up and shot him. So, he doesn't mind being a pain in the ass. They put him here.

Doctor says it's a miracle, no surgery, no major organs punctured. He is doing better than he thought, but he broke the rules, killing a cop. He's fucked one way or another. No one will take his calls, and he's got no hope of getting out of this mess. That's what he told Vera when she asked him, "How'd you end up here?"

And Franklin's answer has two parts. The first part, he trusted someone he shouldn't have, and that's enough to cause what's happened to happen. He should have known better. No, scratch that, he does know better, but the product was just too damn good, meaning the money was too good and he was getting a sweetheart deal, which is what leads to the other part. The other part being that he did business with a friend, and his granddaddy taught him never to do business with friends; *nothing good comes from it.* Franklin tells Vera, "Granddaddy said, 'Friends and business don't mix because you're there to fuck the other guy over without giving up any. Sort of like the head cheerleader and the football star; she's not giving him any, but together they're king and queen—there's power in the art of getting off without giving up a part of yourself.' Not that I understood every one of my granddaddy's allegories, but that doesn't mean I didn't take the lessons to heart. Oddly enough, come Sunday nights, my granddaddy never missed an episode of *Star Trek: Deep Space Nine*, and surprise, surprise he loved the Ferengi and their Rules of Acquisition the most." Franklin explains that he might as well get a laugh out of fucking with someone else. "Why not mess with the guys that put me here?"

Vera would ask him why he has to be so difficult.

"Hey Larry, mind if I piss in that bottle? This one's full," Franklin says, pointing to the Aquafina bottle on the table next to Lawrence while shaking the piss bottle hanging next to his handcuffed hand. "I'll bet you twenty bucks the head of my dick don't even match the top of that bottle, but yours probably slips right inside."

Lawrence—a brother, but you wouldn't know it— gets so frustrated, flustered even, with Franklin that his brown skin turns red, which is a feat in itself as Lawrence says, "Would you shut the fuck up? I'm already missing out on a friend's funeral. I don't want to put up with your fucking hijinks."

Then, he picks up that water bottle next to him and chucks it at Franklin's face. And like a damn cop, he misses. The bottle hits the wall behind Franklin's head, explodes, and covers the bed and him with water.

Franklin yells as Lawrence stomps out of the room. "If I weren't strapped to this motherfucking bed, I'd beat the shit out of you for that!" He jerks on the handcuffs, turning from mock anger to intense laughter. "Hey, Larry, where're you going?"

And then Vera, oh sweet Vera, the rose of his recuperation, flutters back into the room.

Franklin, between a wide grin, yells, "Hey, Larry, Vera and I got to take a sponge bath...Vera, baby, I'm going to be gone to prison for a long time. Why don't you make this one extra dirty?"

"Why do you do that?" she asks, swatting at him. "What did you say this time?" Shuffling over to his bed, with her phone in her hand, outstretched, ready for him to try one more phone call.

Oh, Vera. She's become so invested in him, taking on extra shifts just to be around him, coming in on her days off, working doubles, whatever she has to do just to get a little more of Franklin—working a double now.

He's worked his magic on her, turning the charm on and putting his all into turning her his way. It's not that hard with these health care types and she's no different. Each one wants to nurse this poor, misbegotten and mis-understood being, just like if he were a rabbit or squirrel, back to health, except he's not a rabbit or squirrel, he's a grown-ass man. Franklin won't change no matter how hard Vera tries. And maybe Vera doesn't expect him to change; maybe she thinks he, who she knows isn't a good guy, might just be all right with the right touch and she does have a good touch.

But that's what she doesn't understand; the world doesn't work that way, and it's almost a cruel thing to do it to her now, to Vera, turn her to his corner, coaxing her all the way, finger out under her chin, scratching an itch in her that she didn't know she possessed until he came along. Like one of those funny little fish that live deep under the ocean with the little dangly light hanging from their foreheads, using bio-luminousness—he always liked that word—to trick little tiny fish into their mouth to be gobbled up.

"You must have really gotten under his skin this time," Vera says. "He was cussing and cursing to the elevator."

From the bed, he watches her. "Aren't those the same things, cussing and cursing? Like what's the difference?"

Smiling, Vera touches her stubby index finger to the clef in her sharp chin. "You know, I guess they are. I've never thought too much about it."

"Like is cursing meaning a fella's saying curses like a witch, putting some sort of hex on someone, whereas cussing is the regular *motherfucking* we're all so ashamed we do, thinking that not saying such blasted things makes us seem intelligent or pious?"

Vera rushes to the bed and kisses him, fully on the mouth, taking him by surprise. "Well, my momma always said smart people don't cuss."

He tastes her lips on his, picks up the vague scent of strawberry. It dances across his tongue, tangy and sweet. Franklin asks, "Your momma cuss?"

Vera looks down at him. "Like a sailor."

"Was she a smart woman?"

Vera shakes her head. "No, I don't believe she was. She smoked every day of her life, running through packs like she was always smoking her last cigarette like she might die after that one. Course, daddy did like to put the scare of life in you."

That's just a fancy way of saying he beat the ever-living snot out of her. Franklin's daddy did the same thing; it's how he got his scar. She's only asked about his scar one time, stroking the side of his face after he said "Hey Larry..." so many times that Larry took his dinner down in the hospital café and was gone a whole hour, leaving Franklin all to his lonesome to work on Vera. She asked how he got his scar while running her fingers slowly across the ugly dented skin before tickling his earlobe. He told her he didn't want to talk about it. She asked if he'd ever tell her. He said, "Baby, when I'm free from here, with you in bed, both of us naked in each other's arms, I'll tell you the story, and when I do, you're going to wish you never asked."

He hates talking about his scar. It usually causes a violent reaction. However, with Vera, he might just tell her, but she'll be sorry she asked; she won't like the story, which is why he doesn't tell it. And he doesn't want anyone feeling sorry for him. He doesn't need it. The only person he's ever told the truth to about it was Kevin after Kevin asked him about his scar, and he knocked Kevin on his ass for it. This was on the playground in the sixth grade. But wiping the blood from the corner of his mouth and spitting out a tooth, Kevin said, "So really, how'd you get it?"

Vera leans down again, squishing her breasts just so against his shoulder and neck, smelling today of geraniums. She kisses him. "My momma smoked so much it wasn't much of a surprise when she started coughing up blood and got the big C. She died last year."

"See that's what I'm saying." Franklin wishing his right hand wasn't tethered to the bed, because he'd grab her around that little waist, reach for the bottom half of her that's not little, get her closer to get some more of her sweet sugar she's offering him like a clam opening up for the diver wanting pearls.

She kisses him again to keep him quiet. The lips feel nice. Soft, wet, plump, sort of like her whole body, something he could learn to appreciate if he had the time or inclination. He has neither.

"Let me see that." His eyes on her phone.

She unlocks the phone, pulls up the little digital dial pad, and gives him the phone. "He's going to be gone a while. I can tell." Then, she goes about doing all the things she's supposed to be doing like checking his vitals and updating his chart.

Franklin responds, "Un-huh," while typing in Kevin's phone number, hoping against hope that he picks up this time. He can only call his granddaddy so many times before she gets suspicious.

"The news, this morning," Vera says while doing her work, "said they're burying the cop."

"Who?" he asks, but he knows who. He just doesn't want to talk about killing someone. His stomach turns.

"The one...," she starts to say and then thinks better of it. "Oh Franklin, why'd we have to meet like this? Why couldn't you just have brought your granddaddy to the hospital and run into me and I into you and we start chatting?"

"I make you smile." He hits the call button on the phone.

"Things just would have been better," she says. "You know, I mean, I guess I can come visit you. Do they still do conjugal visits?"

The phone to his ear. "Oh, we're just jumping straight to the fucking parts, huh?"

Vera purrs. "There's no time like the present. Besides, what's the point of writing someone day in and day out if he's not putting it in and pulling it out?"

That makes him smile. He picked the right one. He wasn't sure; he is now.

"They could put me anywhere in the nation," Franklin says. "If it were open, I figure, for killing one of their own, I'd have gone to old San Fran to Alcatraz. It would have been a feather in my hat. People asking me, where'd you serve your time? And I'd tell them, The Rock. I've always wanted to say that. The Rock where old Al Capone did his time, and Clint Eastwood escaped, which is funny, because, considering the way you look at it, that was a popular movie, *Escape from Alcatraz*, but then they go and make that one with Sean Connery and crazy-ass white boy Nick Cage where it's basically the same movie but in reverse with explosions."

"Isn't that a Michael Bay movie?"

"Yes, ma'am. Hence the explosions."

"And Ed Harris. I always liked him as an actor," Vera says. "Reminded me of my daddy."

The phone rings once before Kevin Alexander picks it up. "Hello?"

Franklin holds up one finger to tell Vera he got a connection this time. "Hey, it's me. I've been calling, but you've not been answering."

"I didn't know who was calling," Kevin says.

"Which is why you need to answer. You won't know who it is unless you pick up the phone."

"You could leave a message."

"Like that's going to go over well."

"I'm not supposed to be talking to you," Kevin says. "You're persona non grata."

"Persona non whata?"

Vera, from behind the computer, typing in his chart, says, "Means you're off-limits."

As Kevin on the phone says, "Means you're fucked."

"I know what it means," Franklin says. Then, he whispers so that Vera doesn't overhear. "Which is why I've been calling you, my friend, who grew up with me and who put together the deal with Siriano."

Kevin says, "Then, why'd you ask?"

Franklin loud again. "Don't get funny with me."

Vera says, "That's a funny way to talk to your granddaddy."

Franklin covers the phone with his hand and tells her, "He's hard of hearing and a mean son-of-a-bitch, dementia."

"My memory works just fine," Kevin says. "What about yours?"

Into the phone, Franklin says, "Would you just shut your trap for two seconds and listen to me? I've been calling."

Kevin says, "We've been through this. I know you've been calling, and I've not been answering because I didn't know who it was. Though, I figured it was probably you, somehow. How are you calling me, by the way? You still in the hospital? And why are you calling me? You shouldn't be calling me."

"Yes, I'm in the hospital." Franklin kicks his foot out, which hurts one of the wounds, stretching the sutures. He bites through the pain and makes a noise. "I can't get into it all right now, but I wanted to let you know I'm not going to say nothing to no one."

"Oh shit, Frankie, I know that."

"You know I hate when people call me Frankie. I know you know that; I want you to let him know that."

"He knows that too. He says he knows you didn't let the cops in on what you were doing because there's no business in that, which means Frankie's not in it."

"Oh, good, because when I get to where I'm going, I don't want some dip-shit shoving sharp objects in my ribs."

"I doubt you get that far," Kevin says, nonchalantly.

Now, the opposite of relief washes over Franklin. "What?"

"Renaldo's been dispatched to take care of you," Kevin says. "But if it were me, I'd be more nervous about what Stevie's brother's going to do to you. Word says he wants to kill you."

"Renaldo's a crazy fucker that I want no part of, which is why I dealt with you. You said, hey, these boys they've been verified—verified—you said verified. And I don't even want to think about Stevie's brother. One problem at a time. Pick the biggest problem, take care of it, and work down the list."

"No, I said Casper's sold to them, and he's not had any problems."

"Well, obviously they weren't verified," Franklin says. "You said verified." Kevin said verified. Franklin's sure of it.

Kevin says, "Seriously man, if I could help you right now, I would, but Siriano's already made his decision. You killed a cop. A Fed. That's not going to be forgotten. So, sayonara partner. It was swell knowing you."

"Don't you fucking hang up on me," Franklin yells into the phone. "Don't you do it!"

"What do you want me to say?"

"Tell me how I can fix it."

"What's there to fix?" Kevin asks. "You lost product, you killed a cop, and you're under arrest. What can you do to fix it? What use are you now?"

His friend's right. Franklin's deluding himself into thinking he can fix what's happening. "I want to make this right."

"You want to live. That's something different." Kevin's not as dumb as he plays. "I told you, drive those boys around, see how flexible they were. I don't trust Casper."

"Yeah, well, I didn't think it would go down the way it went down."

"Me either," Kevin says. "But it did. So, I don't know what to tell you. Renaldo's coming for you, and he's going to take care of it. If he doesn't, then you have Stevie's brother to worry about. But Renaldo's good at what he does, which is why Siriano uses him as his man on the outside. Then, he'll go for Casper and take care of him too. But if it's any solace, makes you feel any better, he's going to get that cop's partner just to send a message."

Kevin ends the call before Franklin can ask him what's that going to do. That's just going to make things worse.

Killing a cop's breaking the rules. Franklin knows this. He broke the rules, so he also knows you don't put things right by killing another cop unless you don't trust the people working with you, and you want to send a message to your own organization.

Messages work both ways.

Franklin pulls on the handcuffs on the bed as Vera says, "Everything all right with your granddaddy?"

"No," Franklin says, "but that don't mean that they won't be in time."

CHAPTER FOURTEEN:
TONY MORA

ELIZA LEAVES AND COMES BACK IN THE afternoon, bringing with her Tony's suit so that he can change in the bathroom. Black jacket, white shirt, black tie—the typical attire for such an event. She holds his suit, hanging from a hanger looped around her thumb. "Go change and do it now because you're going to be at the funeral."

"What, at the funeral home?" Tony asks.

Tony tries to take a sip of the scotch Wesley provided, but she takes the glass out of his hand as his lips try to follow it away from his mouth. "That place isn't any bigger than my apartment's living room."

"No, not at the funeral home," Eliza says. "Don't you listen to anything?" She holds up a hand, her manicured nails matching her hot pink blouse under the black jacket. "You know what, never mind. Just go change. I'll drive you. That's an order. One not up for debate."

Nothing ever is with her. He accepts the suit on the hanger and slinks off to the restroom to change.

In the bathroom, Tony recognizes he's a mess, and he's thankful she can't come in, not that the door would stop her. She's just polite. The suit, jacket and pants, hangs off the little hook on the stall door where he's trying to get dressed. He's standing half-naked in the stall with his other clothes scattered around his feet, unconcerned with whatever mess he's standing in because he figured they cleaned the floor last night, right?

He slips an arm in the folds of the dress shirt. The shirt takes him three tries to get the buttons right, buttoning and unbuttoning until the pads of his thumb and forefinger go numb and all the buttons somewhat line up, maybe. Or maybe he just gives up, figuring that's the best he can do even though he's missed one button, although he chooses to think he skipped it, and doesn't do the top one, because why the hell not?

After the shirt's somewhat in place, Tony yanks on the black tie, pulling it from around the collar of the jacket on the hanger. Holding the tie in hand, he uses both hands to flip up the collar and then quickly does the tie around his neck, getting it right on the first try. Well, it's a little short, but because he had so much success with the shirt, that's going to have to do for now.

Then, Tony shifts, trying to slip on the pants, but he can't get his leg to line up right with the pant leg, standing and shooting to slip his foot in three or four times, missing each time, and nearly losing his balance. When he's finally able to get the slacks around his calf and tries to pull the pant leg up around his thigh, Tony loses his balance and falls against the stall door. This is because the room tilted on its axis and is spinning like he's on some rig used for movies like *Star Trek* so the actors can all act like they're falling the same direction. The door lock buckles against his weight, the lock ripping clear from the metal stall, screws flying off in several directions, and he crashes to the red tile floor, landing hard.

Either he's become numb to pain or the alcohol's defused nicely into his extremities because he barely feels the impact or the cold floor underneath. Once he's somewhat positive he didn't hit his head, he rolls from his side to his back and slips his other leg in the pants, easily, pulling the pants up his body while planting his bare feet on the tile and arching his back to lift his waist from the ground.

Tony buttons the front and climbs to his feet where he catches sight of himself in the mirror. He's a mess: cheeks rosy, shirt askew and untucked, pants scuffed white at the knees. Tony wipes the white mark away from his left kneecap and tugs on the bottom of his shirt, straightening the shirt and then pulling the waistband away and tucking the shirttails in place, transforming himself from a hapless hobo to a half-well-dressed man.

He retrieves his belt and loops it through.

Wesley comes into the restroom to check on him, pushing the door open. "I heard a crash."

Transitioning from checking the gig line, Tony folds his collar down over the tie and speaks in the mirror. "I fell."

"You okay?"

Tony nods. Then asks, "Let me ask, did you hear the crash and come to check on me, or did she tell you to come check on me?"

"I don't think 'tell' is the word I would use," Wesley says, smiling.

"No, I guess it's not."

Wesley helps him get the tie right and straight. Tony says thanks. Then, Wesley, looking down at Tony's bare feet, says, "You might want to put your shoes on. With this floor, you never know when the last time it was cleaned."

Tony takes a gander at his feet, rolls his toes on the cold tile, and shrugs it off.

Wesley retrieves his socks and gets Tony back in his shoes.

——

THE VIEWING TAKES PLACE AT A MEGA-CHURCH several miles away, named after the adjoining golf course. Not that the golf course is associated with the church, just the members. The building was donated for use for the funeral because there wasn't a place big enough to hold everyone and the golf-themed church is a failed mall, which means it's plenty big enough and does seem fitting considering Tony spent the morning in the golf-themed restaurant.

Walking in, Tony says, "This place could be bigger."

Eliza tells him to stuff it and walks a little faster, getting ahead of him, telling him to follow her. She knows where she's going and leads him to a back hallway where table and chairs are set up for everyone and some sort of reception, stretching into a room out of his view.

The mall church is busy. Tony passes several colleagues and other people he doesn't know, who all seem to either know him or offer him their condolences before scurrying from his presence.

It seems no one wants to talk with him or even look him in the eye.

Eliza turns a corner, disappearing from view, and Tony finds a large group of people standing in an arched doorway. He peeks around the corner. A group of people are talking with Iris at the backside of the room where the coffin is located, closed now, perched on a small stage decorated with dozens of pictures of Clyde smiling at different points in his life and a white screen hanging above him, playing a slide show, containing some of the same photographs. The room smells of coffee and cake. Hundreds of flowers line the stage and walls and spill out into the hallways. About a hundred people walk in and out of the room, passing him saying nothing.

Tony backs from the doorway, stepping out of view, and fishes Wesley's silver flask from his inner sport coat pocket. He steals a quick swig, readying himself against what's to come. Tips the flask to his lips, unconcerned with who might see, and takes a drink from the flask before Eliza comes barreling out of the room, sees the flask, and at first looks angry and then cools it some as she asks, "Are you sure you're going to be okay?"

Tony stuffs the flask safely back in his inner pocket. "I'll be fine," and then asks, "Is it wise to have cake and a body in the same room? Something about that doesn't seem right."

"I don't know," Eliza says. "They said they're going to wheel him into the main area here in a few, but they wanted to do a half-assed final viewing for bigwigs and people in the know."

"Are we in the know?"

"No," Eliza says.

Tony withdraws the flask again, offers Eliza a drink, and swigs another somewhat final hidden drink from the flask, knowing it's not final, and prepares to round the corner.

He follows Eliza into the room, and he nearly runs into Ed, who's rounding a table and heading toward his wife.

Iris, in everything she wore this morning, but now with heels, turns toward him. She smiles and waves. Tony waves back like he's the beauty pageant winner on a float, hand rotating side to side, not understanding why he's doing it or the fact that it feels good to have her smile at him. He's disgusted and exhilarated at the same time.

Then, Tony shifts his attention from Iris to Ed who's now standing next to her. Ed has a thin frame. He's wearing thick black glasses and a purple shirt with a bolo tie. Ed's eating a piece of cake with a plastic fork from a little paper plate that he's holding between his fingers. He says, "I'm sorry," and takes a step to the side, but he's more worried about the frosting on the cake than the fact that he stepped on Tony's toes as he forks another mouthful of flour and sugar and stuffs it in his mouth.

What's he sorry for? Tony's the one that fucked his wife.

The inebriated version of his brain wants to tell the man all about it, and he even opens his mouth to say something, but Eliza pushes Tony hard on his bad shoulder and does the introductions, saying, "Ed, do you remember Tony? Tony, you remember Ed, right? Seen his picture on my desk."

Tony says he remembers, while Ed nods, finishing another bite of the cake, chewing, and asks, "How are you doing?"

Tony answers, "all right," but thinks, *what the hell kind of question is that?* His friend's lying dead in the room and this fucker's eating cake, and this is when Tony realizes he's not going to be fine. This is too much.

While Ed chews on the last piece of cake staring at him, Tony excuses himself and steps back into the hallway, leaving Eliza with her husband. Eliza excuses herself too, telling her husband she'll be right back.

In the hall, the crowd of people don't look him in the eye.

Tony whispers in Eliza's ear, "You stuffed that picture in a drawer."

Eliza, keeping pace with him by nearly shoving a man to the side, whispers back, "It doesn't mean you haven't seen it."

"All right. I tried. I did. But I can't go in there," Tony says, ducking off into a side hall, this one nearly deserted. He withdraws the flask from his jacket and takes a sip before he takes another sharp turn and dips into an empty room, which has six television monitors already tuned to the worship area. On the screens, he watches pallbearers carry Clyde into the main part of the building and sit him up on a small platform, the funeral director in the wake with a wreath of flowers. He drapes it over the casket, letting it hang off the side of the casket, yellow and white with a purple center. He opens the front half of the casket, revealing the made-up version of Clyde.

Tony turns and takes another hit from the flask.

Coming from behind, Eliza asks Tony, "What the hell was that?" Circling to his front, hands animated and angry. "What's going on with you? Are you going to be able to do this?"

"I can't do it," he says, the flask down at his side. "I tried. I'll just wait out here and then go in the main... say what do you call a mall church's worship area?"

Eliza taps her foot. "Worship area." Then, she comments, "Or something like that."

"See you don't even know," Tony says. "Clyde didn't want any of this."

"Clyde's dead. He doesn't have a say in it," Eliza replies.

"That's what I'm saying." Tony looks over Eliza's shoulder, back at the main thoroughfare. "I think that's the governor. Why's he here? He didn't know Clyde."

Eliza reaches out for the folds of his sport coat and tugs Tony closer. She plucks the flask out of his hand. "I'll hold on to that." And then she checks him over, running her hands over him, telling him to pull it together, but he's stuck on the fact she's touching him all over. She licks her fingers and smooths his hair like a mom spit shining her son's forehead.

CHAPTER FIFTEEN:

IRIS KING

RIS FINISHES TALKING WITH A GROUP OF people and takes her place at the side of the stage to greet the newcomers who ascend the steps. But this is becoming too much, even for her, with flowers every-where and people milling about washed in colognes and perfumes. Every smell is some sort of battlement to fight off the stench of death, which makes the large room smell like a box of potpourri. It's all too much. All this ... *pomp*.

That's what her late husband would call it. He'd say this is too much. Look at this place. No wonder people go into the church business. What other type of business could afford a place like this? God, look at this building. How much does rent for a place like this cost?

Clyde never understood church. He said he never had religion growing up, and he didn't plan on changing that with dying. Then, he'd say, "How'd they pay for a place like this?"

She'd say, "They probably bought it with cash."

But she knows how the church paid for a building like this.

Golf—

—and ten percent to God.

Iris watches the group move over to Eli, stationed at the exit staircase. He greets them with open hands, glad-handing the people, doing the politician handshake, grasping the tallest man's hand, who is dark headed with dark eyes; the man looks like a politician. Eli uses his other hand to grip the guy's forearm. The man looks familiar.

To Iris, it's like everything's happening to her and happening around her so much so that she's not a part of the events. Another out-of-body experience just like when the Cortez woman made the notification as if she's just a figure in a tragic story watching everything where nothing seems to go right, but she's just walking through it all in a fog, doing nothing to change the story.

A crack of Eli's booming voice followed by a loud laugh returns her to the moment, and she realizes that, although she may not be alone, she feels alone. That's what this is. This funeral. Full of people from all over the state, and here she is alone on stage. No one's here for her. They're here for Clyde. Scratch that, Renaldo's here; he's sitting just off the stage staring at her, wearing his brown leather jacket, with a navy shirt, dressed nicely, pleasing to the eye. He's always dressed nicely though, and sometimes it's too nice. It makes her feel like she has to constantly compensate for his appearance. Renaldo being here isn't comforting. He shouldn't even be here. It's more like pouring acid into the wound. He's the reason Clyde is dead.

But she is alone and tired.

Is this grief?

If this is grief, then maybe that explains the irritableness permeating throughout her body. because if she has to listen to another person tell her they're sorry for her loss, she doesn't know what she's going to do. She keeps standing here, shaking their hand, fake-smiling into their face when all she wants to do is cry, but she doesn't cry, not in front of anybody. Just listening to them tell her, "I'm sorry for your loss," and "Let us know if there's anything we can do," and at first, she didn't mind hearing such platitudes, but now, it just makes her want to scream and punch them in the face.

Kind of like her first reaction to that Cortez bitch.

Again, she catches Eli's voice rising over the low roar of the room just loud enough to where she can pick him out of the numerous voices like isolating a French horn in an orchestra, and she realizes the man he's talking to is the governor of the state.

Clyde would hate that.

Eli slaps the governor on the back like they're buddies or he's trying to sell the governor a used car.

Why is he here?

Now, he's descending the steps of the stage to go take his seat in the front, and they're bringing Clyde into the room, wheeling the casket into the large space, the mock-pallbearers walking beside the casket, which contains Clyde in his favorite suit, bring him up on the stage for all to see. One guy pushes from behind. They should be carrying it at least. That's what happens at a proper funeral, isn't it? But they're not.

And not only does she not know who *they* are, but she also didn't choose them as pallbearers, and neither did

Clyde because he didn't want any of this. He wanted something else. Tony was right.

This feels so wrong.

Something rancid pushes its way into her mouth, from the pits of her stomach rolling up to the back of her taste buds: Guilt. Is that what she's feeling right now? She hasn't ever felt guilt, she thinks. Guilt for going against his wishes. Eli said it would be okay. He said Clyde's Will had certain provisions, but being the executor of the estate, he said that she didn't have to worry about the funeral part of things, that he'd take care of it, and that she'll still get the money, but this isn't for Clyde. This is for Eli.

"No," Iris says under her breath, and then louder, unfolding her arms from her midsection—she didn't even realize she'd been hugging herself—she steps closer to Eli. "Stop."

Eli, wearing a dark suit over his bulk, glances her way. His face says that he didn't hear what she said. He's not fat. She's felt the body underneath him. He's solid with a strength that shows he used to be a wrestler. He does Jiu Jitsu now because that's what Teddy Roosevelt did, so he says. But in this suit, he looks massive. His black hair is freckled with gray. He turns his hulking mass. "What was that?"

"Stop," Iris says. Then, she yells at the pallbearers. "Stop!" She stomps her foot. "You should be carrying him. Why aren't you carrying him?"

Everyone's looking at her now. Everyone in the room. The governor. Renaldo. Eli. Everyone.

Now, Eli's at her side, having closed the distance without her seeing him do it, and in a hushed tone, he's asking, "What's wrong? What's going on?"

"This isn't right," Iris says with blood rushing into her cheeks, the heat, the redness, the anger. "We need to stop this."

"Stop what?"

Iris motions to the mock pallbearers. "This. This isn't right. He didn't want this. Clyde didn't want this. You said so yourself, right? He wanted to be cremated and his ashes scattered. That's what you said. That's what the Will says, right?"

"Iris," Eli says, using her name like she's a little kid, "we can't just stop this." His massive hand's on her arm, pulling her to the side, his fingers clamped on her elbow. They hurt and his nails dig into her skin. He tugs on her.

"Let go of me," Iris says, louder and sharper now. "Don't touch me." She swats at his hand with her other hand.

But Eli tightens his grip on her arm. He says, "No, come here," trying to pull her to the back wall behind the stage away from everyone.

The hand on her arm is going to leave a bruise because she bruises easily. Clyde used to tell her, "You're like an old man on blood thinners." So, Iris tries to work her nails under the pad of Eli's fingers to try to pry his hand off her arm. He doesn't budge.

She says, "You are hurting me. Stop! Don't touch me. It hurts."

Eli tightens his grip even more while walking quickly now, and he nearly throws her as he releases her. Iris takes a couple of freewheeling steps, her momentum carrying her forward before she can catch her balance in these shoes. God, she hates these shoes.

Now out of earshot, Eli's tone is sharp and filled with frustration. "What are you doing?"

"What are *you* doing?" Iris says, pointing at him.

"Get control of yourself," Eli says.

Iris rubs the spot on her elbow where it's tender. It hurts. "This is wrong. We need to stop this. You need to stop this right now. He didn't want this." She points her hand toward Clyde's casket.

"We can't just stop this," Eli says. "We're like ten minutes out from getting started. There are nearly a hundred people already here, watching you make a scene. Almost a thousand more out in the hallways or walking in."

"Make a scene?" Iris asks annoyed, ignoring him. "Make a scene? I'm making a scene? You haven't seen anything like that. Don't you tell me I'm making a scene; my husband is dead."

"Which is why we are here, to pay our respects to him."

"Why? He didn't want that. He wanted his ashes scattered at the Grand Canyon. This is ridiculous. Who's even flipping the bill for all this?"

"The building was donated."

"To who? To you? To me? I didn't want it. I didn't sign or approve anything."

Eli lowers his head but raises his tone to something abrasive. "We talked about this."

"When?" Iris says. "In your office when you were fucking me? Or when you had me come in just so you could tell me you're in control of Clyde's Will, the executor, and then, you're telling me you won't execute it the way he wanted. You said it's because you wanted people to be able to pay respects to a great man. Clyde wasn't a great man—"

"—stop," Eli says; now, he's the one saying it. "He died in the line of duty. He deserves a hero's funeral."

"Clyde wasn't a hero," she says.

"Died saving his partner's life."

"Tony doesn't want this either."

"You don't know that."

"He told me this morning. He said Clyde told him the same thing. He said he didn't want this. Clyde didn't want to be remembered as a jackbooted thug, but that's what you're doing to him right now, cementing his legacy as just that. This is wrong, Eli, wrong and you know it."

Eli stops trying to argue with her; he's not going to win. He straightens his back. "What do you want to do? Tell all these people to go home?"

THE CAVERNOUS SPACE, filled with bodies, is just as lifeless as the one behind her in the box. Someone coughs out there, someone in the masses; otherwise, the dull roar of voices has died down to nothing, and it's quiet. Iris steps up to the microphone at the edge of the stage, taking a moment to take in all the eyes staring back at her. As she looks out at the crowd, she can only make out faces a couple of rows from the stage.

In the front row on the aisle, Tony's there with the Cortez woman next to him, pregnant but radiant and beautiful, and next to her sits a man wearing thick black glasses.

On the other side of the room, same row, Renaldo's at the edge of the row near the wall, not too far from where the governor and his people are sitting.

Iris clears her throat and adjusts the microphone, aware of Eli's presence behind her, which is like a weight, gravity, pressing down on her, but he's beside her and that counts for something.

Her eyes wander back to Tony, and he nods to her, and somehow that feels good. But why does that feel good?

With her hands around the microphone stand, small and delicate, compared to the expansive space before her, Iris adjusts the microphone one more time, releasing a soft squeal of feedback through the speakers.

Quiet now.

Another cough from somewhere in the expanse.

Iris inhales through her nostrils. "Thank you all for coming here today," she says, thinking of Eli's words to her. He told her that if she was going to do this then she was going to have to lie and sell it so people wouldn't get upset. In other words, bluff. He asked her if she knew how to do that.

It was just another reminder that just because someone fucks you doesn't mean they know you. She can bluff. It's the truth that's hard.

Playing Keira Knightley again, she starts quiet, clears her voice. "Clyde would appreciate your support and get a kick out of knowing he could fill all the seats. He'd call you suckers for being here."

Cue the mock tears as one lone tear starts its arduous crawl down her cheek. Her own acting skills scare even her. But she will not cry, not a real cry, not in front of all these people. No one makes her cry.

But she detects sadness lurking beneath her calm surface, and Iris realizes she's sucking in on her cheeks, so she takes a deep breath and forces poise. "Clyde never wanted to be remembered as a jackbooted thug," she says. "He was a free spirit that spent his free time either working in his woodshop or dreaming of ways to make money in retirement. But to be honest, I don't think he ever would have retired on his own. He used to say that's why he started working for *The Man* because, at a certain age, you get kicked out of the club. He said then he could be a hippie again and smoke pot, just like his parents."

A soft chuckle ripples from the crowd at the right moments.

"But talking to Tony this morning, he confirmed what Clyde's always told me," Iris says, "He's never smoked pot. I'm not going to talk very long, so please bear with me. This is difficult enough. I will leave the storytelling to the people that knew him longer than I did. However, I will tell you that, yes, Clyde and I met while he was working undercover. It was a poker game. He won. He never played poker with me again. Why might you ask? Because he said if I beat him, I wouldn't respect him." Blank stares. "And because it was a one-time thing. He said he wasn't good enough to beat me, and it was a fluke, kind of like Han Solo winning the *Millennium Falcon*. He said he found the love of his life, and he didn't want to ruin the mystique. But obviously, those that have been married know those barriers are crossed pretty quickly." Pause. "Like going to the bathroom." Pause again. "Although Clyde never wanted that barrier broken either." Chuckles. "After giving this some thought, I thought I would honor my late husband in a variety of ways. Firstly, I want to thank you all for coming. I hope you enjoy the service."

Iris pauses and glances at Eli, who nods urging her to continue. He whispers she's doing a good job.

"Secondly, I wanted to let you know there will be a reception afterward, and you all are invited." She now looks down at the governor. "Yes... even you Governor."

More chuckles.

Iris attempts a smile, but her heart is barely in the performance, and somewhere along the way, her act transforms into something resembling truth, which is unfamiliar.

"Clyde would have liked a party in his honor. He didn't want people being sad for him or his death. So, I ask that you enjoy yourselves at the reception."

Now, her eyes are back on Tony who is staring right back at her.

"Finally," she starts and pauses to clear her throat, "I know there was going to be a graveside service, with the flag and the guns and the honor guards... I'm sorry to all the agencies that sent honor guards and have worked very hard to make this special. Thank you all for coming all this way, but I've decided the graveside service will be cancelled."

Murmurs spread through the crowd like ripples in a pond, people turning to discuss with their neighbors before she's even stopped talking. But Iris's voice grows louder, more confident as if Clyde is with her providing her strength. She didn't mean for him to die, and it hurts knowing she's the reason he's gone. For someone who doesn't normally feel emotion, this confuses her brain.

"I've given this a lot of thought, and I want you all to be happy, not sad. That's what Clyde would have wanted. Did want. So please, after the service today, I want you to enjoy the reception and laugh."

When she finishes, she shuts her eyes. She doesn't want to open them because the room has gone quiet, still, and maybe not in reality, but in her mind, she's alone in a dark room where everything's faded to nothing, spotlight only on her, everything else black. It's how she wants it. Her alone on the stage. Alone in life. Then Eli's voice and presence beside her expand the spotlight and bring the room back into full brilliance, where sounds of shuffling rustling fabric and people reach her ears, and he plays his part because really this is a stage for him. Eli says, "In honor of your husband's sacrifice and to honor the fallen, we'd like to present you with the flag of our nation."

Iris opens her eyes to find the folded flag, the stars, the stripes, the red and blue, in a triangle fold, with Eli's large hand on top, with rings on several of his stout fingers, like a baseball mitt. Beyond the triangle fold, across the canyon, she notices Tony's attention on her, coming through the darkness, giving her a nod of approval, his eyes telling her she is doing the right thing.

She accepts the flag, playing the part fully now, but not having to act anymore because they finally see her cry, and it pisses her off.

CHAPTER SIXTEEN:

TONY MORA

TONY COMES HOME AFTER THE FUNERAL to find Casper hiding inside his house, drinking a beer at the kitchen table, which was fine and somewhat expected. He did tell Gene that he needed Casper. Gene sent him his way because when Tony walked in, the kid's first words are, he didn't know where else to go, telling him Gene said he could hang out here until he figured out what to do next. Casper said that Gene told him he could trust Tony. So now, Tony sits at his kitchen table drinking with the little shit, who doesn't look old enough to drink, but considering everything that's happened, Tony doesn't care. Tony says, "The funeral was terrible."

Casper nods like he's listening. "Does it hurt losing a friend?"

Tony takes a drink. "What do you mean?"

But Casper doesn't answer; he just shrugs. Then, he asks in a small voice, "Do you hate me?"

"Why would I hate you?"

Again, all he offers is another question. "For what happened?"

"I'm not going to get anything out of you," Tony says as he takes a swig from the bottle. "If all you do is keep asking me questions when I ask you questions—what do you mean what happened?"

"Sorry," Casper says like it's painful, and it might be, trying to give voice to thoughts the kid's probably never had before. "But what I'm trying to say—"

"—you're sorry?"

The kid nods. "Yeah, something like that."

"Well—I'm angry at the world. So, if you're asking me if it hurts losing a friend, a close one, then yeah, it fucking hurts."

Casper looks down.

Tony stands up, places his hands on the back of the chair, and studies the kid for a moment before turning to open the small humidor on the countertop behind him, a gift from Clyde. He reaches in the humidor and takes out two cigars, shaking the cigar as he hands it to the kid. "Clyde picked this up in Vegas the last time he was there because everything that happens in Vegas doesn't necessarily stay in Vegas."

Casper accepts it, but his face shows he doesn't know what to do with it, which elicits a smile from Tony.

Tony withdraws the flask Wesley gave him, sets it on the table. "Feel free to drink this, not much left, but I don't own anything nearly as nice. We'll dive into Clyde's Christmas present from last year because why the hell not? It seems appropriate on the day I'm burying him—it was his present."

Tony reaches into the cabinet above the fridge and takes out a bottle of Johnnie Walker Black, which is next to his gold and black pressure cooker. He sits the bottle on the counter. Casper's eyes on him the whole time. Next, he retrieves two glasses and pours some of the scotch in the glasses and walks back to the table, carrying the two glasses by the rim. "That's what any good cop would do, and that's what I want to do. Get blackout drunk."

Tony hands Casper a drink. Casper sniffs the glass and gets right to it. "Are you suspended?"

"Sort of," Tony says, then sips the scotch.

The kid just twists his face, looking at him, showing he doesn't understand, or maybe it's the drink—the jury's still out. Casper blinks a few times.

"Do I blame you?" Tony takes a seat at the table again and gets back to the barrage of questions from earlier. "No, I don't. I don't blame you. I blame myself. I'm the reason my friend's dead." He pauses and adds, "That's still not real to me."

Casper nods like he understands, but he doesn't. How could he?

Tony pauses to sip the scotch. "We need to smoke those cigars with this," he says. "My fucking boss told me what I'm feeling is survivor's remorse, like he fucking knows what I'm feeling. How the fuck would he know what I'm feeling? I don't even know what I'm feeling. Said it is perfectly natural for me to feel this way, but why don't I go home and get some rest, let the shoulder heal, get my head straight, and then come back to work. Like what the fuck?"

Casper shrugs. "But all you want to do is work?" That's a weird thought for him. "That's what Gene said. Said you were in his shop asking for me right after everything. Said he thought it was better I come to you than let Renaldo get me. Said you never take a day off."

"I wouldn't say never," Tony says. "But that's right that is better. Better for you. Better for me."

"But better how?" Casper asks. "What's going to happen?"

"With work or you?" Tony asks.

Casper raises an eyebrow and jerks his head, indicating he doesn't know. "At this point is there a difference? I'm fucked either way."

The kid has a point.

Tony says, "Marque's just doing what supervisors do. All that concern is just a calculated supervisor ploy. He didn't want me in the office when he delivered the news to Eliza and the rest of them that the Siriano investigation's dead. Marque sent me home so that there weren't any unneeded outbursts."

Casper stares at him blankly.

He won't know who any of these people are or what the hell Tony's talking about. It doesn't matter. Tony fills in the blanks for the kid. "Means, I don't fucking know what's going to happen ... with either you or the investigation. All I know is you're in some deep shit, and I need to figure out a way to get *you* out of it."

"Yeah." The kid chuckles. "You sound like Gene. How are you going to do that?"

"I'm not sure yet," Tony admits. "Figured the best way to do this is get Renaldo off the streets. That's what Clyde would have wanted. So that's what I'm going to do. What happens after, I don't know. That's between you and whoever, but if we get Renaldo off the streets, maybe we can get Siriano."

The kid puts the scotch down on the table and takes up a bottle of beer. He puts the bottle to his lips but doesn't take a drink.

"I don't blame you," Tony says.

The kid rocks in his seat. "I figured if you did, you wouldn't be trying to look out for me."

"What else is there to do on the day of the funeral?"

"Not this." Casper throws back the rest of the bottle and chases it with the rest of the scotch.

Again, the kid has a point, and if he keeps drinking like that, Tony might make a man of him sooner than later. The kid starts to open his mouth to say something, but Tony cuts him off. "How do we work this?"

"What do you mean?"

"I mean, how do we do what needs done?" Tony says. "We need to bring down Siriano. That's something that's going to help you get out of this mess, your mess. Gene's mess. Not the only thing, but it's something. It'd make me feel better. Course in doing Siriano, we'd get Renaldo too, and that would make me feel better too. Did you know he had the balls to show up at the funeral?"

Casper just shakes his head.

"We got to figure out how this whole mess began in the first place. How did Franklin know about me being a cop?"

"Did he know?" Casper asks, sounding like Gene.

"I don't see how he would have done what he did if he didn't."

"That's a weird way of saying you don't know," Casper says.

"Don't get smart with me." Tony smiles. "You're not as dumb as you look, are you?"

"I'm not, but it's my ass on the line." Casper points at him. "Not yours."

"It's yours and Gene's."

Casper asks, "Renaldo went to the funeral?"

Tony nods. "Wearing a nice leather jacket and everything. I didn't even know it was him until Eliza pointed it out. I don't know what he was doing there."

"Who's Eliza?"

"She's someone I work with... well... okay... she's more than that and less than that."

"Now I know where Gene gets it," the kid says. Tony asks him what he means, but the kid doesn't explain.

Tony continues, "She found me at the sports bar because I didn't show back up at the funeral home, but she didn't show up until well after they were opened, and I was already pretty freaking trashed. We are ... *friends*." He shrugs. "Maybe more, I guess you could say. I don't know."

"I know what you mean."

"She's great. She doesn't force me to do things. You know what I mean? Like most women are trying to make you into something you're not. That's why I'm still single. Well, I had an ex-wife, but she tried to get me to do things all the time. Eliza's not like that."

"What'd she do when she found you?"

"A lot of talking."

"Why wasn't she drinking?"

Tony gives the kid a look and slaps his stomach to show Casper how big Eliza's belly is. "Preggo," he says. "We talked some more, which always makes me feel better—talking with her. See kid, I might be the reason she's the way she is." He pinches the small ring of belly fat through his shirt. "If only things worked out differently this whole day could

210

have been a bit better—not the part about burying my friend—but the me and her aspect of all this."

"You're the father?"

"Yeah, but don't go spreading that around."

"How do you know it's you?"

"She told me. Also told me I don't have to do this alone, you know; she's there."

The kid just stares down at the table. "I don't have anyone like that. Never have. I kind of always figured, you know, kids have moms or something like that ... grandma ... aunt ... someone, but I've never had that. I've had Gene."

The moment of sincerity and honesty takes him off guard. He pauses, tilting his head to the side to read the kid better.

"Sometimes things happen," Tony says. "Sometimes you just have to get so drunk you don't know where you are. The key is to let things happen the way they should but more the part about doing this alone. If only things had gone differently, I wouldn't be doing this alone. See, talking with her, part of me wants to tell her I fucked up and ask her to leave her husband, be with me, but the other part decides against it."

"Why?"

"I can't stare her in the face... no that's not right... I know I couldn't stand the rejection, especially on a day like this. It'd break my heart."

The kid lifts his head. "Ever hint at it? Like, tell her you want something different but don't say the words?"

Tony nods. "All the time, kid. All the time."

CHAPTER SEVENTEEN:
RENALDO LUNA

R ENALDO WAITS IN THE CAR watching the streetlights shift from green to yellow to red and back again, waiting, frustrated that he hasn't been able to find Casper. He says, "I've checked everywhere and with everyone I can think of to check, including that fuck's pawnshop, looking for that little shit and still nothing. No one knows where he's been."

Mastodon just looks at him from the passenger seat. His way of saying he doesn't know, which is usually the case, because Renaldo doesn't pay Mastodon for his insights. Mastodon may be his man—to him, real name Mattie—who is not strictly affiliated with Siriano. He's someone Renaldo recruited to watch over Iris's poker games, meaning he's Renaldo's guy and one of the few people he trusts—maybe even a friend—but he isn't the smartest person when it comes to running things.

They're both wearing dark suits, white shirts, black jackets, and pants like they're going to a funeral. Nothing too noticeable, something that will help if they need to blend into the city so that they won't stick out.

Renaldo stifles a yawn. "Trust is an important thing. Without it, you're nothing. And you know what? I sure as fuck don't trust Kevin because I don't trust burglars on principle. Those guys are used to fucking people over for their enjoyment, and Kevin's bragged to me about how he does it—shitting on people's floors. Maybe he sent Casper and that shithead Gene to rob the game, punch you in the face."

All Mastodon says is, "Kevin can't dress."

Renaldo squeezes his eyes hard. "You're right. A man who can't dress can't succeed."

Siriano's illegitimate son, Wilson, dresses well. Wilson's essentially a prince in waiting, not an advisor; Renaldo, wants to see power wrested from his control. It all feels like someone's making a move. Alejandro asked him if he felt comfortable working with the white man. Renaldo doesn't, but he's not going to admit that to the old man. He asked Renaldo if he trusted Siriano not to cut him out. He asked if he trusted the others in the organization. Alejandro said that running a crew from prison's doable, but it's hard because people seem to get ideas of grandeur when the boss isn't around. So sometimes, the boss has to cut off the fat even if it's a finger. Alejandro asked, "Do you trust Siriano not to cut you out?"

No, he doesn't, but years of service should mean something. Renaldo's been loyal to him. Siriano has no cause not to trust him, except he does. Iris.

What was he thinking, trying to get in bed with her, trying to get her husband in his back pocket? That's a double strike as far as Siriano's concerned. It shows ambition. No one in power wants to see an underling with ambition. Alejandro taught him that lesson, explaining that's a quick way to a slow death.

Mastodon sniffs and leans against the passenger door. "Focus," he says.

Alejandro provided Omar and Pablo as muscle for tonight's job. The old man told Renaldo, "You can trust them; they're my cousins." Omar's the same Omar who works the kitchen. Alejandro did not explain Pablo, which means he's most likely an enforcer, but Renaldo thinks he's more, an heir. Both of them are trusted underlings. Omar wouldn't work Alejandro's kitchen if he weren't a bodyguard.

Renaldo picks up a small radio and clicks the button on the side. "Everyone ready?" he asks into the radio, and he receives a radio click in return, signaling both Omar and Pablo waiting for his call, parked out of sight, are ready. Renaldo peers over the steering wheel into the night. He sees the ambulance, their target, pull right onto the main street outside of the hospital. The ambulance travels on its own. No chase cars. No convoy. Nothing that would say prisoner inside. But Renaldo knows different. Filiberto called an hour before and told Renaldo they are transporting Franklin tonight. He said he thought there was only supposed to be one guard with him, riding in the ambulance, but he wasn't sure. Renaldo figured there'd be more, but maybe not. One ambulance should be easy enough to handle.

Renaldo motions to Mastodon. "Here they come." Mastodon pulls the masks out from between his legs and hands Renaldo one. He slips the black nylon stocking mask over his face. Mastodon does the same. Then, the big man hands Renaldo the AR-15. Renaldo charges the rifle between his legs. Mastodon does the same.

The ambulance passes them, and Renaldo puts the car in gear, falling in behind the ambulance. Traffic is light. The ambulance stops at an intersection not far from the hospital. In Spanish and over the radio, Renaldo tells Omar, "You're up."

The traffic light turns green. The sedan to the ambulance's left starts to go through the intersection as the ambulance slowly pulls away from the line, starting its way through. Then, a roar of a great engine, Omar's stolen F350 pickup plows into the front passenger side of the ambulance, pushing it to the side, which catches the rear of the sedan, and spins that vehicle nearly 180 degrees and off to the side, the F350 slamming into the fender, driving through it, crunching the front tire of the ambulance, breaking the axle and disabling it. The collision is violent but short. One minute the vehicles are moving through the intersection, and the next, three smoking disabled vehicles sit in the middle of the large multi-laned intersection. After a moment, Omar throws the gears of the pickup in reverse, brake lights blinking on briefly, and he backs his truck up, giving him some space and a vantage point. Then, he's out of the truck, dressed in gray sweatshirt and matching sweatpants with a black stocking mask—same as Renaldo's—carrying an AR-15 too, two magazines sticking out of his sweatpants' waistband. He takes a position from behind his driver's side door to cover the ambulance's passenger side.

Renaldo maneuvers his car toward the rear of the wrecked ambulance. He knows better than to close the distance in his vehicle. He leaves a space. Then, in a flurry of movement, both he and Mastodon exit the car, weapons up. Mastodon covers the passenger side and motions to Omar, who nods, indicating he's seen no movement inside of the cab, but he can only see the passenger side. Renaldo covers the driver's side. In the side mirror, he sees movement as the driver starts to move about the cab. Then, the door pops open and the driver falls out of the cab onto the street. It's not until he's picking himself up off the pavement that the driver notices Renaldo and his rifle. With zero hesitation, Renaldo fires three shots, rifle pulsating against his shoulder rhythmically. The bullets strike the ambulance driver in the chest, burying deep. The gunshots echo off the surrounding buildings, fading into the night, as the man crumples to the ground. He doesn't move. He's dead.

That's when things go differently from what Renaldo planned. The driver of the sedan's up and out of his vehicle now. A white guy with a ball cap and a holster on his side, a gun in his hand. Ball Cap doesn't look like a cop, but it's an open carry state and he's just started a gunfight in the street, so it's probably a scared civilian protecting himself. The guy throws his arms over the top of his disabled vehicle, gun in hand, and points his gun at Renaldo. He fires at Renaldo. The two rounds miss. One chips the pavement next to his foot. The other bounces off the front of his vehicle. Ball Cap fires again, breaking the Renaldo's windshield. Renaldo jumps behind the side of the ambulance for cover. "Stupid fucking redneck."

Mastodon turns to give him a look. "What's going on? A cop?"

Renaldo shakes his head. "No but handle him."

Mastodon switches places with Renaldo, who throws his back against the ambulance and peeks in the rear window. He sees three bodies inside. One is Franklin, strapped on the gurney struggling against the straps, gurney overturned on its side. One that's probably DEA, who's picking himself up off the floor of the ambulance. And the third is a paramedic who's bleeding at the temple and not moving from the seat. The cabinet to his left shows where his head banged against it. Then, Renaldo hears and feels someone else moving inside the ambulance. The passenger.

Renaldo motions to Omar, two fingers to his ear, and then points to the passenger side. Omar nods and steps forward rifle at the ready. The passenger of the ambulance opens his door as Omar advances on the vehicle. He shoots the passenger before he can even get the door opened. The four rounds impact in a tight grouping, one traveling through the door, while the other three slam into the passenger, who sags lifeless against the door.

Mastodon peeks his head out from behind the ambulance to find the civilian, but when he does, everything goes wrong. Renaldo turns from Omar to Mastodon who's just clearing the side of the ambulance and watches the big guy's head snap back in a spray of red mist before his ears even register the gunshot.

CHAPTER EIGHTEEN:
FRANKLIN HAYES

S OMETHING IMPACTS THE AMBULANCE hard, and Franklin and the gurney topple over to the side. Lawrence falls over the top of him. Franklin wishes it were Vera laying over the top of him like when she would reach for something on the other side of the bed, bending low, pressing herself against him, teasing him. He struggles against the straps of the gurney as his face is smooshed against the bench seat, a cabinet near the paramedic's feet. The fall hurts, but at least he's not handcuffed to the bed anymore. That fall would have broken his wrist.

His hands are cuffed together, and the face full of cabinet sucks—it busted open his lip. Franklin spits blood onto the floor of the ambulance. He blinks a few times and pushes himself back from the cabinets, licking his lips, tasting blood. "Hey Larry," he says, speaking into the bench cabinet. "What the hell was that?"

Lawrence shushes him and uses his arms to push down and off Franklin to right himself. "You okay?"

Lawrence removes his weight from Franklin, but in doing so, he's loosened the strap across his upper shoulders. So, maneuvering just right, Franklin's able to scoot his head and upper body down and slip out of the top strap. "Ah, I didn't think you cared," he says. "But hey Larry, I'm on my fucking side. What do you think? I liked it better in the hospital room."

"Shut up!" Lawrence kicks the gurney. The impact jolts and vibrates across Franklin's back. "I wasn't talking to you." Lawrence leans over the body and says, "Hey buddy, come on man, you okay?"

Franklin looks at the paramedic's limp body. "Hey Larry, the paramedic's not moving... you should check on him or something."

"Seriously, shut up." Lawrence fishes his phone from his pocket as he straddles Franklin's gurney to check on the paramedic. Lawrence puts two fingers against the paramedic's neck and holds them over the paramedic's lips to check if he's breathing. Lawrence looks down at Franklin, his eyes showing confusion. "What the fuck was that?"

"That's what I'm asking you," Franklin states, struggling some more against the straps of the gurney. "Why don't you unstrap me?"

"Not going to happen," Lawrence says.

Somewhere up front someone groans and opens a door.

Franklin offers the agent his manacled hands, pushing them up toward Lawrence. "How about un-handcuff me?"

That's when Franklin hears the rifle shots, not just gunshots. No, these have the distinctive pings of rifle rounds zipping through the air leaving behind a lingering echo bouncing off the surrounding medical buildings and cutting through metal.

Franklin instinctively retracts his arms. "Hey Larry, what the fuck was that?"

"I don't know," Lawrence says, but the way he says it indicates he knows exactly what that was, and it was a rifle.

"Was that a fucking rifle?"

Lawrence glowers down at Franklin, and his eyes morph into fear.

"Are you listening to me? Who's shooting? Was that a fucking rifle?"

Lawrence still doesn't say anything.

"Hey Larry—"

"—shut the fuck up," Lawrence finally says, hurriedly dialing a number. He puts the phone to his ear. "Listen, I've just been involved in a collision... shut up... I'll tell you where if you stop talking..."

More rifle shots silence whatever else he was going to say.

The man's distracted. Now's Franklin's chance; he's been waiting for an opening, and a gunfight in the street might be the only one he gets before making it to the jail.

Franklin grabs Lawrence's leg, tripping him up. The phone flies out of his hand as Lawrence stumbles across the floor of the ambulance.

"Unstrap me, bitch," Franklin demands.

Lawrence kicks out twice, striking the gurney and Franklin's shoulder, loosening Franklin's hold, as he says, "Let go of me, you fuck."

Franklin catches a heel to the chin but manages to hold on to Lawrence's pant leg. He tugs on the leg, saying, "Hey Larry, why don't you go fuck yourself... but first come here so I can get the handcuff keys," as he tries to reel Lawrence in.

Lawrence kicks out again, freeing the pant leg, and kicks the gurney again. He retrieves the phone. "If you try that shit again, I'm shooting you right here. I won't hesitate. I'll say you were trying to escape. Nothing will say otherwise"

"He sure won't," Franklin says, motioning his bound hands toward the paramedic. "But alright, I know when I'm beat. It's been a shitty week, Larry."

"It's not Larry...," he starts to say, but then glances to the back door as a shadow passes across the window.

Then, a gunfight erupts outside the doors. Bursts of rifle fire, some popping pistol shots. Metal strikes. Concrete strikes. Even sounds as if a couple of rounds hit the ambulance. A tire pops. Sounds like an epic shootout. Franklin tilts his ear to listen to the gun battle for a moment before saying, "Hey Larry, it sounds like it's a western, and we're the stagecoach. So, I don't mean to alarm you, but I think we're being held up, like being robbed. Or maybe they've come to break me out."

"Or kill you," Lawrence says and places the phone to his ear. "Would you shut up, no, not you, no would you... I'm talking to my prisoner... just listen to what I'm trying to tell you." He steps over Franklin, drawing his gun from under his suit jacket. "Listen to that." He holds the phone out. "That's fucking gunfire outside... just shut up... I said gunfire. Are you going to send somebody or not?"

Lawrence glances out the windows, but he doesn't attempt to exit the ambulance. More gunfire. A rapid staccato of rifle shots slam into something metal. Then, a crunch of a vehicle striking another. Some more random pops of a pistol. A few chasing rifle rounds zinging through the air, striking concrete. Then, the sounds fade, and it's quiet.

"Hey Larry," Franklin says as he works his arms out from under one of the straps to allow him more movement, and he starts working on the straps around his waist, telling Lawrence, "Unstrap me."

"No," Lawrence says.

Franklin expects Lawrence to stop him, but he doesn't.

Then, the back doors of the ambulance swing open, revealing two men wearing nylon ski masks, both with rifles, both pausing when they see Lawrence, who eyes the two as the two eye him; Franklin, stuck in the middle, watching the whole exchange.

No one moves. The pause lasts only a breath, but to Franklin, it seems a lifetime. Franklin rotates his head side to side, taking in the whole scene, and then, he dives under the gurney to use it as cover as both sides trade rounds in a lightning flash of fire and fury, thundering, deafening claps in the small confines of the ambulance; Lawrence unloads his pistol, shooting their way, and they shoot back, but it's two on one. Larry never stood a chance, and it's over as quickly as it began.

Once the gunfight's over, Franklin surveys the cabin and goes to work on the straps around his knees while keeping his eyes on the wide-open ambulance doors. The hospital is off in the distance, he spies a vehicle with some bullet holes, and most importantly, he doesn't see the two with the rifles. Without looking at the agent, Franklin says, "Hey Larry, you okay?"

Nothing.

"Hey Larry...?"

Still nothing.

Just as Franklin is going to risk a peek toward Lawrence to see what the outcome of the gunfight was, even though he knows the man's dead, two figures appear in the doorway again, neither one of them wounded. Their eyes shine proudly at surviving the close quarter's shootout.

"Hey Larry," Franklin squeaks out in a small voice, knowing the agent's not going to answer. He risks a hesitant peep over his shoulder, Larry's chest is a mess of blood, his body slumped in the corner of the ambulance.

One says, "He's not going to be able to help you."

Franklin holds up his cuffed hands. "We can work something out. You don't have to do this."

The one removes his nylon mask, revealing he is Siriano's second-in-command, Renaldo Luna. "I'm afraid I do."

"Oh shit," Franklin says. "Listen, I didn't put those cops on Siriano. I had nothing to do with that whole deal."

"You shot one," Renaldo says, "killed him."

"Well, yeah, I did that, but I didn't put them on the drug deal. I didn't know they were cops. I was just testing the one... kidding with him, you know?"

Renaldo shakes his head. "No, I don't."

"I won't say nothing to no one about the big man."

"Yeah, sure, okay," Renaldo says. "That's why I'm here—to ensure you don't."

Renaldo, rifle up, jammed against his shoulder, is about to pull the trigger, when a third figure, unmasked appears next to him holding a pistol. "This the guy?" the third figure asks.

Renaldo lowers the rifle and dips his chin.

The still masked one says, "I'll get the truck," but Franklin notices he's not addressing Renaldo; he's addressing the other guy.

Franklin knots his eyebrows, questioningly, as Renaldo swivels to the third guy, but just as quick as the gunfight, the third guy raises his pistol, nearly against Renaldo's head, just a gap between them for Renaldo to have a second to comprehend what's happening. Renaldo asks, "What the hell?" But the third guy doesn't give him an answer, he pulls the trigger. Renaldo jerks his head and drops to the ground in a twisted heap. Then, the shooter turns to Franklin, hair cut in a bowl, eyes dark brown and soulless, face rounded angles, skin brown—a beaner, a nobody.

A moment passes.

The shooter dips his chin and steps out of view leaving Franklin alone in the back of the ambulance staring off into the night. Renaldo's not moving. Lawrence doesn't move. The paramedic isn't moving. Franklin realizes if he's going to make a run for it before the cops get here, he has to hurry.

Franklin's fingers lash to the straps around his feet. He kicks his feet and tries to pull on and loosen the strap to free his body. Once he's able to get free, he pushes the gurney back to the side and checks the paramedic for a wallet. He unloads the paramedic of nearly everything he has on his person, laying everything out on the bench next to the guy. He reaches up and dumps one of the small duffle-type bags hanging in the back of the ambulance, spilling all the contents on the floor, like gloves and plastic doohickeys. He swipes all of the paramedic's belongings into the bag and searches the bins and cabinets in the back of the ambulance, frantically, grabbing anything he can use or

might use. He finds an extra paramedic uniform, 511 type blue pants, and a white polo, both too big, but that'll be fine. He searches Lawrence's lifeless body, takes his wallet, keys, gun, and phone, and throws everything else he finds in his possession in the bag. He uses the handcuff keys to free his hands and throws the cuffs in the bag too. He removes Lawrence's holster, badge, and ammo pouch with extra ammo and adds them to his stash.

Before making his exit, Franklin compares his feet to Lawrence's. The shoes are too big, but the paramedic's boots are just right. Franklin unlaces them and tugs them off the guy's feet, tumbling to the side as he tears the first one free.

At the tip of the ambulance, Franklin peers around the edge of the doors, making sure no one is waiting for him, waiting to shoot him. Once satisfied it's clear, he leaps into the street still wearing a hospital gown. The street's quiet, but in the distance, Franklin can hear the sirens of police vehicles. He snatches up Renaldo's rifle and steps over the big dead man in a suit next to the ambulance, searching for the best place to run.

Then, he sees it, a car, sitting still. He runs toward the car in a crouch, carrying both the rifle and the bag, gown open in the back, flapping behind him like a cape, ass to the world. As he nears the car in the intersection, he realizes the car is full of holes. His heart drops. It's useless. That won't be his way to escape. Cops will notice him in no time. This must have been what they were shooting at. The wailing sirens are louder and closer. Then, his ears hear a cough coming from the other side of the car. He rounds the vehicle, careful to avoid glass and pebbles—he should've put the boots on—and finds Leon Gragg sitting against the wheel well near the driver's side door, holding his stomach. "Leon?"

"Frankie?" Leon utters through clenched teeth. "Where'd you come from?"

Franklin nears Leon's downed body. "That's what I was going to ask you. Where'd you come from—I'm sorry about Stevie."

"Don't worry about it," Leon says, waving him off, hand covered in blood, which glistens in the night. "I was following Renaldo."

But something in Leon's face doesn't look right. Franklin doesn't have time to second guess the dying man. He looks back at the ambulance. "Well congratulations, he's dead."

Leon just looks at him.

Franklin runs through his options. He could leave Leon here and run off into the night. He could stay and wait for the cops, or he could figure out a way to make what he has work for him, which is really what he's done his whole life.

"Long story, tell you on the way," he says. "Do you have the keys?"

Leon holds up a set of keys. "Here."

Franklin opens the back door and throws the rifle and the bag in the backseat as the sirens get louder. In the distance, Franklin can see the twinkling reds and blues of the overhead lights, heralding law enforcement's inevitable arrival. He scrambles in the driver's side door and tries the engine. The car coughs to life. Then, out of the car and at Leon's side, he pulls on Leon's arms. "You're going to have to help me," Franklin says. "Come on. You can do it. Get up."

Leon climbs to his feet with Franklin's help, and Franklin lowers him into the car, laying him down in the back seat. His head rests against the bag. Franklin slams the door, jumps into the driver's seat, pulls the door closed, and puts the car in gear.

Franklin scans the rearview mirror. "You got a place we can go?"

Leon sits up in the seat and nods.

"We'll have to dump the car first," Franklin says. "But I think I can make it to Brookside, and then, we'll see what we can get—"

Leon passes out.

Franklin reaches for the bag. Finds it, retrieves the cellphone. Without looking, he dials the number from memory. The call connects. Franklin takes a breath, trying to calm his nerves. "Vera..."

231

CHAPTER NINETEEN:
IRIS KING

RIS IS AT THE CASINO POKER TABLE because her day was shitty and she needed to clear her head, and the best way to do that was to participate in her type of meditation, poker. So, after the funeral, she found the closest Indian casino with an active table and has been here ever since, drinking herself into oblivion, trying not to think about Clyde and trying not to think about crying in front of everyone. About everything. About unintended consequences, Wilson's phrase. That's what he said to her when she called him, asked him to come to the casino. He said that was an unintended consequence and told her to stay the course.

She thinks about Renaldo. About what she's doing to him, her plan.

That's who calls right now, making her phone buzz on the felt table. The dealer gives her a look, but nothing she can't beat back with a look of her own. Iris ignores the phone and goes back to thinking about how she flirted with Tony over her husband's dead body. That'd make a decent joke to tell in the future. It'd be a joke about how she had a change of heart at the funeral and probably embarrassed Eli but fuck him.

"I got up there in front of everyone, and they saw me cry," Iris tells Wilson Notaro. They've been talking for the last hour, trying to figure out how to salvage their plan now that Clyde's in the ground. He wasn't supposed to die. Iris figures that's what's been wrong with her; she's been in shock, and she didn't think that was something she'd feel, grief. "I never cry. No one sees me cry, but I cried. I hate that. If I could kill every last one of them, I'd be able to erase them from seeing me cry."

After drinking through the straw, making a gurgling noise, Wilson says, "That must have been hard. I couldn't get up there in front of everyone and just say, thanks for coming but get out."

Iris folds her cards, tossing the hand into the middle of the table. "It wasn't like that." Even though it was exactly like that, she's just too stubborn to say it was. "You know how it was. My husband was a simple man, had simple wishes. They didn't involve being someone else's entertainment. Clyde just wanted cremation and to have his ashes spread out over the Grand Canyon. That's the least I can do. So, I was standing there and thought to myself, I can do that. Then, I asked myself, why am I not doing that? And well..."

Iris draws her cigarettes from her clutch and the black cigarette holder. She affixes a cigarette to the holder and lights it.

"Is that why you have the pressure cooker?" Wilson asks. He dips the edge of the glass toward the pressure cooker sitting at Iris's feet.

Iris shuffles her feet toward the blue and gold pressure cooker, lets out a puff of smoke. "Have you seen the prices for all that shit the funeral home wants? Like who pays that? An urn shouldn't cost what they sell them for."

Wilson rocks in the seat, doing a full-body nod. "I do. When my grandma died few years back, it put me and my sisters back like twenty-grand 'cause my pops was inside on that State embezzlement thing. This was before he recognized me as one of his own. Twenty-grand was still a lot back then, and I was like that person's dead, what do they care how nice the casket is? Do funerals need to cost that much? I loved my grandma, but she kept money in foil in the icebox. She don't know the difference; she's dead. She'd understand. Hell, she'd get mad if she'd known all the money we spent on her."

Iris considers his story. "Everything for the funeral was paid for," she says, "being it was this big cop to-do, but when I cancelled everything, the funeral home was like, 'you have to pay for the urn.' I asked them why I would need to pay for the urn when they were willing to donate the casket, and they said it's because now the casket's *a used casket* and they're out the difference of whatever they sell it for. I said you can't just clean it and repackage it as new? And they told me it wasn't new—it was now used."

"It's a wooden box," Wilson says. "It's not like it spent any time in the ground. I'm sure it was still all shiny and polished."

"Right?" Iris says. "A wooden box that holds a dead person. I mean, it's not a freaking health hazard for the

consumer. That person's dead. Just wipe it down with some bleach and put the next dead person in it. They wouldn't even know the difference. Like you said, they're dead. But the funeral home told me no, they can't do that. It's against regulations. I asked, 'whose regulations?' You know what they did then?"

Wilson jerks his head.

With the holder between her two fingers, Iris says, "They just requoted the price for the cheapest urn."

Wilson makes a face of disbelief. "How much was it?"

"Too fucking much," Iris says. "So, I ask them, I say, 'Can you hold on to my dead husband for a few minutes while I run out to see what I can find?' They said, 'Since he was a cop, sure,' but they said it like they were being put out. I mean yeah, they weren't supposed to have Clyde anymore since he was supposed to be in the ground, but they don't have to be rude about it. I'm over here trying to do the right thing. And by the way, what would happen if it weren't a cop? No, you have to take the dead person with you? Like who do they think they are?"

The conversation lapses into silence as Wilson buys Iris another drink. The waitress gives Wilson a once over, her critical eye playing over Wilson's crisp navy collared shirt while Iris plays a hand, throwing chips in the pot like they're nothing. The hand doesn't last long. Iris wins. A player gets up in disgust, leaving the dealer and Iris still playing. The waitress delivers the drinks to the table.

"You cried in front of everyone," Wilson says. "You don't cry for no one."

"You know when Clyde and I got married, I didn't cry. Some girls, they cry; they get all teary-eyed and nostalgic or some shit. They fan their hands in front of their faces like if they do it fast enough, they're going to fan the tears away, looking like they're imitating hummingbirds. Like they'd fly away. Yeah, that's it, maybe they're trying to get away from the wedding, hope they take flight or something—that shit's stupid. I don't cry. Not ever. I didn't cry when they told me he was dead, and I sure as hell didn't want to cry on stage in front of everyone..."

Iris falls silent as other players take seats around the table. Wilson greets them cheerfully.

"But you did." Wilson asks, "So why did you?"

"That's a good question," she responds like she doesn't know the answer, except she does know the answer. "I think I did it because I was looking at Tony, and he made me feel so special... like I was the only one in the room. Like I was up there just talking to him. And there was so much warmth and compassion in that face that I forgot about everyone there. And was able to say what I wanted to say. And what I was thinking. Even with Clyde, I never felt like I could say what I really wanted to say. I don't feel that now. But then, I felt that. I've never felt that before, and it was so nearly..." Iris pauses to think of the right word to say.

"Orgasmic?" Wilson jumps in offering the wrong word.

She shakes her head once. "I was going to say transcendental."

"But you mean orgasmic," Wilson says with a sly smile.

"Well, I mean... no... but yeah... no not like that, but yeah, I guess it was kind of like that... I guess you get what I mean... there was just this aura... this glow."

Wilson's shoulders droop as he explains. "Like after an orgasm. I get it. That's why I said orgasmic. Call it what you want, but it was an orgasm." He pauses, placing his hand on Iris's shoulder, his touch warm. "I think that means you like him by the way, but I think you got bigger problems if you're orgasming on a stage in front of everyone."

Iris narrows her eyes. "It wasn't an orgasm."

Wilson cackles and nudges Iris's arm. "I'm just playing with you. I know it wasn't, but it was, you know. Like that's how you know a guy's the guy for you because he makes you feel something you've never felt, why do you think so many first-timers get their cherry popped and then fall in love?"

"Tell that to girls like me," Iris says. "I never fell in love. I don't know what that is. What it's like."

Not even with Clyde. Or Renaldo. She's not loved. She's used. Clyde was safe. Clyde was the best of a situation. Sure she liked him, but love? No.

Wilson says, "It wasn't like that for me either, but I didn't have that, so maybe that's why I've not fallen in love, either."

"You didn't have a first time?"

"I had a first time," Wilson says. Then, he takes a sip of the new drink. "But then I *had* a first time."

Wilson doesn't explain, and he doesn't have to.

Iris is about to let it go when Wilson says, "See, abuse is a hell of a thing. I know you know what I mean... those of us that have gone through it just see the world as something different, you know? I know what it's like, and I know what it does to a person. Can you believe my uncle used to beat the shit out of me? Said I would never amount to nothing? Mad at me for who my father was. Might have been why I was nearly three-hundred pounds by the time I was eighteen? I've worked hard to get down to this size..."

Wilson motions to his body. "Drugs help, but you know what I mean. Lots of working out too.

"I see it in everything you do," Wilson continues. "Maybe that's why you and I have hit it off like we have. I remember the first day Renaldo showed up at your game. I remember the look you gave him. The look you gave me. I think about that a lot. But what I really think about with the stories you've told me, including the ones about the funeral, is that you use men for something. Like you need them to fill something inside of you. Like you're searching for comfort, security, or whatever. I know you do; I'm alright with it. You're kind of like me, how I ate like all that food to heal something inside of me that was broke, through no fault of my own, but wasn't going to get fixed with excess calories."

"Like an addiction?"

"Something like that," Wilson says. He pauses to consider her words. "Do you even like to gamble?"

"Not really," she replies. She receives her new cards and tosses them and her chips into the pot as she folds.

"See, I figured that's what you were going to say," Wilson comments. "I don't care about the gambling. I care about playing the other guy. Getting him to do something that's my idea without him knowing it's my idea. You don't like it because that's not where the joy is for you."

Iris tilts her head to the side, showing she doesn't understand.

Wilson explains. "These are twenty-five-dollar hands. If you cared about the gambling—and by that let's just be clear I mean the money—you'd not be sitting here wasting a hand like that without even looking at your cards. You'd be ignoring me and playing the game. It's about money for

239

you, sure, but it's not. It's about what the money brings you or what the money means. Means you bested a man. Means you don't need them. You don't like men. I mean you like them; you've not complained about what I got going on. But you're not playing poker; you're playing the rich guy on the other side of the cards, which is maybe why we get along so well. We do the same thing but for different reasons. You're using them." Wilson says the last part a little too loud and the scattering of players glance their way.

Iris waves them off.

"See, you play for the power," Wilson adds. "That's where the joy is for you. You want to know why you keep hopping from man to man like they're nothing, why you want an open marriage, or even why you got married in the first place? It's because you like power. I like power, which is why we need to remove Renaldo, but I can't do it like I wanna because then I'd be a rat. My father, he don't like rats. I'll let Kevin be the rat. Let Kevin take him the drives and say here's what Renaldo's been doing, and here's your proof. He used your money and resources to make money without getting it approved. You don't do that. You don't rat. You don't act like a rat even. My pops is a cut-the-arm-off type of guy when it comes to cleansing an infection. But not me. I'm going to say, 'Yeah, I knew but I wasn't going to say nothing.' And that will get me what I want."

"What are you saying?"

"You got married to Clyde. Why'd you get married in the first place?"

Iris doesn't answer.

"You met him at poker, right? You're the most ruthless player I've ever faced."

Iris nods.

"Anyone else ever beat you like he did?" Wilson asks.

"Not like he did, no," Iris says, thinking of the first time she met Clyde. "He never played me again."

"See, there you go." Wilson nudges her shoulder with his fist. "You saw the power in that, and you're searching for that, probably to heal some abuse of some kind of bullshit because, like I said, first time brings love. But as the marriage went on, that need started calling to you, then screaming at you, so that's why you said you had an open marriage and didn't feel anything when he died. Because whatever you and him had, it was gone by then. Sure, you liked him. I like pizza and cake. But just liking those things didn't bring me joy anymore—it didn't bring you joy."

Iris's phone buzzes again; it's Renaldo calling. She retrieves the phone and talks to Wilson while holding it like she's about to answer it. "What's this have to do with the feelings I felt and crying in front of everyone?"

"I'm getting there," Wilson explains. "So here you are, not caring that you're going against Clyde's wishes and your fuckhead boyfriend's out there in the crowd. Not me, Renaldo, and you're up in front of everyone. And then you see someone, who's just as disgusted with *you* as *you* are with yourself, who was as close to Clyde as you were, and who wanted what's best for him—otherwise, he wouldn't have brought that postcard of the Grand Canyon for him, which is super corny by the way. Anyways, you see him, and you say to yourself, what am I doing? This isn't me. And then you get flooded with these emotions that you're not used to feeling and didn't think you would feel."

Iris smiles. "I did, the orgasmic ones."

"The orgasmic ones," Wilson proudly affirms. "You get all these feelings because you've never been satisfied, not like this. He didn't like you flirting and held you accountable, which strangely satisfied you by not giving in to you."

The phone quits buzzing.

"So, you're saying I like Tony?"

"No," Wilson says, loudly, and then holds the next bit out, "*You're saying* you like Tony. That's what you're saying. Those are the first-time feelings I'm talking about. That's fine; I can take the competition. Besides, it's not like he wants you either; you've made that clear. You just got your cherry popped because someone's stood up to you in ways you'd never expected or imagined and said you need to take a closer look at your life. But he's also man enough not to wave it in front of your face, which is why he left after making that remark while he was doing the watch-thing but is also why he could sit there in the audience and look at you and offer you the encouragement to do the right thing and call off the funeral."

"I've never thought of it like that."

Wilson says, "That's why you need me in your life. Talk solves the world's problems."

"I don't know about that."

"It does," Wilson urges, smiling. "My sisters and I wouldn't even know what the problem was. We'd sit there, them being all bitchy and then all of a sudden something would happen, and we'd realize what was bothering them. You know what? It usually had nothing to do with anything going on."

The phone buzzes again. Iris glances down, the screen says, Renaldo. "It's him."

Wilson says, "It must be pretty important if he keeps calling."

"He thinks he's important," Iris says.

242

"You better answer then and see what he wants."

Iris clicks to accept the call. "Hello?"

The voice on the other end isn't Renaldo; it's female. "Ma'am, I'm sorry for bothering you, but you were the last missed call on this phone."

Iris's breath stops in her throat.

"Ma'am," the voice asks. "Are you there?"

Silence.

"Yes," Iris says, remembering she needs to breathe. "Yes, I'm here."

"Can you tell me whose phone this is?"

"Renaldo," Iris says. "This is Renaldo's phone. Why do you have Renaldo's phone?"

"There has been an incident," the voice says with care. "I'm a nurse. We don't know who this man is, but we... I'm sorry... there's only so much I can say. Do you *know* Renaldo? Could you tell me his date-of-birth or his full name?"

Iris looks at Wilson wide-eyed and confused as she answers the woman on the phone. "We're dating, I guess you could say."

"Can you come to the hospital?" the nurse asks.

Iris glances at her watch. "It's late, but I can. Where are you?"

The nurse tells her.

In shock, Iris hangs up the phone, slipping it into her clutch. "I have to go," she says and snuffs the cigarette out before returning the holder to the clutch and collects her chips from the table.

"Everything all right?"

"I don't know." She pushes the chips toward Wilson and leaves.

CHAPTER TWENTY:

ELIZA CORTEZ

E LIZA EXITS THE BACK BEDROOM, and it's the smell of Ed's specialty fresh-ground coffee that nearly sets her off, smells like shit, but then, that smell combines with all her other senses and invokes an intense disgust. She becomes so overwhelmed with irritation that she explodes. Not literally, there aren't bits of her strung about, but it might as well be a true explosion with shrapnel and carnage because she becomes so instantly appalled at the state of her union, her house, her life, that an overwhelming desire overtakes her to dismantle her life brick by brick, but more importantly, it leaves her with one thought: how could she bring a child into this? What is she thinking?

Eliza hasn't been happy for a long time, and Tony's called her on it and continued to call her on it. He keeps calling her on it. Asking her why she hasn't talked to Ed. Why she won't tell him?

And here, she's tried to rationalize it to herself and him, but it hasn't made any sense and she hasn't given him a real reason. She thought about it all night. Couldn't sleep because of it. Because yesterday, drunk Tony wouldn't let it go.

She doesn't know why she has not told Ed.

Besides, it's not like she has not asked herself those same questions. It's just she keeps coming back to the same answers. She's afraid. She doesn't want to lose what security she has.

But really, what's keeping her here? Things haven't been right with Ed for a long time. It's not that things are just hard. Marriage is hard and is a lot of work, but it goes beyond that. It feels like her marriage is dead, and it has felt that way since she found out about everything.

Sure they've worked on it. Tried to at least. And sure he's tried to change, but then again, has he? Really? Can people change? Do people change? Is counseling enough?

But Ed couldn't even do that, couldn't be bothered, convinced, badgered, or guilted into it. So has he changed any? Maybe? Maybe what little counseling they've had is enough. But is it enough to save their marriage? Maybe in another marriage, the changes would be greater, but in hers, have they really happened? If the changes have happened, they've been minor.

It's not like they've ever worked on things in counseling anyways. Ed had all sorts of excuses as to why he couldn't attend this counselor or that one. Ed would question, "Why do we need to spend money on that? Why are we telling some stranger our problems?"

To which she would say, "To save us."

Then, Ed would reply, "It costs too much money."

And she would come back with, "What's your marriage cost to you? Is there a price on being married to me?"

He would argue, "I don't like talking to a man about my problems with you. I can't let my guard down. What will he think of me?"

To which she would say, "That you are human. Have feelings."

And then Ed's response might be, "I don't feel comfortable telling a woman about us having sex."

Then, she would remark, "Why would that bother you? You went out and paid for it."

So, this morning, it's not just his coffee that bothers her, that causes these repugnant feelings to bubble to the surface, filtering through her mind as she walks into the kitchen, but it is the spark that lights her fuse.

Sure, his coffee has disgusted her ever since she found out she was pregnant, no scratch that, it smelled like shit before she found out she was pregnant. It's how she knew she was pregnant, stopping to throw up every time she picked up Starbucks on the way to work, the only thing outside of her house that came close to the quality of Ed's coffee. She was puking on the side of the road. How humiliating. Eventually, she figured out it was the coffee. It took her longer than it should have, but it was a hard habit to break. Her doctor tried to explain to her that it had something to do with a chemical in coffee that is also found in broccoli and Brussels sprouts and shit vegetables like that, and as a result of the pregnancy, her sense of smell was better and caused nausea. The doctor was drinking coffee as he explained it, which smelled like vile shit, sneering, and laughing at her the whole time as he told her how she

felt. It triggered her morning sickness right in his office. He didn't laugh after that.

Now, as she walks into the kitchen, Eliza finds Eduardo on his phone, face buried in his phone, seemingly amused at whatever he's reading, his coffee sitting on the table next to his other hand, steaming and freshly brewed. The smell. The rage builds. The kitchen is a reflection of her life, and her blood pressure spikes, head pounding, and like careening into an invisible curtain, her stomach turns as the aroma of feces assails her, mixed with the slight sulfur smell from Ed's boiled eggs—two, to be exact, on the table in little holders. The trash is full, and he left the lid open again, banana peel on the top. Also part of his breakfast.

"What are you doing?" Eliza snaps, sweeping past him, slamming the trash can lid shut as she passes. "Why can't you shut the lid? It's not a hard thing. It won't hurt you to do it. I ask you to shut it so it doesn't smell. You know I'm really sensitive to smells right now. Why can't you do that one thing? It's not that hard."

He doesn't look up from the phone. "It's not just one thing."

"What do you mean by that?" she asks. "You know what? No, it's not. There are other things you don't do. But do I complain about them? No. I put up with it. But really, the trash? That's going to hurt you to bring the little white lid down with your fingers?" She acts like the trash bit her, and she waves her fingers in front of her face like she's hurt, blowing across her nails. "Oh no, I lost a finger doing it."

Eduardo rolls his eyes. "Don't be like that."

He may not have said the phrase, but his tone communicates it, and her ears translate it to him calling her dramatic. "Be like what? Overly dramatic?"

Ed raises an eyebrow. "I'm not calling you dramatic; just don't make a big deal out of something that isn't."

"I've told you the coffee makes me sick to my stomach, but you still make it. I'm fine with that, but I need you to start listening to what I'm telling you and at least try to act like you care."

Eduardo shrugs. "What's the big deal? It's just the lid to the trash."

"Except it's not," she says. "And really, you're not even going to respond to what I just said? Do you not care? You act like you don't"

Eduardo shakes his head. "No, I care." Then, he sighs and takes off his thick glasses, pretending to clean the lenses with one of the cloth napkins from the table, buffeting the lenses, rubbing them.

"Then, why can't you close the lid? Or be bothered to clean out the dishwasher? Load the dishwasher? Put the dishes away? Or act like you want to be here? Do any of the chores? Hell, why the fuck can't you just put the dishes away in the right place or hang your towel up?"

She's not really mad about any of that, at least that's what the counselor told her. Counselor said that wasn't what was bothering her. No, it's the fact that those things indicate to her that Ed doesn't care about her.

Except every single one of those things pisses her the fuck off.

Eduardo stares at her for a few heartbeats as he silently cleans his glasses, stalling, processing what she's said. He has to process everything. Work it through his big head. Poke the hamster with the cow prod to get it moving in the wheel. He's an accountant. Numbers are his life. Birthdays. Account numbers. Passwords. Phone numbers, he never had trouble with those, no little black book for him. How could he remember nearly everyone's phone number, but he can't remember to do the simple things?

And she can't take it anymore.

Eduardo fastens the glasses back on the bridge of his nose and scoots away from the table. "What do you want me to say?"

"I want you to care," she says.

"I do care."

"You have a funny way of showing it. You care more about numbers, your job, your sluts, than you do about me."

"What... why... when will you let this go?" he asks. "You can't keep bringing this up. Eventually, we will have to move past it."

"Let this go," she repeats, her voice getting louder with every syllable. "What am I letting go? The fact that you are a cheating bastard? The fact that you did the one thing I asked you not to do? Told you, you couldn't do, the thing that absolutely crushed me. What the fuck do you want me to do, Ed? Do you think I'm just going to be the good Latina wife and let you walk over me? I should just forget this and move on—I'm not forgetting this."

"You could at least forgive," he quips, picking up his phone. "But it's early, and I don't want to fight with you right now." He points to the trash can. "I'm sorry I forgot to close the lid." His eyes and attention drop to the phone, signaling the conversation's over, but that's not how arguments work.

Eliza moves to the fridge, opens it, and retrieves the Brita filtered water container. "What are you doing?"

Eduardo looks up from his phone. "Just checking e-mails."

Eliza frowns and raises an eyebrow. "Work e-mails?"

"What other types of e-mails would I be checking?" he asks with a heavy sigh, stopping what he's doing. He should know what she's accusing him of. He puts the phone back down on the table. "They are work-related, yes."

Eliza selects a glass from the cabinet and fills it with water. She faces him. "But you're at home."

"I am, but I missed a lot of work yesterday going to the funeral with you."

"You didn't have to go." She pauses to sip the glass, holding it with two hands. "You could have gone to work. You could have decided not to be with me rather than pretend it's some great burden."

"I know I didn't have to go, but it was important to you. He was your friend. I felt I needed to go, needed to be there."

Eliza drops the glass from her mouth. "Out of obligation?"

Eduardo opens his mouth to say something but then snaps it shut. He drops his chin to his chest and takes a short breath, halfway between a sigh and something someone would do when they're counting to ten, gathering his thoughts. "That's not... now don't... why do you have to be like that?"

"Like what?" Eliza says. "You didn't answer the question. That's not what I asked you."

"What did you ask me?"

"You heard me."

"Seriously, we're going to do this now?" Ed says. "It's not even eight in the morning. Why? Why are we doing this now? Can't this wait? Can we not go twenty-four fucking hours before you jump all over me?"

"So you don't want to talk about whatever it is that you meant."

"You know what I meant, but I have work to do," Ed says, dismissing her and going back to the phone. "I'll clean up the kitchen when I get a chance, but right now, I'm going to enjoy my breakfast, answer some e-mails, calm down, and then go to work."

She puts the glass on the counter behind her and uses the counter to hold up her body. "Do you even love me?"

Eduardo's head whips her way. "Why would you even ask that?"

"Because they say you don't cheat on someone you love. They say if you cheated on me then you don't really love me."

"That's not what was going on... we were in two different places—two different people."

"Do you love me?"

Eduardo jumps to his feet, pushing the chair backward, and takes a step toward her, arms out to hug her, to hold her, to tell her he does, but she waves him off, telling him not to touch her, and she slaps his hand away.

"Why are you even asking me this?" he says. "Look, we had a rough patch. That's what it was. We weren't getting along. I couldn't reach you. I couldn't talk to you."

"So, you reached for someone else," Eliza says sharply. "But what I'm asking you is do you love me?"

"I only reached for someone else because you are too consumed with your career. You weren't home. You never were and when you were home, you weren't home if you know what I mean. You were so distant. So guarded. So strong."

Eliza's voice drops to a wishful hush, knowing he should have said *yes,* the minute she asked. This time, quieter, from a well of disheartenment because she knows what the answer is. "Do you love me?"

"Yes," Ed says in a similar tone to hers, but tinged with a question as if even he doesn't believe his words.

"It took me asking you multiple times before you answered. It shouldn't take multiple times." Then, she says, "Why did it take multiple times?"

Ed exudes impotent apathy, not knowing what to say. They both know what this moment is, a death. The death. The death of their marriage, of who and what they are. Yesterday was just an act, get along for the funeral, play nice, but they aren't a couple anymore, not even roommates.

Instead of feeling despondent or upset about the revelation, Eliza's heart soars with courage born from her despair. It rises in her, replacing her sadness with joy, hope, and thoughts of Tony. Thoughts of how Tony wants the best for her, of how hearing him yell out on the radio and seeing him utterly wrecked over Clyde's death broke her heart and how all he wanted was her comfort. And how she enjoyed being there for him, how it felt right, is right, how it should be. Eliza's eyelids flutter the tears away, and in a small voice, growing bolder, louder. "The baby's not yours."

It's like she slapped him. Ed takes a half step back. Blinks once. His jaw tightens.

But she can't look him in the eyes, so she looks down, closes her eyes, and says, "You may want a DNA test or whatever to be sure, but I'm sure." It's all happening right now, not like she planned, not how she ever imagined it, but somehow, she's calm, serene. "The baby isn't yours... *he's* not yours. I'm sorry."

Ed doesn't speak.

The baby, a boy, is all Eduardo's ever wanted.

Does Tony want a boy? In all the times he's asked if she knew the sex, he's never said, and she's never thought to ask him.

Eduardo's lips curve to form the question of who, but his throat contracts so tightly he's unable to make a sound.

Then, she slips the knife, putting the wounded animal out of its misery. "The baby's Tony's, Ed," she says to answer his question. The words becoming easier to say as they come out. It feels like she's throwing up, her body exuding all the shameful foulness from her system, purging herself of the truth, "I so was angry at you... angry for what you did... it happened when you moved out. I... I'm sorry. There's nothing I can say."

Neither of them knows what to say. There isn't anything to say. Their marriage ended long ago, and they've been living with the corpse ever since.

With that, Ed blinks again, once, and then twice, and leaves without saying anything. He doesn't slam the door, doesn't yell or scream, doesn't make a scene. That's not him. He's never been like that. Perhaps that was the problem, no passion. He never fought for them; why would he fight now? He just left. One moment he's standing in the kitchen arguing, and the next, he's in his car backing down their driveway and gone. All of it in seconds.

Relief washes over Eliza as she realizes she's alone.

Her phone rings; it's Marque.

CHAPTER TWENTY-ONE:

TONY MORA

TONY JERKS HIS HEAD FROM THE KITCHEN table. Knocking wakes him up, and it is not a great way to wake up. He blinks a few times to clear out the cobwebs. Think about what happened last night. Casper was here and they talked. They drank. He got bombed, doing what cops do. He's not sure if he feels any better now that he's done it. He smoked half a cigar, which is still between his fingers, long cold. That could have been bad. That's how fires start. He drops the cigar and his hand swipes against an empty glass bottle; scotch, oh yeah, the drinking. If the empty bottle wasn't enough of a reminder, the pounding headache coming on in a sudden surge would've made him remember.

So he drank a lot. Maybe too much. A hell of a lot. But when did he pass out?

Tony rubs his eyes with his index finger and thumb, pulling the fingers together to the bridge of his nose.

The knock comes again.

"Yeah," Tony says, gathering himself and sitting up in the chair, "I'm coming."

The change in altitude makes the headache worse. Standing makes it worse, and he has to stop. The room lurches to the left and to the right before spinning a few times and then slowly fading to black. Reaching forward blindly, he puts his hands out to steady himself, grabbing hold of the chair to avoid falling. All he can do is ride it out and wait for his vision to return.

Tony closes his eyes, his blood pumps thickly through his aching head. His face hurts like a hand is pushing from the inside out. He's not sure if that's from the drinking or sleeping on it. When he opens his eyes again, everything's a bit too bright.

He turns from the mess of the table to find more empty bottles littering the kitchen counter. Some still have liquid in them. Some unopened. Some empty. He must have emptied the cabinet, looking to clear out the last contents of whatever he had after the scotch was gone. Did he take the pressure cooker out of the liquor cabinet? When did that happen? But the entire cabinet's empty, so he must have done it.

The knock comes again.

Tony ignores the knocking and puts the pressure cooker and bottles back into the cabinet, hoping the minor pause in walking will help him overcome the raging hangover. It doesn't. He takes a swig of whiskey to combat fire with fire.

The doorbell rings.

"I'm coming," Tony yells. "Hold up. Will ya?" Before closing the cabinet door, he takes a second swig of whiskey and places the bottle back in the cabinet. He collects the empty ones by the necks, as many as he can gather, and drops them in the nearly full trash can.

Where's Casper? Guest room? Tony told Casper he could stay in the guest room.

So on the way to the front door, Tony checks and finds Casper asleep, fully clothed, shoes still on, lying on the bed on top of the comforter. Tony pulls the door nearly closed.

The knock comes again.

Tony opens the door and finds Iris standing on the other side cradling a pressure cooker and dressed like she was yesterday. Black dress, no makeup, hair frazzled but still presentable. Desirable. Like that's some sort of superpower of hers to look completely rundown and still good. Do some girls learn how to do this? Or are they born with it?

"You okay?" Iris asks, adjusting the blue and gold pressure cooker, held under her arm, using her hip to bounce it up farther on her waist, further securing it to her armpit.

Tony blinks a few times. "I feel like I left the diaphragm open on the camera and everything's overexposed," he says.

"So you're hungover?"

"Something like that."

Iris peers around the opening of the door, looking to see if he's alone. "Mind if I come in?"

Tony shakes out of his stupor and pushes the door open. "Sure," he says. "I'm sorry; you caught me at a bad moment."

"You look like you just woke up."

"That's the bad moment," Tony says. "Waking up with a monster hangover like this." He pauses. "I didn't expect to see you again anytime soon."

And watches the comment land wrong; her face drops and cheeks redden like she's ashamed or sad. Then she tip-toes into the house.

Closing the door behind her, Tony asks, "Sorry, my mind's not working right. Everything's still running a bit too slow. What's the polite thing to do when someone visits?"

"Well in the movies and down south, in a situation like this, you'd offer me a drink or something," Iris says, playfully. "But don't feel like you have to. I am the one dropping in on you. I'm sorry about it. It's early, but I just... I needed to talk to you."

Tony lifts his hands in mock surrender. "So, you want a drink?"

Iris smiles and says she would love a drink. Tony steps past her, telling her to follow him, and shows her the way. They walk down the hallway to the kitchen. "I don't have much... and after last night, I don't know what's left, but I do know there's some liquor, maybe some milk, tap water, and I could make coffee."

"I would love some coffee," Iris says, stepping into the kitchen behind him. "I've been up all-night thinking about yesterday. Thinking about you. Thinking about Clyde. Just thinking. Poker helps me think. I went and played some poker to blow off steam and think some more about..." She pauses to examine his kitchen with judging eyes, the mess. "Sorry again about dropping in on you. I just... I needed to talk."

Iris deposits the pressure cooker on the counter next to the stove. Relieved of the burden, she quickly adjusts and fixes her hair while inspecting her reflection in the microwave. Tony prepares the coffee and retrieves clean mugs from one of the cabinets. The whole process takes a few minutes, and they pass it in silence as he eyes her without getting caught, and she eyes him without getting caught, except both know, but no one wants to acknowledge it or break the silence. The moment passes.

At the sink, Tony passes his hand under the sensor to turn on the water, washes his hands. "Not trying to be rude," he says, "but why are you here?"

"I needed to talk to you," Iris says. She stops to look around unsure if it's safe to have this conversation here or someplace else. She glances toward the guest bedroom door and then at his bedroom door. "Is there someplace we could sit down? Talk?"

The sensor shuts off the water. The kitchen table is covered in empty beer cans, bottles, and ash and won't do. Wiping his hands with a towel, he motions behind her at the wall of windows, opening to the backyard and his covered patio. "We can go on the back porch. Is that all right with you?"

Iris faces the windows. "Works for me."

They wait for the coffee to finish brewing, the conversation pauses. Once done, Tony pours two mugs' worth and leads the way to the back porch. He opens the back door and leads the way to two outdoor wicker rocking chairs with plush lime green cushions. "It's not much, but I call it home."

Iris says, "It's nice."

Tony offers a seat. Iris chooses the chair closest to the door. Tony takes the other one. "I pride myself on picking outdoor furniture."

"I didn't know it was a passion for you," Iris says as she makes herself comfortable. She pulls her feet up under her, folding one leg under the other. Once settled in the seat, she lets the coffee linger under her chin, grasping it with both hands. She closes her eyes and is quiet. The steam drifts off the surface of the liquid and swirls under her chin.

Tony notices the goosebumps on her arms and how little her dress covers. "Are you cold?"

"Yes," Iris says, tracking his eyes to the goosebumps on her arms. "And no. I feel like I should be, dressed the way I am, but I'm not really."

"Would you like a blanket? There's one just inside the door."

"Oh, you keep them there for all the girls you bring out here?"

Tony doesn't answer.

She accepts Tony's offer. He places his coffee down on the small table in front of the chairs and steps back inside to retrieve a blanket from a cedar chest near his back-door. Outside again, after shutting the door, he wraps the blanket around her shoulders. Then, sitting, he retrieves his coffee from the table. The whole time Iris is quiet and looks content.

Tony sips his coffee, waiting to see where this conversation's going.

Finally, Iris opens her eyes and says, "You were right."

"About?" Tony asks.

"About everything. About Clyde. About..." her voice trails off. She takes a sip of the warm drink. "You were right. I wanted to come here and tell you thank you."

Tony tilts his head to the side. "You're welcome."

Iris sighs and looks around the backyard for a moment. "Yesterday wasn't easy."

"You're telling me," he says, lifting his coffee mug. "But what part are *you* talking about?"

"Getting up in front of everyone and kicking them out."

"I was surprised you did that."

"So am I," Iris says. "You're the reason I did it. Clyde thought so much of you. He really did. He was happy to be your partner. You know the other night we were talking and... I don't know... I guess I made a pass at you."

Watching her struggle to find the words is amusing, and she totally did make a pass at him, a disgusting one at that.

"You guess?"

"Okay, I did make a pass at you," she admits. "I don't know why I did that. It wasn't right, especially with Clyde laying right there."

"I don't think he minded," Tony says. "Besides I have a theory about that." Not telling her how tempting her attempt at flirting with him was at the time and how disgusted he became at himself for liking it.

Iris jerks her head toward him. "Do you?"

"Well, not just about you." he laughs, getting comfortable in her presence. "But I would say it applies. Eliza doesn't like when I talk about it because she thinks it's bullshit. But it's a theory. Has to do with people having sex."

"Care to share?" Iris asks, interested.

"Well, see, you know the Five Love Languages?" he asks. Iris nods. "It talks about people's love language. How some people like words of affirmation. Some gifts. Some acts of service or whatever. Some like touch."

"You're saying I like touch." Iris reaches out with one hand and places it on Tony's knee. He looks down at her hand; he can hardly believe her, coming over here to make an apology for making a pass at him and then doing it again.

"Yes, but it's more than that. See, when something traumatic happens, it causes stress. People handle stress in different ways. Some people, they drink. Some gamble. Some like to fuck."

"You're saying I like to fuck?"

Shit, he's screwing this up.

"Yes... no... I'm... you know what, why don't you apologize, and then, I'll tell you the rest of my theory."

Iris sips the coffee. "No, this is getting too good. Why don't you finish?"

Tony smiles. "So, people handle stress differently. You handle it by finding comfort in others. Is that a better way of saying it?"

"Better than saying I just want to fuck?"

"Yeah."

"Yeah, that sounds better. So, you're saying that I handle stress by finding a man and having my way with him."

"Something like that," he says, not missing that her hand's still on his leg slowly moving back and forth. "You know Clyde told me never to play poker with you."

"He did?"

"Said you can't be beaten. Said he only played you once. Beat you. It was luck. Had to be. Said he wouldn't play you again because if you beat him, you wouldn't respect him. Said you don't respect any man who loses to you. I kind of figured that out the other night when you made a pass at me. You were so ... subtle."

"Did you like it?"

Tony looks away; his eyes would betray him. His nerves are sensitive to her hand, warm on his leg. When he turns back, he finds her eyes on him, grinning.

"Is that what you are doing right now, trying not to play me in poker? Is that what we are doing?"

"Isn't that what this is?" Tony asks, turning it around on her and giving her a look. "You're playing me right now. This may not be a card game. We may not be sitting around a table staring each other down, but this is a game and you're playing me. Just like at the funeral home. I beat you then. Didn't I? That's why you did what you did later in the day. You realized how shitty you had been and how Clyde deserved better. That's what's happening right now, isn't it?" He motions from him to her. "That's what you are doing; we are playing again except I didn't know it until just now."

Iris retracts her hand fast and bristles some, but she also gives him a look of acceptance. "I came here to apologize."

"By making another pass at me? I'm not sure if I'm upset with you or not for doing it."

Iris closes her eyes and drops her chin and shoulders. She nods while biting at her lip. "Fair enough. I don't know why I did that."

Tony tells her it's okay and not to worry about it. "My theory explains it."

"Your theory just says I want to fuck."

He lifts one finger to correct her. "No, you use people."

Watching her, she doesn't get upset, and here he thought she'd at least frown or something, but no, she lets the observation wash over her. "You are the second person tonight... I mean today that's said that."

"It's true, and I think there have been others that have said that. Eliza said that to me," Tony says. "Said that's what you do. You use people."

"That woman does not like me," Iris says. "Do you think I'm using you?"

"I don't see what the endgame is, so I don't know," he says honestly, but he knows she is using him. That's what she does. He just doesn't know what she is using him for.

"I used you yesterday," Iris admits. "I got up there and said those things... that took a lot for me to do that by the way... I said those things and told those people to get out and the whole time I was doing it I was looking at you."

"I know. I was there."

"You can be an ass."

"That's what your husband told me," Tony says. "He used to complain about how I could be an asshole, show no mercy when it came to pointing out the painfully obvious."

Iris with a flat tone says, "He's dead."

Tony concedes. "He is."

"I should have realized what was happening when Eli wanted to do the whole parade. He did it for himself. Not Clyde."

Tony says, "Bucky's all about himself. This is his life. Everything is for his ego. He has nothing beyond this."

"Isn't he married?"

"Did that stop you?"

"No," she says, blushing. "I guess it didn't."

Tony leans forward and puts his hand on her knee over the folds of the blanket, turning the whole scene back around on her, making the second move. "Look, nothing personal, but I don't look at becoming Eskimo brothers with Bucky or Clyde." Then, he takes his hand back.

"I don't know what that means."

Leaning back, he says, "And I'm not going to explain it."

Iris pauses and takes a moment to search his face.

Tony does the same, looking her over. He notices how her nose turns up just so. She isn't bad looking when it comes down to it. She doesn't need makeup. She's a wash-and-wear type of girl. She looks good in the dress. Tony understands what Clyde saw in her. If it weren't for Eliza, he'd see the same thing.

Iris asks, "You don't hate me, do you?"

"Why would I hate you? Why would you even ask me that?"

She looks down, searching for an answer, waiting before answering. "For ... I don't know..."

"For you doing what you do?" Tony asks. "Why would I hate you? Clyde loved you. He knew who you were. He knew you were the best thing that was going to happen to him and that, frankly, it wasn't going to last. Sure, he dreamed of it lasting, but he dreamed of a lot of things. Clyde was all about dreams, living big."

"He's in the pressure cooker," Iris blurts.

"He's what?" Tony asks.

"On the counter... I didn't know what to do... The urn was so expensive."

"He's in my house?"

She nods and Tony glances over his shoulder back toward the kitchen.

Iris says, "I want you to take him to the Grand Canyon."

"You want me to do what?"

"Take him to the Grand Canyon. That was in his Will. I had to make sure it happened. That's what it said."

"What do you mean it was in his Will?"

"This is going to take a lot longer if you keep questioning everything I say," she says. "Eli read me his Will when I was in his office. He said there were some money and other matters that would be coming my way, but they depended on some stipulations. One of them is you taking Clyde's ashes to the Grand Canyon."

"Why me?"

"Well, actually it was you or me, the *or* being the important part of it, but after lugging that thing around all night, I can't do it. It's too much, and I've already screwed up. Eli was convinced we could do the funeral and shit and still get the money, but it wasn't right."

"You don't think you're going to get Clyde's money?"

"Clyde didn't have money."

"You know what I mean." Tony says, waving the comment away. "So, is that all you came over here to do?"

"No," Iris says.

She opens her mouth to say something but then decides not to.

"What else is there?" Tony asks.

"I wanted to say thank you for yesterday," Iris says. "That's what I've been trying to say."

"You said that already."

"Yes, but you distracted me," Iris says. "Look, I let Eli lead me astray. I shouldn't have done that. Then, I was standing up there shaking hands and looking at you, and I realized you are a better friend than Clyde probably deserved. There's things about him you don't know about."

She stops for a moment to gather her thoughts, and she must have seen the questions forming in his eyes and at the tip of his tongue.

She says, "No, I'm not going to tell you. If you find out, you find out, but I'm not going to be the one that tells you, and if it never comes out, then that's probably for the best."

"That's why you are here asking me to take him to the Grand Canyon?"

"Yes, because you didn't forget about him." Iris reaches into her bra and withdraws a folded piece of paper. Tony recognizes it as the postcard. "This was sweet. I thought about putting it in the urn now that he's not in the casket, but I thought I'd return it to you with Clyde's ashes and tell you you should just go out there and make this a real thing."

Iris attempts to hand him the postcard, but Tony doesn't take it right away. He lets it hang there in the space between them for a few heartbeats. Then, just as her hand is about to withdraw, Tony accepts the postcard.

Iris says, "I could never have done what I did yesterday without seeing you in the audience and giving me the courage. That's what this is. What I'm doing. The right thing. You know, talking with Clyde, we talked a lot about crime and criminals and doing the right thing. I don't do the right thing, Tony. I'm not a good person, but Clyde saw something in me that was there and no one else seemed to see..." her voice trails off again.

"He could bring out the best in people. He always told me to calm down. Don't let every insult be the spark that lights my dynamite."

Iris chuckles. "What does that even mean?"

"I don't know. He had some weird notions about how the world worked."

"See, that's the thing," Iris says. "We talked about doing the right thing. Clyde would say being a good person is about doing the right thing ... but that it wasn't about doing the right thing on the big stuff. I mean, that is important too. Like do you shoot this person or not? Do you steal or not? Do you have sex with him or not? No, he said it was always about making the little decisions in life.

If you don't make the right little decisions, how will you make the right big ones? To be a good person takes work."

"It does."

"Clyde saw that in me. Saw that I could be a good person."

"Do you want to be a good person?"

Iris hesitates. "Yesterday, you had that same look. Maybe it's because I like you and not for any of the reasons I like anyone else. Maybe it's because you remind me of Clyde. You're his legacy. Maybe not. Maybe it's all bullshit, and I'm losing it. But you have that look. You look at me like you see so much potential in me that I don't see, but it's not like potential because it's happening. It's already me." She rubs the back of her neck. "I'm sorry; I guess I'm not making any sense."

Tony squints. "No, I think I understand."

"So anyways, thank you for giving me the courage to do what I had to do."

"The right thing," he says.

"The right thing," she repeats.

Iris finishes her coffee and stands up, stretching her legs and rolling her ankles, but she keeps the blanket wrapped around her shoulders. "Can we talk more later?"

Tony stands and says they can.

"I'm sure your head hurts, and I have a friend that needs help. But I'll leave Clyde here for now."

"I can't go right away," Tony says. "I mean the Grand Canyon. I have some work things to take care of in the wake of his death."

"I understand."

"But if you decide you want to come out there with me. We can do it together. Not like you want but together." Then, Tony turns the conversation back around. "But I'm not going to have sex with you. We could go out there together, as friends, and do this for Clyde, but I'm sorry; my heart belongs to someone else."

"I know," Iris says. "Not that it will stop me."

Tony doesn't say anything.

Iris taps her nose. "Women know these sorts of things." She gathers herself. "Probably why I want you so much. I can't have you." Half-chuckles.

"What are you going to do now?" he asks.

"Go see my friend in the hospital, and then, I don't know … do some soul searching. What are you going to do?"

"I don't know," he admits.

As he shows her out, he asks about the pressure cooker, and Iris tells him the story about the funeral home.

CHAPTER TWENTY-TWO:
ELIZA CORTEZ

E**LIZA DIALS TONY'S NUMBER** for the fourth time and holds the phone to her ear. She's calling to tell Tony what's happened—she asked Marque to let her be the one to do it—except Tony didn't pick up on the first three phone calls and doesn't on this one. So she gives up and finishes getting dressed. But then, on the sixth attempt as she slips her gun holster on her belt and adjusts it to the side of her stomach, and cradles the phone between her shoulder and neck, Tony does answer the phone.

He asks, "What's up?"

Eliza hears a giggle in the background. She slips the gun into the holster. "It sounds like I'm interrupting something," she says, pausing to inspect herself in the mirror. The female voice in the background sounds familiar. "Am I interrupting something?"

"No," Tony says, quickly, but then hesitates. "What's going on?"

"I didn't expect you to be up this early..."

Her mind searches for the right words, but how do you tell someone their friends are dead? What is the right way to break the news to him? It shouldn't happen over the phone, but it is what it is. So, she starts where they left off yesterday.

"Are you sober?"

Tony chuckles. "Hey, you're the one that called," he says. "And yes, I'm sober. Or sober-ish. Sober enough. I didn't expect to be up this early."

The leftover irritability from the blowup this morning stomps on her mood. Maybe it's the pregnancy, but it's almost like she can smell the alcohol through the phone. Eliza says, "You promised me, Tony, you promised you wouldn't go home and drink. That's what you did, isn't it? You went home, and you got hammered."

Eliza envisions Tony on the other end of the phone stiffening with the chastisement. With defensiveness in his voice, he says, "My friend died, and I had nothing better to do. Besides, what's it matter to you? I'm not anything to you. You made that clear yesterday. You make that clear every moment you don't tell Ed. If I were something to you, you'd tell Ed, and we'd see what happens... Maybe it's what you need. Him finding out, getting angry, and you and I figuring out what this is. But right now, I'm pretty fucking hungover. I don't want to do this with you today."

Eliza says his name, almost pleading into the phone. "Tony."

Tony's voice hardens. "Why did you call?"

"No one wants to do this today," she says.

The events of this morning are still fresh in her mind. Her emotions are running rampant, and it feels like she's on a rollercoaster, flipping and looping. With a deep breath, she takes a step back from the dresser and sits on the edge of the bed. Part of her wants to yell at him, to tell him she told Ed, to tell him how she feels now that it's in the open. The other part of her wants to scream at him to tell him he's such a fucking asshole sometimes, to tell him she's in love with him and has been since their night together. Then, the last part of her just wants to cry.

Her bitter morning pushes through in her tone. "Whose voice did I hear when I called?" she snaps, realizing she sounds just like she did after Eduardo broke the news to her when they started working on their relationship. She can almost hear herself yelling at her husband, ex-husband, separated, whatever they are now. Asking him, where are you going? Who are you talking to? What are you doing?

Tony says, "Iris," too quickly before he can hear how it sounds.

His admission hits her hard and hurts.

"Did she stay over? Fuck you too like she's fucking Bucky?"

"Why do you care?" Tony says. "What's that matter to you? We aren't anything."

"I don't know what we are. We aren't anything right now, but..." But her words fizzle to nothing.

"You said we aren't anything."

"Then, why's it hurt?" Eliza asks but doesn't give Tony time to process what she just said. "You know what, never mind, it doesn't matter to me. You're an adult. You make your own decisions."

"It's not like that," Tony argues in a small voice. "It's not what you think. She came by this morning. She didn't spend the night. It's not like that."

Eliza detects something else in his voice, some sort of longing, a determination like it's a revelation.

"Well, what's it like then?" Eliza asks, sounding harsher than she meant, meaner, but at the same time relief creeps into her voice.

"She wanted to thank me for yesterday," Tony explains. "I gave her the confidence or strength or whatever to do what she needed to do."

"To call off the funeral?"

"Yeah, but it was more than that."

"Like what?"

"Do right by Clyde."

"How can you do right by Clyde?" Eliza asks. "You were pretty much hammered the whole freaking day, yesterday. How could you help? How could looking at your dumb face help anyone?"

"She said that I helped her do the right thing."

"I don't think she knows how to do that," Eliza says. They are off topic. This isn't why she called. She called for a reason. "Tony, listen, I need to tell you something."

But Tony goes on, "She said I made her believe in herself."

"Tony," Eliza says.

But he keeps going like he didn't even hear her. "She brought me Clyde."

"She what?"

"Clyde," Tony says. "Well, his ashes. Brought them over this morning so that I can take him to the Grand Canyon."

"What?" she says. "His ashes? Grand Canyon?"

Tony says, "In a pressure cooker, that's where his ashes... that's where Clyde is, on my counter."

Eliza shuts her eyes and holds her hand tight against her forehead. "Why a pressure cooker?"

"She was explaining that when you called."

He's completely derailed what she was about to say, but she can't put it off any longer. She yells at him, "Tony—just shut the fuck up. Something's happened."

"What's going on? Are you okay?"

No... she's not okay... Eliza wants to tell him about all the ways she's not okay, to tell him about her argument, about how she's finally told Ed, about how he left. About Marque. About Lawrence and Nader. About everything. Her voice comes out as a squeaked plea. "Tony—"

"What's going on?" he asks, rolling through whatever she was going to say.

Eliza takes a deep preparatory breath because it feels like punching him in the gut. That's how it felt for her when Marque called. She speaks quickly. "Lawrence and Nader are dead."

Silence.

"They're what?"

"Dead," Eliza says, taking another wheezing inhale. "They were killed."

Silence.

Then, she hears Tony gulp. "When?"

"Last night."

Silence, again.

Tony tries to understand the news. "What do you mean they're dead?"

"They were shot to death."

"How?"

"That's what all of this is about." Eliza drops the phone to her chest as she leans forward on the dresser, taking a moment. Then, talking down to the wooden surface of the dresser, she says, "I'm calling to tell you they are dead, and it's all hands on deck. I found out this morning. Marque called."

"What happened?"

"There was some sort of shoot-out last night while transporting Franklin Hayes from the hospital to the jail. I don't know many of the details. Actually, I don't know anything. Marque didn't go into details on the phone, but he said there's going to be a meeting. Everyone's expected to be there."

"Do we know who did it?"

"No," she says. "And Tony?"

"Yes."

"Franklin's gone."

CHAPTER TWENTY-THREE:
GENE ORR

GENE IS DRINKING HIS MORNING COFFEE
and sitting at his kitchen table when Kevin steps into
the room, appearing from the stairs on the bedroom side of
the house. "Jesus Christ," Gene exclaims, bolting upright,
jumping in his seat, and spitting the fresh drink back into
the coffee cup. He didn't know Kevin was here, in his
house. He slams his coffee down on the table. "What the
hell? Where did you come from?"

Kevin doesn't answer. He is dressed as always, flat-bill,
black sweatshirt, and baggy blue jeans.

Gene runs his tongue over his teeth, the coffee burnt
his tongue and lip, and he spilled some of the coffee down
the front of his shirt and bumped his knee against the edge
of his kitchen table. Catching himself and fixing his reaction, Gene sits up a little straighter, trying to calm his heart
down, telling himself to pull it together. Don't let Kevin
see him sweat. No need for him to know about Casper.
He can still fix this. Get Casper out without fucking the

kid over. The question is, can he do it without sacrificing himself in the process?

"What are you doing here?"

Kevin slides into a seat at the kitchen table. "You should lock your bedroom window." He throws his upper body across Gene's table and picks up the toothpick holder, selects one toothpick, and pulls it out of the holder. He jams it in the side of his mouth while leaning back in the chair and crossing his legs, getting comfortable.

"Why the fuck should I lock my window?" Gene asks. "It's on the second story." He pulls at the front of his blue shirt with one hand as he spits on the coffee stain. Then, he reaches forward, sets the mug down, and grabs a napkin off the center of the table. He dabs the spot a few times, spitting and rubbing the spot on his shirt.

"Right," Kevin says, removing the toothpick from his mouth as if he's instructing a class, waving the pick around as he talks, conducting a symphony of his own. "That's how I got in. Someone wanting to rob you blind do you some harm... even kill you... that's where they'd come in. I'd guarantee it."

Gene's fingers pause from rubbing vigorously, working the stain, and he glances up without raising his head, "Are you wanting to rob me blind?" He starts rubbing the shirt again.

Kevin shrugs, saying he doesn't know, hasn't decided yet, and puts the toothpick back in the left side of his mouth. "Listen, we need to talk. Now, I've been patient. More so than I'd normally like to be, but I can't be patient no more, you know? We need to talk."

"Oh, that's why you are here?" Gene gives up on the stain. He picks up the mug again. "Because we need to talk? What do we need to talk about?" Gene sips the coffee. It's bitter and he's lost the sensation of taste where he burned his tongue when Kevin appeared.

"Casper. The drives. That's why I'm here."

"I'm disgusted that you've ruined my morning coffee," Gene says, setting the coffee cup down on the table a second time. "So let's do this. Why don't we talk about how you even get in the window? Let's talk about that. What made you think it was okay to come in the window? Come in uninvited?"

Kevin stares at him. "I didn't think you wanted to be seen consorting with me. I climbed your neighbor's fence."

"The fence doesn't come close to my place."

"Their roof does."

"You jumped from one roof to another?"

Kevin nods while using his tongue to push the toothpick from one side of his mouth to the other, which makes a soft sucking noise and a click against his teeth.

Gene takes a deep breath, regaining control of his emotions because he has to play this smoothly. He can't let Kevin know that he tipped Casper, but he also has to string Kevin along just long enough to satisfy him so that he can save Casper. "How do you even do that wearing all that? How do those pants not get stuck on something and rip?"

Kevin uncrosses his legs, dropping his foot on the floor. "A talent."

"It's something."

Kevin says, "You haven't called. You haven't texted. Now, I get it. I do. You want to avoid letting Renaldo on to what's going on. I respect that. Keeping me out of things, arms distance, but I've left you messages. I've called. Texted. Asking where the drives are. Where are the drives?"

"I don't have them."

Kevin throws his toothpick at Gene. "I want the drives."

"That's great and all." Gene pushes the chairs front feet off the floor, playing it smoothly, or trying to—if he were watching this from the outside in, he imagines he looks something like Harrison Ford in *Star Wars* talking to that green alien just before shooting him first when they were bickering about the money. Delivering the line the way Han Solo did, playfully and sardonic, Gene says, "But I don't have them."

"We've talked about this. I need the drives. Last I heard, you were going to go talk with Casper and get them? Did you talk to Casper?"

"I don't have them."

"That doesn't answer my question," Kevin says, leaning forward. "Did you talk to him? That's the question."

"I talked to him." Gene debates how he's going to talk his way out of this one. He could tell Kevin the truth, tell him how Casper's started playing his own game, how he wants to negotiate. Or he could be obtuse and see if he can buy some time to get the drives back from Casper and save them both, but something inside him says if he doesn't play it right, someone's going to end up dead. So he says, "He won't give them up."

"What do you mean he won't give them up?" Kevin asks, "Why not?"

"He's not as dumb as I thought," Gene says.

"So you've talked to him?"

"Yeah, I've talked to him. He figured out we were going to play him, so he's laying low somewhere, but I don't know where. He wouldn't tell me. He said he wants to trade the drives, but when I asked him what he wanted to trade them for, he didn't have a clue as to what he wanted, which is pretty typical of his thinking." Gene touches his temple, tapping his finger against his head. "No forward-thinking with that one. He's all about the now. But he wouldn't give them up."

"What do you mean he wouldn't give them up?" Kevin says. "What's there to give up? He was hired to do a job. He did it. Give us the shit, and he's on his way."

"Except he wasn't ever going to go on his way," Gene says. "You were going to throw him to the wolves so to say. Sacrifice him. Get him killed. He's dumb, but not dumb enough to not see the play coming, and so he said he's taking some steps to keep himself in the game."

"Steps?"

"I don't know what that means. The kid watches too much television. What's important is he feels he's going to be thrown out like bathwater."

Kevin waves his hand in front of his face. "Yeah, but he didn't know that was the plan."

"That doesn't change how he feels."

Kevin stands and stretches, hands massaging his lower back. "I think I pulled something bending over to get in your window."

"Do you want me to call an ambulance?"

Kevin fake laughs. "You think you're funny, but no, I don't need an ambulance. I need to get laid. Take a shit."

He steps around the chair and takes a few steps toward Gene's counter while Gene asks, "In that order or do you prefer to do it all at the same time?"

Kevin doesn't say anything.

Throwing a hand up, Gene adds, "To each his own."

Kevin glances over his shoulder, silent, and then starts to search Gene's cabinets.

Gene, watching from the table, asks, "Can I help you find something?"

"Coffee?" Kevin says, opening one cabinet, rifling through it, before moving on to the next one and letting the doors slam shut, "Looking for a mug."

Gene points. "The mugs are above the sink to the left."

Opening the cabinet and finding what he wanted, Kevin retrieves a coffee mug. He pours himself some coffee. "I need those drives. This whole thing won't work if I don't have them."

"Casper said he hid them," Gene says. "I don't know what that means or where."

"What do you mean he hid them?"

"He took them, and he hid them. He's not as dumb as he looks. What do you mean what do I mean? What does it mean when you hide something?"

"You're not as smart as you pretend?"

"What's that supposed to mean?"

Kevin ignores the question. "Look, things are in motion. I need the drives. Where do you think they are? Excuse me... where do you think he hid them? Any chance of him turning them over to someone else?"

"Like who?"

"The cops."

"I don't know."

"Where is he?"

"I don't know that either," Gene lies.

Kevin pauses to think about Gene's response for a moment. Does he see the lie?

Kevin says, "Okay, well let's try this. What *do* you know?"

"Not a whole hell of a lot." Kevin's normally gray skin gains some pink undertones, showing he's upset. Gene's known Kevin long enough to know this. "Look, I'll get the drives, but I need some time."

Kevin says, "I don't have time to give you. Like I said, this has nothing to do with me. Shit's happening, and shit's rolling. I mean it does have to do with me, but you know what I mean. This has to do with everything that's happening and well ... things are happening. We don't have time to fuck around. I need those drives. It's bad enough that the girl wasn't there to get kidnapped, that would have distracted the spic fucker, but things change. We did what we should have done—adjusted. But still, things have to happen, and I need the drives to make that happen. I'm on a time limit here," he taps his wrist as if he were wearing a watch, "tick-tock, tick-tock. I'm running out of time and patience."

"What are you leaning on me for? Go find Casper. I've done everything you asked. If you want to make a power play, make it. What do you need the drives for? What do you need me for?"

"You're the kid's protector," Kevin says, but by the way he says it, it doesn't sound right. It sounds like he's implying something.

"What's with you?" Gene asks. "Just because... because you and I didn't work out... doesn't mean I'm banging the kid."

"I didn't say that."

"No, but you just heavily implied it."

"You think I have hard feelings about us not working out." Kevin pauses to take a drink and sets the mug down. "Why would you think that? Man, I came to you because I trust you. I told you what's going on because we're friends. You and I... that's the past...we work better as friends anyways."

"Friends."

"Business associates, what the fuck do you want from me?"

"I want to know why you're putting the pressure on me. I want to know that I'm not getting fucked here. I want to know that whatever move you're making or not making isn't going to end up with me in a ditch somewhere."

Kevin's eyes flare. "It's not."

"What do you need the drives for?" Gene asks.

"To prove Reni's ambition."

"What ambition? The fact that he's doing his own thing, fucking some girl? What are you proving that isn't already out there? Isn't you doing this proving you have ambition too?"

"Not the same," Kevin says. "Not that type of ambition. I have a different type. There's a huge difference between a *yes* man who wants the corner office and a parking space, and the guy that wants to kick the boss off the top floor—I simply want to enjoy the finer things in life."

"It's not the same? What's the difference? Ambition's ambition."

Kevin moves to the table to stand behind one of the chairs; his fingers drum against the back of the chair.

"No, what I'm doing and what he's done are two different things," Kevin says. "Siriano will see the difference... *does* see the difference. I mean, here's this spic fucker, this guy that's worked his way up to the second position in a highly powerful criminal organization, who is not only not content with how things are going but wants to take advantage of the boss being locked up. Like, doesn't he know who he's dealing with? You know we've heard Renaldo trying to get someone in prison to shank the boss? That shit makes it back to the boss. No? Well, he's over here talking shit and then trying to start up his own network of guys while bonking a government employee's wife—a DEA agent at that."

"How do you know all that?" Gene asks.

Kevin snorts. "She brought him to those poker games. He cut her out, but she didn't seem upset about it. So, why's she not upset about it? I'll tell you why." Kevin lifts the mug toasting Gene as if he's about to make a major point. "The guy goes to the DEA agent's funeral, which mind you is fucking bold. So, he's not only there but sitting in the front row."

"How do you know this?" Gene asks, but Kevin just smiles. "Did you go to the funeral?"

"Would it matter if I did?"

"I told you when you started this, it wasn't a good idea. There's only so many ways this goes right, and so far, nothing's gone right."

"Just because you got a dumb fuck that doesn't know when to die," Kevin complains.

"The way I see it." Gene leans forward to retrieve his mug and takes a drink. "Casper can't die now, not yet, not if he's hidden the drives."

"Oh, I'm not going to kill him."

"Renaldo might."

Kevin laughs once. "Renaldo's got bigger problems."

"Like you fucking him over?"

"Yes, but I'm not the only one."

"Let me ask you," Gene says, sipping the coffee again. He's been thinking about all this because something's been bothering him about Kevin's little plan. "How are you going to pull off this coup of yours? What legitimizes your position? Like I get that you can knock Renaldo off and then take his place as second in command, but what makes you think Siriano's going to go for that?"

Kevin's lips curl into a smile. "What makes you think I'm knocking Renaldo off for myself?"

"What do you mean?"

"I told you, things are happening. I need those drives to make them happen, but there's other things happening. You don't act like Renaldo's been acting without making a few enemies."

"Enemies like you?"

"Enemies like some people make when they do too much business and overextend themselves."

"There's already a dead DEA agent," Gene says. "How many other people are going to have to die before you get Renaldo pushed out?"

"Don't put that on me," Kevin says. "Frankie wasn't supposed to shoot anyone. Remember, the plan was to do the deal, put the DEA on Siriano, blame Renaldo, and let the dominos tumble. But to make all that work, I need the drives to hammer home Renaldo's incompetence."

Gene takes a sip of the coffee and leans back in the chair. "But that didn't happen. You don't have them."

"No, it didn't." Then, quiet for a moment, Kevin states, "I don't have them, but I need them."

Gene reminds Kevin. "Death touches everyone. What are you going to do if Renaldo sees what's happening?"

"Handle it."

"And if Frankie figures out you fucked him?"

"Luckily, I don't have to worry about that. Frankie's going down for that DEA fucker. Sucks, I like him, we're friends, been friends for a while, but it is what it is."

"Just going to throw people away casually?"

Kevin shrugs. "Hey, it's business. Business is business. He'll understand." He opens the back door because he can't be bothered to leave like a normal person.

But before Kevin leaves, Gene says, "You sure about that?"

CHAPTER TWENTY-FOUR:
FRANKLIN HAYES

FRANKLIN SIPS HIS WHISKEY not saying anything, eyes closed, savoring the moment—it may be one of his last—the whiskey's bitter against his tongue. Nina Simone's *Wild is the Wind* plays on the stereo next to him, turned up loud, letting the jazz fill the room.

Seated on Vera's couch, staring out the balcony door of Vera's third-story apartment and watching the sunrise off in the distance as the morning passes into day, Franklin lets the music flow over him, soothing his troubled mind—troubled because decisions have to be made... hard ones. And then things have to be done. The music is filled with melancholy, and the sound exerts a certain gravity on the space, weighing the room and the mood down.

Leon stirs on the couch next to him. Leon's bare arm and hand are draped across his naked midsection, and he's wearing one of Vera's ex-boyfriend's t-shirts around his neck, which is hanging loosely over his chest, arms not in the sleeves. His wounds are dressed in nice white cotton and duct tape. Leon swallows hard and keeps his eyes shut.

Vera patched up Leon as best she could, telling Franklin the man needed a hospital, but she could stop the bleeding and make him comfortable. She did that. Then, she put the music on and told him that she had to get back to the hospital before disappearing to the back bedroom to get dressed. Now, she's dressed in purple scrubs and saying, "I signed up for a double because I thought I would be watching you, but with you not there and the mess pasted across the morning news stations, I don't want to bring any attention to myself. Have to pretend things are normal."

Franklin tells her that's for the best. "Get to work. I'll be here when you get back."

Except that's a lie. He won't be here.

Vera kisses him on the cheek. He kisses her back on the mouth.

Vera leans into him. "I'll be back as soon as I can. I'll play like I don't feel good. Take a sick day. Come home."

And then Vera's out the door. He watches her go. When the door shuts, Franklin takes a sip of the whiskey. "It's a shame."

With sleepy eyes and gritted teeth, Leon grimaces and fights whatever pain he's feeling, he says, "What's a shame?" He shuffles his body up on the couch, awake now.

"I like that girl," Franklin says. "I've never met anyone like her. She's something special. At first, I befriended her because she was pretty. Thought I could use her, but she's something, you know? Really something."

Leon's fingers fiddle with the edge of the tape on his stomach, nails scrunching one of the corners while the pad of his finger smooths it again. "She has the touch."

Franklin, dressed in the extra paramedic uniform he found in the ambulance and wearing the dead man's shoes, turns his head to look at Leon's dressings, blood seeps through the white cotton. "You're bleeding. You need a hospital."

"No," Leon says. "You know what it's like. I can't go there. They'll call the cops. Then, it's going to be how'd you get shot? What were you doing? Where did it happen? They'll be expecting me to come in."

"Man, you're going to be bleeding all over this poor woman's couch if you don't do something about it."

Leon considers this and dismisses Franklin with a half-wave of the hand. "She can change them when I get back."

"You may not make it that long."

Leon drops his head to his chest and rolls it to the side slightly. To Franklin, this man's dying; he just doesn't know it yet. Franklin says, "Look, about your brother—"

Leon lifts his hand from his lap cutting him off, fingers still darkened with dirt from the road. "Don't."

"No, I need to say this."

"Don't! I don't want to hear it. He's dead."

"I liked your brother."

"You missed the funeral," Leon says, chuckling to himself, causing pain.

Franklin laughs. "I bet there were Black & Mild's everywhere."

Leon pauses. "Don't sit here and tell me you liked my brother. Don't lie to me. He was an idiot. Look at how he got himself killed."

"I'm not lying to you. If I say I like someone, I like someone. What kind of bullshit is that? I'm over here trying to explain to you that I feel bad your brother was killed, and you're over there telling me no, don't talk about it. What kind of shit is that? I feel responsible."

"That's because you are," Leon says, bitterness in his words. "But I just don't want to think about it right now."

"I do."

Leon risks pain to lift his head in a defiant look.

Franklin looks right back at him while sipping his whiskey. He swallows and says, "Yeah, I know what you were trying to do. I know why you got shot. You can sit there, and you can tell me your stories about going after that man and saving me, but we both know that's bullshit and not why you were there. I didn't know it at first, but now I've had time to think about it. I've had a drink. Had some quiet. Listened to good music. You know, relax. My mind's worked it over, turning it this way and that. I know what you were doing."

"And what's that?" Leon leans away from Franklin, daring him. "What was I doing?"

"I'll tell you; you weren't there for Renaldo."

"No?"

"No, because I've heard about you," Franklin says, returning the stare. "Stevie would talk about you. Tell me these stories. How you can be violent and how you were like this professional killer. Like *Leon the Professional.* You see it? With a baby Natalie Portman? Fucking Gary Oldman? You see it?"

"Missed that one."

"Now that's a lie," Franklin says. "Guy going around with a reputation like you, named Leon, not having seen the movie with a guy with a name like yours. That's a bald-faced lie if I've ever seen one. See, Stevie loved you. The way he talked about you all the time. He thought you were the bee's knees and other redneck cracker bullshit. It's that movie with that French dude who takes young Natalie on as a protégée after she witnesses her family murdered. Weird movie, really; couldn't be made today. Some majorly pedo-overtones. And Oldman's Oldman, you know? Way over the top. Like his career's the opposite of Pacino's. Like he's going backward... from loud to quiet where Al's getting all loud and BANG! Hooah!" He does his bombastic impersonation of Pacino. "Later on in his career, but you know, he started subdued, intense, a simmering fury. Like in his first big movie. You see it in the *Godfather*. Man, I watched that movie every Friday night with my best friend growing up. We wanted to be that. Those guys."

"That's Hollywood bullshit."

"It's what we did."

"It's bullshit. Things don't work that way."

"You know what, you're right," Franklin says. "Crime don't work that way. Not anymore. No, my friend and I, we figured that out." He pauses to take a drink, finishing off the glass, savoring the experience. "Not for people like us—me black and him a fucking fairy."

Franklin pops to his feet in a sudden flurry of movement. "Crime works differently now, you know? Less structured. Less connected. But don't let anyone ever tell you it ain't organized."

Franklin floats toward the wet bar, which is a converted TV stand with some bottles and a bucket of ice stolen from a cheap motel. The whole time, Leon's eyes stay fixed on him. Motioning to Leon with his glass, he goes on. "Except for me, I don't work for others," he continues. "I'm in business for myself. Business oh... it can be so sweet. Stevie was with me. Like a driver. Like he's driving Miss

Daisy, but I'm Miss Daisy, me, the black man, and him the driver—a fucking hillbilly Morgan Freeman, giving his opinion on this and that, fucking annoying at times."

Leon chuckles to himself. "Stevie couldn't drive worth shit."

"I'll toast to that," Franklin says as he fills a new glass with whiskey, spilling some of the whiskey over the rim. With the bottle in his hand, he turns suddenly, raises the glass, and toasts to Leon. "Couldn't drive to save his life— so to say," amusement stretches across his face, "but he was loyal. I'll give him that. You should know, when it mattered, he went for his gun. Now, at the time, I didn't understand what was happening. I was struggling for my life."

"You and the cop?"

"Me and the cop." Franklin turns back to the table, setting the bottle down. He closes his eyes and rocks his head to the music beat, taps his foot right along with it. "That was a mistake. I guess before what's about to happen, happens, you should know that. Maybe deep down you do know that." Franklin shrugs. "Maybe you don't."

"What happens?"

Opening his eyes, Franklin stomps his foot, with finality. "Stop that."

"Stop what?" Leon asks while trying to sit up on the couch.

"Stop pretending what was going to happen wasn't going to happen. Stop pretending,"—He draws the word out. "All you're doing is just delaying the inevitable, and personally, I don't know about you, I don't like the suspense."

"What are you wanting me to say?" Leon asks.

"You don't know?" Franklin asks, sweetening his words as he steps forward, sipping on the glass.

"Thank you for saving me."

"We both know I was saving myself, but I'll accept the apology because you are welcome." Franklin standing and playing to the room, to the wounded man, who only stares blankly up at him.

"Then, what do you want me to say?"

Franklin drops his head, shaking it side to side. "You really don't know, do you?"

"No," Leon says.

Franklin becomes animated again. "All right, let's try it this way: I'm sorry for Stevie's death. Yes, I'm sorry. I've apologized. I didn't intend for Stevie to die. Stevie died because I was fucking with the cop, putting that gun in his face, saying, listen motherfucker I know you're a cop."

"Did you know?"

Franklin slaps his side. "I had no idea. I mean, you always suspect such a thing, suspect someone could be a cop. You feel it. It's like before it rains, a pressure, a certain apprehension when it comes down to working with someone and unless you've seen that person do some truly fucked up shit you never know. I like to test people. I test their patience. I test their resolve. I test their loyalty—"

"Like my brother?"

"I tested him," Franklin says, nodding. "I made him mad. I put him through hell. You know, one of the last things he said to me was that he wanted to be my friend. Wanted to know what was going on in my life. I think that's sweet. I've thought a lot about it when I was in the hospital. Stevie wanted to know what was happening to me, despite all the shit I said to him, despite how I treated him, fucking give the man a cigarillo and some whiskey," he examines the glass, "like this one, and he'd be happy. Smoked like a fucking chimney... really I couldn't stand it."

"Then, why'd you have him around?"

"Because he was a good person," Franklin comments. "Not in the moralistic view of things. No, he wasn't doing the right thing. He'd just as soon drive by you broken down on the highway than stop to help. He littered. He fucking loved being loud. He smelled awful. But he was good to have around. There was a certain gravitas to the way he did things." Franklin bending over, flexing his shoulders and chest the way a bodybuilder would, showing Stevie's girth. "He was a big boy if you know what I mean, but most importantly..." He lets his voice trail off as if he's asking a question without asking.

"...he was my brother," Leon says.

Franklin clicks his tongue against his cheek and points at Leon, making pistol fingers. "Bingo goes the doggie-o. He was your brother. The brother of Leon Gragg, the boogeyman, a regular John Wick-redneck-hillbilly-white-trash-motherfucker. If someone could upstage Keanu, it'd be you. Out there head shootin' people."

Franklin's body shivers from his knees up to his waist, to his chest, arms flapping out, and then to his neck. Then, Franklin looks at Leon, a stare really; eyes are the windows to the soul.

And Leon stares back.

"I wasn't there for Renaldo," he finally says.

Franklin cups his hand to his ear. "I didn't hear you. Say it again."

Leon narrows his eyes. "I wasn't there for Renaldo."

"Good, you see where this is going." Franklin pauses to take another drink. "But no, I'm not going to do the talking in this little confession. Does the priest tell people about their transgressions? A counselor tell people what their parents did to them? A parent about why the kid wanted the cookie from the jar? No. You have to say it. I want to hear it. You want to say it. Let's speak up here. After all, we're friends."

"We are not friends," Leon says.

"Funny, that's what your brother told me just before he died. He said we weren't friends. Said I didn't confide in him. Said some other things, but you know, that's all kind of been negated with everything that's happened since."

Leon says, "I was going to kill you."

"There we go." Franklin paces in front of Leon on the couch.

Leon tracks Franklin side to side. "Then, I was going to kill Renaldo."

"That was your plan. No mistake," Franklin says. "Things didn't go right. They never do, not after you meet the enemy, and let me tell you, I know how fucking annoying cops can be, especially when it comes to executing your plans."

"But if I hadn't intervened, you'd be dead."

"The way I see it, I was still strapped to that bed when they busted in on me in the ambulance. Renaldo, with a rifle, ready to use that itchy finger of his." Franklin wags his index finger with the glass hand. "But it wasn't you who put a stop to it. It was some other beaner fuck who put the gun to Renaldo's head and pulled the trigger." Franklin reaches into the bag from the ambulance and withdraws Larry's gun. "He put the gun to his head," he says and closes

the distance to Leon, with the glass in one hand and the gun in the other. He places the muzzle against Leon's head to demonstrate what happened. "Like this, putting it right here and Renaldo... he didn't know what was happening. I think that's not fair... guy not knowing why he's about to die. He should know. I want you to know."

Leon says, "Because is business..." and his voice fizzles out. He could say more, and he should. They'll be his last words, but he doesn't.

"Business is business, motherfucker," Franklin says, pausing to sip the whiskey. "But if you don't stop a man trying to kill you then that man's still going to try to kill you." What he's about to do has nothing to do with business. "And when a man tries to kill you, it stops being business; it's all personal."

Leon closes his eyes. Leon knows he's right.

Franklin pulls the trigger; he doesn't hear the gun. He blinks a few times after, generating mental pictures of the scene, which isn't as gruesome as TV makes it out to be. Some blood on the wall behind him, but mainly, Leon, sitting, shirt wrapped around his body, head slumped against his chest, blood pouring out.

With that done, Franklin finishes the whiskey with one strong gulp, turns away from the scene with the ringing in his ears, and crosses the small room. He sets the gun down on the TV stand, gets a refill of whiskey and sips it, and thinks about what comes next.

No. Not what. Who.

CHAPTER TWENTY-FIVE:

RENALDO LUNA

RENALDO BLINKS, gulps, and takes in his surroundings: a nurse off to his side, wearing purple scrubs, types on a computer, a shapely woman, but not bad looking, her eyes say hello at seeing him awake. The rest of the room is out of focus and blurry, tan and cream colors, with machines, and a strident antiseptic smell. Renaldo blinks a few more times, trying to order his mind.

The nurse says, "Oh good, you're awake."

"What ... where?" Renaldo tries to ask, but the questions die in his throat.

"Hospital," the nurse says as she pushes the computer away and gives him her attention. "I'm Vera, your nurse." She tucks a strand of hair behind her ear, her face a mask of friendliness and concern.

Renaldo surveys his body. No straps. No cuffs. No nothing. "How did I?"

The last few moments of his memory flash through his mind like the blast of the gunshot. Pablo turning on him, delivering the message, and carrying out the act.

Alejandro, how could he? Why would he do this to him?

"Police found you. Brought you in," Vera explains. She laughs to herself as if she's enjoying an inside joke. "Anyways, they were worried about you."

"What happened?"

Sliding off the stool, Vera stands and steps next to the whiteboard with his name on it. "Renaldo Luna, correct?"

Renaldo nods and pain starbursts behind his eyes. "How'd you know?"

"You're lucky," Vera says as she crosses the room to check his vitals. She withdraws a blood pressure cuff and affixes it to his arm to manually take his blood pressure. "Shot in the head." She affixes the ear portion of her stethoscope to her ears.

Renaldo touches the side of his head, expecting to find bandages, but nothing. Instead, he finds rough skin, puffy to the touch, as he explores the stitches.

Vera squeezes the bulb inflating the cuff and holds the stethoscope to his arm. "They had to shave your head to do the stitches and clean up the wound, but hair grows back."

"Yeah, sure, okay," Renaldo says, retracting his fingers from the side of his head. He closes his eyes while she finishes taking his blood pressure. The lights in the room are too bright, and now that he's awake, he notices the slight tolling pain, wafting at the edges of his psyche.

"Headache?" Vera asks.

Renaldo doesn't open his eyes. Just nods.

306

"You have a concussion. Probably a pretty bad one since you've been out of it for the last couple hours, but you did get shot in the head, so I'd consider that a win—waking up only having pain that is." She laughs to herself, softly.

"Shot in the head?" Renaldo asks. His mind returns to the moment Pablo pulled the trigger. Franklin's face was just as surprised as he was. Renaldo reflexively leaned back at the last second. Then nothing.

"Do you remember how that happened?"

"No," Renaldo lies. "Where are the police?"

"They said something about holding on to you, but that meant an officer had to hang out here and wait for you to wake up. They weren't interested in that. Figured you weren't going anywhere anytime soon, so they left a card. I'm supposed to call them when you wake up. Or the doctor is, that is."

"You going to call them?"

"I have to call the doctor first," she says. That doesn't answer his question. He opens his eyes and glances at her as she explains. "The doctor's going to have to clear you first. Head trauma and all. I'm still amazed you're alive."

"Yeah, me too," Renaldo says.

"As far as how we got your name," Vera says, "I hope you don't mind, but one of the other nurses called a contact in your phone. That's how we know your name. She was up here until just a little while ago. She said she had to run an errand. Go change clothes. Or that's what the other nurse told me. I just got here." Vera motions to the computer and continues talking. "I was just updating everything."

"Concussion?"

"I'll let the doctor explain it to you. You know, give it to you in doctor speak. They have a particular way of saying

things, and I don't want you to believe I'm practicing medicine or something outside of my duties. After all, I'm just a lowly nurse... ha... but the way it was explained to me was the bullet entered here," she touches her temple, then traces her finger across her forehead, "hit your skull, deflected, went along here, and exited here."

Renaldo says, "I'm not dead."

Her lips stretch into a kind and pleasant smile. "No, you are not dead."

"I thought I was dead."

"We thought you were dead too," she says. "A gunshot to the head isn't something a lot of people survive, but you'd be surprised how many times it happens. Kind of amazing. A miracle, you know?"

Renaldo nods again, this time the pain fades some. "Yeah, sure, okay. A miracle. That's a way to put it."

"Only way it makes sense."

Someone knocks and both Renaldo and Vera turn to see who it is. Iris says hello while leaning against the door-frame. She's wearing a white t-shirt and blue jeans with her hair pulled back and no make-up, her face full of concern.

"May I come in?" Iris asks not stepping into the room. Renaldo's not sure if she's asking him or the nurse. "You okay?"

Vera nods for him and says he just woke up.

Renaldo wants to speak, but his mind's elsewhere, processing how he's feeling, or better, what he's feeling. The realization hits him that somewhere along the way he fell in love with Iris, which isn't much of a surprise considering how defensive he's been about this whole deal and why he's not wanted Siriano to know about her, but still... when did that happen?

Vera smiles brightly again, saying, of course, she can come in, and she takes the blood pressure cuff off Renaldo's arm and steps back toward the computer.

Vera taps on the computer keyboard a few times and then excuses herself, saying she's going to call the doctor and have him come up to check on him. Iris tiptoes into the room. After an awkward silence, Renaldo's eyes shift from the door to Iris as she comes to his side. "I'm sorry I wasn't here when you woke up." She reaches out to touch his shoulder.

"It's okay," Renaldo says, shrugging away. "I..."

What was he going to say? What is there to say?

Iris says, "I had to run an errand. I... I needed to change clothes too. I went home and tried to hurry back here."

"I didn't think...," he starts. "I'm surprised to see you."

Her cheeks blush a pale red. "Reni, I care about you."

"I wasn't aware of it; that's all." Renaldo turns away from her because his emotions are a swirling mess.

Iris strokes his arm. "I wanted to make sure you were okay."

"I'm okay," he says. "I think. Actually, I don't know. I got shot in the head. Can I be okay?"

"You don't have to be okay."

"I don't feel okay."

"What's wrong?"

Renaldo wants to confide in her, but what's he going to say? His mentor ordered his death and betrayed him? How's she supposed to process that? What could she say to make that better? What is there to say?

"I feel so alone," he admits. He is alone. As alone as he has always been.

"I'm here for you." Her voice is soft and full of concern.

"Yeah, sure, okay," Renaldo says. "I appreciate that. Don't think that I don't."

"But there's something else going on?"

"Things are just difficult right now. There's a lot going on."

She chortles. "You're telling me."

"How did the rest of yesterday go?" Renaldo asks. "I was surprised you did what you did, but I guess I understand it. If the person I was married to wanted something to happen and that wasn't happening, I guess I could see myself doing what you did ... standing up for myself. But I might have done that before the room was full of people."

Iris smiles. "It was hard."

"I'm glad I could be there to help."

Iris pauses. "Me too."

"When did they call you?" he asks. "The nurses, what time?"

"This morning ... early. I was playing poker, so I was awake. I haven't slept in two days."

"You need sleep."

"I could say the same thing about you," Iris says. "They say that's the best medicine for a head injury. Sleep and rest."

"My vision's a bit screwy, but everything seems to be okay, I think."

"Have you tried to walk yet, stand?" she asks.

He tells her he hasn't. "What errand did you have to do?"

Iris pauses before answering. "Clyde, I needed to drop him off with Tony... Antonio." She half-laughs at herself as she purrs his full name. "Clyde wanted to be taken to the Grand Canyon."

"His body?" Renaldo asks.

"Ashes," she says, but before Renaldo can ask for an explanation, she places her hand on his chest. "He wanted to be taken there. I'm not going to do it. Maybe if someone made me, but left to my own, that's not my thing. That's not me."

"But that's Tony?"

"Tony would have done anything for Clyde."

"Did Clyde ever talk about work?" he asks. He might as well see what she knows. That's why he was in this relationship in the first place.

Iris retracts her hand. She lifts her chin toward him and looks into his eyes. He looks back, putting emotion in his eyes, not hard to do because he loves her, but he sees the truth in her eyes—she doesn't love him. She can't. It's not in her. It's not her nature.

"He didn't like to talk about it. He didn't want to be a... he just didn't talk about it," she says.

Renaldo nods, which causes a slight shifting of pressure in his skull.

Iris adds, "He did say Tony set up the whole thing."

"What thing?"

"The thing that got him killed. Said Tony set it up. It was his informant. Clyde just ran the operation. Tony's informant set it up. That's the last thing Clyde told me."

"Who's Tony's informant?" he asks.

"Some pawnshop owner said Tony's worked him for years, said he'd get the guy's kid or something to set up the deal."

"Kid?"

Iris shakes her head. "Clyde wasn't clear on the details. Something about the meet. I don't know. Might be why a young man is sleeping in Tony's house. Maybe Tony's protecting him, you know, since everything went to shit."

"Wait, what?"

"When I was at his house dropping Clyde off, Tony got a phone call, and while he was talking on the phone, I peeked in the guest bedroom because the door was open. And, well, I'm curious about Tony. I wanted to see more of what he's like. You know the things he doesn't show people."

———

IRIS STICKS AROUND FOR A FEW HOURS, but when she dozes off lying in the bed next to him, Renaldo wakes her up with a gentle nudge and tells her to go home and get some sleep. She nods with heavy eyes and says she would be back.

Once she is gone, Renaldo picks up the phone and makes the call he's dreaded since regaining consciousness. It rings once and then the line picks up. No hello. No nothing. Just an expectant void, waiting for him to speak first.

"Alejandro," Renaldo says, leaning back in the bed, stretching the coiled cord out, his head against the pillow. "It's me."

The line remains quiet for a long moment, and finally, Alejandro's voice, not surprised, states, "You're alive."

"Yeah, sure, okay," Renaldo says, trying to figure out what else to say to the man who ordered his death. "A miracle they tell me."

"A miracle… you could call it that."

Renaldo doesn't know what he expected the old man to say. Maybe explain. Tell him why. Give him a reason.

Any reason. What was his transgression? What did he do to his mentor to warrant such a betrayal?

But nothing. Just silence.

Then, Alejandro clears his throat. "Is there a reason for this call? Or were you simply informing me Pablo failed?"

"What I want to know is why? Why did you do it? Why did you order it?"

Alejandro repeats the question in a quiet voice so familiar and reassuring to Renaldo in his youth, but now it sounds callous and uncaring, nearly mocking. "Why? Why? Why? Deep down, you must know why? Think hard, Reni, why do you think it happened?"

"Did Siriano get to you?"

"*No!*" the old man says. "But the time was right, so I made the call. I want you to know this business had nothing to do with your business or your white man and was very much personal to me. Painful if you must know. But that's how decisions like this go. Good men sometimes die to serve other needs. Someone's making a play against you, this we agree. Unfortunate for you. But whatever turbulent tide has washed you upon my shores once again is a transgression that cannot go unpunished."

"You were like a father to me," he says. Alejandro was more, a mentor, a teacher. Renaldo was like his son.

"And you are no longer," Alejandro says, wearily, crumbling to Spanish and remaining there. "I am no longer a father to you or a mentor. You made this clear. I am nothing to you, so you are nothing to me."

Renaldo cringes. "I'm glad to know you ordered my death. Glad to know it was painful and personal. I can hear how distressed you must feel at knowing I survived."

Alejandro half-laughs. "Don't act self-righteous. You asked for this."

"Asked for this? How did I ask for this?"

"And if I must be honest, part of me gladdens at hearing your voice. I did not wish for this to happen, but events rarely follow intention. You have no idea what pain this has caused me. But your impudence couldn't go on, not after all that has happened."

"Impudence?"

"You left me," Alejandro says, tone harsh. "You left me to go work for the white man. I told you not to go, but you ignored me. Then, gone, you don't come visit. No calls. You never acknowledged me in your rise in the white man's kingdom, making me feel like that man young Henry ignored. Made me feel like your own personal Flagstaff. You go off to your new kingdom of power and glory groveling at the gout-ridden feet of your king, leaving me and mine behind as if we never existed ... your mother included. But then you come back in your moment of trouble and great need—the kingdom is threatened—asking *me* for *my help*, like your time away, your exile from home was nothing, asking me to help you handle a problem you created for yourself."

"That's not what happened," Renaldo argues, but even before the words leave his mouth, he knows Alejandro's complaints are warranted.

"It is what happened, Reni," Alejandro says. "You are an arrogant young man who ignored those who raised him, casting us aside at the moment it served your ambitions, but when you needed help, we were the first you chose to visit. It's insulting. You were everything I ever dreamed of having in a son, an heir. I am old. My time is short. What I have built was to be yours. Yours, Reni! But you abandoned me. You cast my humble influence to the side because it was not what you foresaw for yourself. And to tell you the harsh truth, it is not what I foresaw for you either. You were everything I wasn't. But you ignored me. And you only came to me when you had nowhere else to turn. Your problems are your problems. You know what I've always told you about a man treading water. I taught you better than this."

Renaldo mumbles, "A man that treads water drowns slowly."

"You must pick a direction and swim. But you chose to drown, so drown."

CHAPTER TWENTY-SIX:

TONY MORA

ONY SITS AT THE CONFERENCE TABLE
next to the windows in a black low-slung swivel chair,
which squeaks under his weight, dressed in blue jeans
and a white t-shirt. He senses Eliza's eyes on him as she
enters the conference room, and she struts around the
large cherry red table and sits in the seat next to him. The
chair snags Marque's attention who is at the head of the
table, standing, dressed in a black suit. He glances up at
Tony as Tony ignores Eliza's judging eyes. Marque doesn't
speak and continues to shuffle his papers preparing for the
briefing, flicking eyes down.

Just a few weeks ago they met here to talk about the
operation at McDonald's. Clyde led the meeting then,
pointing to the whiteboard like a teacher in school, giving
everyone their positions. Larry and Nader cracked jokes
about Franklin's knock-off shoes and how Gene Orr's
pushing the shoes is further proof the guy's a rat. Tony
told them Gene's not a rat, just an informant. Eliza said

it was the same thing. Clyde told Tony, "You're in the car." Clyde laid the whole thing out, talking about what would happen if things went bad... all of that seems so long ago.

Now, the last to arrive, Eli Buchanan shoulders his way into the room like a bull entering an arena, carrying a large folder and a laptop and huffing, dressed in a nice cool suit, electric blue, dark hair stiff against his forehead. He joins Marque at the end of the table.

Bucky nods his head, giving the cue to begin.

Marque glances at his assistant and gives a silent command. She removes the doorstop from the door. The door shuts with a click. The projector whines to life, and its bulb illuminates the whiteboard in a ghostly glow. Marque clicks a button, and the slides of the PowerPoint change in time to Bucky's presentation as he lays the whole thing out. "TPD is taking point on this investigation," he says. "It happened in their city, and you all aren't homicide dicks. FBI assisting, but I don't know what their Special Agent in Charge is going to make of this. We've lost three brothers, and I'm asking this office to stay out of any investigation for the time being and focus on mental health. You all need to mourn and heal."

Both Bucky and Marque glance at Tony.

Marque clicks the remote and the computer whirs as the PowerPoint shows the street outside the hospital, and Bucky breaks down what happened: "Nader was in the passenger seat of the ambulance. Larry in the back. Gunmen disabled the vehicle here in this intersection. They had rifles. No cameras. No witnesses. Nothing. Something happened, but investigators don't know what. Whoever got Nader didn't give him a chance to exit the vehicle. Shot him dead. Larry's a different deal. Larry was able to shoot back. But we don't know if he got any of them. Didn't look like it. Renaldo Luna was found at the foot of the ambulance, shot in the head. Don't know what his involvement is, but Matthew Elizondo, aka Mastodon, was found dead on the east side of the ambulance. Elizondo is a known associate of Luna's. He was shot in the head; we don't know who did that. Investigators believe a third-party but are not sure yet. The gunshot to Luna's head didn't kill him. He's at the hospital now. We can't hold him because we don't know if he was involved... even though we know he was involved. Nothing on the crash vehicle. Stolen yesterday. Larry's gun and other effects are gone, and Franklin didn't stick around. Currently, we're working on a warrant to ping Larry's phone to get a location. Maybe we can get Franklin back and get some answers."

So, they have nothing but dead bodies and questions.

Eliza kicks the underside of Tony's seat to get his attention. "What are you supposed to be today?" she asks, gesturing at his clothes. "I told you to dress nice. You look like you stepped out of a cigarette ad from the fifties. Is this a look? What the fuck are you wearing?"

"I'm wearing clothes," Tony says. He doesn't understand how his wardrobe could elicit such a strong response. "And what do you care? I'm supposed to be off, so I guess I look like a guy that's off" He runs his hand over his chin, highlighting the stubble.

"You look like you just rolled out of the trash," Eliza says. "You know, I thought you having that beanbag chair would be a bad idea, seeing you got it confused with a trash bag."

Tony can tell she's upset about something. He says, "What's wrong with this? I look nice. I put on clean clothes. What else do you want from me?"

"How about you look like a fucking adult."

"That's a bit harsh."

"I'm all out of sweetness."

Tony scoots his chair away from her and rubs the base of his neck, processing what she just told him. "You sound better when you cuss."

Bucky slaps the table. "Tony, Eliza, anything you'd like to share with the group?" he asks.

Tony glances back at Eliza. He says nothing.

But not Eliza, she leans forward in the chair, glancing at Tony as if to say watch this. "Yes, actually there's something I'd like to share."

Tony swivels in his chair to watch Eliza as she pushes her chair back and struggles to her feet. The pregnancy's getting to her, limiting her mobility. Somehow she looks more pregnant than yesterday. Certainly more tired.

Under the confines of his taut electric blue suit seams, Bucky stares at her as she struggles to her full short height. He says, "Well what is it?"

With her hands on her hips to support the weight in her midsection, Eliza asks, "Did you have sex with Clyde's wife?"

Bucky coughs, choking on the sudden lack of oxygen in the room. Tony almost falls out of his chair. Marque simply looks down.

Eliza smiles. "I ask because, if you did, that's a huge issue when it comes to talking about her boy toy on the side, Renaldo Luna, and going after Siriano, and it raises some interesting questions about your character."

With his eyes locked on her, Bucky swallows and exclaims, "Excuse me?"

Marque says in a quiet voice, "Give us the room," but no one moves. Marque half stands, hands flat on the table, and with more force, "Give us the room," shaking the others out of their stupor. The others glance at each other, and then one by one, they stand, gather their things, and exit.

The room empties.

Eliza says to Bucky, "You should be excused. Like from this conversation. I'm asking a simple question."

"That's not a simple question," Bucky says. "That's inflammatory, and I don't understand what bearing it has on this meeting."

Eliza waddles to the side toward the door and yanks on the string for the blinds, shutting out the rest of the world. "It has a great amount of bearing on this meeting."

Bucky smashes his lips together. "How so?"

"You just have to answer that question first," Eliza says.

Bucky starts, "Why do I—"

"—because I'm sick of all the bullshit. We've lost three friends, I had a shitty ass morning, and I just don't fucking care what you have to say anymore," Eliza declares, shaking. Tears form at the corners of her eyes, and her normally pale cheeks redden. Her whole body trembles with rage and passion at the accusation.

Bucky observes the body shake too and sees the involuntary movement as some sort of sign that he's in control. He sees her emotions as a weakness. A satisfactory grin sweeps across his face. "Well, if you don't care what I have to say, why does my answer matter?"

"It matters."

"How so?" he asks, visibly pushing his outrage down into the soles of his feet, trying his best to keep a calm appearance even if he's a few shades brighter.

Instead of stepping toward her, as he would normally do in a conversation, as he does in the courtroom when he's challenged, his raging hulk to her delicate flower, he decides the better thing for him is to sit at the table, stay calm. Normal. Controlled.

Bucky nods a few times, extracts a seat from the table. Eliza waits for him to take his seat next to Marque, even waits for Bucky to pour himself a glass of water and take a sip before speaking again

"Answer the question," Tony says.

Bucky swallows hard and puts the glass down on the table, placing both hands, palms down, on the surface next to the glass ... buying time. With his large hands resting on the table, Bucky shifts his gaze toward Tony and slowly enunciates the next words. "Don't tell me what to do. I'm a goddamn United States District Attorney."

Tony, un-swayed by his blazing glower or blistering tone, corrects him. "*Assistant.*"

"Excuse me?"

Tony adds, "If you're going to start yelling titles, you have to get it right."

Bucky shakes his head, dark hair unmoving, forehead glistening. "What's gotten into the two of you?" he asks, turning in his seat to look at Marque, who has his chin tucked tight against his chest, as if Marque could offer some sort of assessment to what's happening. "Are you two trying to get fired?"

"No," they both say at the same time.

Eliza says, "Just trying to get everything out in the open."

"Anything else you'd like to get in the open?" Bucky asks.

Tony looks up at Eliza and stands. "She's carrying my baby."

"What?" Bucky says.

"My baby." Tony points to her midsection. "My baby."

The non-sequitur shakes Marque out of his observational trance as if the bell's rung, and he's trying to throw in the towel. He rockets to his feet. "I think this meeting is over."

Tony says, "Come on now, Marque. We haven't even started yet because I, too, would like to know if he's fucking Clyde's wife. I just felt you needed to know where I stand with all this, and if we expect you to tell the truth, then I might as well tell you something true."

"Bucky doesn't understand what Tony's saying," Eliza says.

"What is he saying?" Bucky asks.

"Iris is fucking Renaldo. You know that, right?" Eliza says. "I mean you had to know that. He came to the goddamn funeral." Then, to Marque she adds, "He wore the same jacket that was draped over the sofa at Clyde's house when we did the notification."

Marque says, "Even if he did come to the funeral, what about him? What does any of this have to do with Eli?"

Tony asks, "Why aren't we on him?"

Bucky asks, "What do you mean?"

Tony explains, "Cuz the way I feel, and the way I see it is ... if she's fucking you and fucking Renaldo Luna, then maybe you might be compromised. And that might be why every time Clyde and I tried to get something going on Siriano, it got shut down."

"Even if I was," Bucky starts, "it would have nothing to do with the investigation."

Tony says, "Appearances."

"So why don't you let me look at your phone?" Eliza says. "That would answer our questions. Does she text you? Call you? Give you smoke signals? How do you know when she's ready for you? How do you know when it's booty call—"

"Where are you going with this Mrs. Cortez?"

"How long has this been going on?"

"I'm not your cheating husband ... or you for that matter," Bucky says, dropping the insult in the space between the words.

Eliza is straight-faced. "That's not going to be my name any longer."

Tony makes a T-sign with his hands, asking for a sidebar. He reaches for her arm, pulls her down to the side.

Eliza leans into him, turning her face away from Bucky so he can't see her smile, she whispers, "I ended my marriage this morning."

But before Tony can process what she said, Bucky snaps his fingers. "You two want to come back to this conversation?"

Leaning forward in the chair, Marque says, "I think things have gotten out of control."

Bucky tells Marque, "No, let them talk; it's just starting to get interesting."

Eliza whips around and tells Marque, "I don't want his blowhard ass to get up here and tell me how two more friends of mine have died and how it couldn't be avoided when he's been screwing Iris, who I'm pretty sure has something to do with Renaldo Luna and Siriano."

Bucky shifts his attention from Marque to the other end of the table. He feigns composure to conceal his escalating anger. "What's going on with you two? Yesterday, we were all one big happy family grieving a loss. Where's all this coming from?"

Tony says, "Yesterday, you orchestrated a public spectacle, despite what Clyde—you know, the dead guy—wanted, just so you could shake hands with the governor and show off how big your dick is."

Bucky opens his mouth to voice a retort, but Eliza steps in and says, "So why don't you go fuck yourself?"

"Excuse me?" he asks.

"Don't worry—Iris has been giving it to you well enough as it is." She adds, "Renaldo too."

Bucky leans back in the chair, silent for a few moments while he studies Eliza. Then, he brings his hands together in front of him as if he's praying, eyes shifting back and forth from Tony, who can't believe Eliza said what she said, and Eliza, who despite seemingly not believing it herself is doing a pretty good job of putting on a convincing face that she means every word.

Eliza, capitalizing on Bucky's lack of words, delivers another blow. "Is that why Siriano's not facing new charges for drugs?"

Bucky shakes his head. "My relationship or lack of relationship has nothing to do with this investigation."

But it's Marque who says, "I'm going to have to disagree with you."

"What?" Bucky glances at Marque in distaste and disbelief. "Not you too?"

"No," Marque says, cutting the silent accusation off at the wick. He adjusts in his chair, pulling on his belt over his stomach. He reaches into a folder and withdraws photographs. He places them on the table.

Each photograph is of Iris and Renaldo: One is of a poker table where Renaldo is standing behind her with his hand on her shoulder. Another is of them on a date, drinking wine. One is risqué and perhaps X-rated. Another is of Renaldo sitting in the front row of the church at Clyde's funeral.

Marque says, "It does seem Iris King does have a relationship with Renaldo Luna, who is the second in command of the Siriano organization. So, it does open avenues for certain questions."

Bucky interjects. "Where'd these photos come from?"

Marque continues while layering additional photographs out on the table. Iris and Bucky. Iris and Renaldo. Renaldo and Kevin Alexander. Kevin Alexander and Franklin Hayes.

"Clyde made me aware of a possible attempt at recruitment. He asked that I keep it to myself while he looked into it. He took these photographs, all except this one," he points to Renaldo at Clyde's funeral, "which is confirmation of Clyde's theory." Marque clears his throat, holding a hand to his mouth, and adds, "A funeral Clyde expressly did not want."

"This is ridiculous," Bucky says.

"These are the facts," Marque says. "If you are uncomfortable with them, perhaps you should be more aware of the people you consort with outside of this office."

Bucky's body straightens. "I'm a United States *Assistant* District Attorney; I think I know how to handle myself."

Marque, showing balls, says, "But you aren't a Drug Enforcement Agent working organized crime. Criminals have a way of trying to corrupt, turning good to bad."

Tony leans forward. "I thought she was sleeping around, but I never imagined it was Renaldo."

"No one did," Marque says, "except for Clyde. He figured it went like this. Iris ran her poker games. She met Clyde and was supposed to have stopped, but what Clyde thought happened was she didn't stop as much as let Renaldo run them, not knowing who he really was. Except, we know who Renaldo is and who he works for. Clyde figured Renaldo found out he's DEA, and so he sees an opportunity to try to get close to Clyde through Iris, quite literally."

"To do what?" Eliza asks. "To get information on us?"

"Perhaps," Marque says while collecting the photographs into a stack. He pushes the stack toward Buchanan. "Perhaps it was to get information on Siriano. So, then it becomes like Tony said ... *appearances*."

CHAPTER TWENTY-SEVEN:

GENE ORR

G ENE REALIZES HE'S TIRED when he opens the
door to his shop. The stress and paranoia have taken
a massive toll on him. He's exhausted. Not to mention
he's hungry and sick to his stomach at the same time. He
has not eaten much over the last few days or taken a shit
because his schedule's all jacked up. And Kevin's visit this
morning didn't help things either, not that it ever does. He
made everything lock up, squeeze tight, but that's how it's
been since he started playing his game of kings and thrones.

He withdraws the key from the slot and drops the key
into his pocket. A thought keeps tugging at the back of
Gene's mind: Who's backing Kevin? Because someone's
backing Kevin.

Gene steps inside, switches the sign from closed to
open, and flicks on the lights. But when the lights blink
on, slowly flickering to life, buzzing, casting a dull cheap
fluorescent blue over the ruined showroom, Gene sees the
shelves knocked over and the display cases smashed. Glass

from the cases is scattered across the floor intermixed with the merchandise, littering nearly every inch, and sitting in Gene's computer chair, pulled around the edge of the counter and parked in the breach between the showcases, sits Franklin Hayes, wearing a paramedic uniform. Sitting in the chair like he's been sleeping, he looks, at best, disheveled, and at worst, happy to see Gene. He lifts his head, and with one hand, he motions to the destruction, proud of it.

The uniform throws Gene for a moment. "Frankie?" he asks, taking a step forward.

"Welcome to work," he says. "You're late. It's about time you got here. I didn't want to do all this, but things have been a little fucked up lately. I've been fucked up lately. You know, that's what happens when your world dissolves around you because there's some ratty ass people fucking you in the behind, but I guess you know all about that."

Surveying the damage, Gene lets the insult go; he's heard shit like that his entire life. Right now, he's more upset with the state of his store. Screw Franklin's mock bigoted indignities. "What the fuck, man?"

Franklin's eyes drift across the damage.

"I got bored," he says, as he kicks his feet and swivels in the chair. The chair spins, turning away from Gene as Franklin explains. "No, scratch that. I got angry. Like hit shit angry. Break shit. Once you kick one shelf over, the others have to go, it fucks with the feng shui otherwise."

The chair circles back around, coming back face to face with Gene, except now Franklin's produced a gun. He plants his feet, stopping the chair's turn.

"Really though, I just wanted to get your attention."

Gene steps forward, eyes on the gun. "I'd say you have it. Guns have a way of capturing one's attention."

Franklin chuckles to himself and looks at the gun and back at Gene. "If that didn't work," he motions to the debris, "I thought this might." Franklin taps the gun against his leg. "Like the gun? It came from a cop, from a *Law*-rence." He emphasizes the law in Lawrence. "I called him Larry."

"He give it to you?"

Frankie smiles and throws his body forward, coming out of the chair and to his feet in one big surge. He tucks the gun in his waistband. "Something like that. I kind of figured he wouldn't need it anymore. But enough about Larry. He's dead. I want to know about you—how you been, Gene?"

"Busy."

Franklin steps forward, nodding his head. "Trying to fuck someone over?" Franklin lets the question sit in the space between them as he steps around Gene, trying to make him uncomfortable, invade his space.

Gene won't give in to intimidation.

"Yeah, that'd count as busy. Could be considered work in some circles. Work makes a man thirsty." He smacks his lips together. "But busy, yeah, I know you are," he adds circling him.

Gene starts to say something, but Franklin places a hand on Gene's shoulder, silencing him.

"I know it because that Casper kid really fucked my shit up," Franklin says. "I mean here I was sitting with a good friend of mine, dead now, some say it's my fault—won't say that anymore—but a good friend nonetheless. He always wanted more from me than I was willing to give. You know how that is don't you, with you and Kevin and all?"

"You would know about that, wouldn't you?" Gene says. "Kevin and you are best friends."

Gene still can't believe Kevin was going to do Franklin like he was, set him up with the cops to take a fall.

Franklin hesitates a tick. "Anyways, everything was copacetic, I just got new shoes—from you—but that's not important yet, but then here comes your boy toy to ruin my day."

Gene tries to follow Franklin's conversation, but he can't focus on what the man is saying.

"The ones you sold me," Franklin says. "Surely, you remember ... the white Jordan's."

Gene remembers. "I sold them to you."

"That you did." Franklin taps Gene on the shoulder. "They were nice too. Good shoes. But I got to ask you, were they fake? I heard they were fake—were they?"

Gene starts to say they weren't, but Franklin stops him with an upheld hand.

"You can stick to a lie," he says. "I'll give you that; that's what you do. Stick to a lie no matter the consequences. You play the role to the end. You don't give in. You just say anything that gets you out of the trouble you're in. Every time you've sold something fake to a customer, and that enterprising soul decides to get it appraised, inevitably discovering its inauthenticity, you stick to the lie. You don't have to say nothing; your face says it all. Says they were fake."

Gene closes his eyes and stretches his neck. "Look, I don't know what you're talking about."

Franklin places his hands on the base of Gene's neck, almost as a caress, like he's going to massage the spot. His palm is hot and moist against Gene's skin, breath rank.

Franklin tells him to stay with him. To open his eyes. To focus. And then Franklin slaps Gene's left cheek a few times.

Gene stares at him.

"Surprised I know?" Franklin asks. "Well, old *Law-rence*... Larry had a buddy. Some dipshit that thought it'd be funny to throw that out—that they were fake—rub it in my face. You know a real kick a guy when he's down type... get it?... kick? No? I'm sorry. I thought you were a funny guy... being you're out there fucking people over and selling fake shit and calling it real."

"I don't know what you are talking about," Gene says. "He told you the ones I sold you were fake? They're not fake."

Franklin slaps Gene one more time, harder than he did before. He grabs the base of Gene's neck and tugs him forward, putting their faces within inches of each other. "Were not," he says. "Past tense, were not fake. They no longer exist. Except they were fake. Doesn't matter now. They're gone now. Some paramedic cut them off my feet. He could have unlaced them or something. But no, snip snip." He makes a pair of scissors with his fingers, mock cutting fabric. "Course they were covered in blood, so I don't know I probably wouldn't have wanted them. They'd be ruined, but it's the principle of the matter."

"I'm glad you're all right."

"No thanks to you." Franklin drops his hand to the side and pulls the gun from his waistband. Pats the gun against his thigh as if he's trying to decide what he's going to do next. He clicks his tongue against the roof of his mouth. "You ever been shot, Gene?"

Gene closes his eyes and gulps. He answers, "No." Then, he opens his eyes.

"You want to be?" Franklin asks, bringing the gun up, putting it in Gene's face, finger on the trigger.

The blackness of the barrel steals Gene's voice.

And then Franklin breaks and lets the gun hang loose to his side. "I thought I knew what being shot would be like," he comments. "It was nothing like I ever imagined. Barely felt it, to tell the truth. Shot five times. Five times, Gene." He counts the wounds on one hand while pointing to each section of his body where the bullets struck him. "Five times. And all because of your little boy Casper."

"I don't know what you're talking about."

"Like you don't know about the fake shoes?"

"They were real Jordans," Gene says.

Franklin lets it go. "You know what's real? That fucker messing with me when I was laid up in the hospital from the five gunshots. Here, I'm sitting in a hospital bed and some Pakistani fucker is over there teasing me about the shoes you sold me, telling me, asking, did you get those from Eugene? Like it's some big fucking inside joke. Like it's a question he already knew the answer to. He's asking but not asking. Says you're known for your knockoffs. I didn't know that. Who knows that?" Franklin points at Gene. "The cop leaves that shit out there like he's doing it to make me wonder. Torture me. Like it's something everyone knows. Made me lay there in that bed, shot five times, thinking about it. I'm shot five times, and I'm there thinking about those damn shoes."

"Means they were good shoes," Gene says.

"They were good shoes," Franklin says. "Made me happy."

"So, what's it matter if they were fake or not?" Gene asks, trying to turn the conversation. "If you couldn't tell, then no one else could have either. And if you can't tell and they make you happy, then why's it matter if they're fake?"

"It matters," Franklin says. Then, offhand, he slaps Gene's arm. "It matters to me because I've come to appreciate appearances."

Franklin turns away from Gene and throws himself back in the computer chair. The chair's casters carry his momentum backward, rolling across the floor.

"Appearances matter; maybe not in your world, but in mine, they matter. They matter a lot. So, you embarrassed me by giving me fake shoes. I can't have that. Even if I don't know. They're fake and others know."

"They weren't fake."

"You really going to argue with a man that's got a gun?" Franklin trains the gun on Gene, using the armrest to lazily prop his arm up in a half-hearted attempt at intimidation.

Gene stays quiet.

"Good choice," Franklin says. "They were fake. That's fine. They were. Don't tell me otherwise or I'm going to shoot you right now. Right in your fucking faggotty fucking face because I'm done, Gene. I'm done being screwed over, and I want some answers. I want to know how this all happened."

"How what happened?"

Franklin elevates his arms as if he is praying to God, both hands to the ceiling. "All this, this, how I came to be here, wearing this, with a dead man's gun, talking to you about appearances. How did we get here? Where is here? What is here? Questions with answers. Questions that need to be asked. I want to know. Enquiring minds want to know. I need to know."

"Last I knew, you were in the hospital."

Franklin sighs. "I was, and then I wasn't," he says. "Guess you wouldn't know anything about that. It's not like the guy getting fucked over by the police is told what the police are thinking. No, that comes later when they write their reports and lie." Franklin shivers, acting as if a chill is running through his body. "I feared for my life ... or, get this part, it's the important one ... or others' lives. Great line. Know what it means. This means they can kill with impunity. That's it. That's all she wrote. The fat lady sang. So, I get it. They don't tell you what's going on, but that's not how it is for your side of the conversation, is it?"

"I don't know what you mean," Gene lies. He knows exactly what Franklin's saying.

Franklin drops the gun on him again in his half-assed way. "You want to play games?" Gun lazily bounces with his words. "Do I really need to stand up, walk over there, and put this to you just to get you to tell me what I already know? I've already killed one man; you want to make it two?"

Gene shakes his head.

"Good choice," Franklin says, taking the gun off him. "I'm tired, Gene. Being shot does that to a person. But what I want to know is how did this all happen?"

"I—"

"No, don't answer," Franklin says. "It's not one of those conversations. I know how this happened. I just want to tell you about it before I kill you. What do they call that in the movies? Like when James Bond would do it? You know I could never get Kevin to dress nicely. I'd say to him... 'Look at you. You're white. You could look like that,' and I'd point to Sean Connery. He'd say that he didn't care. Why didn't he care?"

"Frankie, I'm having a hard time here," Gene says.

"Following me?" Franklin says. "Guess you would."

Franklin sinks in the chair. He snaps his fingers. "Monologuing," he exclaims. "That's what I'm doing, but I'm not really because I do have a purpose. I want to know how this happened."

Gene tilts his head to the side.

"You're working with the cops, right?" he says. "I mean that's how this had to go. You work with the cops; they've got you by the balls or something. Yeah? Okay, but you don't want to set them up with Siriano because... well we know how he feels about appearances... so you make your protégé do it. That's how part of what happened, happened. I think." Franklin winks. "Only you can tell me for sure."

"You're on the right track," Gene says.

"What I need to know is where Casper is," Franklin says, "Where is he?"

"Are you going to kill me?"

"Haven't decided yet, but seeing I'm here and you're there, I'd say chances are likely."

Gene could fight him on it, but that'd just enrage him more. Or... he could come clean and see if Franklin's mood changes again. Gene says, "Tony's."

"Who's Tony?"

"The cop that was in the car with you. Casper's with him."

"Why is he... you know what, never mind," Franklin says as his face twists, perplexed. "Where's he live?"

Gene says nothing.

Franklin smiles. "Backbone. Nice. I like seeing that. You don't take shit from no one, do you? You just work both sides to stay out of it, but I'd say you're in it."

"I can give you the address," Gene says. "And it helps to know some things others don't think you know."

Franklin leaps to his feet.

Gene stands his ground, legs like putty.

Franklin sticks the muzzle of the gun against the side of Gene's head. "Did you ever love my friend?"

Eyes forward and without hesitation, Gene says, "With every inch of my heart."

"Pity, he never felt the same way about you," Franklin says.

"That's why it didn't work out."

With the gun against his ear, Gene doesn't move, not one muscle, except his heart pummels his ribcage. Time passes slowly. Then, Franklin removes the gun and chuckles. He steps around Gene to leave.

"You want to know how it happened?" Gene asks as the door opens but doesn't close. Gene concentrates on breathing as he dares to turn around, and when he does, he sees Franklin hasn't left the store. He has one hand still on the handle, one leg out the door. "Kevin set you up. All of it. His idea. Even the cops."

CHAPTER TWENTY-EIGHT:

IRIS KING

RIS ASKS RENALDO, who sits at the foot of his hospital bed before getting dressed, "Something has changed hasn't it?"

"Yeah, sure, okay," Renaldo says, dismissing her in the way he usually does.

It's afternoon. She stands near the window looking out over the parking lot. The dying sunlight casts its winter glow across the pavement below the window. This is her favorite time of year when she can step outside to smoke, wrap herself in something warm, and feel the cool air wash over her skin. She talks into the window. "I mean yes, I know you got shot in the head, that would change anyone, but something's going on. Something's bothering you. What's going on?"

Renaldo doesn't respond, so she turns around to face him.

And he just looks at her as he buttons his salmon-colored dress shirt, fingers working, not saying anything. He's been like this since she came back to the room.

"I can see it. Something's bothering you, and I'm trying to figure out why you won't tell me," Iris says. "When I walked in after you woke up, your eyes lit up. You were happy to see me, but now, something's changed. I can tell." She pauses. "What's going on? You can't just call me, tell me you need some clothes, and expect me to hop without any explanation. Are you sure you want to check out?"

"The hospital isn't a hotel."

Iris says, "You know, in all the time we've been ... doing whatever this is, I don't think I've ever been to your place. It was interesting walking through it. The landlord let me in. The door opened, and it was like stepping into a new world, like that book about the wardrobe, but without the satyrs and shit, like seeing a whole new side of you for the first time."

What struck her the most was how empty his place was. Sure, his closet had clothes and cabinets had dishes, his rooms had a bare minimum of furniture, and the place had the expected appliances, but something about it was empty. Almost hollow. She realized there was a whole side of Renaldo she didn't know anything about. She'd heard about it, been told about it, and Wilson explained how he might react when they started this, but she'd never seen it. So maybe the change she's seeing now has nothing to do with the head injury and everything to do with him and how he got to be the bagman for Siriano.

But then again, maybe it does have to do with the head injury.

"Maybe you're acting the way you are because you were shot," Iris says, guessing at the matter. "The doctors said traumatic brain injuries can do that in someone like you, someone who's taken a bullet bounced off their skull." She repeats what happened to him to try to press upon him the seriousness of the injury. "Doctor told me there's no telling what's happened or how much damage could be lasting. Said right now you have a pretty severe concussion but seem to be doing fine. But they said there was one guy who took a nail in the skull, three inches into his brain. Said his wife told them he was a nice man before that. Now, not so much. He's prone to violent mood swings and severe anger, but the upside is he's now a well-respected painter. He couldn't paint before. The doctor said that's the nature of such injuries and the aftereffects. Said they're still medical mysteries."

Renaldo interjects, "Did they stay married? The guy with the nail in the head?"

Iris shakes her head. "The doctor said the wife didn't love the stranger her husband had become."

All Renaldo does is nod to her story as if everything she said just washed over him without leaving an impression. He finishes with the shirt and pats his thighs with both hands before standing. He sways a bit. He mechanically tucks the shirt into his slacks.

"So why can't you tell me what's going on?" Iris says. "You seemed fine before I left, but now, now you seem so much more determined, focused. What's going on, Reni?"

"We need to leave," Renaldo says. "I don't have time to explain."

"To go where?" she asks, crossing her arms. Clyde hated when she did this, called this a preamble to a fight, her digging in and battening the hatches. "We've been through this six times over the last hour, and you've not said anything that makes sense. They don't want you to leave. You got shot in the head for goodness' sake."

"We just need to get out of here," Renaldo says.

"Why?" Iris asks, even though she knows better. He won't tell her. He's been like this since she got back with his clothes. He even threatened to leave naked when she wouldn't hand them to him without an explanation.

"Police might show up," Renaldo says. "I need to get out of here before that happens."

"Bullshit," Iris says. "If that were true, you would have told me the first six times, but each time I ask, your answer changes. First, it was just because. Then, it was so we could run off. Then, it was so you could go talk to someone. Then, it was you were scared to stick around; the people that shot you might come back, and now it's the police. If it were just one answer it would be the same, right? Plus, why would they show up? And just how did you get shot in the head?"

He doesn't answer.

So, Iris presses. "Is it because of what's on the news?"

She's referring to the reports of the shootout outside the hospital, the two dead DEA agents, and the escaped prisoner.

"I'm not stupid. I know it has everything to do with that, but I want you to say it. I want to hear it. I have to hear it. It's not about being right; it's about what you're willing to tell me. Do you even trust me?"

Renaldo's eyes scan her body, which makes her almost uncomfortable, but for the first time, she sees the man she's heard so much about: the dark pupils, the expressionless features.

Does he trust her? He should but he shouldn't but trusting her works for her plans. But then, that just means she's using him. She uses everyone. Clyde trusted her and look where that got him, an unintended consequence.

"You can trust me Reni, but you have to talk to me. Talk to me."

"I trust you." Renaldo picks up his left shoe.

Iris purses her lips. "Do you?"

"I do." Renaldo pauses just long enough to reinforce his words. "But there's no truth in who we trust. No choice either. Nor in those we fall in love with."

Iris presses harder. "Do you trust me enough to tell me what's going on?"

"We need to get out of here."

"Where would we go? And that doesn't answer my question."

Renaldo slips his other foot into the shoe. "I wasn't kidding about the police," he says. "Do you want to know what's going on?"

"God, you are frustrating at times but also beautiful, even with that bandage around your head. That's why I'm asking; I want to know what's going on with you."

"Do you?"

This reminds her of arguments with Clyde, circular.

Iris says, "I wouldn't say it if it wasn't true."

Renaldo stiffens and drops his hands to his side. He faces her, trying to decide if he's going to trust her or not, even though he already told her he does. But nothing in his body language says that's true.

"I don't even know why I am here," she says, going over her actions over the last twenty-four hours, or even the last week. Everything feels like it's her fault, and if she were capable of accepting responsibility, she might agree, it is her fault. But of course, she's not capable of it.

Tony was right; she uses people.

She tells Renaldo, "I just buried my husband. I shouldn't be here. Just as you shouldn't have come to the funeral. Except when I received the phone call telling me you were in the hospital, I came running. I don't know why I did that. There was no thought, no hesitation, nothing like I'd expected. Even when that bitch told me my husband was dead, I didn't react, but when the nurse called and told me you had been shot, I came running."

What she doesn't say is how much that surprised her. Then, when her senses returned to her, at the first opportunity, she dumped her husband's ashes off with Tony without a second thought as if grieving Clyde's death was as easy as ending a book: close the cover and put it away. That surprised her too.

Is she a terrible person?

Do terrible people think they are terrible? Do they know they are bad, or do they just lie to themselves and pretend they're something they aren't?

Iris asked Wilson if she's terrible for being the reason her husband's dead. Wilson told her people lie to themselves all the time. They tell themselves they're something different, but they're not. They're who they are, and that's all they are. He said people think they're free, but they really aren't; they're all imprisoned one way or another. People don't go around telling themselves they're the bad guys. They go around living their lives, lying to themselves about who they are, and at the end of the day, they do what they do.

A shadow flicks across Renaldo's face as if he's about to admit he's been cheating on a spouse for years. He says, "I used you," while at the same time his whole body collapses under the strain of the admission, shoulders sinking, chest collapsing in on itself like it's causing him physical pain. "I used you to get close to your husband. I didn't know I'd fall in love with you. So, if you want to know what's going on, then I might as well start there so there's no misunderstandings between us."

"What's that mean?" Iris asks, even though she's already figured it out and accepted that about their relationship. Why doesn't he see she knew? That's why she invited him to the house.

"It means I love you, and that scares me."

"Why would that scare you?" she asks, and then says, "Wait what?"

"Honesty, being honest scares me. I've had no one my entire life I could trust. My mother worked nights. She left me in the care of strangers. Oftentimes, I'd sleep in some attorney's office, under a desk, or under something in the building she worked at. Sometimes sleep on their waiting benches and couches. Sometimes on the floor. Sometimes I'd help her clean, but I spent my time there. Not at home. Not with friends, but with her."

"You've never mentioned your mother before." Iris uncrosses her arms and takes a step towards him. "Does she live ... live close?"

Renaldo checks himself in the mirror. "Works three miles from here and owns the building now." He points out the window. "But that's not... forget about that. Just listen. As I got older, you know school gets harder, teachers assign you homework. I guess that's not much of a thing now, but you know what it was like growing up then. They assign you homework and send you home with hours and hours of reading and math."

Iris perches herself on the edge of the bed. She crosses her arms. "School wasn't much different for me."

"Well, my mother didn't think it was right for me to be doing it up at her work," Renaldo says, "but she didn't want me to be too far away either, so she sat me down at a counter in a café in the building she worked. One of those little neighborhood places tucked away, and well-traveled, that sort of place that never closes except when they do. So, if you want to know what's going on with me, that's part of it—you need to know where I came from to understand how I got here." He motions to the room. Then, he points to the phone. "The person I stayed with, Alejandro, became like a father to me. He ran the café. Gave me my first job. Took me in, treated me like I was one of his own. When you left, I called him."

"I don't understand," Iris says.

"Yeah, sure, okay," Renaldo says. "I called him because he's the one that put me in the hospital."

"He shot you?"

"Not him, but someone associated with him," Renaldo says. "He cut me out and tried to kill me."

"Oh my god," Iris says, playing her role, doing it like Keira Knightley, just like she did when that bitch came over to tell her Clyde was dead. "Why?"

Renaldo hesitates before answering; he hides his face from her. "I work for a guy named Siriano. Ever heard of him?"

"Clyde and Tony mentioned the name a few times."

"He's in prison; I take care of his interests on the outside," Renaldo says. "Your husband died doing a deal that was supposed to start an operation into Siriano."

"He what?" Iris asks, nearly overplaying it.

Renaldo tilts his head to the side and raises an eyebrow. "Don't pretend to be stupid," he says. "You know who I work for. That's why you let me take your games from you. Siriano money backed your bank. You can't go against him."

Iris knew that from the beginning, but he was so cocksure about taking her games from her, she had no idea what the ramifications of it would be. He wants to think he was using her, but no one uses Iris. She pastes a mask of understanding on her face while throwing in just enough of a questioning raised eyebrow. "So, what's the problem?"

She'd kill it in a close-up, emoting without talking, allowing the audience to know exactly what she's thinking. They'd have to guess, but they'd know.

"The problem is Siriano doesn't know his money backed your bank."

"But he runs some gambling operations, right? How could he not know?"

"Right, which is all lucrative, but there was more money to be had. Bigger pie and all that."

"You used me to make money?"

"Not just money," he says. "I used you for that and for the sex ... which I guess you used me for that too... We're alike in that, using people, but I used you for your husband as well."

"My husband?"

"I knew he was DEA, Iris."

"You did?"

"And now he's dead," Renaldo says, stepping toward her. "I'm sorry about that, by the way. If it matters, I had nothing to do with that deal. Siriano went around me."

Iris plays like she doesn't understand what he's saying, leading him down her path, asking, "Around you?"

Renaldo struggles for the right words. "He allowed ... someone else to set up the deal. I didn't know about it until later."

"Why did he go around you?" Iris asks, even though she knows the answer.

"That's the question, isn't it?"

"And that's what's been bothering you?" Iris says, filling in the blanks. "Is that why you've been so absent the last week?"

"I loved Alejandro, and I asked him for help. This is what happened." He points to his temple. "That's his version of help. He doesn't understand why I'm the way I am—"

"—what about Siriano?" she asks. "Does he know about the games? The money you've basically skimmed off the top?"

"That's part of the problem. On the day your husband was killed, someone robbed a game and took my computer drives."

"The ones with the player information?"

Renaldo nods.

Iris lunges toward him and wraps her arms around him, squeezing him tight. "Thank you for trusting me."

"Yeah, sure, okay," Renaldo says, with her on him, looking up into his eyes. "So, you see I'm in a pickle. Siriano wants me to take out the person responsible for setting up the deal." Renaldo uses his fingers to count. "He told me to kill that person, the person who killed your husband, and he wants me to kill your husband's partner as well. But it won't matter that I hadn't gotten close to Clyde. Siriano's all about appearances. If that gets out, I'm a dead man. And with the robbing of the game and taking the drive, someone's trying to destroy me. Because if you add our relationship on top of the poker operation, I'm fucked no matter how I look at it."

With her hands wrapped around his neck, Iris licks her lips. Should she kiss him, a reward for trusting her? "Do you know who robbed your game?"

"I do," he says. "And I think he's with Tony."

"What? Why would he be there?"

"Because he's the one that set up the drug deal and, I think, robbed my game, which means he's probably linked to Tony. You said it yourself: Tony's informant had some kid do it, and so that means Tony's protecting him."

"How do you fix this?"

"I get him, and I get the drives, and then, you and I get out of town," Renaldo says. But before Iris can respond, he adds, "There's nothing here for me. I'm a dead man if I stay. I gotta go."

Iris bites her lip. "What exactly are you saying? Are you asking me to go with you?"

Renaldo places his hands on her shoulders. "I love you."

Iris kisses him. "If I go, can we stop off at the Grand Canyon?"

CHAPTER TWENTY-NINE:
ELIZA CORTEZ

T HEY PULL INTO TONY'S DRIVEWAY after
the disastrous meeting with Bucky and Marque, neither saying a word to the other; there's nothing left to say.
Tony's in the driver's seat, and Eliza's in the passenger seat.
They sit in the quiet acceptance of something greater than
friendship, which unfolds slowly like the blooming of a
beautiful flower: something right and perfect, with a warm
center, vibrating in the excitement of not knowing what
comes next—an ember of contentment.

Eliza breaks the silence. "Could I have handled
that better?"

Tony shifts the car into park and turns in his seat to
look at her, which nearly melts her. His look usually does,
but this is different. Before, Eduardo held them back, not
physically, but the idea of her marital betrayal held her
back from committing fully to how she feels about Tony.
Tony was a temptation, and Eliza was determined to pre-
vent what happened from happening again.

But now, that love is attainable, and the car idles, vibrating in time with her heart.

"Don't give me that look," Eliza says. "You know what I'm talking about. That meeting."

Tony says, "I know what you are talking about."

"That doesn't answer the question, now does it?" Eliza says, shifting in her seat. "I mean, yes, I guess I could have handled it better, but that's not what I want to hear."

"You handled it perfectly," Tony says, switching the car off.

Her heart hammers on. She didn't know feeling this way was possible. "Don't patronize me," she says. "Besides, it doesn't matter right now. I've never felt this way."

"What way?" Tony asks.

Eliza brushes a strand of her dark hair out of her face with a swipe of her hand. "You stood up for me; that means something," she says. "Thank you for standing with me. Not only that but also through everything that's happened and going on. You've been patient with me, understanding. You haven't forced me to make up my mind or gotten frustrated at the fact that I didn't know what to do. You let me choose. You haven't been a pushover about it either. You have resisted, but just barely, and only enough to show me you are a gentleman and not a jerk."

Tony rotates more in the seat, getting comfortable, and slips an arm around the back of her headrest. "Of course."

"I couldn't have done what I did in there without you."

Tony's face breaks, and whatever tension was there is now gone. "I'm still surprised you did what you did."

"Although, I could have done without you announcing to everyone that I'm pregnant with your child. That took me by surprise."

Tony half-smiles through a blush and stammers, "I got carried away at the moment."

"But I appreciate the support," she says, quieting her heart and controlling her breathing. "I don't have that at home. Not with Eduardo. I don't think I've ever had it. I think I thought I did, but then, I realized he's never supported me. I didn't have it."

"That's why you have to find that, someone to support you."

"Makes you wonder, you know, about things," Eliza says, "about life. Makes you think about how people build this world around them, these relationships, and you have to wonder how many people find that with someone else, and it passes them by."

"What do you mean?" Tony asks.

"You have your theory—"

"The love languages?" he asks. "You hate that theory."

"I didn't say it was a good theory."

"It's a great theory."

"It's really not," Eliza says, giving him a silencing look. Then, with pursed lips and narrowed eyes she says, "Shut up. Please stop talking for a moment and let me say this. You're going to ruin it with all your talking."

She's thought a lot about this over the last two years, and after today, with what happened between her and Eduardo and then confronting Bucky, now is the right time to tell Tony how she really feels.

"Be quiet and listen," she says. "I have something I need to say to you, but I don't know how to say it. When you start talking, rambling, you ruin it."

"Like I nearly did the night you kissed me," Tony says. "You remember when… when you and I got together? I walked you to your room."

"Only because we stayed up too late at the hotel bar drinking, I remember. Eduardo was furious about the amount of money I spent on drinks. He bitched at me for two months about it. I mean he's an accountant, so on one hand, I understand how he wants everything to be balanced just right, but on the other, I could have done without him bitching at me, asking me how I could have spent two hundred dollars in one night."

"I spent as much too," Tony says. "That hurt my wallet. Why do drinks at a hotel cost so much?"

"Do you remember when we were outside my room? I remember, I remember how you were going on about something. Do you remember what? I don't remember what. It's funny how that is. I've thought about that night a lot. I mean, I kind of have to, every doctor's visit, every time I get dressed, every… I've thought about it, but I don't remember what you and I were talking about on the way to the room."

"About a book I read," he says. "The best-seller about the mob guy who meets the housewife in Oklahoma right after JFK was killed. They're being chased by this hit-man."

"Was it any good?"

"If you'd had listened to me then, you'd know my opinion on it."

"Was I any good?" Eliza asks, catching him off guard.

She remembers the kiss in the hallway, how it felt like a rocket ship exploding in her chest, and the next thing she knew, they were inside the room, undressed and lying in each other's arms. The first time happened so fast that she didn't really enjoy it; there was no time. It was over in minutes, leaving them both exhausted but strangely satisfied too. After a few minutes, they tried again, and it went much better. Does he play it on a loop in his head? Does he even think about her?

Tony says, "After you told me to shut up and kiss you?"

She nods.

"Yes, you were the best."

Her heart sores at hearing his words. Then, Tony's face darkens. He says, "I'm sorry."

"For what?" Her chest tightens.

"For everything. For putting you through this." He motions to her body.

Eliza looks away for a second to force herself to relax. "You didn't do anything."

"I feel like it's my fault: you, Ed, us. I feel like I screwed it up. Screwed us up. Ruined our friendship."

"Screwed certainly is the right word." Eliza chuckles. "But I had a choice in the matter."

Tony furrows his brow together. "I guess I feel like I took advantage of you, took advantage of you in your moment of weakness. You know we talked about Ed all that night. You were going on about him sleeping with all those women."

"I remember."

"And I suggested that you should sleep with some men."

"I remember."

"And then you did."

"Tony," Eliza says, "I remember."

"I feel like I pushed you in that direction," he says. "I flirted with you. I wanted you to sleep with me."

"We didn't sleep."

"You know what I mean. I wanted you, and I took advantage of you. I guess I had intentions. You were drunk and heartbroken, and I used that to my advantage."

"Tony, I wasn't drunk," she says, stressing he must know it was her decision just as much as his.

"Okay, okay, you weren't drunk. I'm just saying, I took advantage of you to get something I wanted—you."

"I'm not a commodity."

The conversation lapses into a familiar valley where neither of them knows what to say next, but they don't want to get out of the car or move, or speak, because no matter how cold it is outside the car, the bubble of warmth inside the car is so encompassing.

Eliza says, "Look, I'm not saying what happened wasn't something special. It was. You made me feel... God why are we even talking about this, right now? How do I tell you how you make me feel? How do I tell you what I'm feeling? Don't look at me that way. You know what I mean. Special? Appreciated? Like I'm the only woman in the world and I'm all that matters. Do you know why I never said anything to Eduardo?"

Tony shakes his head.

"I felt wonderful when I was with you," Eliza says. "The whole next day at that conference, I deluded myself into thinking this was something that could work, me and you. That's why I nestled up next to you in the classes we attended. Took hold of your arm and rubbed my cheek on your shoulder. You smelled good. I was trying it on. I liked it. It was comfortable. Felt right, almost, but it was going to end, we had to come back here, back to our own lives. Did you ever tell Clyde about us?"

"God no."

"Did you want to?" she asks. "Why didn't you?"

"He wouldn't have understood."

"I feel like he would have. I feel like he would have been happy for you. He would have said, 'Antonio, it's about time.' I feel like that would have been his reaction."

"I don't know about that. He always seemed to resist mixing work with pleasure."

"He was a strange man. I mean, look at who he married," Eliza says. "Do you know why I never told Eduardo? When I got home, I was a wreck. I cried the whole way back home. What was I going to say? Hey, I fucked a coworker. You and me, we haven't been working for a long time. I feel disconnected and out of sync. I don't even think you love me, but with Tony ... there's something."

Tony places a hand on her shoulder. "There is something here, isn't there?"

Eliza smiles and places her finger against his lips, shushing him. His lips are so soft and stretch into a wide smile under her touch. "Shut up. Don't talk. I need to tell you this," she says. "I couldn't tell Eduardo. I wanted to tell him. I intended to tell him. Part of me was so sick to my stomach that you and I did what we did. Not that it disgusted me, but there was that too. Still, it was more that you and I did it, and now I have to go home. That I have to go to him. I was so sick with guilt that it felt like someone punched me in the stomach, then jumped on my stomach. I almost threw up. I thought I could handle it. Then, I knew I couldn't. I cried. I lied to myself. But I knew the truth. This wasn't something I could hold on to, but then I got home, and he started bitching at me about the money spent at the bar, asking me what I was thinking, what I had been doing. He was being... an asshole... yeah, that's the right word. He was an asshole about it. We had a huge blow-up where I thought, *fuck you dude, I'm not telling you anything about what happened.* Anger became the plug. It kept me from saying anything. We fought. We went to our corners: him the bedroom and me the bathroom.

"Then every time after that," Eliza continues, "when I would think about telling him, when I had worked myself into doing it, I got to thinking. Thought about then. Thought about the anger. Anger became the way to keep it from coming out. First, it was the bitching about the money. I get that it hurt our budget, but at a certain point in life when you have things going on, fuck a budget. It's not important. But then it became, how could he? How could he cheat on me and not feel what I'm feeling? That made me angrier. I tried to hold on to it. Push it down, like way down to the point I gave myself a sour stomach. I might have an ulcer. But every time I felt weak enough to tell him, I got to thinking about what it was doing to me, about how it was tearing me apart on the inside, and then I got to thinking about how he did it and how it doesn't seem to faze him. He cheated on me for two years before I found out. And that pissed me off."

"So, is that why you didn't tell him?" Tony asks.

Eliza shakes her head and returns to her earlier point. "I think the key to any great relationship, a marriage, is support. Like the woman beyond the man type-of-shit. But how many people are like me? Blinded by love and to what opportunities are out there, to what's out there? How many miss opportunities like you? Like the girl that falls for her high school sweetheart—that's me by the way— how many of those stories are out there? Makes me wonder, what if? You know, what if the universe puts your person there, right in front of you, but either through ignorance or devotion, you don't see them, don't see *it*, because of your self-contained and whole built commitments." She uses air quotes, "Like out of *duty* you ignore your heart?"

Tony shrugs. "You are talking about me ... about us, right?"

Eliza backhands his chest.

"I just wanted to make sure I knew where you were going because I'm a bit confused as to what this is and where we're at."

"Well smart guy, we're at your house," Eliza says.

"Not that, I'm just saying," he says, "I wanted to know if you're saying you're happy, like happy, we found each other? Or happy you broke things off with Ed? I guess none of that matters because I just want to know that you are happy."

"Can't it be both?" she asks. "I mean, I am happy I found you."

"Is that why you got jealous?" he says.

"Jealous? Who gets jealous? I was never jealous."

"Not of Iris?"

"Did you think I was jealous of Iris? Why would I be jealous of her?"

"For hitting on me."

"She slept with Bucky. Trust me: you can do better than anything he can pull down."

"So, you wouldn't go to bed with a United States district attorney?"

"*Assistant* and no, I wouldn't," she says. "I wasn't jealous of Iris."

"You weren't?"

"Okay, I was jealous of Iris," she admits, "but I was also worried I made you wait too long for me to figure out what this was, what I felt. But I knew you only had eyes for me, even if I'm a fat cow."

Tony moos.

She slaps his stomach. "Did I get carried away with Bucky and Marque?"

"Perhaps, but then perhaps not," he says. "It needed to be said. Someone needed to address what was happening ... what we all saw. Thank God Marque backed your play and had those photos. I had no idea Clyde had done any of that surveillance work."

"I think that was sort of the point," Eliza says. "There are only so many things you can share with the people closest to you, and you don't want to be embarrassed like that. Like how you didn't tell him about us. He couldn't tell us, 'Hey, I'm chasing this major criminal organization, and by the way, I think my wife's fucking the second-in-command.' Can you imagine having to come out and say something like that? That's a major eat a shit-pie moment."

"Still, it's like Marque knew you were going to bring it up. You know, with him having the folder ready to go and everything."

Eliza says, "We talked about it before the meeting, he said he called the meeting for a reason, not to stroke Bucky's ego, but to clear up some things. I had no idea it was going to be that."

"Those pictures were wild."

"Gives a whole new meaning to a small world."

"I wonder why he never said anything."

"Probably the same reason you never said anything. He was embarrassed."

Eliza reflects on that for a moment. "We should go inside. It's getting cold. Why don't you show me around?"

"You've been in my house," Tony says.

He's cute when he doesn't get it. This will do them both a lot of good.

Eliza smiles. "Tony, if there's one thing I didn't expect about pregnancy, is how God-awful horny I've been. Eduardo and I had sex six months ago. If you find me attractive at all, great, if you don't... I don't care, but I want to go inside your house and see the inside of your bedroom."

Tony removes the keys from the ignition. "Well, when you put it like that, let's go inside."

Eliza opens the car door and exits, shutting the door. She takes a moment to ready herself for what comes next. It may not be comfortable. She doesn't feel sexy, but they both need this, and in a way, she doesn't think Tony's going to mind whatever happens. He'll be happy either way. Maybe they do what she intends to do, maybe they don't, but regardless, Tony's going to enjoy his time with her, having her with him, because that's all he's wanted the last few days. That's all he wanted at the hospital, and that's all he wanted at the funeral. She didn't give it to him then, but now she can. All Eliza cares about is making him happy. It's all she's ever cared about. It's why she treated him the way she did yesterday, why she helped him through his grief.

Outside of the car, the air is crisp and new, the sun bright and warm, the breeze cool and refreshing, and the smell of rain accents the air, but off to the west, clouds are moving in, the signs of a coming storm, but one they can ride out together because that's all she wants right now is to be together.

This feels right.

Then, she stiffens at the sight of the open front door. "Did you leave your front door open?"

CHAPTER THIRTY:
RENALDO LUNA

THE HINGE SQUEAKS as Renaldo lifts the latch with two fingers and nudges the gate open on the chain-link fence, waist-high, cheap, and mass-produced. The gate is on the eastern side of the single-story dwelling filled with Alejandro's life, his family, his wife, his children, his grandchildren, and Pablo. The latch falls back in place as he steps through the gate and marches toward the darkness of the side of the house, each step careful and planned. He can't risk discovery, not now. He never thought he would end up here. He never saw the old man as anything but a beloved teacher, but Pablo meant to kill him. He failed. It's Renaldo's turn to return a favor for a favor.

Even though it is winter, he is shoeless, and the grass is lush under his feet but cold against his skin. The grass shows the level of care and maintenance Alejandro takes in his residence. It is distasteful and an example of someone Renaldo once feared who has morphed into a cranky old man who values only what remains: his garden, his yard, visions of the past, willfully ignorant of the future. Alejandro had been someone Renaldo loved, admired even, but Renaldo couldn't live in the old man's shadow forever. He wanted to be his own man. He wanted to be someone. Siriano offered this to him, and he took it.

What was wrong with that?

But now that's gone.

From the shroud of darkness, Renaldo concentrates on the back corner of the house, his breath crystallizing in the cooling temperature as a cloud of vapor escapes his lips. The night is dark. No moon. And the only light is from the porch and the star-spotted pinpricks of the neighbors' houses. Much of the neighborhood has bedded down for the night.

Renaldo treads forward, unsure of the yard's layout and relying on memory, but memory is a fickle way-finder prone to betrayals and missteps. Each step he takes now is with careful consideration, if not hesitancy. It has been years since he was here last.

The grass is a dark carpet that leads him farther into darkness, and as soon as he steps into the porchlight, he's committed. There will be no turning back, not that there ever was a chance for him, not now. After Pablo, there is no turning back. No before. No return. A line was crossed. A bullet fired. And like that bullet, once fired, it is beyond recantation. Now, whatever happens, happens.

Alejandro should have known it would come to this. He should have seen it the moment they talked on the phone, but the old man's overconfidence will be his undoing. Either Renaldo succeeds in doing what he's doing tonight, or he fails; either way, tonight marks a break in who Renaldo was. The bullet marked the beginning, and the old man's death will record the end. There was Renaldo before, who cared for the trivial things, expensive clothes, exquisite food and exceptional drinks, the loyal hound; now there is this Renaldo, the one who comes after, who cares about one thing: Iris.

Kevin had told him she would be his downfall. Kevin had said girls can kill you, and he was right. Iris killed the man he was; Renaldo's someone different now.

On the way over to the Sporting Goods store where his poker games are held and where Renaldo keeps a stash of weapons and extra cash, he told Iris that Alejandro had to answer for what he did. She said he doesn't have to do this. He told her that he needed to see the old man and finish what he had begun. She told him to let it go. Go home. Get his things. Leave. She told him to grab what he wants at his apartment and leave—leave with her, leave tonight— echoing what he asked of her in the hospital room.

But he can't leave, not yet. Not now.

Alejandro needs to answer for what he's done.

The anger is blinding. The anger is an emotion, which was something Alejandro always preached against, saying emotion kills you. Emotion weakens you. Emotion serves no purpose. But it's too late for him; emotion's taken over and dictates his actions now. The phone call only cemented this decision. Alejandro will pay for his betrayal.

His head, still wrapped in the bandage, pounds at the temples, pulsing against the bandage, and he shivers with anticipation.

From the shadows, he watches Alejandro exit his house, moving with the stunted grace of a man in the winter of life: shoulders tight, legs awkward, and gait stilted. He makes out Pablo at a table, sipping on a bottle of beer through the kitchen's hexagonal window. The old man turns on the external water faucet. A hose runs to the inflatable blue, white, and sea foam green kiddie pool with a clear plastic rim along the middle. The type of pool that fathers spend their summers squeezing plastic valves together and blowing into to inflate. Alejandro turns to go back into the house, leaving the water running. Then, he's back, closing the sliding glass door on his way out of the house with one hand and holding a metal tray in the other hand. The hand that closes the door is carrying a beer. The door opens and closes with prefabricated cheapness, and Renaldo hears the old man grunt and groan while the running water provides an underlying rhythm to the sounds of the night as the cool evening stillness lifts the smell of peppers and spices off the tray, through the backyard, and into Renaldo's nostrils, triggering an intense collage of memories of his life before Siriano. Memories of the diner. Memories of another time. Memories of Alejandro.

The old man carries his tray to the charcoal grill; the flame, orange and red, flickers in the grill's abyss. Alejandro rests the tray on the shelf next to the grill and closes the lid, snuffing the flame, and after a deep sigh, he collects a chair from the side of the house and drags it across the patio. He positions the chair in the middle of the pool. He returns to the grill, opens the lid, lays the strips of meat on the rack, and closes the lid. After shutting off the water, he returns to the pool, removes his shoes, and rolls up his pants legs. He retrieves the beer, grabs the chair, and steps into the pool. He plants the chair in the middle of the pool and sits.

Renaldo emerges from the darkness with gun in hand, pointed toward the old man's head. He tiptoes into the pool, careful not to splash, but the water is cold against his skin and soaks his pants legs.

He won't make the same mistake Pablo made. He won't make a sound.

Unaware of Renaldo's presence, Alejandro sips the beer, gripping it at the neck. As the bottle leaves his lips, Renaldo squeezes the trigger. One small pop in the night. The bottle drops into the pool as Alejandro's body slumps in the chair. Renaldo repositions and fires once more into the crown of the old man's head.

The door to the house snaps open, and Pablo rushes out of the house. Renaldo pivots and puts the gun on the bodyguard. "Stop!"

Pablo stops mid-step. His eyes shift from Renaldo to Alejandro, dead in the chair bleeding into the pool, and then back to Renaldo.

"Think about it," Renaldo says. "He's dead. It's over."

Pablo remains quiet, but fury radiates across his face.

"It's yours. I'm done."

Pablo tilts his head to the side.

"He's dead," Renaldo says, gun on him. "You don't need to die either. You're the heir, yes? You don't want this. I don't want this. I'm done. I leave tonight. This was between him and me. I don't blame you for what you did. It was only business. This wasn't that. It was something else."

Pablo steps back from the pool with his hands up and backs into the house, Renaldo directing him with the gun. Pablo eyes him as he slides the door shut, the glass pane cutting them apart. With a flick of his wrist, Renaldo motions for him to lock it. Pablo does. The lock clicks. Then, Renaldo motions again, and Pablo dissolves from view, backing into the house. Only then does Renaldo lower the gun and step out of the pool.

———

AT THE DOOR TO THE APARTMENT, Iris grabs his hand, drags him back, and kisses him in a long passionate kiss. Iris breaks the kiss. "I'm really happy we are doing this. I've wanted to do this for a long time. Since the moment I saw you."

"Me too," Renaldo says. "I think this is right. It feels right. I'm done. Either Alejandro was going to try again, or Siriano would come after me. Leaving is the best option."

Turning from her to the door, Renaldo slips his key into the lock and turns the key. He opens the door and steps inside, swiping his hand against the light switch and stopping in his tracks when he sees a pile of shit in the middle of his living room and Wilson Notaro in one of Renaldo's chairs, legs crossed at the knee, staring at Renaldo with an amused look.

Then, a gun barrel is against the side of his head. Cold. He shuts his eyes because, suddenly, everything makes sense. Everything that has happened over the last few days has led to this moment. He realizes he was played from the beginning.

Wilson, Kevin, and … Iris?

Renaldo, in a resigned voice, says, "Yeah, sure—"

CHAPTER THIRTY-ONE:
TONY MORA

T ONY THOUGHT ABOUT CALLING THE
police for the kicked in front door, but Eliza and he
were in a moment, a long-overdue moment, so he talked
himself out of it. They shut the front door as best they could
and continued on with what she wanted to do, which was
fun. Then, they laid in his bed talking about what comes
next where she realized how late it was and told him she
would stay over, but she wanted to take a shower and drink
some tea first. She said that decaf tea helped her sleep. The
shower was for what they had just done. He volunteered
to make her tea while she got cleaned up. He used his electric kettle in the kitchen. Now, a tea bag is seeping in her
mug next to his on the kitchen table, steam wafting out of
the top of the mug. Eliza is in the shower. Tony, dressed
in a blue cotton robe, lifts his mug to his lips with both
hands and sips it. Tony doesn't like tea, so he has cold water
in his mug.

Who and why would someone steal a pressure cooker full of ashes? How will he explain that one to Iris? Nothing seems to be missing except for Casper and the pressure cooker. Everything else was how he left it. So why kick in the front door? The door says someone wanted to get inside badly; it suggests that person was determined.

From the darkness of his front room, he hears a familiar voice. "I thought you would have fixed the door or something by now. Bolted it at least. Not just leave it like that. That won't fool no one."

Tony glances up and discovers Franklin in his kitchen, wearing a paramedic's uniform, a gun at his side, the scar on the side of his face.

"Or keep them out," Tony says, playing it cool, unconcerned with Franklin's presence, but this feels vaguely familiar: Franklin with a gun. Tony playing like it isn't a big deal. This time there won't be any last-minute rescue. No code words. No Clyde.

Franklin looks determined. "I mean anyone could just waltz in at any moment and do whatever they wanted."

"I take it you kicked my door in."

"I needed Casper."

"Did you find him?"

"I did."

"What did you need him for?"

"To answer some questions about some things that are going down. The kid knew some things and was just a pawn in a larger game of fuck the donkey. Seems we all were."

Tony keeps steady eye contact. "He wasn't my informant."

"I know Gene was—oh, don't look like that. Gene told me. Told me where the kid was. They're both okay, but I needed what the kid was hiding."

"What was that?"

"Let me ask you," Franklin says, "what sort of sick fucker puts ashes in a pressure cooker?"

Tony shrugs. "Funerals are expensive."

Franklin bounces the gun off his thigh. "I mean, here I thought I finally got things going my way. Your buddy shot me five times. I'm still alive. Free now. You know, I got the kid, I got the goods, or so I thought, cause the kid told me he hid the drives in a pressure cooker in your kitchen. Did you know the kid isn't a guy but a girl playing a guy? I didn't. And I guess you probably don't know about the drives... let's just say there's been some hanky panky happening off stage that didn't involve your lot, but it means a whole hell of a lot to what's going on. Explains everything in a way. The kid said they were in here, in a pressure cooker. He said he hid them after you passed out drinking last night. So here I am happy as a clam to have things going my way. I grabbed the pressure cooker off the counter, grabbed the kid, and went to an undisclosed location to plan the next step of my little revenge plan. Don't worry. It doesn't involve you or at least it didn't."

"But you didn't think I'd be awake when you returned."

"It was always possible." Franklin steps forward nodding. "I mean, it is your house. I thought I'd wait until it got late. That way if you were here, you'd be asleep. Why are you up so late?"

Tony glances toward the bedroom door. He hears the shower water running but says nothing.

Franklin tracks Tony's eyes to the door, and he must hear the water too. "Oh, you aren't alone... well, best way to deal with grief, huh? That's what my Granddaddy always said."

"Ever hear of the Five Love Languages?"

Franklin shakes his head. "I don't have time to be having no friendly conversations with you," he says. "You and me, we aren't friends. We're not doing this right now. Right now, I've come for something."

"And I wasn't supposed to be awake." Tony takes a drink from the mug, hearing Clyde's voice telling him to stay calm. "Wasn't supposed to be sitting here."

"No, you weren't supposed to be doing none of those things, and we sure as hell aren't supposed to be talking about having some quality he'ing and she'ing time to deal with our grief."

Tony nudges Franklin back toward his goal, acting interested but disinterested. "You came for the drives."

Franklin steps forward. "I came for the drives," he says. "Here I am, happy as a pig at an all-you-can-eat buffet. I opened the lid to the wrong pressure cooker. Saw what I thought was sand. I thought 'all right, that's strange but hey maybe it's for protection or storage,' you know, in case it gets dropped. Thought that's not a bad idea. Put the drives in a little plastic baggie. Put them in something no one would think about them being in and add some filler in to keep them safe. You know, absorb any blows. That kind of thing. So, I stuck my hand in, deep. Felt around. I realized there's nothing in there but me wrist-deep in a dead guy. It was ashes—not sand—and that's when the kid decides to tell me that isn't the pressure cooker he put the drives in. He said that one looked different from this one."

"To your right," Tony says. "Next to the microwave. My liquor cabinet. Top shelf."

"You keep a pressure cooker in your liquor cabinet?"

"Where do you keep yours?"

Franklin waves the gun from side to side. "So, you won't mind me taking that off your hands, do you?"

Tony says nothing.

"Right, well, I'll just be grabbing that and be on my way," Franklin says. "Why don't you do that thing where you... Freeze motherfucker!" Franklin laughs. "I've always wanted to say that to a cop... Nah, just do that thing where you keep your hands where I can see them and all that shit. I'll get what I came for and be on my way. No problems. No hard feelings, yeah?" Franklin turns to retrieve the pressure cooker from the cabinet, still keeping eyes and the gun on Tony.

Tony knows that he needs to stay calm. This won't work if he gets excited. It won't work if he tips his hand. "What are the drives for?"

"They're Renaldo's drives." Franklin glances at his wrist like he's wearing a watch happy to spill the story. "I got time."

Franklin pulls a seat from the table across from Tony.

"Seems our mutual friend has gotten up to some nice little side deals old Siriano knows nothing about. Seems Renaldo didn't know about our little deal. Guess someone was trying to set him up to get taken down by the cops. Funny, how you were using Gene to screw him over, and someone else was using Gene to screw Renaldo and you over. Both of you not knowing you were being screwed. Seems sad not knowing when you're being fucked over. But then again, I guess you got yours."

Tony offers a polite smile. "The drives, what are they? Why are they important?"

"Those drives have books or something on them, financial shit. Gene tried explaining it to me, but all I heard were that they were important. Siriano's going to want them. I want to be the one to deliver them, so I don't end up dead for killing your partner. Which reminds me, seems at the same time we were shooting at each other... oh wait, you didn't shoot at no one. That was me shooting your friend."

Tony glares at him.

Franklin presses his lips together in a slight frown. "I'm sorry about that by the way," he says. "That was just business, you know? I was just messing with you to see how you handled yourself. I didn't think you were a cop. I never expected it to go that way. Anyways, seems as we were shooting at each other and dealing with what came next, your little butt buddy Gene was robbing one of Renaldo's poker games with Casper's help. They were supposed to hit the game, make it look like a robbery, take money and computer shit, and kidnap Renaldo's special lady, except she wasn't there. Casper was supposed to be the fall guy... girl... whatever, but Gene couldn't go through with it. The faggot's got a heart or at least a soft spot for the kid. He sees the best in people. Loves the wrong sort-type."

"He told the kid to hide at my place while he tried to figure out how to get out of the mess he made? Gene wouldn't do something like that on his own."

"No, he wouldn't," Franklin says. "But his ex-boyfriend would, who just so happens to be my best friend or ... I thought we were friends. I don't know now."

"He used you just like he used Gene."

Franklin dips his chin. "Seems so. I'll have to have a conversation with him about it."

"So what's the next move?"

"I guess that's all dependent on how the rest of this plays out. I'll have to talk to Kevin about setting me up with the cops. I still have to meet with Siriano's people to get out of my mess."

"You killed a cop."

"And there's no coming back from that," Franklin says. "That's what my Granddaddy used to tell me, but if I can get Siriano off my back, I got a little lady I might just try to run away with."

"But you need the drives first." Tony delicately removes the teabag from Eliza's tea, dabbing the teabag twice, aware Franklin's eyes watch him the whole time, every movement, every twitch. Steam drifts from the surface of Eliza's mug.

"I need the drives first," Franklin confirms.

"And I'm awake catching you in the act." Tony deposits the tea bag on the table and a brown puddle forms under the bag, spreading across the grain of the table. The sweet smell of green tea fills the kitchen.

Franklin says, "You weren't supposed to be awake."

"You think I'm going to try to stop you."

Franklin shrugs; the gun shrugs too. "Crossed my mind."

Tony picks up his mug and takes a sip, still playing it cool. "You with the gun and me sitting naked in my robe."

"You look nice in the robe," Franklin says, eyeing Tony. "But yeah..." his voice trails off as he rocks back and forth in the seat, unsure of how he wants to handle this situation.

"Let me ask you," Tony says. "Do you like pineapples?"

Franklin's face changes from amusement to contempt. He glances over his shoulder to see if someone's there, awarding Tony the opportunity he's been waiting for and what the whole conversation's been building toward.

Franklin's face comes back around, the contempt collapsing into dangerous glee. Tony tosses the contents of his mug into Franklin's face. Franklin's hands snap to his face, stupidly thinking the water's going to be scalding like Eliza's mug, but it's not. He should be more observant. Tony springs to his feet and lunges across the table, one hand going for Franklin's gun hand and pinning it to the table while the other grasps Franklin's head. Tony slams the man's face into the table with everything he has and wrenches the gun out of his control.

Franklin yells and grabs the edge of the kitchen table. He flips it to the side to get to Tony. The table collides against the wall. Tony kicks Franklin's chest as Franklin starts to stand, knocking him back in the chair, then Tony steps back while rising the gun and pointing it at Franklin. Blood runs down Franklin's nose. Wearing nothing but a towel on her head, Eliza rushes out of the bedroom, naked and concerned.

Tony says to Franklin, "Seems the tables have turned."

Franklin chuckles and rushes forward at Tony's midsection in a clumsy attempt at a double leg take-down, but Tony sidesteps, the fabric of his robe billowing behind him. He hammers the back of Franklin's head with the butt of the pistol.

Franklin tumbles to the floor.

Tony steps on Franklin's ankle, adding all his weight to the man's leg. Tony warns that if he attempts to get up, he'll blow his head off. "It's my turn to say keep your hands where I can see them."

With his cheek pressed against the tile, Franklin chuckles. He arches his back like he's going to get up but sighs and places his hands out wide, palms down on the tile.

CHAPTER THIRTY-TWO:

ELIZA CORTEZ

ELIZA SITS ON THE WHITE COUCH. The room assaults her senses now as it did two weeks ago when she first sat here: white here, gold there, sterile and hard. Everything competing for dominance; rugs, carpets, and blankets, some of which imitate animal fur. All of it just as lifeless and cold as the rest of the room and perhaps the woman who lives here. A living room dressed to be anything other than somewhere anyone would want to live.

Eliza says, "It seems like a lifetime ago since I was here last. So much has happened since then."

"A lot has happened since the last time you were here," Iris says.

Eliza chuckles. Her life has imploded around her and, at the same time, blossomed into something she never imagined existed.

"So much," she says.

"Would you like some tea or something?"

Eliza brushes past Iris's attempt at playing host. "Sorry, if I woke you. You look like you just got out of bed."

Like last time, Iris wears a sheer robe, a pale pink bra and panties underneath, which blend into Iris's natural skin tone, bold stitching in select areas and lace in others, nothing overtly sexual, but not what Eliza would consider common pajamas. Even if it were, Eliza wouldn't wear something like that this far along in her pregnancy.

Another difference between the two women.

Iris pauses for a moment before answering. "No, no, no trouble. I was just getting around. Seize the day."

"Funny you should say that. Seize the day. Seize the moment. Seize the power. Right?" Eliza's tone sours. "Everything that has happened ... started right here in this living room."

Iris lifts her head to the side, giving a sidelong glance. "Excuse me?"

"You heard me," Eliza says, struggling to stay civil.

"What do you mean, everything that has happened started here?"

"Just something Tony and I were talking about."

Eliza places her hands between her thighs. She doesn't feel good today: bloated, gassy, uncomfortable. There is about a month left in her pregnancy, so she figures this is how she should feel. She's glad she is doing this now because had she waited until later into the day, she might not have felt up to it. She just wants to sleep.

"You mentioned something about wanting to talk?" Iris says, gesturing to Eliza, which is nothing more than an offer of encouragement for Eliza to get on with whatever she has to say. That is fine; Eliza doesn't plan on being here long. "You said it was important. What did you mean by that?"

Eliza tells Iris, "You can smoke if you want. I won't mind. It's your house."

Iris's eyebrows arch as her face breaks into exaggerated concern. "I didn't want to..." she breaks off as she leans forward and motions toward Eliza, hand outstretched, "with the baby and all. I didn't want to cause you any harm or anything like that."

Both women pretend this is a friendly conversation, but it is not.

"It's your house," Eliza says. "Please. If you feel the need to smoke. Don't worry about me."

With her neck straight, Iris crosses a leg over the other while stretching an arm along the ridge of the couch, rotating the empty cigarette holder between her fingers. "You said it was important?"

Another clumsy attempt at trying to get to the heart of this conversation, which suits her. She might as well make this quick. She can't guarantee it will be painless. Her lips pull back into a polite closed-mouthed smile. She withdraws her hands from between her thighs and holds them up to talk.

Eliza says, "Before we begin, I was just wondering... for my own sake... there's no one else here, is there?"

Iris holds her eyes on Eliza before answering, tight-lipped. "No?"

More a question than a statement, implying Eliza is hinting at some sort of impropriety, pretending she does not understand. But she understands.

Eliza clears her throat. "You really aren't very good at this, are you? I can read you just fine."

"I'm sorry."

"You should be," Eliza says. "But the reason I was asking if someone else is here, and the only reason I ask is I want this conversation to be just between us. You know, between two women. Just us girls. The last time I was here... well you weren't alone, and I wasn't sure if that person was here or not. No, don't worry. I am not one to judge. What you do as an adult is what you do."

A smile forms in the corners of Iris's mouth. "He won't be around any time soon."

"No, I guess he won't be; he's dead," Eliza says, but before Iris can comment, she adds, "I'm here on my own."

"Excuse me?"

Eliza cradles her stomach. "I'm on leave, maternity leave. After last week, Tony insisted I go ahead and go on my scheduled leave. The office is a mess right now. I planned on it, but he knows me well enough to know I sometimes don't do what's best for me. I can be stubborn. They still need me. Need him. I'm stubborn, and he convinced me to do it for my own good. Sometimes the stubbornness can be unhealthy for me."

"Like letting me smoke around you, who's pregnant?"

Eliza nods. "Like that."

"Is Tony doing okay?" Iris asks with concern in her voice while trying to turn the conversation.

Eliza isn't sure if she is genuine or not. "He's doing fine," she says. "Clyde's death hit him hard and then Larry and Nader... we both struggled. Hit him harder than me, but I have other concerns on my mind. Tony's had a hard time with the deaths. Clyde more than the other two, but he liked Larry and Nader. After the funerals on Monday,

Tony decided he would take a few weeks off ... to spend time with me."

"Are you two...?"

Eliza smiles. "Yes, we are."

"Is he?"

Eliza nods. "Yes, he is."

"Oh my. I never would have guessed."

"I doubt that."

Water starts running upstairs; Eliza hears it, Iris hears it, and they both lock eyes.

"It couldn't be sweeter," she says. "Just like last time, you are predictable if anything, at least for someone like me who sees through your bullshit. I can see why Clyde didn't bring you around."

Iris's face twitches, but she manages to hold the innocent stare.

"You can look at me that way if you want. You think if you stare at me like this, eyes locked, I'll pretend you didn't just lie."

"I don't have to explain myself to you," Iris says.

"Works better this way."

"What's that mean?"

"We have the drives."

"What drives?" Iris asks. "What are you talking about? What do you mean?"

"I read you correctly."

"If you are going to speak in riddles, then I think we are done here, yeah?"

Eliza holds up her hand. "Tony and I discussed this, me coming over here. Tony was against it... said we should just let the cards fall where they may and let the dust settle.

I told him that was bullshit. Said she needs to know. Clyde was my friend too. She should know we know."

Iris regards Eliza for a moment with a sharp eye and then leans back in the seat, her cigarette holder between her fingers. No cigarette. She flips it between all four fingers, tumbling it end over end. "What should I know?"

Eliza leans forward and pats the table situated between them. "That we know."

"Know what?"

Eliza fans her hands out wide in front of her. "Everything."

"Which would be what, exactly?" Iris asks, letting her voice die toward the end of the question. She leans forward at the waist, careful not to disturb her robe, and not wanting to break whatever spell she thinks she's capable of weaving or has weaved.

"It's cute," Eliza says, unaffected by Iris's charm or lack thereof, "thinking you can charm me. I know it all. Like I said, we have the drives. We have witnesses. We know what happened. We know it all."

Iris reaches for a cigarette pack lying on the table and withdraws a cigarette and a lighter. "It all? What do you know?"

"About what happened," Eliza says.

Iris puts the cigarette in the holder. "If you know it all, then why are you here?" Iris flicks the lighter, holding it to the cigarette, and puffs it to life.

"To tell you to your face," Eliza says. "To tell you I know and ask you if Clyde was in on it."

Iris closes her eyes and lets the smoke out through her mouth, slow and soft. Then, eyes open, she uncrosses her legs and leans back against the cushion, with the cigarette holder off to the side of her face, level with her chin. "If he was in on what? My dear, you are not making any sense. I'm sorry. I'm not following."

"Is that the face you make when you bluff?" Eliza asks. "Is this your act? Pout your lips, lean forward, show off some cleavage? I mean, I can see what you are working with, your body. You look good. You kind of have a Blake Lively thing going on. How could you not be alluring to someone like Tony, Clyde, Renaldo, or whoever else? I can see how they may fall victim to your charm. A spider is what you are. You are much prettier than I am. Even when I'm not... like this... but I also see through all that. Mark it up to me being female. Mark it to the fact I don't give a flying fuck about you. I don't know you. I'm not your friend. I wasn't your husband's partner. I didn't spend time with you or play in your poker games."

Iris deposits the cigarette on the table, the end of the cigarette breaks into a wash of ash, and she stands. "I think it's time for you to leave. We are done here."

Eliza sighs and stands too. "That's fine. I can leave, but we know—"

"Leave."

"You're not curious what we know?"

"Couldn't care," Iris says, with a wave of her hand. She ascends the three steps toward the front door. "You need to leave."

"Do you know why your charm didn't work on Tony?" Eliza asks. "It's because he is in love with me. That's why you couldn't use him."

"Use him for what?" Iris asks. "What would I use him for?"

"That's what you do. You use people, and when you can't use them, you like them even more. The thrill of the chase and all that, but it didn't work with him."

"I do not use people."

Eliza steps toward the front door and Iris. "You don't? You didn't use Wilson Notaro to get back at Renaldo?"

"I don't know who that is."

"Siriano's son." Eliza stops at the front door.

Iris opens the door.

Eliza says, "You didn't use Wilson to get back at Renaldo for taking your poker game? Didn't orchestrate this whole thing? Even the drug deal with Clyde?"

Iris shakes her head and bites her lip. She closes her eyes. Speaks in a small voice. "Leave, please."

Eliza takes a step toward the door but turns at the last moment, with one foot in the doorway. "So, Clyde didn't know?" She waits a moment for Iris's face to supply the answer. "Okay, I had to know. I had to know if he knew. He didn't know, did he? He had no idea what you were doing or how spiteful you can be. He had no idea what sort of black widow he married. Renaldo took your poker game and that upset you, so you seduced him, slept with him, and then, tore him down brick by brick. It's masterful, really. Used Wilson to convince Kevin Alexander to set up the deal with Clyde and Tony, and then, you had Kevin have someone rob the poker game to get the evidence needed for Siriano. What were you going to do, have Kevin take it to Siriano to show him what Renaldo had been doing? Wilson acts as a witness. He's believable. He's the boss's son. Who will take over now that Renaldo's gone—oh Wilson's right here. That's some devious shit." Eliza points up the stairs. "I bet Wilson is up there, so let me ask you, how long will it be until you use him up? Betray him?"

Iris crosses her arms. "Leave."

Eliza slips the last knife in. "Was it worth it?"

One lone tear trails down Iris's cheek. "Was what worth it?"

"Clyde's death?" Eliza leaves before Iris can answer.

BIO:

MARK ATLEY WRITES CRIME STORIES. The characters he met on the streets meet those he drew in his head, interacting with exhilarating results. The ride is wild and entertaining, and the dialog bounces like an old pickup in a pothole-ridden back alley. Mark's first novel The Olympian was positively received. A Bright Young Man will be published by Close to the Bone in 2022. His short fiction appeared in Punk Noir Magazine, Bristol Noir, and others. Mark works as a detective for a suburb of Tulsa, Oklahoma. He graduated from Oklahoma State University with two degrees in journalism. Follow Mark on Twitter @markatley and visit markatley.com.

More books from
4 Horsemen Publications

Cozy Mysteries

Ann Shepphird
Destination: Maui

Destination: Monterey

Detective and Noir

Joe Davison
Mike Strong Series

Mark Atley
Siriano Saga

Horror, Thriller, & Suspense

Alan Berkshire
Jungle
Hell's Road

Erika Lance
Jimmy
Illusions of Happiness
No Place for Happiness
I Hunt You

Maria DeVivo
Witch of the Black Circle

Witch of the Red Thorn
Witch of the Silver Locust

Mark Tarrant
The Mighty Hook
The Death Riders
Howl of the Windigo
Guts and Garter Belts

Steve Altier
The Ghost Hunter

YOUNG ADULT FANTASY

BLAISE RAMSAY
Through The Black Mirror
The City of Nightmares
The Astral Tower
The Lost Book of
the Old Blood
Shadow of the Dark Witch
Chamber of the Dead God

Shattered Start: Story of Sera
Sins of The Father:
Story of Silas
Honorable Darkness: Story of
Hex and Snip
A Love Lost: Story of Radnar

JOE DAVISON
Cold Front

C.R. RICE
Denial
Anger
Bargaining
Depression
Acceptance
Broken Beginnings:
Story of Thane

VALERIE WILLIS
Rebirth
Judgment
Death

DISCOVER MORE AT
4HORSEMENPUBLICATIONS.COM